THE NAMELESS WAR

Book One of the Nameless War Trilogy

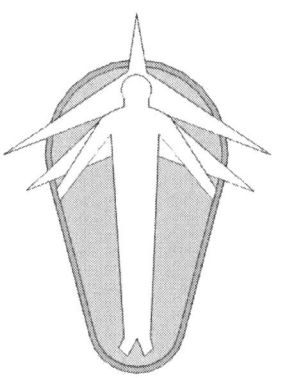

By Edmond Barrett

First Print Edition

Copyright © 2012 Edmond Barrett

All rights reserved. Except for use in any review, the reproduction or utilization of this work in whole or in part in any form by any electronic, mechanical or other means, now known or hereafter invented, including xerography, photocopying and recording, or in any information storage or retrieval system, is forbidden without the written permission of the author

This is a work of fiction. Names, characters, places and incidents are either the product of the author's imagination or are used fictitiously, and any resemblance to actual persons, living or, business establishments, events or locales is entirely coincidental.

ISBN: 1477645977
ISBN-13: 978-1477645970

DEDICATION

With thanks to my parents for their support, to Phil, for his abusive text messages during the editing, Ray Hammill for his extremely generous help with the 2nd edition and Jan with 4th edition

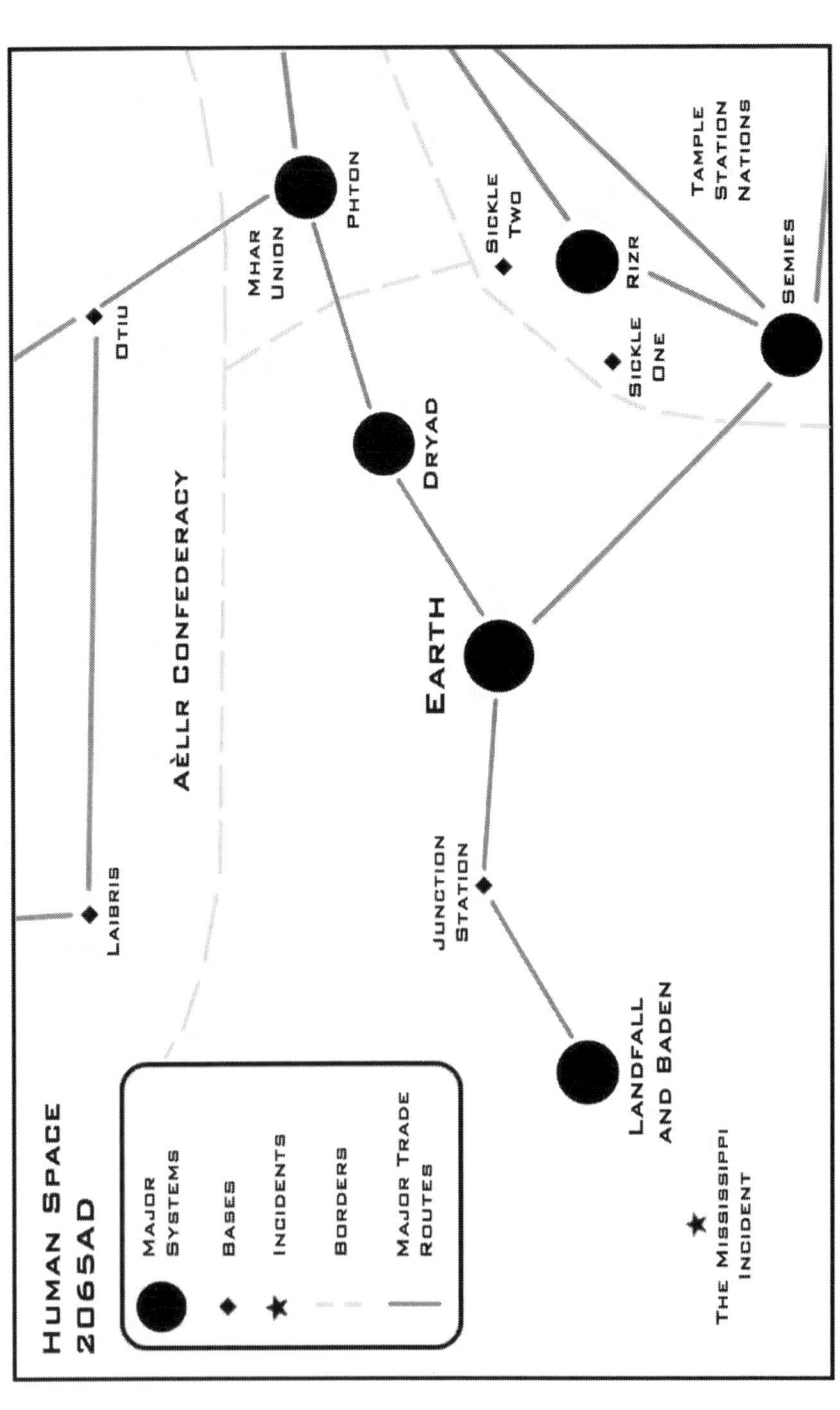

CONTENTS

1	The Mississippi Incident	Pg 1
2	Cause and Consequence	Pg 37
3	Echoes and Ashes	Pg 52
4	The Old Lady	Pg 90
5	Baden	Pg 98
6	Storm Warning	Pg 138
7	The Geriatrics	Pg 163
8	The Dubious	Pg 177
9	Scorched Earth	Pg 192
10	On the Eve of Battle	Pg 219
11	Silent Running	Pg 229
12	Contact	Pg 264
13	Blooding the Guns	Pg 286
14	Wing and a Prayer	Pg 323
15	The Lost	Pg 355
	Epilogue	Pg 368
	Glossary	Pg 384

Chapter One

The *Mississippi* Incident

Date: 12th August 2065
Vessel: *Mississippi*, River Class Light Cruiser (seconded to the Science Directorate)
Location: System A046-026
Mission: Exploration, Sampling and Stella Cartography

The *Mississippi's* four plasma engines slowly pushed the ship away from the third planet of the system, driving the ship far enough away from the planet to allow the jump drive to be safely engaged. Starlight glinted from the gunmetal grey hull of the two hundred meter long vessel. The ship had all the usual features of a Human warship: a pointed ram bow, a slab sided armoured hull with a centrifuge buried within, turreted plasma cannons and missile launchers mounted above and below the hull and four wings with the vessel's thrusters mounted on the tips.

In his small cabin Captain Ronan Crowe was lounging comfortably in his chair, reading a report from the ship's purser. A short stocky man in his mid-forties, Crowe was far from what most people would expect a fleet captain to look like. A native of New Zealand, years in space under artificial light had given him a pale complexion, while his tightly cropped hair was already both receding and greying.

On his belt the communicator started to buzz urgently. Without interrupting his reading he put his earpiece into place, before reaching down and flicking the switch.

"Crowe here."

"Officer of the Watch, sir. We're picking up an odd contact on radar. Five light seconds out on a convergent course."

Crowe stopped reading and looked towards to forward bulkhead as if he could see through the metal to the Bridge. Five light seconds was close by space standards.

"You're certain it's not natural or one of ours?" he asked.

"Definitely not natural, sir. We've already observed a slight course correction; there's no sign of a transponder or an IFF return, which makes any of ours unlikely. Although it's hard to say for sure at this range, it looks pretty small for a jump capable vessel," came the reply, "Big enough for a drone though."

"On my way up."

Two steps took the Crowe out the door of his cabin. Quickly he made his way down the narrow corridor towards the Bridge. Set into the bulkheads on either side were ratings' bunks, from some of which came the gentle snores of members of the off duty shift. Commander Berg, the *Mississippi's* second-in-command, was standing on the starboard side of the Bridge examining the main radar display. Seeing her superior out of the corner of her eye, she straightened and turned to face him. Of Turkish descent but a native of Bremen, the Commander was on what was likely to be her final tour with Crowe. With two years aboard the ship and excellent appraisals, she would in all probability soon be offered her own ship.

"All right Carol, what have you got for me?" Crowe asked as he pulled on his jacket.

"This, Captain," Berg replied turning back to the radar screen. "We picked it up about four minutes ago at a range of just over the five light seconds mark. We initially thought it was an asteroid; then it made a course correction towards us. Passive sensors aren't sure yet, but they think they may be picking up signs of engines on standby. It's already travelling at three times our velocity."

"Any idea on size?"

Berg looked down at the sensor operator.

"Phillips?" She prompted.

"I think somewhere in the region of shuttle sized, sir. Fifteen to twenty metres perhaps? It's now coming up at four and a half lights seconds, sir," Phillips responded without taking his eye off the screen.

"If manned that's only just big enough for an in-system jump drive, way too small for a full interstellar capable vessel," Crowe muttered, "and there's no reason why an in-system ship would be running around this far out without a mother ship."

"Going at a fairly serious velocity too." Berg added. "We're not picking up anything else from it, no radio, radar or FTL signals. I wonder how the hell they're even seeing where they're going."

Crowe watched the blip on the screen for a few moments. Then he reached down to his belt and flicked onto the main ship intercom channel.

"All hands, this is the Captain. Suit up and close on stations; repeat close on stations. Professor Rey and Mr. Copland to the Bridge."

Around the Bridge all the personnel were pulling on their own suits with a speed that came from regular drills. The survival suits allowed a ship to decompress most sections before action. This drastically reduced the chances of secondary explosions and fire, allowed damage control teams to move around without having to work their way through multiple airlocks. They also gave a crewman at least some chance if the hull was opened up in their section.

"Do you intend to stay here skipper, or move to the conning tower?" Berg asked as she instinctively ran her fingers down the seals on her suit. Although the conning tower was one of the most heavily armoured points on the ship, the whole concept of a conning tower on a cruiser was pretty outdated. Modern cruisers were burying their battle bridges deep inside the hull. The day bridge was inside the centrifuge, which meant it had gravity. However if the ship started getting thrown around by weapons hits or wild manoeuvring, the spikes and troughs in the artificial gravity could be wildly disorientating.

"Not until we know what we're looking at; retain pressure in the centrifuge, depressurise the rest."

Berg nodded and pressed a red button on a console. A mournful siren echoed through the ship. As she did she glanced across the lighted board showing the various ship chambers, all glowing a steady green.

"All sections report closed up for action, sir," she reported.

The aft hatch clanged open and Professor Rey and Alfred Copland hurried though, slamming it closed behind them. Both were carrying rather than wearing their survival suits, a sight that caused Crowe to stifle a sigh. Deep space exploration might be the reason he joined the fleet, but he frequently found it bloody irritating to have to deal with civilians who sometimes displayed all the survival instincts of a depressed lemming.

"How can I help?" Alfred asked as he started to struggle into his suit.

"We have something approaching us on a convergent course. We've observed a course correction so natural phenomenon seems unlikely," Crowe told him.

"So a ship?"

"That is one possibility."

"That's very little to work on Captain. What do you expect us to tell you?" Professor Rey replied unhelpfully. "I expect you to put your suit on and be ready to offer an opinion when I ask for it," Crowe told him firmly before turning back to his holo display.

"Captain, target is now coming up at the limits of our cameras," one of the sensor operators called out. Crowe nodded towards him and the main holographic display but whereas the others looked at the image of the approaching object Crowe's eye flicked towards a small group of figures being projected in one corner of the display, which read: 'COMPUTER ENHANCEMENT 50%.'

The screen image wasn't much more than a best guess, as the computer attempted to fill in the parts the powerful cameras still couldn't make out. What they could see however answered some questions. The object was definitely something constructed; it also bore no resemblance to the design style of the other three known space faring races. The computer enhancement figure started to slowly count down as the object approached.

"Curious," Professor Rey commented looking interested for the first time. "It doesn't appear to correspond to anyone's design philosophies. You know, this may well be someone totally new."

"Captain, we should back off," Copland said in a sharp voice. "We're not equipped for a first contact situation. I strongly advise we leave this system at the earliest time possible. We need a diplomatic ship, not a warship. The regulations are very clear in this area." The part time diplomat looked around defiantly as if expecting someone to leap up and start debating the matter with him. Crowe suppressed the strong urge to frown at him. There was definitely something about the man that rubbed most people up the wrong way. But it didn't mean he was wrong. After the disaster at First Contact, it had been decided that in the future, such situations would, wherever possible, be handled by specially formed diplomatic missions. However the professionals hadn't done all that well with the early contacts with some of the Tample star nations, and in the end a more robust action was taken.

"I know the regulations Mister Copland, thank you for your contribution," Crowe replied flatly before turning to one of his officers. "Navigator, how long till we cross the Red Line and can jump out of here?"

"At present velocity, sir we will exit the planetary mass shadow in just under two hours."

The unbreakable nature of the light speed barrier meant that for a ship to cross-interstellar distance in real-space would take decades, centuries or even eons, depending on the intended destination. Jump drives offered a means of travel that would get a ship to its destination in a more practical time frame. When activated the drive would form a conduit from one point in the galaxy to another that the ship then travelled along. These linkages greatly compressed the distance between the two points and while the ship's actual velocity remained low, the relative velocity was many times that of light. Thus Einstein was neatly sidestepped and starships could cross-interstellar space in days rather than decades.

The system did, however, have certain limitations, the most significant being that no ship could enter or leave jump space while inside the gravitational effect known as the mass shadow. Caused by planets or even large asteroids, its size or depth was directly proportionate to the mass of the planetary body generating it. The planet *Mississippi* had been surveying was a third larger than Earth and its mass shadow correspondingly deeper. Which meant the ship was still a long way from being able to make its jump.

"Can we avoid the contact getting within a light second of us?"

The navigator tapped in a series of commands. On his screen the computer flicked through their possibilities and after a moment he shook his head.

"Negative sir. The contact has too much velocity on us, assuming it adjusts its course to match," he replied.

"Okay let's see if we can test that assumption and see how determined it is to intercept. Helm, increase engines to one hundred percent normal. Navigator give an adjusted course to the edge of the mass shadow."

"Adjusted course laid in, going to one hundred percent normal in five, four, three, two, one, firing." Everyone on the Bridge automatically leaned forward to keep their balance as the deck shuddered beneath them.

There was a pause of several seconds while they waited for to see what the contact's response was.

"Captain! Radar contact is adjusting course to match."

"Passive sensors! Contact has just activated plasma based engines."

"Plotting. Contact is still on an intercept course. Time to intercept thirteen minutes."

Crowe cursed quietly under his breath.

"Navigator?"

"New time to safe distance from planet is one hour twenty seven minutes."

"How the hell did it adjust so quickly?" Berg muttered. "That thing made a course correction immediately but it takes several seconds to get any sort of radar return."

It took Crowe a moment to take in what his first officer had said. Radar, like everything else on the electromagnetic spectrum, travelled through vacuum at light speed. That meant it had taken over four seconds for their radar beam to reach the contact and other four seconds for the reflection to return, so they only saw the course correction nearly nine seconds after it had been made. But the contact had adjusted to their increase in acceleration instantly, rather than with the nine-second lag that there should have been.

"My word! That's impressive," Professor Rey commented from where he was standing at the rear of the Bridge. Crowe and Berg exchanged looks of concern.

"Professor. Any idea how they're doing that?" Crowe asked quietly.

"Gravitation perhaps?" Rey replied after a moment of thought. "But to pick up something as small as a ship, that's impressive. Whoever they are they're clearly highly advanced, who knows what else they can do."

Yes, who knows? Crowe thought to himself. If there was one thing he didn't want to have to do it was make first contact with a superior ship. He'd much rather it was something too feeble to be tempted to take a crack at the *Mississippi*.

"So they're technologically ahead of us," Berg said quietly.

"Well, not necessarily, Commander. They may be ahead of us in scanning technology but it isn't a given that superiority is across the board." Rey gave a shrug. "We'll only know that when we get a closer look."

"Yes, interesting. But currently not something we would choose." Crowe turned to Copland. "All right it looks like avoidance isn't a runner; we're going to make contact whether we want to or not. Time to brush up on your diplomatic skills." Copland started to go pale.

"Cap... Cap... Captain we have to avoid contact. W...we can't make contact," he stuttered.

"That doesn't appear to be our choice any more. We could turn our engines into molten metal and we still wouldn't pull away." Crowe flicked on his intercom. "Radio room, start transmitting the standard greeting message with a secondary language stream. Let's see where that takes us."

"Confirmed Captain. Now transmitting. Earliest time to reply is nine seconds."

Crowe forced himself to sit down. Transmission lags were one of the biggest irritants of deep space work, but there wasn't much you could do about it. Faster Than Light (FTL) transmitters were simply too big to put into anything but a dedicated hull and Emergency Message Drones (EMDs), were only useful for calling for help across interstellar distances. "Just have to hope we can make some sense of what they say," Berg murmured. "Our diplomat is looking a little pale."

"Bridge. Radio Room, reply possible any time from now," squawked the intercom.

"Sensors. Any change of contacts profile?" Crowe called out.

"Negative sir. Still nothing but static on any radio frequency."

"Hmm," Berg started. "If this is a truly new alien species, then they possibly could be using some system that can't send or receive radio."

"But everyone still uses radio. Everyone," Copland objected. "Even the Aéllr. "

"In the case of a new race that does not mean anything. They could have discovered something better," Crowe replied.

"It might also explain why they're not using any sort of radar," Rey added. "They might be operating on something completely different."

"Sensors. Time to intercept?" Crowe called out

"Eleven minutes to course convergence, sir."

"We could try putting a communications laser onto their hull and see if that gets a response from them," Professor Rey suggested.

"That could be taken as a hostile action," Copland said nervously.

Crowe nodded slowly as he considered it. "Almost anything could be taken as hostile Mister Copland, but unless their hull is made out of tinfoil, a coms laser isn't even going to mark the paint. Try one pulse per second, see where that takes us."

Another two minutes crawled past without any response from the approaching contact.

"I wonder could it be some sort of deep space probe," Professor Rey finally broke the silence. "Maybe we've got completely the wrong end of stick."

"What do you mean?" Berg asked.

"Well maybe instead of being advanced, it's actually primitive. Perhaps this was launched from another star system. Ships have after all been reporting picking up distant radio transmissions from an unknown source for a couple of years now. This vessel could have spent centuries crossing interstellar space."

"Any probe would have only limited fuel or reaction mass. This would have to have made some big course corrections to intercept us," Berg replied dubiously. "Seems a bit unlikely for something designed to make a real-space passage across interstellar space would also be programmed to chase after starships."

The image on the main display was getting much clearer. The approaching object was made up of flat angular surfaces, with almost no distinguishing marks, no view ports or anything else. There was what looked like a radar dish set into the nose of the object, and a pod of some sort protruding from one side of the upper surface.

Crowe drummed his fingers against the armrest of his chair. He was starting to get seriously worried. This thing was coming, barrelling towards them at a hell of a speed without giving any indication of its intentions. What most people didn't realise was that 'alien' didn't simply mean humans who happened to be little green men. It meant everything: physiology, history, language and culture. Making a high speed run straight at someone might well be an alien's idea of a friendly hello. On the other hand it could be an attack. Either way he had to make a decision within the next few seconds, the kind of decision that no amount of training or experience could prepare you for. Crowe could feel his flesh crawl. Well that was what they paid him the big bucks for.

"Captain, the contact will now intercept in four minutes, it will enter plasma cannon range in thirty seconds, and point defence will be in range in two minutes fifteen." The voice of the ship gunnery officer echoed over the intercom.

Crowe waved Berg over.

"What do you think?" he asked her quietly.

"I'm starting to get worried," she admitted in an equally quiet voice. "At that velocity they're going to fly by us unless they have one hell of an engine."

"A fly by is not what's really worrying me."

"You think they could be hostile?"

"I'm open to the possibility."

"We have no readings that resemble weapons."

"That doesn't prove anything."

Berg looked concerned.

"They'll crucify us if we get this wrong."

"No they'll crucify *me*," Crowe replied. "Sensors. Any change?"

"Negative sir. Approach track remains consistent."

Crowe looked around his bridge and wondered whether the next few minutes would see the end of his career. The lights on the weapons readiness board glowed the orange tone for standby.

"Button up the port side radiator. Guns, load and charge primary armament, load point defence batteries, fire only on my command," he ordered.

"Captain what the hell are you doing?" Copland burst out as he pushed forward.

"Taking precautions," Crowe replied tightly.

"You're planning on opening fire!"

Crowe gave the diplomat a cold look.

"I'm planning to protect this ship any way I can. Now get back there and shut up!" he finished with a snarl.

"Damn it! Your trigger-happy kind started the last war," Copland screamed.

"Control yourself or get off my bridge!" Crowe roared back at him.

There was sudden ping from one of the main sensor consoles.

"Contact has just started emitting Doppler radar!" one of the sensor operators shouted.

"Contact's acceleration is increasing… its engines have gone full burn!"

Crowe's eyes widened as it all finally clicked and the sense of unease that had been building suddenly turned into outright horror.

"Dear God! That's not a probe, it's a missile!" Crowe shouted. "Point defence! Commence! Commence! Commence! Engines all ahead emergency power! Helm hard to port, bows up forty-five degrees! Countermeasures full spread!"

A steady thumping noise echoed through the hull as the point defence guns started to launch explosive charges at the approaching missile. All four of the main gun turrets started turning to bear. The barrels of the six plasma cannons began to glow as highly energised plasma was pumped into the firing chambers. On the main view screen the point defence projectiles started to burst around the missile. The pod on the top of the missile was ripped away, the front mounted radar dish was turned into a sieve but the missile kept coming.

The missile came curving in as the *Mississippi* twisted desperately to avoid it. But the evasive manoeuvres had been left too late.

"It's going to hit," Berg shouted as she tried to belt herself into her chair. "All hands brace for impact!"

The blast was deafening, as every surface of the ship became a giant soundboard. Control panels and light bulbs shattered, sending out sprays of glass and metal, cables were ripped from their mountings and crew thrown across ship chambers. Screams and cries of pain came from several parts of the Bridge.

Berg got to her feet and cradling her right arm staggered over to the main damage control display.

"Mutter des Gottes!" she said shakily as she reviewed the mass of flashing lights. "Hull breaches, conning tower plus Decks One, Two and Three from Frame C through to Frame E. The port cargo pod and port wing are gone. Fire in Junction Room Two. Upper radar array is offline. Passive Sensor Arrays One and Four are offline. Engines One and Four offline. Turrets A and B offline. Reactor One and Generator One both offline... Oh God. The jump drive is offline."

More than half the ship's critical systems were out of action. Crowe knew that damage on that scale could only mean heavy casualties among his crew and after two years with few personnel changes he knew every one of them. He tried to contact engineering but the intercom crackled uselessly. Behind him he could hear Berg issuing instructions to her damage control teams runners. The forward display was now only showing half a sphere.

With the dorsal radar arrays out of action they were blind into the upper arc.

"Helm put us into a slow roll. One complete revolution every thirty seconds," he snapped before trying his intercom again. Several minutes crawled by before the Lazarus systems found a working connection and re-established the main intercom.

"Bridge to Chief Engineer."

"Chief Engineer here," it crackled back.

"Chief. What's our situation with the jump drive?"

"The lads in the drive compartment have reported that they took a power surge. I'm moving forward now to see the lie of the land."

"What about the rest of engineering?"

"The port side engine room is a wreck. Engines one and four are probably both write-offs. Reactor one and generator one are both none functional."

"Any hope of the reactor or generator going again?" Crowe asked.

The Chief quickly stamped on the hope.

"Not a prayer skipper. The reactor's control board is in component parts. Plus the port side radiator is terminally cabbaged and we've suffered a major fluid leak to the aft radiator, so it's only working at about half efficiency. To top it all off the exchange lines to the number two sink have been severed so we don't even have enough capacity left to run two reactors anyway."

"Get back to me once you know the situation with the jump drive," Crowe ordered.

"Will do. Chief out."

Crowe switched his intercom onto a different channel.

"Bridge to fire control. Guns. What's the situation?"

There was a long pause on the line before an unfamiliar voice answered.

"The gunner's dead, sir," came a shaky reply.

"Who's this?" Crowe asked.

"Sub-lieutenant Mamista, sir."

Crowe mentally cursed. One of his most junior officers was now in control of the ship's remaining armament.

"All right Mamista, you're going to have to manage back there for a while. What's your condition?"

"About as bad as it could be, sir. It looks like both A and B Turrets are total losses. C and D are operational but the command lines have been broken so both turrets are on local control. We still have control over the two missile turrets but both auto loaders have jammed. I have their crews trying to free them up now. The Lazarus systems are bringing what's left of the point defence guns back on line. They are about the only thing I have direct control over right now."

For all the fear in his voice Mamista seemed to be making a fair job of holding it all together.

"Good work sub! Keep at it. We'll get help to you as soon as possible. Bridge Out."

Crowe had just started to turn back towards the damage control console when a shout came from across the Bridge.

"Contact! Bearing two, zero, five, dash, one, seven, three! Profile matches first missile!"

"Time to intercept?" Crowe shouted.

"It's coming at full burn sir. Three minutes twenty to convergence!"

Berg turned towards him and called out: "we have forty percent of port side point defence and ninety of starboard."

Crowe shook his head.

"Point defence was no bloody use the first time. The missile was bracketed several times without effect." Switching on his intercom he asked: "Bridge to fire control. Sub, what's our chance of hitting the contact with plasma cannons?"

"On local control sir. Our guns have almost no chance of hitting a target of that size and speed," Mamista replied.

"Captain. All that damage means we're putting out a hell of big radar profile on our port side," Berg said. "If we keep our starboard side to the missile that might give us a better chance of spoofing it."

"Not with the cargo pod. The first one got a solid lock on the port side pod," Crowe replied as he fought down a rising sense of despair. The *Mississippi* was badly hurt. He could see it on the damage control display and feel it through the soles of his boots. What the hell were his options? Shooting his way out wasn't a runner. They probably couldn't take another one like that, hell they'd probably been lucky to take the first one. Spoofing it didn't seem that likely with that big lump of a supply pod providing a nice big radar return...?

"But what about...," Berg started.

"Yes!" Crowe shouted. "Activate the bracket charges. Prepare to jettison the pod on my command." He switched his intercom to ship wide. "Captain to all hands. Prepare to cut to silent running. Fire Control. When the missile comes into effective range fire your charge then power down your guns. Countermeasures. Prepare to fire a full spread when the missile gets within two hundred clicks. Helm. Complete roll and present our starboard side."

"Missile two and half minutes from convergence."

Crowe forced himself to sit down and wait for his orders to be carried out. On the holoscreen the red blip representing the missile continued to close in on the small green sphere at the centre of the holo.

"Two minutes."

"Plasma cannons firing." Three green bolts hurtled away from the ship but all of them missed the missile.

As the plasma bolts sped past the missile Crowe felt himself relax. For better or worse he was now committed.

"Are any of the EMDs still operational?"

"Yes, sir. One is still responding to commands," replied the navigating officer.

"Download our logs right now. If this doesn't work launch it. Don't wait for the order, just use your own judgement," Crowe ordered.

"Yes, sir."

If *the Mississippi* didn't survive then at least the fleet would still be told what had happened to them.

"Ninety seconds."

"Jettison charges ready."

"Silent running and jettison charges on my mark," Crowe ordered. "Fire counter measures now."

Three small chaff rockets blasted away from the *Mississippi* to explode a hundred kilometres in front of the missile, laying down a glittering curtain of silver foil strips.

"Incoming Doppler radar!"

The missile adjusted minutely as it started to receive data from its terminal guidance system.

"Now!" Crowe shouted.

Two muffled thumps echoed through the hull as charges severed the brackets holding the pod to the ship and propelled it away from them. The starboard side thrusters fired, pushing the ship away from the pod. At the same time thin metal screens started to slide forward, mostly screening the outlets of the engines and armoured shields closed over the heat radiators. For a moment the missile seemed to hesitate between its two choices as it pushed through the curtain of chaff. Then it made the tiny alteration needed and slammed into the cargo pod.

The missile detonated only two kilometres from the *Mississippi's* hull. The pieces of the cargo pod punctured several sections of the hull and the ship was once again rattled from stem to stern. Several members of the Bridge crew let out brief cheers, before being silenced by a scowl from Berg.

"We may have dummied the missile Captain, but not necessarily the launcher," Berg said quietly.

"We'll know in a few minutes either way," Crowe replied. Noting his first officer's tight expression, he turned to one of the ratings, sitting uselessly in front of the upper radar array display. "Garrity. Go down to sickbay and get a sling for the first officer."

Berg nodded her thanks as the crewman left.

"Navigator. How long till we coast clear of planetary mass shadow?" Crowe asked.

"On our current track sir, with the engines shut down, approximately two and three quarter hours," she replied.

Berg nodded to herself. "Drift clear then bug-out as soon as we can," she said.

"Assuming the Chief can get the jump drive going again." Crowe switched on his intercom. "Bridge to Guinness. Chief report please."

"Chief here. Have we finished rocking and rolling yet?" The Chief Engineer asked in a dry voice.

"We're waiting to find that out ourselves. What's the current news on the jump drive?"

"Luckily the circuit breakers protected the drive itself but the motors that lower the control nodes took the full force of the overload, sir. They aren't just burnt out; each one has been fused into a solid lump."

"Can you fix or replace them?"

"Certainly can't fix 'em, they're all utterly cabbaged. We only have a couple of spare units so I can't replace them all. Best bet is cut the motors off the top of each node then manually crank them into position."

"How big a job is all this?" Crowe asked.

"It's not big, but it is slow, sir. We can't use a cutting lance in case we toast a node as well, so we're back to the old fashioned hacksaw. There's only room for two of us in here so it gonna be two or three hours work."

"All right Chief let me know if there is any change. Bridge out." Crowe turned to Berg. "At the earliest opportunity we are going to bail the hell out of here. Whoever they are, they're hostile."

"Not necessarily Captain," said a weak voice. Professor Rey unwedged himself from a corner of the Bridge. "The actions are hostile but the fundamental intent might not be. But I agree this isn't the time to try to find out."

"What does our diplomat have to say?" Crowe asked.

"Very little I think, sir," Berg replied, pointing to the floor. Copland lay with his neck bent at unnatural angle. She knelt awkwardly and checked for a pulse. After a few seconds she shook her head.

Crowe had been far from fond of the diplomat, but his safety had been Crowe's responsibility and he had failed him.

"Any idea on casualties yet?" Crowe asked quietly as two crewmen pushed the diplomat into a corner of the Bridge.

Berg shook her head.

"The surgeon hasn't reported yet, sir."

Crowe sighed and flicked on his intercom again. "Bridge to sickbay"

There was a long pause.

"Sickbay here what the hell is it?" The surgeon's voice snarled.

"Report." Crowe snapped back.

"At least five confirmed fatalities, with two more to follow, eleven seriously wounded and Christ only knows how many minor wounded!"

Crowe winced. The *Mississippi* had a total crew of only seventy. Including the walking wounded anything up to a third were probably already killed or hurt. In the background Crowe could hear someone screaming.

"Damn it I'm being swamped up here… no. No. NO! Just shut the hell up and give her morphine! She's had it… Damn it Captain! I need more assistance here."

"We'll get some to you as soon as we can. Bridge out." Crowe looked round his bridge. The surgeon had been on an open line so the entire bridge crew had heard. Every face wore the same expression, one of relief that they were alive and guilt for being grateful that someone else had been killed or hurt. Crowe shook off the thought of the task of letters writing to husbands, wives or parents and finding the right words. This might not be over yet and he couldn't afford to let himself be distracted. Right now he couldn't afford to think of them as human beings, only as warm bodies for keeping his ship going.

Turning to Berg he ordered: "Commander, arrange a head count as soon as practical. See what we have left in the way of a crew."

"Yes, sir," Berg replied. "I'm going to have to…" She paused as Rating Garrity handed her a sling. Then tried for a moment to pull it on one-handed.

"Here let me." Crowe took it from her.

Berg nodded her thanks as she turned to allow him to loop it around her neck. She then carefully lifted her useless arm into the sling.

"You were saying?"

"I need a lot extra hands to flesh out my damage control teams."

To expand their range the ship's compliment had been reduced, plus much of the damage control teams had been replaced with civilian science personnel. They hadn't expected the *Mississippi* to get into a fight out here and as a result she simply wasn't manned for battle line duties.

"With all the systems we've lost we may have spare crewmembers in weapons, sensors and engineering. Take as many as you can without degrading what we have left."

Aside from the remains of both cargo pods, the main display remained empty. The surviving sensor systems were attempting to cover the gaps left by the damaged ones, but they were still blind in several arcs. Unfortunately there wasn't much they could do about it. Rolling the ship again would mean firing the engines, possibly revealing their position. Minutes slowly ground by as the crewmembers manning the surviving passive sensors studied their displays with intense concentration. Every slight anomaly was compared against the record database of the first two attacks. The intense silence was broken as the helmsman coughed, causing several of the crew to start violently. He looked around and gave a sheepish smile as several people cursed him quietly.

The next hour crept slowly by, but without incident.

On his bridge Crowe listened to the steady stream of damage reports. It steadily became more apparent just how badly they had been hit. Guinness had briefly appeared on the Bridge to give a full engineering report before disappearing below to supervise the work on the jump drive. If the damage had seemed bad at first, closer examination wasn't improving the view. The structural strength of the hull was seriously compromised in several places. Whiplashing of the hull had ripped control and power lines from their mounting all over the ship, leaving its infrastructure almost fatally compromised. The Lazarus systems were designed to automatically reroute power and command signals around damaged sections. But for them the ship would have lost all power immediately and have been left helpless against the second strike. But the system had been pushed to its limit. As it was the system throughflow display now looked a mess as the computer shunted power and command signals through whatever remaining connections it could find. The result of this was that there was simply no slack left in the *Mississippi's* systems. Another bad hit, even if the hull held together, could see them left dead in space.

    The sickbay had finally given a toll on their losses. Ten of the crew were now known to be dead and nineteen were seriously injured. Worse still two members of the ship's civilian science crew were missing. They had been in a section that had been opened up to space and Crowe could only pray that they had been already dead before the remaining pressure had blown them out. The alternative was literally the stuff of nightmares. Finally three ratings were still trapped in B Turret. So far Berg hadn't been able to spare a damage control team to cut the buckled hatch out of its frame. With the ship's crew complement virtually gutted, any walking wounded personnel were having the stay on duty. The ship simply didn't have enough healthy crew left to run without them.

    Sub-lieutenant Mamista had reported that number one missile turret was completely jammed by a, fortunately uncharged, missile that had more or less been mashed into the loading system. Number two missile turret was also jammed but the Sub-lieutenant was confident it could be released by, to quote, "brute force and unreasoning violence." The work on the jump drive was continuing slowly, but on track. Crowe would have liked to be able to allow some of his crew to stand down from action stations, but the speed of the first two attacks made clear that if there was a further missile, seconds would count. That meant that the crew had, in most cases remained sealed up in their suits.

Of their attacker they saw nothing. Despite fatigue and tension the operators of the passive arrays barely blinked as they hunched over their consoles. What remained of the science crew analysed the readings taken from the missiles. Crowe didn't expect their analysis to yield any immediate results but it didn't hurt to try.

Two and quarter hours after the attack Crowe felt his bridge crew start to relax. Everyone was still razor sharp, but the atmosphere of fear was starting to lift. The navigator was starting to make the necessary calculations to work out the most efficient course back to Baden Base. The air on the Bridge was getting fairly stale as the recyclers operated at minimum power. With the centrifuge only freewheeling, gravity had dropped to about half Earth normal. Crowe and Berg had been stood at the back of the Bridge quietly discussing damage control priorities, but now Crown stood silently, looking around his bridge, listening to the hum of equipment and sounds of his crew, committing it all to memory. For five years this had been his bridge. For five years he'd pushed back the borders of space. He'd seen good times on this bridge, but those days were over now. To hope otherwise would be a lie.

"How the hell am I going to explain this one to the HQ Commander?" he asked quietly as he stared down the length of the Bridge to the main holo.

"You followed the rules of engagement to the letter, sir. They can't fault you for that," she replied.

"You can always be faulted Commander. There are elements of the Council that have never wanted Battle Fleet ships on exploration duty. They fear that a trigger-happy soldier would start another war. This will play right into the hands of those elements."

"They didn't communicate with us sir. They just fired. It's not too much of a stretch to say that they would have shot at a Science Directorate or a national ship."

"We must have missed something Carol. We must have. People don't open fire without a reason."

"Humans sometimes do skipper. Aliens? Who knows?" Berg replied with a shrug, then grimaced as her wounded arm objected.

Crowe didn't respond. Instead he continued to stare into space.

"What are you thinking sir?"

"I'm wondering what the hell to tell the families. Twelve people are dead and I have no idea why." Crowe shook his head and added flatly: "someone will have to be held responsible. You've been good first officer Carol. I'll do my best to ensure this doesn't hurt you career."

Berg seemed shocked at the despair in her captain's voice and unsure how to respond.

There was a sudden beep from passive array control console.

"Contact! Bearing two, zero, seven, dash, two, six, four!" the petty officer shouted out. "It's coming out of our blind spot."

"Is it a missile?" Crowe asked sharply, springing forward.

"The system doesn't think so sir. Profile does not match that of the first two. The contact is decelerating. I'm reading a larger engine burn but a much shallower acceleration curve. I can't be sure, sir, but I think it's a ship."

"We thought the first one was a ship PO, bring up the projected track on the main display," Crowe ordered. With the first beep from the sensors he had suddenly felt adrenalin fizz through his veins, blowing through his despair. Despair would return but for the moment it was sidelined.

A blue line appeared on the main holo display. Crowe immediately noted with relief that the track did not intersect with the *Mississippi's* projected course. But it was going to get close, too damn close.

"It's going for the debris field. Probably to see if there is anything interesting left of us," Berg said. "That is going to have them coming to rest relative to us. It's not quite going to be course convergence, but the range will be less than two hundred and fifty clicks and...."

"And if they had more than three brain cells to rub together, they'll realise that isn't enough debris for an entire starship. At that range they'll see us even if all they do is look out the bloody window," Crowe finished sourly. "Navigator, how long till we're out of the mass shadow?"

"Another forty minutes, sir. The Chief says the jump drive will be on line in about fifty minutes."

"No point sparking up the engines if the jump drive isn't operational," Berg muttered.

"Contact will be inside two hundred clicks in twenty six minutes sir," the sensor operator called out.

"Have we anything on visual yet?" Crowe asked.

"We're picking up the afterglow of their engines, but not the vessel itself sir."

Crowe sat down and looked up at Berg.

"Any thoughts?"

Berg carefully adjusted her arm in its sling.

"The missiles went for the cargo modules rather than the main hull. The stealth coating on the hull might be fooling their radar... or whatever the hell they're using. If we play it cool sir, we might be able to slip clear yet."

"Two hundred clicks is well inside the effective range of visual scanners," Crowe replied as he glared at the holo.

"That's also well inside the effective range of our plasma cannons and missiles." Berg shook her head. "God I wish we had a railgun as well."

"A railgun is a distinctly 'take no prisoners' weapon Commander," he replied as his mind raced looking for a way out. If bringing back a badly damaged ship was bad, then actively opening fire on an alien ship would be catastrophic. But there weren't any alternatives. Unless their luck changed drastically for the better they were going to make contact. A distance of less than three hundred kilometres would be the starship equivalent of knife fighting range.

"We don't really have many choices Carol," Crowe conceded. "If we can we drift clear we'll do so, but if they give even a single indication that they have spotted us, we start shooting. No hesitation this time."

He flicked on his intercom.

"Sub-lieutenant Mamista, status report."

"We've nearly cleared the auto loader on number two missile turret sir. We may have reconnected C Turret to central fire control, but D Turret is definitely still on local control."

"*May* be reconnected Sub?"

"Sorry, sir. We won't know till we turn the whole system back on, sir," Mamista replied apologetically.

"All right sub. Order the gun crews to hand crank the turrets onto the target bearing," Crowe ordered.

"Hand crank sir?"

"We don't want to put out any avoidable power signatures Sub," Crowe explained patiently.

"Very good sir. Fire control out."

"Well that's one positive thing," Berg commented. Crowe looked at her questioningly. "I think our Sub is working out well."

"There is that. Remind me to put in a good word for him later."

As the two central turrets started to slowly swing round towards the approaching alien, Crowe once again forced himself to sit and wait. The alien ship slowly came into focus on the holo display. It was approximately wedge shaped rising to a tower arrangement toward the stern. On each side of the vessel were large cylindrical tanks, probably for fuel or cargo, each one about a third the length of the hull. Just aft of them were outboard engine assemblies each mounted on a short thick column.

"Estimated length, sir, is between seventy and hundred and twenty metres," a sensor operator called out.

"That's pretty small to be lobbing fifteen metre missiles," Berg muttered. "It could just be a scout with the big guns behind it somewhere."

"Or just carry very few reloads," Crowe replied.

"Contact is continuing to decelerate. They will reach the outer edge of the debris field in seven minutes," the sensor operator announced.

"With any luck they'll be too interested in the wreckage to see us," Berg commented.

Crowe nodded before clicking on his intercom.

"Bridge to Chief Engineer."

"Sir," Guinness responded after a moment.

"Chief, get back to engineering. I'm probably going to need to crash start the engines in a few minutes."

"Roger that sir. About to get a bit hairy is it?"

"Something like that Chief. Bridge out."

Several more minutes inched by. The alien ship had now come to a near halt within the debris field. The cameras caught the occasional glimpse of a robot arm reaching into the debris. The Bridge of the *Mississippi*, aside from the hum of machinery, was now absolutely silent. They watched their sensors intently as the alien ship continued to pick slowly through the remains of the cargo pod. Crowe kept his concentration focused on the visual display. It was unusual to get so close to an enemy ship that visual was useful. Space combat was mostly about firing at a radar blip. But here and now he could see the alien, and perhaps feel her captain's mood. When the alien's engines were idling the ship was little more than indistinct grey shape. Then the engine pods would rotate on their mountings and fire for a moment, throwing the ship into high relief. Slowly the alien investigated every piece of the pod that was bigger than a man's fist. Suddenly the alien's engine pods spun and did a long burn. The ship turned to face the *Mississippi*.

"*Shit*! We've been spotted," Crowe snarled. "Start up sequence: targeting radar, search radar, weapons, engines, life support now!"

"Captain! It has an aperture at the front. It matches the size of the missiles. Its hatch is closed," a sensor operator shouted.

The alien had just made one hell of a mistake. They probably caught a faint signal from the *Mississippi*'s hull and thought they were just another piece of wreckage. If they'd realised they had a ship within arm's length they would have spun and fired or backed off. Instead they had started to approach, which meant that they were pointing their missile launcher right at the *Mississippi*. It left Crowe with no option but to open fire or lose the capacity. At this range the fight could only be short and vicious.

"Guns charged."

"Guns fire at will!" he barked into the command frequency.

The three plasma cannons immediately stabbed out. Only one of the glowing green bolts hit the ship, striking high on the tower assembly. The bolt punched straight through the tower and exited from the back. *"No armour,"* Crowe thought as atmosphere gushed from the breaches.

Four missiles, far smaller than the one that had near crippled them, streaked out of launchers set into the flanks of the alien. In unison they turned towards the *Mississippi*. The cruiser's point defence immediately rattled into action, sending out a hail of explosive charges. The four missiles crossed the space between the two ships in seconds. The shrapnel from the point defence projectiles destroyed two of them. The other two hammered into the hull.

"D Turret is hit!" Berg shouted.

"Captain they've brought a targeting jammer on line. It's not powerful enough to effect main fire control but it's going to screw with D Turret," someone else shouted.

Another plasma bolt spat from the *Mississippi* and punched into the alien ship. Several seconds later a second bolt was fired. Crowe glanced towards the damage control board and cursed inwardly as a red light lit up beside one of D Turret's guns.

The forward facing hatch cover on the alien ship started to open. The alien was going to fire one of the big anti-ship missiles. At this range there would be no chance of avoiding or intercepting the missile.

"Guns! Target their forward launch bay!" Crowe ordered. The reply was a garbled affirmative. If the alien succeeded in hitting them with another big missile it would all be over. Another hit on that scale would probably cause the hull to fold.

A shot from C Turret knocked yet another hole in the alien's hull. The alien had been hit at least six times, but clearly they hadn't hit anything immediately vital. The launcher hatch was now completely open and from deep inside the launch bay came a deep orange glow. C Turret fired again. It struck close to the launcher but as the glow continued to build, Crowe knew it hadn't been close enough. The plasma cannon wouldn't have recharged by the time the missile launched.

The big missile erupted from its launcher at the same moment D Turret, now completely out of step with C, fired. What happened next was almost too fast for the human eye. The glowing green bolt clipped the missile just as it left the launcher. The missile jolted sideways, then wobbled and finally started to cartwheel madly out of control. There were brief cheers on the *Mississippi's* bridge as the missile tumbled away from them.

Up to that point the alien had been holding a steady course, finally it started to take evasive action. Their engine pods rolled into a new position and fired, pitching the nose up. The *Mississippi* started to roll to keep the alien within the firing arc of the remaining weapons.

As the alien passed beneath the *Mississippi* it spat out another three small missiles. They were now so close that counter measures didn't have time to fire off chaff rockets. Point defence destroyed one missile, the second burst against the armoured belt without effect, but the third went into the front of C Turret.

"C Turret is offline, sir!" Berg shouted as the ship shook from the impacts. That put them down to one partly working gun in D Turret. However the alien was now also showing signs of serious damage. Plasma and atmosphere were leaking from several of the holes in the hull and the alien's jammer, that had been wreaking such havoc with D Turret's ability to shoot straight, had ceased transmitting. Its engines remained intact though.

Slowly the two ships twisted and turned around one another. With her wingtip thrusters, the *Mississippi* should have been able to turn on a dime but they were mostly gone. Instead the cruiser was limited to slow lumbering turns, as the alien manoeuvred to stay outside the firing arc of the *Mississippi's* last gun.

"Keep rolling to port. Engine four to two thirds," Crowe ordered before calling back over his shoulder. "Berg, any hope of getting C Turret working again?"

"No. The acceleration coil is smashed and the turret crew are out," she shouted back.

"Damn it!" Crowe cursed as he watched. It wasn't going to be fast, another five or ten minutes, but the alien was inevitability going to out turn them and cross their stern. When that happened, even those small missiles would smash either the engines or the radiator. Once that was done they would have all the time in the world to hammer the cruiser without fear of counter fire.

"Fire control to bridge!" Mamista crackled over the intercom.

"What is it sub?" Crowe asked.

"The missile launcher is up, but not many of the designators are working. I'm putting the available fire arcs up on the main holo."

Crowe glanced at the holo. It looked like only two of the six targeting laser designators were still working.

"Good work sub. Now as soon as you get a shot take it. Bridge out."

The alien had continued to edge further round. They hadn't fired for several minutes, so obviously they'd seen their chance and were keeping their missiles up the spout, ready for the fatal shot. Getting out of his chair Crowe moved over to the helm terminal.

"Can we go into a vertical spin along our beam axis?" he asked as he leaned over the helmsman's shoulder.

"No sir. The wingtip motors on the dorsal and ventral wings are both knocked out. We only have the starboard motor." The man replied without taking his eye off his console.

"Okay, okay," Crowe muttered to himself. What to do? This was well outside any predicted scenario. It had been assumed that with weapons that could start hitting an opponent at one hundred thousand kilometres, action couldn't possibly get so close. But then the alien had fired from at least five light seconds away, so might be even more unaccustomed to close combat…

"Okay people, we're going to reverse our turn. Hopefully get the missile to bear before they can react. Helm. Prepare to throw everything into a port turn, main engines, wing motors, docking thrusters … the lot. Burn them out if you have to."

"Sir it's an obvious move. They're going to see this coming," Berg cautioned.

"Maybe, maybe not. Either way it's the only card we have left."

Crowe turned on the intercom as the helmsman started to program the manoeuvre. "Bridge to fire control."

"Yes Skipper?" Mamista replied instantly.

"Sub. Prepare to engage with the missile to port."

"Aye sir."

"Helm ready sir!" the helmsman called out.

Crowe quickly returned to his chair and buckled himself in.

"Helm, fire control, now!"

There was a sudden lurch as the main engines went hard astern. Anything not bolted down was pitched across the deck, everything else vibrated madly and across the Bridge the crew clung to their consoles. Relative to the *Mississippi* the alien suddenly rocketed across the cruiser's stern. Two missiles shot out from the alien and hammered into them.

"Just lost engine two!" Berg screamed over the din.

The alien must have realised what they were trying and attempted to put their ship into a relative dive. However the *Mississippi's* helmsman rolled the cruiser without waiting for Crowe's order. For barely two seconds the alien crossed into an area covered by one of the laser designators. The low powered laser speared out, painted the target and a Long Lance missile blasted out of the turret. The alien tried to intercept the missile with one of its own but the range and response time were too short and their missile burst harmlessly behind. The Long Lance punched into one of the alien's side mounted fuel tanks. For a long moment nothing happen.

Then there was a sudden blinding flash as the tank went up. The vacuum of space snuffed out the fire almost immediately, revealing the damage. Almost the entire port side of the alien ship had been ripped open, exposing the decks and chambers. Atmosphere and fragments of shattered hull tumbled away from the terrible wound. Slowly, and almost gracefully the mutilated alien spiralled away. Silent.

D Turret was still turning to bear so there was no final shot. One moment fighting for their lives, the next watching their defeated enemy reel away. Crowe suddenly became aware of just how much adrenalin must have been pumping through his veins as his hands started to shake like an old man's.

"Damage report," he whispered.

There was a pause as Berg listened to her frequency.

"Chief says engine two has taken damage to its control surfaces. He can give you one-quarter power ahead or half power astern. The missile turret has jammed again. D Turret reports fractures in their plasma lines, they can still fire but recharge between shots is going to be at least five minutes. Two thirds of the starboard side manoeuvring thrusters appear to have burnt out," Berg reported as she came over to him.

"I just hope to God they've had enough," Crowe muttered. "Because we certainly have."

"Captain! The alien is starting to regain control," one the sensor operators reported.

Slowly, over the course of ten minutes, the alien pulled itself out of the slow tumble.

"Fire Control to bridge. What are your instructions Captain?"

"Wait for the order," Crowe replied. "Let's see what they do."

The *Mississippi* hovered close by, her one remaining gun tracking the alien.

Slowly the alien ship started to limp away from them.

"Skipper. They have a stutter in their remaining engine. I'm reading several major radiation leaks and significant atmosphere bleeds," a sensor operator reported. "I don't think they're going to get very far, sir."

"Now what the hell do we do Commander?" Crowe asked. It all seemed a little surreal. After hours of tension and with their ship damn near coming apart at the seams, they had the alien at their mercy. "That ship is a hulk. If we leave them we will probably condemn their crew to death."

Berg gave her commander a worried look.

"I hope to God sir that you're not planning to board them," she said. "I strongly recommend that we retreat."

"I know Carol, I know. I just wonder whether we can salvage this."

"We've got only one sort of working gun. Sir. We're in no condition to dictate terms."

"I know Commander."

Crowe stared at the image of the shattered vessel. Up to now there had been no time to think only to react. Only now could he think and try to find a way to make this... better. But he couldn't see a way and instead his thoughts kept returning to his crew. If he'd only ordered better or ordered faster then perhaps a dozen men and women would still be alive.

"Bridge. Radio room!" the intercom squawked out. "Contact is transmitting on a FTL frequency!"

"What's it saying?"

"Nothing we can make sense of Skipper."

"Bridge to fire control. Knock out that transmitter!" Crowe ordered.

"Captain! This could be an attempt at dialogue." Professor Rey objected.

"Or it could be an attempt to call up reinforcements," Crowe snapped back.

"Fire control to bridge. We can't identify the position of the FTL on the alien ship. Err... its just stopped, sir."

"Right, we're out of here!" Crowe muttered. "Navigator. Plot best course to edge of mass shadow. We are not hanging around to find out what they're calling up!"

"Captain! We can't abandon survivors!" Rey objected. "The diplomatic situation might be recoverable and we could learn a lot from that ship."

"They've been able to signal they're in trouble. We can't and we're in no condition to take on reinforcements."

"Course to edge of mass shadow plotted Captain."

"Transmit to helm. Helm lay in that course as soon as you have it," Crowe ordered.

"Captain, the contact's engines have shut down. They're drifting."

"Perhaps if any of the shuttles are still working we could board?" Rey persisted.

"Professor the answer is..."

A flash from the holo lit up the Bridge for a moment before the display cut out. Screens around the Bridge also shut down for a moment as the pulse hit them before restarting themselves.

"Contact has exploded sir!" a sensor operator shouted. "Explosion profile consistent with fusion reactor breach."

"Escape pods?"

"Negative. There's no sign of any escape pods."

Fusion reactors were pretty stable beasts. If they went wrong they generally just shut down. The only way to get them to explode would be if the reactor's core were literally ripped open while running. But the *Mississippi* hadn't fired for several minutes. That left only one possibly.

"They self-destructed," Berg said in a hushed voice. "There must have been some of them alive but they blew themselves away."

"Helm, get us on course." Crowe ordered. As the *Mississippi's* bows turned towards Earth he added quietly: "we need to tell everyone what we have started."

Chapter Two

Cause and Consequence

28th September 2065

"Did we get any reason for the meeting reschedule?" Paul Lewis asked as he shrugged on his jacket.

"None was given, sir," Sheehan replied as he passed the Admiral his cap. "I believe it might have been at the request of the US State Department."

"Thank you. I take it that scandal in Washington is still rumbling on?"

"It certainly is," the staff officer continued. "He is considered to be a key ally to the President so obviously…" Sheehan shrugged.

"We get bumped because some senator can't keep his trousers on," the Admiral replied dryly. "Good to know that people have their priorities straight." As Command-in-Chief of the Home Fleet, the dour Englishman was the officer most directly responsible for the defence of humanity's home world, a role that brought him into more contact with politics than he entirely preferred. Which made the monitoring of those political factors an unofficial part of his chief of staff's job.

"Is the shuttle…"

"Already being prepped, sir."

"I assume you've already shuffled the rest of today's timetable."

"Pretty much, sir. I'm just waiting for Rear Admiral Brian's staff to get back to me."

"Good, and how are preparations for our transfer to Resolution coming?"

"Everything is on schedule, sir." Sheehan made a slight face. Lewis's peripheral vision was excellent and he caught the expression.

"Problem?"

"I'm just not really looking forward to being shoehorned into Resolution sir. I just hope our new home is commissioned on time."

The Admiral smiled briefly. "Yet the Resolutions seemed so big when they first came into service," Lewis commented as he checked his watch. "Time to make a move. Oh and can you arrange an uplink to my wife's office? Lunch is going to have to be rescheduled as well."

Ten minutes later a shuttle detached from the flank of the battleship *Titan* and started to drop down out of high orbit. Within moments the shuttle was lost among the starships, shuttles and stations crowding Earth's orbit.

The headquarters of Battle Fleet was a collection of large ugly concrete buildings situated to the north of Dublin. Locally nicknamed The Fortress, it had been built as a temporary home for the fleet during The Contact War. Intermittently it was proposed that the fleet move to a new purpose-built home, or at least a set of buildings that didn't look like it was designed to withstand an orbital strike. But each proposal had bogged down in committees and instead new extensions were added. As his car drove in through the main gates, passing the saluting marine, Admiral Cody Wingate, the most senior military officer of the fleet, doubted it would ever move.

As the car turned the light shifted and for a moment he saw his face reflected in the glass. It was funny how even after thirty years and a dozen plus operations, it could still take him by surprise: an African American man now in his mid sixties, average height and slightly overweight. A far cry from the mental picture he had of himself, frozen in his late twenties. As the car stopped he fumbled for a moment with the handle before getting it. Somehow Wingate found that he missed the fingers of his left hand far less than he missed his face.

His staff captain, Anna Barker was already waiting for him when he reached his office.

"Good morning, sir. Did you get my message?" she asked as he walked into the room. Wingate paused in the act of tossing his briefcase into a chair.

"What message Anna?"

"The Council has moved this morning's meeting forward an hour to accommodate the Chinese premier."

Wingate sighed.

"I wish someone would accommodate us for a change. Has it been passed up to *Titan*?"

"Yes, sir. Secretary Callahan is out of his office however and seems to have his phone off. I've left a message but I have no idea whether he's received it."

"If we've done what we can it's not our problem Anna. He's our oversight not vice-versa."

Wingate turned slightly as the door of the conference room opened and Lewis stepped into the room looking in poorer humour than usual.

"Sir," he murmured as he sat down.

"I thought you were going to miss this," Wingate commented.

"Orbital control is all screwed up again," Lewis replied in an irritable tone that suggested that someone was going get it in the neck later.

Behind him officers and various civilian support staff were filing into the room.

"You've seen the meeting plan?"

"I think you're asking whether I've seen that we're being blamed for doing what we were told?" Lewis replied with a ghost of a smile. "Yes I have. The words 'after the horse has bolted' spring to mind."

"Unfortunately it's more serious than that Paul."

"With politicians it usually is."

"It plays into the hands of those who continue to believe the fleet is inherently trigger-happy," Wingate shrugged. "We'll have to try to stop them from going off on a tangent about armed explorers."

"With respect sir, but I have yet to see one of these meetings where someone doesn't attempt to send it off in some strange direction." Lewis looked around. "Where's Secretary Callahan?"

"He doesn't seem to have got the message about the change in time."

"Well that's something," Lewis grunted.

Even at the best of times the C-in-C and the Fleet's civilian head only really tolerated each other. Lewis's record in the last war had got him as far as his current role, but his unwillingness to play the political game would see him go no further. Wingate had often reflected that it was probably just as well that Lewis seemed to have no such ambitions.

Battle Fleet was in many respects a political and military aberration, a fleet not answerable to any single government and in essence a formalised mercenary force. Due to some questionable wording in the original treaty that founded Battle Fleet, the roles of First Admiral and Secretary of the Fleet overlapped somewhat. Some previous First Admirals and Fleet Secretaries had waged near war over the all-important definition of what constituted operational details. But Wingate had found Callahan more of an ally than an opponent, a shrewd operator who saw his role as a bridge between the military officers and the civilian government they answered to.

There was a chime from the ceiling and a voice said: "ladies and gentlemen can you please take your places." There was a short pause as people found their chairs. "Ladies and gentlemen please rise for the Council."

As people got to their feet the eight hologram pads on the opposite side of the table started to shimmer into life and take form. In the centre sat the hologram of the President of the United States. To her left were the Prime Ministers of China, India, New Zealand and South Africa, and to her right those of Canada, the UK and Italy.

"Thank you everyone, if we could get started," President Ruth Clifton said briskly. "We're here primarily to discuss the incident that took place on the 12th August 2065 in the system tentatively identified as A046-026. As you all know a Battle Fleet vessel, the *Mississippi*, on a routine exploration mission was fired upon and severely damaged. The *Mississippi* returned fire resulting in the complete destruction of an alien vessel of unknown origin. We are here to discuss our response to this incident."

"Our response must be the complete and immediate withdrawal of all armed vessels from exploration duties. The policy of supplementing Science Directorate vessels with armed explorers always ran the risk of just such an incident. Now possibly our worst fears have come to pass," the Indian Prime Minister Faisal Farooqui said firmly.

"With respect Mr Prime Minister, but that is not the immediate issue."

"I must disagree Admiral. Sending armed vessels into sovereign territory is virtually guaranteed to provoke an alien race. To continue sending ships in that direction risks further antagonising them and risking war."

"With respect, sir, that is an assumption," Lewis answered him sharply. Wingate shot his subordinate an irritated look, the answer came across as far too defensive.

"A reasonable assumption based on the actions of a Battle Fleet officer. A Battle Fleet ship encountered a ship of an unknown race and destroyed it. What more is there to say?"

"Again with respect, sir," Wingate interrupted. "The logs and witness accounts show that Captain Crowe held his fire until he was certain he was under attack. He then made all reasonable attempts to extract his ship without getting into further conflict."

"When he encountered the alien ship directly, he made no attempt to communicate. His own logs admit this," Farooqui countered.

"Admit is a strong term Prime Minister. The ship's log also show that the direct encounter took place at a range of less than three hundred kilometres. If I may remind the council, the alien's missiles were observed crossing that distance in less than two seconds."

"Yes but…" Farooqui attempted to cut in.

"Also may I remind the Council that *Mississippi* had sustained severe damage to all major shipboard systems? Captain Crowe held his fire until the alien turned its main armament towards him. At that point *Mississippi* had to fire or surrender his ship to destruction."

"There is also nothing to indicate that an unarmed explorer wouldn't have been met with the same response. The difference being that an unarmed vessel would almost certainly not have survived the encounter," Lewis added flatly.

"Can we be sure that no attempt was made to communicate with *Mississippi*?" the British Prime Minister Michael Layland asked.

"We've had three independent teams from Battle Fleet, Science Directorate and the North American Space Agency go over the logs, communication, radar and sensor records, with a fine tooth comb. We know they had a Faster Than Light transmitter, because we detected an FTL transmission being made just before the ship blew. However the logs give no indication that any such transmission was directed at *Mississippi* before they were fired upon. In essence, even with the benefit of hindsight, we haven't been able to find anything the crew of *Mississippi* missed."

"Do you believe that this is an inherently hostile species Admiral?" The President asked.

Wingate sighed and leaned forward.

"In truth Madam President, what we know about this species is the sum of very little. As you say this could be an inherently hostile species. Equally this incident could be the result of mistaken identity, it could be a single captain losing his nerve or even a weapons malfunction. We simply do not know."

"Then perhaps it would be wise to stay away from their borders."

"With respect Madam President, but where is the border?"

There was a pause for a moment as everyone considered the Admiral's question.

"It should be noted that this incident took place within twenty-five light years of Landfall and Baden Station," Admiral Lewis added. "There is no guarantee they don't already consider those points to be within their sphere of influence."

"Was there anything in the system that they might have been attempting to protect?" the Italian Prime Minister asked.

"*Mississippi* was of course only performing an initial survey but there was nothing to make us hurry back. Seven planets, two of them gas giants and no planets in the Liquid-H2O band. No indication of native life or any particularly exciting ores."

"I think perhaps we should accept that we cannot currently answer why *Mississippi* was fired upon and move on." PM Layland paused before continuing. "The question is response. We can either cease exploration in that direction for the time being and wait to see what, if anything, comes of it, or investigate to determine whether diplomatic relations can be opened or what the level of threat is."

The Chinese Premier Wen Jiabao spoke and they waited for the translation to come through.

"What can we currently determine of their military capabilities?"

Wingate nodded to one of the officers down the table.

"Commodore Tsukioka has prepared a brief on this topic. Commodore if you please."

The small neat Japanese officer stood up.

"Ladies and gentlemen, our full report will be forwarded to your respective governments at the conclusion of this meeting. For the moment I will cover only the main points of my report, which is based on the reading taken by *Mississippi* before the aliens' destruction. Obviously there are limits to what those readings can tell us."

"Yes, yes, we all understand the limitations," Clifton interrupted. "Can we get on?"

"Yes ma'am. Based on the *Mississippi's* readings the alien ship appears to be a mixture of technological levels. We have evidence of some systems we don't understand even in principle, while others appear to be several steps behind our own technology," he continued unflustered.

"The most interesting point is their scanning technology. It appears to offer both Faster Than Light feedback and greater range than any technology we are aware of. It is also apparently small enough and cheap enough to use in a missile guidance system. The only possible way to achieve FTL scanning that we know of, even in principle, is by gravitational detection. However to detect something as small as a starship by this means is well beyond our understanding. As a result we don't have any active counter. *Mississippi's* experience indicated that a ship might be able to avoid detection by powering down its systems but this is far from certain. The tactical advantages of a scanning technology that is not subject to transmission lags obviously cannot be overstated. However one possible ray of hope is the apparent use of conventional radar for terminal guidance. Our hypothesis is that the FTL scanner is not accurate enough for final approach and the radar they were observed using is at least a jammable technology."

"So they would be able to see one of our ships without it being able to see them?" the Indian Prime Minister asked.

"The current information would indicate yes."

There was a murmur of conversation.

"If I may continue?" the Commodore asked in the tone of a schoolteacher. The conversation stopped. "The second area where they appear to have an advantage is in Faster Than Light transmitters. The alien was observed making a FTL transmission. The transmission stream was far more complex than our one-point-five pulses per second and our smallest FTL transmitter is bigger than the entire alien ship. However the technology does appear to be within shouting distance of our own. The opposite is true of their conventional engines. While they did appear to be like ours plasma-based systems, the performance was far inferior. The alien proved only marginally more manoeuvrable than *Mississippi*, even after she had two engines disabled. This plus the fact that the alien's hull was clearly unarmoured indicates that the power-to-mass ratio on their engines is significantly lower than ours. Possibly lower even than our first generation engines. One last factor that we find very interesting is the explosive yield of the long-range missiles. For all the size of the missile it wasn't very impressive, hinting at either a small warhead or a relatively weak explosive. Also the explosion wasn't focused against the hull of the *Mississippi* so the bulk of the yield was effectively wasted."

"Is it possible that this could be an attempt at misdirection by one of the alien races already known to us?" the Chinese Premier asked.

"We believe that is very unlikely, sir," Commodore Tsukioka replied flatly. "The Tampel and the Mhar would have to make major technological advances in almost all critical shipboard systems in a very short timeframe without us picking up on it. For the Aéllr to make the necessary technological developments is more possible but it would be very much out of practice. They have always placed a high premium on ship and crew survival."

"Not to mention they already know they can take us in a stand up fight but we would hurt them a lot. Politically it would take a lot for them to be willing to have people coming back in body bags again," Admiral Lewis added. "If this was an attempt to trigger an incident it would be closer to their own borders."

"This is all very interesting but what does it mean in practical terms?"

"If I may venture the observation," Layland added. "*Mississippi* is a comparatively elderly ship and yet she dealt with the alien. This is surely a positive sign."

"Perhaps or perhaps not Prime Minster," Wingate replied. "You are correct. The Mississippi is an ageing design, but even our most modern ships are built around the same premise, namely combat at relatively short range with energy weapons. These aliens would apparently have the ability to detect and attack us from a safe distance. However I have to qualify that by saying this was only a single ship. It could have been their newest and best or another ageing vessel, nearing retirement. We also have no idea on the overall strength of their fleet."

"Does this mean you're looking for extra funding?" the Prime Minister of New Zealand asked sourly.

"For the moment, no," Wingate replied, ignoring the looks of faint surprise he got. "What we really need right now is information. What we have is so patchy we could easily head down the wrong track. What we in the fleet are advocating is sending a single ship with a full science and diplomatic team to discover and if possible make friendly contact with this species," he continued. "If friendly contact proves impossible to achieve, they'll complete an analysis of the level of threat they pose."

"I presume you are suggesting an armed ship," the President replied. "That could be seen as a hostile act."

"I believe, Madam President, it has to be armed ship or no ship at all. They have already fired at one of our vessels. If we sent an unarmed ship we would be trusting to luck that they are definitely not hostile without any information to confirm or disprove that assumption. We are suggesting using a single Herald Class scout cruiser to investigate and if possible make contact. If I may remind you they are about the same size as a River Class but with less armament and more importantly greater acceleration."

The President pursed her lips for a moment before looking up and down the table at the other council members.

"Admiral, there are real concerns that Battle Fleet is not the organisation to lead any search for this race."

Wingate heard Lewis let out an irritated hiss.

"Yes ma'am. I've notice the debate in the media. I've also noticed most of them have ignored that fact that *Mississippi* was fired upon first."

"Yes Admiral but the fleet does have a certain… history."

"Yes ma'am but the salient fact is we are the only armed human fleet. If the Council opts for an unarmed ship, it can be a Science Directorate vessel or one from the national fleets. If armed, it has to be us."

"Very well Admiral. Do you have anything else to add on this subject Admiral?" she asked.

Wingate glanced at his own people.

"I don't believe so Madam," he replied.

"Very well. Moving onto the next item, the proposed tracking station on…"

It took nearly another hour to work through the rest of the agenda. Halfway through the meeting Secretary Callahan had finally turned up looking flustered. When the Council members disappeared into a virtual conference room to discuss the matters raised privately, Lewis let out a sigh and sat back in his chair. Around the room other people were starting to gather up their papers. Callahan was reviewing the minutes of the meeting to get some idea of what he missed.

"What do you think?" Wingate asked his subordinate.

"That one of these days we are going to end up with political commissars on our ships," Lewis replied sourly.

"Council has to be aware of public opinion Paul."

"Being aware of it is one thing, pandering to it is another," Lewis replied in the same tone. "I'll be sorry to see the Chinese finish their period on Council. We get less messing from them than anyone else. They're reluctant sir, but their choices are limited."

"Pardon?"

"They don't want to send us anything but unarmed…" Lewis shrugged, "Might simply disappear into the black."

Unfortunately such prejudices had some backing, Wingate reflected as he rubbed his scarred face. The Contact War had probably been history's most avoidable conflict. For various reasons the military leaders of the day had advised a course of action that resulted in armed forces being put into the same piece of space as an extremely rattled alien taskforce. What followed had been as tragic as it was inevitable.

Mississippi herself had finally come home only two days earlier. Even after the temporary repairs completed at Baden Station her wounds were all too apparent and that might have focused a lot of minds. It had been nearly fifteen years since a Battle Fleet ship had fired a shot in anger and not since the end of the Contact War had a human ship staggered home so mutilated. It had affected the fleet; such an event couldn't fail to. Most of the enlisted personnel and all the junior officers now serving had joined the fleet after the war and they had never seen the effects of battle damage in, so to speak, the flesh. However if there was new a feeling of unease there was also one of pride. One of their own had taken a terrible beating but had emerged victorious. Wingate had been in the main Battle Fleet control room when the battered cruiser had limped into the system under her own power, resolutely ignoring the two deep space tugs sent to escort her.

"There is one final thing I wanted to speak to you about, Captain Crowe," he said.

"Well the man will likely have to be given a desk job," Callahan said briskly.

"I'm sorry Daniel. I forget but when was it exactly that we court-martialled Captain Crowe," Wingate replied.

"What's the alternative exactly?" Callahan said looking up from the meeting minutes as he took a seat. "Simply give him another ship, ignore any protests? And before you say anything Admiral Lewis, yes I did read the report."

"Yet you still seem to be taking the idiot press's interpretation," Lewis replied coldly.

"No, I believe the Captain did his best in an impossible situation. But the reality is a lot of people have reservations about Battle Fleet. If the fleet gives Captain Crowe a frontier posting, it will be thumbing its nose at the world and lining up for a showdown with the Council. Is Captain Crowe worth that?"

"So presumably we lynch him," said Lewis.

"Colourful as ever Admiral," Callahan sighed. "I am merely suggesting Captain Crowe be assigned a desk position. At least until things have calmed down again."

"That would be a mistake," Lewis said in as he started to gather up his own papers. "Crowe spent the last six years playing taxi driver for the Science Directorate. A man like that isn't going accept a desk job."

"Accept Paul? I didn't think the fleet worked on consensus."

"He could opt to resign his commission with the fleet, and probably would."

"That would be a possibility."

Lewis frowned at the Secretary.

"Yes I'm sure it would be politically convenient for Crowe to be hounded out of the fleet without any messy due process. I however would be somewhat reluctant to see the only skipper we have who has seen combat against this race, being sacrificed to quiet the mob!" he snapped back.

Callahan's mouth opened to shoot back a reply but before he could speak Wingate raised his hand.

"Please gentlemen, let's keep this civil. With respect Mister Secretary, Admiral Lewis, neither of you are wrong," he said. "In his determination to avoid an incident Crowe held his fire. That's a far cry from trigger-happy. To dismiss him either directly or indirectly would be unfair and unwise. Are we really prepared to tell every captain in the fleet that they can under no circumstances defend their ships?"

"No, of course not." Callahan said with a shake of his head. "My office will be spending the next few weeks trying to portray him as a hero, but sending him back out will make that much harder. So at the very least he is going to have to be kept closer to home."

"I accept his next posting will be subject to an unusual degree of public scrutiny. You can be assured your office will be informed of the Captain's next posting," Wingate conceded.

"Would you like to join me for dinner before you head back to *Titan*?" Wingate asked Lewis as the two officers walked along the corridor from the Council Chamber after parting from Callahan.

"I'm due to join my wife in… about half an hour," Lewis replied, "although I could do with a drink of something to wash the politics out of my mouth."

Wingate looked up at his taller subordinate.

"You seem to be getting more intolerant of our leaders as you get older."

"Laura has been saying the same thing for years," Lewis replied with a rare smile.

"Hmm… A thought occurs. If we transfer Crowe to Science Directorate completely, even the Council couldn't claim he'd get up to much mischief in an unarmed sh…"

"Not a prayer," Lewis interrupted. "Laura told me last week that officially Science Directorate accepts our findings that Crowe was not responsible for the incident. Unofficially, despite the work he's done for them, those hypocritical bastards won't touch him with a bargepole." The disgust was clear in Lewis's voice.

Wingate nodded to himself.

"Well that's no great surprise," he said after a moment. "Alright, change of subject, how are simulations coming along."

"Not really much good news on that front either. They're going badly, worryingly badly," Lewis said seriously. "I've got every tactical officer in the Home Fleet working on it and so far the results have been poor. Even such large missiles are very small targets for plasma cannons. So far only the much maligned Luna class have fared well, but I don't think we can place too much reliance on only six ships."

Wingate grunted an affirmative.

"It would be useful if we could lay our hands on some more flak ships," Lewis added. "There's a thought. Might also solve the Crowe problem."

"Oh?"

"Flak ships don't wander around on their own. If we could put him onto one of the Lunas, that would keep him somewhere useful and under the watchful gaze of a senior officer. Might keep the Council happy," Lewis explained

Wingate looked at the ceiling for a moment.

"Yes I can probably work that deployment out. What about the sims?"

"Bottom line is if it's a long range fight they win and if it's short range we win. In this case we think attack would offer the best form of defence. If we could pin them against something they have to defend, we could probably force them into our weapons range. We'd take some licks but we would do damage. If they attack however, it wouldn't be pretty. Missile fire would probably be the first indication they were there."

"The Council would have a collective fit if they heard you talking about attack," Wingate commented.

"They're perfectly welcome to ensure I don't have to attack anyone," Lewis replied with a faint smile as they turned into the Admiral's dining room.

Chapter Three

Echoes and Ashes

2nd February 2067

    The marine on duty at the main access hatch of the Herald Class cruiser *Harbinger* watched impassively as the officer drifted down the access way towards him. Behind her came a rucksack on a towing line. With an occasional touch she corrected her drift until she reached the marine. Then twisting gracefully she caught hold of the guide bar and arrested her movement. Reaching back she stopped the pack with a touch.
    "Commander Faith Willis reporting for duty aboard the cruiser *Harbinger*," she said as she passed the marine her storage drive and pushed herself down until her boots made contact with the deck plates. The magnets in her boot held her down in a standing position as the marine plugged the drive into his pad and examined her posting orders carefully.
    "Very good ma'am," he replied after a moment. "Permission to board. I'll inform the Second Lieutenant that you've arrived."
    "Thank you," Willis replied flatly before pulling herself through airlock and into the ship. The marine watched her go before shrugging to himself and returning to his position.

    Captain Marko Flores woke with a start as his intercom buzzed. The book he'd fallen asleep reading fell off his lap and landed with a soft thump. It buzzed again as he tried to get the earpiece into position.
    "Captain here."

"Officer of the day. Sorry to bother you, sir, but our new First Officer has arrived," said the Lieutenant at the other end of the connection.

"Already? Good. Give me five minutes then send her in."

"Yes, sir."

After pulling on his jacket Flores quickly ran a comb through his hair and checked his beard was neat. The fleet wasn't all that keen on facial hair and in the early days had made a stab at banning it outright. A storm of protests from Muslims, Sikhs and a few other groups had seen the idea dropped fairly abruptly. So instead the fleet contented itself with vaguely frowning upon beards, something Flores had long since decided he could live with.

Moving over to his desk he switched on his computer screen and called up the copy of Commander Willis's file that had been sent to *Harbinger* the day before. The fact that the ship even needed a new second-in-command was something of a disaster. Until five days ago *Harbinger's* First Officer had been the highly capable Commander Martin Wilfor, a man who had served with Flores for nearly three years. Unfortunately Wilfor was subject to a single failing: when busy he could become spectacularly forgetful. Five days earlier he'd been hurrying to examine a potential problem in the dorsal radar. Upon reaching a ladder he needed to go down, he stepped out onto fresh air expecting to push himself down. Unfortunately the ladder in question wasn't in the zero gravity environment of the main hull, but in the centrifuge. Commander Wilfor crashed down two decks, sustaining two broken legs and a broken jaw. He was probably lucky not to have broken his neck, although Flores doubted he was currently feeling lucky at all.

It was an easy mistake to make when you crossed from zero G into gravity and back a dozen times a day. Certainly Flores had himself made the same mistake many times, albeit less drastically, attempting to put things down in mid air when in gravity or failing to stick them down when not.

Still it left Flores with the major problem of replacing his second-in-command. He would have dearly have liked to replace Wilfor with one of his existing officers. They had all meshed well together, but they lacked experience, particularly given the importance of their assignment. Normal procedure at this point would have been to get an officer from another ship. Given that they were docked at Baden, the biggest fleet base outside Earth's solar system, this shouldn't have presented a problem. Unfortunately bad fortune once again smiled on them as most of the Third Fleet was out on manoeuvres around Landfall. Those ships that remained didn't have the calibre of officer he needed.

Finally after two days, and one fairly direct transmission from Headquarters asking what the hell *Harbinger* was still doing at Baden, a replacement was found. Commander Faith Willis had been on a courier heading back to Earth for her next assignment when the urgent signal had turned it around.

When her file first arrived on his desk, Flores was certain he had found the solution to his problem. Her record was impressive, with excellent reviews and a startling number of technical courses successfully completed. It was only after he said yes and went back over the file that he started to develop reservations.

Her previous assignment had been as a staff officer at the fleet's ground base on Landfall. Previous to that she had served for just over a year as the First Officer on board the Heavy Cruiser *Odin*. Her superiors from both these assignments had written favourable appraisals. Yet they seemed to Flores to be slightly… cool. Nothing he could put his finger on, indeed he might simply be reading things into the accounts.

There was a tap on the door.

"Come in."

A woman in a commander's uniform walked in, came to attention and saluted.

"Commander Faith Willis reporting sir."

"Thank you Commander, please pull up a seat."

Flores took the opportunity to study his new first officer. She was approximately average height with a slender build and auburn hair cropped short. Her features were pretty in a delicate sort of way but currently flat and expressionless.

"Well Commander, welcome aboard. I'm sorry we had to drag you back out here. I expect you were looking forward to seeing Earth again," Flores began.

"Thank you, sir. The reassignment was something of a surprise," she replied calmly. "But I am looking forward to getting started." Her voice was quite soft but a Northern Irish accent remained detectable.

"How much do you know about our assignment?"

"Only what I've read in the media, sir."

"You'll need to read through the mission profile in full, but for the time being I'll give you the abridged version. We are to seek the aliens that the *Mississippi* encountered…"

"The Nameless, sir." Willis interrupted.

"What?"

"The media are calling them the Nameless," Willis explained.

"Oh… Not very imaginative by their standards," Flores shrugged. "Anyway we're to find them and if possible make contact. Alternatively we are to gather information about them. Either way, at the first sign of hostility we turn around and run like hell."

Willis nodded, her face expressionless. Flores frowned inwardly, any officer would treat their new captain with caution until they figured out what made them tick, but this interview was starting to feel very laboured.

"We're also more heavily manned than normal. As well as our regular crew we also have science, diplomatic and marine contingents. So it's going to be hot bunking all the way."

"I'm sure people will manage. Are they already aboard?"

"No. They've been on our tender while we were waiting for you. I'll be honest with you Commander; these are not best circumstances for a new officer, particularly a first officer. I'm going to need you to get up to speed pretty much immediately. We are going to be getting under way tomorrow afternoon, barring any more disasters. Do you have any questions?"

Willis looked thoughtful.

"I don't believe so, sir. It sounds like I have a lot a head of me," she commented. "With your permission I'd like to get started."

"Find Chief Benson. He'll help you find you way around. I'll see you in the morning."

"Thank you. Goodnight, sir."

When she was gone Flores remained in his seat, his fingers drumming on his desk. The slight reservations he had were upgrading themselves to serious concerns. She seemed very… reserved and Flores wasn't sure he liked that. Then he shrugged to himself. People sometimes just sucked at interviews, hopefully that was the case here.

Even in the age of modern interstellar travel there were still strict weight limits on personal belongings. One positive thing about these restrictions was that they made it very quick to unpack, Willis reflected to herself as she closed her cabin's small storage locker. Loosening her jacket she lay down in her bunk with hands behind her head. The cabin was tiny, little more than a two-metre cube, but in the cramped confines of a warship to have such a space to yourself was a rare privilege. On *Harbinger* only the Captain, First Officer and Chief Engineer had their own cabins. The rest of the officers were two to a cabin with the ranks in three separate messes.

After a few minutes she blinked as she realised that the low rumble of the centrifuge was lulling her to sleep. As she roused herself to change she thought about the interview with her new captain. It seemed to have gone reasonably well and it was certainly her good fortune that the posting had come her way. The ship itself was extremely interesting. The newest cruisers in service with the fleet, the Herald Class were designed to serve as the eyes and ears of the main battle line. They weren't particularly well armed or armoured, but they had unrivalled acceleration and the best electronic warfare systems of any human ship. It was those systems especially that Willis was looking forward to getting her hands on.

Seven weeks later

"This isn't going to cut it, Bosun," Willis said as she examined the computer pad. "I want this reorganised... properly this time."

"With respect ma'am," replied Bosun Daler, "this was signed off by Commander Wilfor." There was a weary note in the Petty Officer's voice.

The two them were in the Number Two Storage Hold. Around them, filling almost every cubic centimetre of the chamber, were boxes and storage bins. As the storage holds were situated in the main hull, containers were attached to every surface, including the ceiling. It was the nature of those attachments that was bothering Willis.

"Commander Wilfor is no longer serving here Bosun," she replied frowning, "so I'm not interested in what he signed off. Single bindings are not strong enough."

"Yes ma'am for the heavier containers I agree, but it's unnecessary for the lighter ones. It's also going to make it a lot more difficult to get anything."

The Commander looked completely unmoved by this argument.

"I'm not interested in a debate Bosun, just get it done before the end of the next watch."

Without waiting for an answer she turned and pulled herself out of the chamber. Once Willis was safely out of earshot Daler allowed himself a heartfelt sigh. It had been nearly a week since he'd been subject to the last 'Willisism,' as the crew had taken to calling her orders. He'd almost started to hope that she might have toned things down, but no. From a certain point of view the order made sense. If a ship were hit hard the containers could break loose, damaging their contents and anyone who happened to be in the cargo hold. But in the case of a light ship like *Harbinger*, such a blow would probably cave in the hull, making the lashing down of containers a moot point. His wasn't the only department getting the Commander's attention and while some had benefited from her expertise, others would have been better off if she had just left well enough alone.

"Excuse me. Commander Willis?"

At the sound of her name Willis turned around to Professor Bhaile, leader of the civilian delegation. A short, fat and balding man in his mid-fifties, he always seemed to favour clothing cut slightly tighter than Willis thought suited him. Whenever, such as now, she saw him in zero gravity he always reminded her of a rubber ball she had as a child.

"Yes Professor. What can I do for you?"

Bhaile brought himself to a clumsy halt beside her.

"I wanted to have a word about what you said to Leah Moir. She came to me in a very upset state. She said you actively threatened her..."

"I believe my exact words were that if I found her gear in the access way again I'd heave it out the nearest airlock and her after it," Willis replied.

"Commander I don't believe that language is at all appropriate!" he replied with indignation.

"Professor, Ms. Moir has been told more than once not to spread herself across the entire deck. Blocking a main access way, even temporarily, is unacceptable."

"She isn't a soldier, Commander."

"But this *is* a warship. One that may be required to go to action stations at any time. I'm not prepared to see someone being carted off to sickbay because they tripped over one of her belongings."

"I don't think an emergency is very likely while we're in jump space Commander."

" By its nature an emergency tends to be unexpected," Willis replied wearily.

"NOW HEAR THIS. NOW HEAR THIS. ALL SENIOR PERSONNEL, TO THE OFFICERS' MESS," the intercom squawked.

"You'll have to me excuse Professor," said Willis as she started to push herself down the corridor.

"Yes we'll continue this later."

Willis brought herself to a sharp halt and looked back over her shoulder.

"No Professor, we won't. This conversation is finished."

"I'll keep this quick," Flores began as he looked around the table. "We'll be jumping into the next system in about ninety minutes."

"Do we know anything about this solar system?" asked Major Tigran, commander of the ship's marine contingent.

"No. We're now well beyond any previous telescope observations," Flores replied.

"Are we realistically expecting to find anything in this system?" Chief Engineer Cian Seoige asked.

"Not likely Chief. We were only thirty light years away from our last location in real-space. There was no sign of any radio transmissions so the best we can hope for is to pick up the trail again."

So far the mission had been maddeningly unproductive. For several years ships operating beyond Landfall had been reporting radio transmissions of an unknown origin. The transmissions had been strong enough to confirm that they weren't natural but too weak to be legible. But they had offered *Harbinger* an obvious place to start their search for the Nameless. Like Hansel and Gretel following the breadcrumbs *Harbinger* had started to track the steadily strengthening transmissions back to their source. Then abruptly the transmissions had stopped.

It was inexplicable.

There was only one plausible reason why they were no longer picking up radio signals. No one was transmitting. Yet that didn't make sense. The only way a civilisation could stop sending any radio transmissions would be to go pre-industrial.

The exact cut out point was undoubtedly currently somewhere in interstellar space, so instead they had backtracked to where they had been receiving the transmissions. They then travelled 'sideways' in an attempt to get a second bearing on the source. Unfortunately the distance was simply too vast to get a decent triangulation. So Flores was forced to make his best guess and grope forward blindly.

"Anyway it's going to be the usual drill. We'll be making re-entry at the twenty light hour mark and seeing if there is anything of interest. The crew will close up on stations in about an hour."

"Captain, how much further are we planning on going this run?" Willis asked.

"This system will be the last stop before we head back. The only question is do we top off from the supply ship again or do we head all the way back to Baden?"

"From the mechanical point of view everything's good. For my department there is no reason to return yet," Seoige replied.

"Good." Turning to Willis, Flores asked: "Commander, what about the crew?"

"The regular crew are fine. The civilians are a bit more of a problem," Willis replied. "They're getting a bit surly about the hot bunking. It doesn't help that there is nothing for them to do apart from staying out of the way. It would probably help if we could drop some of them off until we definitely find something."

"Not really a runner Commander, sadly. The Council's instructions were pretty specific," Flores replied with genuine regret.

Hot bunking was a process by which two crewmembers on different shifts were assigned to the same bunk. When one got up to go on duty the other would go off duty and go to bed. As a ship designed for long range operations *Harbinger* did have enough bunks for the normal crew to have one each, and with the compliment swollen by civilians hot bunking had been the only way of packing them all in.

"If there is nothing else people then we may as well get on with it." As everyone rose to their feet he added: "Commander, can I have a quick word."

Willis waited, her expression carefully blank. Flores's expression was equally unreadable. Seven weeks in space and she remained as unknown to him as the day she stepped aboard.

"Commander. I want to have a word with you, regarding your performance."

"May I ask in what respect sir?" Willis replied with a note of caution in her voice.

"Your disputes with the crew and civilian staff."

"I didn't realise complaints been made, sir," she responded stiffly.

"Only from the civilian staff, who tend not to pay much attention to the chain of command. The details I've received indicate that you were correct in all cases. What concerns me is your handling. It... lacks subtlety and generates unnecessary friction. They are civilians, and while I agree that doesn't mean they can do what they like, the handling needs to be different."

"I see, sir."

"Which brings me to the second point: your relationship with the rest of the crew. I noticed your command style is very abrupt."

"You said no complaints had been made, sir."

Flores smiled slightly.

"I hear the ship grapevine as much as anyone else commander. You aren't getting the best out of people and your relationship with the ship's NCOs in particular is worrying me."

"I will attempt to improve that, sir."

Flores stared at her for a moment.

"All right, Commander. I'll see you on the Bridge in a while."

He watched her leave the cabin with a frown on his face.

"All hands prepare for jump in."

Commander Willis's voice came over the intercom as Captain Flores pushed himself down the corridor toward the Bridge. Around him ratings were moving quickly to their stations. While the chances of hitting something in the vastness of space were incalculably small, it was the policy of the fleet that when jumping into an uncharted system all hands wore their survival suits and closed up on their combat stations. In theory by spreading the crew across the ship it reduced the number of people any single strike could kill. It also meant that if they found themselves in hostile territory they would be as ready as possible to defend themselves.

Entering the Bridge Flores pulled himself along the hand bars of the ceiling towards the command chair. Terms like 'up' and 'ceiling' were of course extremely subjective in the zero gravity environment of the main hull. However it had long been recognised that humans were designed to think in precisely such terms. Therefore all starships had one direction designated as 'up' for all non-centrifuge sections.

"We are now at twelve minutes from real-space re-entry, sir," Willis reported as she pulled herself out of the command chair. Their earlier conversation certainly didn't seem to have broken her composure, Flores thought to himself.

"We're still on track for re-entry on the twenty light hour mark."

Flores nodded to himself satisfied before a thought occurred. He gestured Willis closer.

"By the way, who's due to win the sweep if we find something?" he murmured, referring to the small betting ring on board that he officially knew nothing about.

Willis thought for a moment, her expression one of clear disapproval. The ship's betting ring was something Flores had heard of before her, another bad sign regarding her working relationship with the NCOs, and he had stopped her from closing it down. Flores believed such activities offered a harmless diversion.

"PO Hedges and Rating Sharma I believe, sir. Oh and Rating Mesa still has a chance to win if our first encounter with these people is incoming missiles."

"Gloomy beggar. All right Commander, you'd better be going."

As Willis headed aft toward the auxiliary control centre. Flores pulled on his survival suit.

"Deceleration for jump out complete, sir. Jump out six minutes," the Helmsman reported.

Flores watched the shimmering tunnel of light of the jump conduit on one of the smaller screens.

"Thirty seconds to real-space re-entry," called out the Helmsman.

Flores put on his helmet and flicked on the main intercom.

"All hands brace for re-entry," he announced before closing his helmet visor.

The deck trembled as the jump drive started to strain to push the ship back into real-space. The main displays blanked out as the computer received the usual surge of data it couldn't make sense of. Flores felt his stomach lurch uncomfortably. Then with a final jerk they were through. The displays lit up again and their operators launched into feverish activity. The first minute or two of any jump in was always the most dangerous. Effectively a ship was blind while it systems re-established themselves and waited for the first radar returns to come in. If by some mischance there happened to be something unfriendly within firing range of the jump in point, the first you'd probably know of it was when their first shot hit you. However, as with the rest of the systems they had already investigated, *Harbinger* was confronted with lots and lots of nothing special.

"We are showing all clear in all quarters Captain," the Senior Sensor Rating announced.

"Any radio traffic?"

"Nothing coming up on the initial sweeps but background noise Skipper."

"Damn it," Flores muttered to himself. He hadn't realised just how much he had been expecting the pick up the trail. "Looks like we've struck out, again," he sighed. "Take us out of combat stations. Tell the science team they're up. We might as well have a decent look around since we're here. I'm going to go for a wash. Give me a buzz on the off chance we see anything worthwhile."

The initial charting of a star-system was one of the most boring jobs in exploration. It involved holding position at the edge of the system while the ship's various scanning systems found the major planetary bodies, then tracked and extrapolated their orbits. It was slow but necessary work. The effects of accidentally attempting to jump out inside a planetary mass shadow would, if you were really lucky, be very unpleasant and more likely fatal.

Three hours after their arrival in the system, Flores was examining his face in the mirror and wondering whether he needed a shave. The ship had settled back into the usual day routine but already the system was looking more interesting than the previous ones. The science team weren't certain yet but there appeared to be a planet in the Liquid Water Band, more often referred to as the Goldilocks Zone. If confirmed, it would be a valuable find in its own right. In every solar system there was a narrow zone in which water could exist in its liquid form. Too close to the local star and water would boil off, but too far and it would freeze. The exact distance of this band depended on the star's strength. Most planets in the Universe fell outside the band but those few that did offered the best prospect for future colonisation. Certainly the finding of a future home for humanity would be enough for this trip to be considered at least a limited success. He was just lifting the razor when the intercom on his belt buzzed.

"Flores here."

"Sorry to interrupt you Captain. I have a request from Professor Bhaile for a radar focus," said Willis

"For what reason?"

"He believes he has detected an object that's point of origin is the second planet."

The second planet was the one possibly in the Goldilocks Zone.

"Interesting, how sure is he?"

"Err… at the moment the system's reading sixty nine percent sure, sir."

"Tell him if it gets up to eighty five percent he can have his radar focus."

"Yes sir."

An hour later Flores, Willis and Professor Bhaile were studying the main holo display. The computer estimate of whether the object came from the second planet had topped out at eighty seven percent. The search radar had been brought to bear on the object and almost immediately the results had been exciting.

"Well that's either the strangest shaped meteor I've ever seen or it's a vessel," Flores murmured trying to suppress a growing excitement. The news had sprinted round the ship literally within minutes and the sense of weariness on board had evaporated instantly.

The radar focus could only provide a picture of the surface of an object. But what it did show was interesting to say the least. The object had a pod-like front followed by a disc shape behind that might be a small centrifuge. The rear however was indistinct, possibly damaged.

"In real-space it's at least five hours away captain, if we go for a least time approach," said Willis, pre-empting the next question.

"What do you think?"

"Strange that we're spotting something artificial in a place with no other sign of life in the system. Still definitely worth a look Captain." She pointed to the rear of the object. "If this is wreckage we might be able to get a very close look at it, maybe even board it."

Flores nodded slowly to himself.

"I think we'll go for a slow approach. Keep our thermal signature down. No point advertising that we're here," he said.

All around the display there were nods of agreement.

The anticipation was so strong Flores could almost taste it. Their plotted course to the object took nearly seven hours to cover. He attempted to go below to do some paperwork but found himself back on the Bridge every twenty minutes to look at the slowly improving scans. As the range lessened, any doubt that this was a major find dropped away. Up close the object was most definitely a spacecraft but it looked a far cry from any sort of interstellar capable ship. For one thing it was small, barely half the size of *Harbinger*. There was massive damage astern however, to the point that it wasn't immediately clear what kind of propulsion system the vessel had used.

During the approach the science team had barely moved from their displays. Flores had heard a dozen theories developed and discarded as improved information was received. Finally they got within a hundred kilometres of the contact and Flores called Bhaile and his senior officers for a conference.

"Well Professor?" Flores queried.

"This is certainly very, very interesting," Professor Bhaile said. "Have you ever seen the pictures of the Mars mission ship NASA was planning to build before first contact Captain?"

"I don't think so," Flores replied after a moment of thought.

"I have," Willis said. "This ship does bear similarities, or at least what's still there does." She shook her head. "I'm sure this is fascinating from the academic standpoint and this would look wonderful in a museum, but compared to what took a pop at *Mississippi* this is a relic. I don't think we're going to learn anything useful from it."

"I don't know about that Commander," Bhaile murmured. "Optical can you focus in on… grid reference G15 please? Thank you."

The view on the main screen focused in on the required part of the alien ship.

"That's definitely a hatch," Bhaile said firmly. "And it's one designed to be reopened."

The Professor had a point. Hatches on a probe didn't include hand wheels. Why waste the mass that no one would ever use? On any kind of manned vessel however, a way to open the outer hatch was generally a desirable feature.

"We could come along side and send a team aboard," Bhaile suggested.

"I wouldn't recommend that Captain," Willis quickly objected. "We don't know what else is out here and I don't think we want to risk the possibility of trying to dodge missiles from a standing start."

"Okay. So we send one of the shuttles over," Bhaile said, looking at Willis and Flores.

"Equally bad idea Professor," Willis replied. "If something jumped us we'd either have to bug out and leave the shuttle and crew behind, or hang around to pick it up again and possibly get taken out."

"However I think you're right about going inside. If that's a ship it might have the remains of a crew so well worth a look. We'll send out the Doppelganger and circle the ship. Coxswain Benson?" Flores looked round.

The ship's Helmsman looked around.

"Sir?"

"Get suited up."

Doppelganger was a system originally developed by NASA at the start of the twenty-first century, which sought to marry the flexibility of a human with the go anywhere capabilities of a probe. Basically a Doppelganger was a human shaped robot, directed by its operator back on the ship wearing a control suit that transmitted to the robot the movements of the wearer. The Doppelganger mimicked these movements exactly. Obviously there were some limitations. The speed of the radio transmissions limited the range to a few thousand kilometres at best, before the response lag made the system unusable. However it remained the best way of getting human capabilities into places you wouldn't send a human, albeit with a pretty hefty price tag. A captain would be filling out a lot of paperwork if he lost or broke one.

Chief Coxswain Wallace Benson checked the display mounted on the right arm of the interface suit and nodded satisfied. The control room for the Doppelganger system was located outside the centrifuge. However the various cables of the harness system kept him fixed in position while still allowing him to move freely. Beside him two of the engineering crew were completing the checks on the Doppelganger itself.

"Are you ready?" Commander Willis asked stiffly from the corner where she was holding herself to avoid getting in the way.

Benson glanced towards the starchy commander. She'd been prickly enough at the best of times over the past few weeks, but now she looked in particularly poor humour. That struck Benson as strange. Now they had finally found something the ship was abuzz with excitement but the Commander didn't seem to share it. Still he had heard that this was her first posting on a scout ship, and no matter what the manuals claimed, that was very different from being First Officer on a battle line vessel. From what Benson could see, it was taking the Commander a while to figure that out. Still he'd seen a lot of officers on their first tour as a Commander and it took most of the starch out of them. Willis was the stiffest he'd seen to date, but despite that, in his experience she wasn't the worst by any stretch of the imagination.

"Just have to fit the self-destruction pack then we're ready to roll ma'am. Two more minutes," Benson replied.

Willis nodded slightly. The self-destruct backpack was slotted into place and Benson pulled the visor down over his eyes. The Doppelganger came on line and immediately mirrored Benson's exact stance. He felt the usual disorientation as all of his senses told him he'd just jumped two meters to the left. He looked to his right and felt the other usual disorientation as he saw himself suspended in the network of cables and supports. One of the engineers looked towards the big display screen showing what Benson saw and gave a thumbs up.

"Okay good to go," Benson reported. Unhitching from the docking frame he guided himself towards the airlock. One of the engineers pulled the outer lock open and the Doppelganger/Benson floated in and pulled the hatch closed after him. He heard the sound of pumps die away as the air was sucked out of the airlock.

"We're cracking the lock now, Cox," Willis's voice said in his ear.

"Roger that."

The outer lock swung open and Benson pushed out. Grasping the edge of the lock he took a moment to find his bearings. *Harbinger's* main sensor array gave him the direction to look in for the alien ship. The built-in laser rangefinder flicked out.

The alien ship was a mere one hundred and twenty clicks away. Benson plotted the course and engaged thrusters.

For ten minutes he drifted. He loved these moments. Even though he was still safely in the ship, it felt like he was out there with nothing between him and the stars. As he closed, he started firing the thrusters to bring himself to a halt relative to the alien vessel. Up close the vessel looked more of a museum piece than ever. A quick burst from the thrusters pushed Benson towards the rear.

"Careful, Cox," he heard Willis say, "we're picking up high levels of radiation back there."

Benson backed off about a hundred meters and continued to curve round the stern of the ship, which was a mass of wreckage. The Doppelganger's Geiger counter started to click urgently in his ear. Benson quickly jetted out from directly astern of the ship.

"That's a really strange looking engine system. I can't make out what heck I'm looking at," Benson commented. There seemed to be a big round plate of a slightly larger diameter than the main hull. It looked like it had been positioned directly behind the hull on a series of mental columns. Now it was nearly ninety degrees out of position, and only held on by two of the columns. "This bucket definitely came off second best against something. I can see what looks like a radiation shield but not what makes this thing go."

A new voice cut into the intercom link.

"Actually Cox you can," said Flores. "Someone up here recognises it. It's Nuclear Pulse Propulsion."

"Never heard of that one, sir," Benson admitted.

"Wouldn't imagine many people have. That circular shield is a pusher plate and the columns are shock absorbers. You lob a small nuke out the back and ride the shockwave. The Americans experimented with the idea in the mid twentieth. Never came to anything though."

"That's a seriously retro propulsion system, sir."

"In the case of this one it looks like something clipped the edge of that pusher plate. Retro is about the right description, but it would however indicate that they have developed nuclear weapons, sir," Willis observed.

"Yes it would. Carry on." There was a click as Flores closed the connection at his end.

"All right Cox. I saw what looked like view ports at the front. See if you can look in and find out if anyone is at home."

"Roger."

Benson very gently jetted forward again and landed on the alien ship with barely a clunk. Engaging the foot magnets he walked over to the nearest view port, then moved onto the next and then the next.

"Something covering the inside of the ports. Can't see anything in there," he reported.

"I see it Cox. Let's have a look at that access hatch."

Benson started to walk round the hull toward the hatch. He had just reached the port when he paused and changed direction toward the centrifuge. Something had knocked a fist-sized hole in the metal. Judging by the way the metal was bent outwards it had been a something on the way out. Streaks of frozen gas surrounded the hole. Walking round to the far side of the centrifuge he found another hole, this one with the edges bent inwards. Something had punched all the way through, probably a piece of the engine when it was destroyed.

"Doesn't look like we'll have to worry too much about the airlocks," Willis commented as Benson turned back toward the airlock. "Science team is requesting we get some samples of the frozen gas, but have a look inside first."

"Roger that."

The handles for the lock were the wrong shape for a human hand, making them awkward to get a good grip on. At first he couldn't shift them but at a command the support crew increased the strength to the Doppelganger's limbs and slowly the mechanical strength forced it round. Inside the airlock was a tight fit but the inner door of the lock was already open and Benson was able to push through into the cabin. There were a few drifting ice crystals that helped to defuse the Doppelganger's lights a little but mostly Benson could only see what was directly in front.

The inside was cramped and utilitarian. Not a square centimetre of space had been allowed to go to waste. As with the outside of the ship, the inside reminded Benson of the pre-contact human spacecraft he'd seen, but there was also a subtle… alienness. He turned towards the stern of the ship to investigate the centrifuge. As he did a nightmarish form lit up.

"Sweet Jesus!" Benson scrambled away desperately. He felt the Doppelganger's back crash into the side of the ship.

"Easy, easy Cox!"

A hand closed on his arm and the visor was flipped back.

"Easy Cox it's all right," Willis's face was directly in front of him. "It's all right Cox it's already dead."

He looked pass the Commander towards the monitor. The horrible form was hanging motionless. It was clearly an alien and just as clearly dead.

He let out a nervous half laugh.

"Sorry about that Commander. That was a bit horror film moment."

"That's all right Cox. We all damn near jumped out of our skins as well," she replied with a rueful smile. "At least now we know there's a crew."

Another thought occurred to him.

"The whole ship's watching this aren't they?"

"Afraid so Cox."

Benson groaned quietly to himself. The Commander's smile changed to one of rare amusement.

"Ready to carry on?"

"Better hang on a moment ma'am," said one of the engineers, "his heart rate is still racing."

Benson took a few deep breaths then pulled his visor down.

"The Bridge is asking for you to take a couple of close-up shots of the body then head forward to see if we can find a cockpit," he heard Willis say as she moved back away from the control frame.

The effects of hard vacuum on a biological life form were never pretty and at times like this it was good to know that what was right in front of your eyes was actually over a hundred clicks away. The alien was a strange looking creature. It had a long, almost horse-like head on a thick neck. Its body looked massively powerful, as did its six limbs, two of them dedicated arms, topped with hands and opposable thumbs. The other four limbs were the creature's trunk-like legs. Once Benson circled the body he turned and headed towards the front.

He quickly found the cockpit and the rest of the crew. There were two of them, still strapped in their seats. The alien on the left had merely bled out of every pore but the one to the right must have tried to hold its breath or something. Its chest had basically exploded, which explained what was covering the inside of the view ports.

"What now Commander?" Benson asked.

"Hang on Cox, it's just being discussed now. While you're waiting see if you can find their computer core," Willis replied.

"Roger."

Benson spent several minutes opening up access panels while the intercom link hissed quietly in his ear.

"Chief. You're to bring it back in."

"Do you want me to collect samples?"

"Negative Cox. We're going to head towards the ship's point of origin. We're going to see if we can find some live aliens."

The planet was a purple and green jewel hanging in space. A single moon slowly orbited around its parent planet and parked in geostationary orbit on the dark side of that moon was *Harbinger*.

For two days they had sheltered in the moon's shadow. After leaving the wreck they had made another jump deeper into the system. Their re-entry had been a discreet distance from the planet, nearly a light minute, well beyond the edge of the planet's mass shadow. Then they coasted into a lunar orbit unpowered. Once there they deployed several probes to allow them to look round the moon without exposing the ship directly.

What those probes had revealed had been both fascinating and puzzling. Even at a glance the planet was supporting massive amounts of life. It was also clearly the point of origin of the wreck. Artificial satellites surrounded the planet, everything from burnt out rocket boosters to a primitive space station. The relatively weak optical scanners on the probes were also picking up signs of cities on the planet beyond. There were massive urban centres on every one of the planet's continents. There was however one thing they weren't picking up that was conspicuous by its very absence: radio traffic.

The passive sensors on *Harbinger* were among the best available to humanity. If there was even a single radio, mobile phone or transmitter of any description being used on the planet, *Harbinger* would be able to hear it. Instead all they were picking up on the radio bands was the background hiss of the local star. Not only were there no radio signals, there was no sign of life on the surface. When night fell there was no light on the surface that could not be attributed to natural sources. It was frankly a little eerie and a few members of the crew had been heard to refer to it as the ghost planet. Finally, after recovering the probes, Harbinger carefully slid out from behind the moon and approached the planet.

Another two days later and the mystery was still just that. They had deployed ground survey probes and done a complete topographical survey of the planet's surface. Several of their probes had dropped low enough to burn contrails of fire across the alien sky. Not a single inquisitive radio signal was received. Their survey had mapped several hundred major cities all over the planet, and thousands of large towns, but not a single one showed any sign of life. Most disturbing of all however were the craters.

Going by the roads that could still be seen, each one must have been a major population centre but now it was as if a giant ice cream scoop had gouged twenty-two, eighteen kilometre wide lumps out of the planet.

Finally Flores called together his senior officer and the heads of the civilian teams to decide what their next course of action would be. They were all packed into the officers' mess. A large holo display had been temporarily installed and pictures of the surface were stuck across the bulkheads.

Flores was the last to arrive. The others were standing in groups speaking quietly as they examined the pictures.

"Everyone take your seats and we'll get started."

Once they were all seated around the holo display he looked towards Bhaile.

"Professor, can you give us a quick run down of your findings so far."

"Certainly Captain. All right the basics first. This planet is approximately fifteen percent larger than Earth. Gravity at sea level is roughly one point two Gs. The planet's atmosphere is thicker than Earth's, meaning air pressure at sea level is approximately ten percent as much again. The atmosphere is a breathable mixture of oxygen, nitrogen, and carbon dioxide. At this point it looks like this planet could support humans indefinitely."

"Let's not get ahead of ourselves. What about the original tenants?"

Bhaile spread his arms in a gesture of puzzlement.

"We have nothing. We have identified towns, cities, power stations, farmland, airports and ports. Not one of them has shown the slightest sign of activity. *Harbinger's* look-down cameras are powerful enough to see creatures on the surface but they aren't the same species as the one we found on the wreck."

"Hmm... Okay. Referring to those craters, could we be looking at the aftermath of a nuclear exchange?" Flores asked. "Could these people have wiped themselves out?"

"On the first point definitely no. This planet has not suffered a nuclear war." Bhaile's tone shifted as he became more certain of his subject.

"How so sure?"

"Firstly we aren't detecting the right radioactive isotopes. Secondly we've seen craters like these all across our own solar system wherever an asteroid or comet has collided with a moon or planet. These were caused by physical impact, not an explosive blast. For a single asteroid to score a direct hit on a city is possible but pretty unlikely. For twenty-two to manage it goes went well beyond improbable.

"Orbital bombardment," Willis murmured. "I wonder did someone redirect asteroids at them?"

"No," Bhaile replied shaking his head, "all of the craters are of almost identical size and shape, indicating the impacters were all the same mass and travelling at the same velocity. If it were redirected asteroids, we'd be seeing a lot of variety in terms of size and shape of the craters."

"Large calibre railguns maybe?" Willis asked.

"Possibly, or simply drop a lump of metal out of orbit. A side effect is that the planet is in the midst of at least a minor ice age, probably caused by debris thrown up into the atmosphere by the impacts. If you look here and here, you can see cities that are being engulfed by the expanding ice sheet."

"Alright. What about this being self inflicted?" Flores asked.

"Well... if we go by the wreck then such a style of attack might be within their capabilities. These craters are spread across the entire planet."

"An alien version of mutual assured destruction perhaps?" suggested Major Tigran, commander of the marine contingent.

"Those impacts destroyed twenty-two cities. That alone would have killed tens of millions. Cooling of the planet would have had disastrous effects on agriculture, probably resulting in millions more starving. But I believe this planet supported billions. I'm not seeing anything that would account for every last one of them."

Flores sighed and put his hands behind his head lacing his fingers together.

"Any idea on timeframe?" he asked.

"There are heavy concentrations of dust particles in the upper atmosphere but we don't have the modelling software to determine the length of time since the event. In all honesty Captain, I think we're reaching the limit of what we're going to learn up here," he admitted.

"Landing parties?" Willis asked.

"We're running out of alternatives."

"Captain we have received no invitation to land," the senior diplomat objected.

"If you can see someone to ask please point them out," Willis replied sharply. "If you're planning on waiting for an invitation we're going to be sitting here for a long time. This is our best lead to date. We can't simply turn around and leave without at least trying to find out what happened and whether it is relevant to us."

"I am merely saying that we should consider returning to Baden and seeking authorisation from the Council."

"We already have authorisation to take what action is deemed necessary. The only reason to return to Baden would be to avoid having to take responsibility for a decision," Willis replied coldly.

"Commander." Flores's voice held a note of warning.

Willis took the hint and sat back in her chair.

"We will make landing. It is our duty to see if we can come up with some answers."

"We should drop mobile probes into one of the craters and another on one of our landing zones to take some air readings," Bhaile added.

Flores glanced towards Willis.

"It will take a couple of hours to prep the landing teams so launching probes wouldn't delay us much," she replied with a shrug. "If there is something nasty down there, I'd rather find out with a probe than in person."

"Okay. But where to land?"

"I would suggest here and here," Bhaile said, pointing to cities on opposite sides of the planet. They seem to be the two biggest surviving cities."

"We only have two shuttles and one ship," Willis reminded him. "We'll want to put the landing parties close enough together to offer some mutual support. How about we keep one of your cities and also look at this town here, about ten clicks away?"

Bhaile studied the display. "Okay I'll go with that," he agreed.

"Alright. Commander Willis will lead the team into the city. Major Tigran," Flores nodded to the Japanese officer, "will command the second group. Major, make sure your men keep their safety catches on. We don't need to make first contact by riddling one of the locals full of holes."

The major nodded seriously.

"Alright everyone. Let's get started."

Commander Willis ignored another sickening jerk as the shuttle rammed its way into the atmosphere. The fires of re-entry threw a flickering light across the cargo space and the civilians in the shuttle kept looking nervously at the portholes, clearly half expecting the flames to eat through the hull. The regular crew and marines with long experience ignored it. Technically the shuttle could have taken a slightly longer but much smoother re-entry curve, but radar didn't work all that well during re-entry and if someone took exception to their presence they would have less of a chance to dodge any incoming fire.

"Coming out of re-entry, ETA seven minutes," the pilot called out over the intercom.

Willis looked over towards Benson, who was performing system checks on one of their two Collapsible Wheel Vehicles, usually refer to as CWVs.

"All set Cox?" Willis bellowed over the noise. He gave a quick thumbs up. Willis switched over to the intercom. "Pilot I want you ready to dust off as soon as we clear. Then go into a holding pattern at five thousand metres until we give the all clear."

"Roger that commander. ETA six minutes."

Willis clicked her intercom back to receive and shouted back to everyone in the cargo hold.

"Everyone listen up. Touch down in six minutes. Everyone mount up."

They all settled onto the two CWVs waiting for the forward ramp to drop. Willis looked back around. The marines all had their suit visors down, concealing their faces but all of them were still and patient. They could all feel the shuttle decelerating hard. The docking clamps attached to the wheels squeaked hard in protest. There was then a thump as the shuttle hit the ground. Instantly the forward ramp dropped with a crash and the wheel clamps popped open. The marine driver in the front vehicle immediately floored the accelerator and roared down the ramp. As they cleared the underside of the shuttle one of the marines in the back stood up and locked the 12mm railgun into firing position. The second, slightly larger CVW with the science and diplomatic staff bounced out immediately behind. As the two vehicles got clear, the shuttle opened its throttle and pushed itself up and away.

Willis had decided that the foliage was hard to get used to. In many respects it was similar to terrestrial plants but then there were almost as many differences. The first they'd noticed was the colour. The foliage was a deep and varied range of purple. Up close the difference became more apparent, the leaves of individual plants were thicker and fleshier than those on Earth and when one of the Marines leaned against a tree the whole thing had bent over as if it were made of rubber. The air was cold and crisp, like a spring morning back home in Belfast. After nearly two months of recycled ship air it was a refreshing change.

Three-quarters of an hour after landing they had settled themselves into a defensible position on the outskirts of the city and established contact with the ship and the second party. They had approached the city via a wide concrete roadway. Once settled they watched the city for any signs of life. Nothing stirred and Willis felt safe enough to send the shuttle back up to the *Harbinger*.

"Any thoughts?" Willis asked Benson and Marine Sergeant Martinkus as she examined the city through her binoculars.

"I've seen livelier graveyards," Martinkus replied sourly. "If there was any kind of a party here, it's well and truly over."

"Yes, looks like we've missed it all right," Benson agreed. "Private Brijnath, have you seen anything?"

There was a rustling from the branches of one of the more rigid trees.

"Zip, zilch, nada, Elvis has most definitely left the building," Brijnath called down

The city loomed in the distance, dark and foreboding. Even through her binoculars many of the buildings looked dilapidated. Her breath misted in the cold air, momentarily blotting out the city. She had expected answers to become obvious once they got down, but the mystery loomed as large as ever.

"Going on the orbital scans this place looks big enough to support a couple of million people easily. So where is everyone?" Willis muttered to herself. "Sergeant, you, me and four of your men are going to scout into the city. The rest of the party will remain here until we give the all clear."

"Are you sure that's good idea Commander?" Martinkus asked in the tone NCOs use with officers when they're thinking 'this isn't a good idea.' "You're not trained for ground operations, ma'am."

"Yes but I'm going anyway," Willis replied in a tone that made clear disagreement wasn't going to get him anywhere.

Instead he saluted before turning and bawling at his troops.

It took two hours for them to work their way towards the centre of the city. The marines sat in the CWV facing outward, their weapons ready. Although they had images taken from orbit that gave them a crude map, many of the streets were choked with abandoned vehicles. In a few places buildings had collapsed into the street, forcing them to backtrack and find another route. The buildings themselves were squat, blocky and, to human eyes at least, ugly. Almost all of them had the weather beaten, crumbling look that structures get when they have been abandoned for a few years. As they headed further into the city, the buildings started to become more high-rise, but there still wasn't any sign of life.

Finally they drove into a square and Willis signalled to stop. The fuel cell motor that drove the CWV wasn't particularly loud but the silence when it was shut down was intense. It wasn't the silence of something waiting to happen, but the more disturbing quiet of there being nothing left to make any noise. The building in the square looked slightly grander than those they had seen before.

"We're not going to learn very much riding round the street. We're going to have to start poking around buildings," Willis said.

"We've a whole city to look at Commander," Martinkus grunted. "Just 'cause it's big doesn't mean there's anything important in it."

"It's got to have local government offices somewhere," Willis gestured around the square. "This looks like somewhere to start." She took a step forward but Martinkus's armoured gauntlet closed round her arm.

"With respect Commander, my boys will take a look around first. Make sure there are no surprises. Lee, cannon. Brijnath check it out."

"I don't think there are any aliens ready to jump out at us," she commented impatiently as the three marines quickly disappeared into the building.

"Yeah but I'd get some serious earache from the Major if you fell through rotten floorboards, ma'am," Martinkus replied patiently.

Reluctantly Willis had to admit, at least to herself, that as much as she wanted to find answers she had to acknowledge that dirtside wasn't her area of expertise. Once the marines had given the all clear, the rest moved in. The first few buildings they checked had nothing in them aside from mouldering furniture, rusting machinery and peeling paint. Five buildings in they struck gold. The building appeared to be some kind of library. Certainly there were shelves upon shelves of books. The first one Willis picked up fell apart in her hands. Clearly it had been used as nesting material by some creature. Most of the books however seemed to be intact. Slowly they swept through the room.

"Sarge!" called out one of the marines. "I've got a body over here."

It was in a small room towards the back of the library. The body was slumped across a desk. Aside from a few leathery looking tendons the body was little more than the skeleton. Its general shape seemed to be about the same as the bodies found on the space ship. Something had dropped out of the alien's outstretched hand.

"I was starting to wonder whether that damn spaceship's crew were just their equivalent to the chimps we sent up in the first rockets," Willis muttered.

Martinkus picked the object out of the body's hand and then turned the skull round. There was a hole in the side.

"Suicide?"

"Looks that way," Martinkus replied, fiddling with the object. After a few seconds the sergeant managed to open it up. "Looks like a gunpowder based weapon, some kind of semi automatic."

Willis looked at the body. "Have you seen many corpses here Sergeant?" she asked.

"Aside from this one, no."

"I wonder where everyone else is then?"

"Rotted away I guess."

"Why is this one still here then? This building isn't air tight or anything," Willis challenged. "No I don't expect you to be able to answer that Sergeant."

"Sarge," one of the marines called out. "It's starting to get dark."

Willis glanced at her watch with surprise. "What, already?"

"Only a twenty-hour day on this rock. Also this hemisphere is in its autumn, plus the nuclear winter effect," Martinkus calmly explained.

Willis cursed herself for forgetting that and making such a bloody stupid comment.

"We'd better head back to the camp. It seems to be safe so tomorrow we'll bring in the whole team."

Martinkus looked around the library nodding slowly in agreement.

"This is reasonably defensible. Not that there seems to be anything to defend against."

It took longer to find their way back out of the city than expected. The unlit buildings loomed threateningly over them. The Sergeant was unwilling to reveal their position by turning on the

CWV's headlights, so instead the driver relied on his helmet's night vision goggles. Lacking goggles of her own, Willis sat in the darkness. The darkened building loomed over her threateningly and Willis found herself shivering, and not just because of the cold.

The camp was blacked out when they got back. Martinkus grunted with satisfaction as a sentry challenged them. Those who had spent the day at the camp quickly gathered around. While the scientists had spent the day happily examining the local plant life, the diplomats had been left twiddling their thumbs. Willis found herself giving a brief run down of what they had found.

"A library, that's great!" burst out one of the linguists, a young woman called Alice Peats, when Willis described their main find. She then blushed when everyone turned towards her.

"Well we haven't seen a live alien, so their written record might be all we have," she muttered.

"Fair point, Ms Peats, fair point."

"So are we going to shift into the city, Commander?" Martinkus asked.

"I'm going to speak with Flores now. If the Captain has no objections we'll move the camp into the city," Willis replied.

The *Harbinger* was sitting in geostationary orbit above the planet's equator. The position had been carefully chosen to allow the ship to maintain direct contact with both ground parties. It took a minute for the transmitter to find *Harbinger* in the night sky and there was another slight delay as the signal was rerouted to Flores's cabin.

The Captain rubbed his fingers through his beard as he listened to Willis's report.

"Good work finding that library," Flores replied after a few moments thought. "If in your judgement to shift base to there is safe then I am authorising you to do so. Major Tigran's team has found nothing of worth so I'm going to direct him to relocate to your position. This library of yours currently looks like the best source of information, so I want both sets of civilians working on it."

Flores paused for a moment. "This is damn strange Commander. Where the hell has everyone gone?"

"That's certainly the big question, sir. With two teams we should be able check more buildings here, see what turns up."

"Okay. Tigran should reach you by the middle of tomorrow. While the two of you are checking the town we're going to perform a more detailed scan of the planet's surface around your current position. This planet has been subject to some kind of apocalypse but there is nothing to suggest that it couldn't support at least some survivors."

"Hopefully we'll start finding some answers instead of more questions tomorrow sir," Willis replied with a greater note of optimism than she felt.

Alice Peats sat on the floor surround by piles of books, humming softly to herself as she made notes. The second team had turned up mid-morning and they were now slowly sweeping through the city, block by block. The scientists were busy examining the body of the alien over on the far side of the library hall. For an hour or so there had been the whine of a drill against bone, a sound that had set Peats's teeth on edge. Fortunately they seemed to have finished that for the time being. She'd already had to move once after finding herself unable to concentrate as long as she could see the bones and dried flesh of the dead alien.

The scratch of her pencil on the pad slowed and finally stopped as her thoughts began to drift. What thought had once passed through that now desiccated skull? Had it been filled with dreams of the future, of family and friends? Or was its mind so strange, so alien, that she could never have understood it? Were there still members of this species hidden somewhere on this world, or did this library represent the last echoes of an extinct race?

"Any progress Ms Peats?"

Peats nearly jumped out of her skin as the speaker walked around the closest set of shelves into view. Commander Willis wasn't a particularly tall woman but she could move like a ghost and now loomed over Peats. Her expression was disapproving.

"Err, yes, well, I'm making some progress towards getting what looks like their alphabet."

"And?" Willis enquired.

"And what?"

"And how long before you can expect to read some of this?"

Peats stared at the commander for a moment.

"Commander if this is a dead language we'll be lucky if we can read any of it in under ten years!"

"I thought you were among the best Ms. Peats," Willis replied coldly.

"I am the best but this is not the same as a spoken word!" Peats hissed, aware of the drop in volume on the other side of the library. "It took decades to find a way into ancient Egyptian, and they were human."

Willis let out an irritable sigh. Behind her Major Tigran and a squad of his marines plodded back into the library.

"Alright Peats. Stay at it. But keep an eye open for anything that might offer some quick answers. I need practical results, not a long drawn out academic exercise." She turned on her heels and walked away.

Bloody soldiers, Peats thought to herself, *they never understand anything they can't either shout or shoot at.*

Ignoring the fuming linguist, Willis headed towards the corner of the library where the scientists had been examining the body. Professor Bhaile saw her coming and moved to intercept.

"Commander. Before you ask we are making some small progress."

"Good. What have you found?"

"Going by our testing so far, our subject here has been dead for between fifteen and sixty years."

"That's a pretty wide margin Professor."

"We should be able to narrow that down a bit once we get some of the samples under the equipment we have in the ship, and find out just how active the local micro-organisms are. It is interesting though. Even with the bottom end figure, after fifteen years you would think there would be some signs of a population recovery."

Willis sighed heavily.

"I was really hoping that some answers would be turning up by now."

"We've also been pulling apart some of the computer equipment we found. It looks very similar to the silicon microprocessors we had at the end of the last century," Bhaile told her.

"Any thought on where everyone has gone?"

Bhaile shook his head.

"Sorry Commander on that one your guess is as good as mine."

"Commander, Major," Benson called out. "Call from the ship."

Captain Flores's face was already on the small view screen when Willis reached their communications equipment set-up.

"Ah Commander. Anything new to report?"

"Not really, sir. The science team have a few bits but nothing big."

"We've got something," said Tigran.

Willis stepped aside and waved the marine forward.

"We've just finished surveying the surrounding area. We've established that we're in some kind of government or administrative centre. We've noticed something disturbing. In every building there are signs of a bonfire and there were the remains of computers and files. It looks like someone has made a concerted effort to destroy all government records."

"Government buildings?" Flores looked puzzled. "Can you be sure?"

"Not one hundred percent, sir. They were offices but their government status is an estimate," Tigran admitted. "The burns were done carefully however. The fires weren't allowed to get out of control. Apart from those buildings, it's like people simply opened their doors and walked away."

Flores pondered this for moment and then shrugged. "Well we've also found something strange. There appears to be a collection of temporary structures about fifty kilometres north of your position, and it's massive, at least twice the size of the city you're now in."

"You think we might find something there?" Willis asked.

"It's being suggested up here that maybe these aliens were wiped out by some sort of epidemic, but that's only a theory. These temporary buildings might be where refugees were sent if the cities were abandoned. If you and the Major judge it safe I'd like you to take a look."

Willis glanced towards Major Tigran.

"I see nothing to prevent us from going," the marine replied after a moment's thought.

"Alright. We'll move out at first light with two of the CWVs, half the marines and a couple of the civilian team. The rest can stay here and continue with what we have."

"Okay. We'll speak again in…" Flores glanced toward the ship clock, "…eighteen hours."

Willis didn't sleep well that night. Several times she woke to hear the comforting tread of the sentries. Ghosts were a subject that hadn't crossed her mind in a long time, but if ever a place could be haunted this entire planet felt like it. When it came, Dawn was something of a relief. First light found Willis, Tigran and half the marines cruising down a reasonably intact road. Vegetation had broken through the concrete in a few places and there was the occasional abandoned or burnt out vehicle but they made good speed. They had spotted a herd of some kind of creature. Like the city builders they had six limbs and were clearly some kind of animal native to this world.

Willis pulled on her helmet and engaged the command radio frequency. She closed the helmet visor for some privacy.

"Major. What do you think we'll find here?" Willis asked.

The marine officer was riding in the leading CWV. So far he had not offered any kind of opinion.

"I don't believe we're going to find anything," he replied quietly. "Whatever has happened, someone has wanted to cover their tracks and not leave any indication who they were. That has... sinister implications."

"You don't have much faith in the disease theory?" Willis asked.

"Can you imagine a disease that requires government files to be burned?" the Major challenged.

"No I can't. But if something like ethnic cleansing has happened, where are the cleansers?"

"As I said I don't think answers are going to be found."

Willis didn't have any answer to that. The atmosphere on the planet was oppressive and affecting almost the whole landing party. People talked as quietly and respectfully as they would in a graveyard. Something unknown had come to this place and destroyed it. When they left the library, the six marines and seven ship's ratings being left behind had started to fortify the building. Neither Willis or the Major had ordered such work but everyone felt the desire to defend him or herself.

Eventually they turned off the main road onto a dirt track.

It led straight to their destination. When they got within a kilometre of the buildings they slowed down to walking pace. Half the marines debussed and deployed into a skirmish line ahead of the vehicles. Slowly they made their way into the mass of crumbling buildings. They all seemed to have been built out something that resembled wood and were laid out with military precision. Willis stepped into one of the huts. They were all the same: a smell of rot and a few disintegrating bunks.

Several times they crossed through the remains of wire fences that sub-divided the camp. There had also been the remains of a very strong perimeter fence all round the camp. By now everyone was on foot except for the two drivers.

"This is starting to look less and less like a refugee camp and more like a prison camp," Willis commented to Major Tigran as the two officers examined the top down view supplied from the *Harbinger*.

"Yes it is," the Major agreed. "I suggest we head for this cluster of buildings. They look like more permanent structures. If there's anything worth finding here, it's there."

Peats's back let out a sharp click as she straightened up. Sitting on the floor was playing hell with her spine but the alien chairs were just too weird a shape to be comfortable. She needed at least a quick break to clear her head. Six hours of staring at alien text would fry anyone's brain. Happily the fleet preferred its coffee thick enough to coat roads and strong enough to raise the dead. With mug in hand she wandered back to her notes. She paused at the desk the dead alien had been slumped across. There was something like a newspaper spread across the desk. The alien had bled heavily across the paper, obscuring most of the text. There was however also a picture which she hadn't seen many of in their work. The old blood covering it made it impossible to see what the picture showed. She carefully prised up the stiff paper and glanced towards her scanning equipment. If she could look past the blood perhaps she could get enough of a quick answer to get the Commander off her back.

It was over two hours after entering camp that they finally reached the centre. The building complex was huge and made of some sort of concrete-like material. Its appearance was strictly utilitarian. It had a number of industrial sized chimneys that sent a chill down Willis's spine. The building material was the same as they'd seen in the city, but the style subtly different. It took time to find their way into the complex. There were several entrances but each one was fused shut by rust. Willis was just about to order Tigran to blast an entrance when they came to a door hanging off its hinges. Inside was unlit and like everything else showed signs of long abandonment. The floors and walls were of bare concrete, and looked roughly and hastily finished. Slowly they started to move through the giant building.

From the moment she saw it Willis had an uneasy feeling that she knew what the purpose of the building was. She kept her feelings to herself but several of the marines looked like they were thinking the same thing. They found several chambers that looked like showers, complete with nozzles in the ceiling. But no drain in the floor. Finally they reached the basement level, and there they found where the population had gone. There were dozens of large ovens set into the walls, the last of which was stuffed with the partially cremated remains of several aliens.

"My God. This isn't a refugee camp, it's an extermination camp," Willis said quietly.

Peats's computer emitted a little ping as it finished applying the software filter. She drank the last of her now cold coffee before looking at the screen. And when she did her mouth immediately went dry. The picture was of a wedge shaped starship.

That looked just like the one that had attacked the *Mississippi*.

Chapter Four

The Old Lady

1st May 2066

The great hatches at either end of the Gemini Construction Platform's Number One Dock were open, ready for the launch. But with most of the lights inside the dock switched off the great ship lurked within darkness. The launch was scheduled for 1.32pm Greenwich Mean Time, carefully chosen as the moment when the dock would come out from behind Earth's shadow. The Sun would illuminate the great ship as she left the dock for the very first time. With all the money spent on the ship, people tended to feel that at the very least the fleet should put on a good show.

In the main observation lounge the armoured shutters that normally protected the large window had been retracted, offering an unrivalled view of the launch. Occasionally sounds of laughter could be heard from the access way. Above in the station centrifuge, the yard managers were entertaining the various officers, diplomats and assorted other dignitaries that always seemed to turn up for these events. Going by past launches, about a third of the guests wouldn't actually make it as far as the observation lounge, unwilling to subject themselves to the discomfort of freefall. Even those who did would wait until the last minute, a fact that suited the current occupants just fine.

Admiral Lewis waited, staring out into the darkness of the dock. Apart from Staff Captain Sheehan, Lewis was alone. The only movement inside the dock drew the Admiral's eye. A single space-suited worker was making some last minute adjustments, not to the ship, but the bottle launcher. Lewis smiled slightly. You couldn't argue with tradition, no matter how daft. The launching of a ship, particularly a future flagship, demanded the breaking of a bottle of champagne, which in a hard vacuum wasn't all that easy. Considerable effort had been expended to make sure that bottles wouldn't either explode or freeze solid. Plus after one early cruiser spent its career sporting a dent caused by a part frozen bottle, they were careful to fire the bottles at a new ship's heaviest armour.

Lewis's reverie was broken by the sound of Sheehan clearing his throat in a very deliberate manner. He turned in time to see Admiral Wingate pulling himself through the hatch followed by Secretary Callahan and Admiral Charlotte Naismith, Third Admiral of the Fleet and the officer responsible for ship design.

"Afternoon, sir."

"Paul. Sorry to keep you waiting. It took us a while to shake off the Indian Ambassador," Wingate replied as he pushed himself over the view port. Lewis, Callahan and Naismith joined him looking out into the dock, behind them their respective staff officers spread out like a destroyer screen to keep any casual wanderers at a distance.

"I'm sure you're looking forward to getting aboard her," Wingate said after a few moments.

"Yes, sir, I must admit I am. The designer promised a lot. I'm interested to see how she'll shape up in the trials."

Wingate turned away from the view port.

"Alright to business. You've read the report from *Harbinger*?" Lewis and Naismith nodded. "Unfortunately with the US election and various other diary clashes, it's going to be at least six weeks before the Council can meet to discuss the matter. For once Secretary Callahan and myself are in agreement. We can't sit on our hands while we wait for Council. But we also agree that it wouldn't be appropriate for this to show up on any set of meeting minutes, particularly since they want this kept under wraps if possible."

"They're going to be disappointed," Lewis commented. "This is too big to keep quiet. Evidence of an alien race systematically wiped out! The Press are going to lap it up."

"I agree. And when it does hit the new stands the Council are going to want answers," Callahan replied, "and they're going to want them quickly."

"They're going to be disappointed there as well," Wingate said seriously.

"Why's that?"

"*Harbinger* brought back a vast amount of data, but much of it raises more questions than it answers, something that even Captain Flores admits," Wingate said. "We know this race, call them the Centaurs, were a nuclear-capable civilisation. They were exterminated between thirty and fifty years ago. Before that extermination the Centaurs came into at least limited contact with the Nameless. That is the full extent of what we definitely know. After that you're talking theory and guesswork."

"Well we do also know that the Nameless must have been involved."

"No Mister Secretary, we don't," Lewis replied sharply.

"There is no evidence to directly tie the Nameless to the extermination, only that the Centaur civilisation came to an end shortly after a Nameless ship was sighted. That's circumstantial evidence at best," Wingate added.

"We aren't taking this to a court of law Cody."

"No, but stating at this point that the Nameless were definitely involved would have consequences."

"People keep accusing the fleet of being trigger-happy, but if we tell our captains and diplomats that the Nameless have committed genocide, it will colour their actions in the event of a second encounter. But the information supplied by *Harbinger* doesn't give us a smoking gun so to speak. The contact between the Centaurs and Nameless could just be a coincidence," Lewis said.

Callahan looked at him with surprise.

"I didn't think you'd be a man who believed in coincidence Paul."

"And broadly speaking Mister Secretary, you'd be right," Lewis shrugged. "But if you can rule everything else out, then coincidence may be all you have left. We aren't in that position. Put simply we don't have enough information to support any kind of solid conclusion."

"I wonder could this have been a war between the Centaurs and the Nameless?" Naismith asked.

"If it was, it was one-sided," Lewis replied. "It looks like the Centaurs were at roughly the same level we were at when the Contact War began."

"Well they came off a lot worse if it was war," Callahan said sourly before glancing at Lewis. "What about that ship? It was primitive but relatively lightly damaged. Given how damaged the *Mississippi* was…"

"Doesn't prove anything," Lewis replied with a shrug. "There's no saying it was even fired upon by weapons of equal power to those used against *Mississippi*. Also the nature of the Centaur ship meant if they managed to turn their stern towards incoming fire, the pusher-plate would simply laugh at any conventional explosive. It looks like what took them out was something clipping the edge of the plate."

"Alright, returning to the planet. If someone was determined to commit genocide why go to the trouble of setting up an extermination camp? Why not simply scorch the planet from orbit?"

"Well, we can make a reasonable guess at that," Wingate said. "Planets capable of supporting life are too rare to destroy. A large scale nuclear or kinetic bombardment would destroy a planet's biosphere."

"But there was a bombardment," Callahan countered.

"Which was apparently concentrated against a number of major cities. In all likelihood, these were the seats of the major governments. Their destruction would have decapitated those administrations and once those were gone any resistance was likely to have been ineffective and disjointed. That left the liquidation of the population, which would have presented its own problems had they wanted the planet to be useable afterwards." Lewis's voice was unemotional. "The long term problems of nuclear weapons are obvious. Biological warfare requires a pretty sophisticated understanding of the target species, plus anything powerful enough to wipe out a race might well cross the species barrier and decimate the biosphere. Finally, chemical warfare requires impractical quantities, even for high-density areas such as cities. If you want to wipe out a race, death camps are quite simply the most efficient way to do it," Lewis sighed. "The poor bastards probably had their heads in the noose before they even knew what was happening."

Callahan shuddered.

"If someone wanted the planet why did they abandon it after wiping out the Centaurs?" Naismith wondered out loud.

Wingate shrugged.

"Perhaps they found something not to their liking."

"Or perhaps they're waiting," added Lewis. "Maybe they don't need the planet now but might do in the future. In that situation it's better to wipe out the population when they don't really have the means to fight back." Lewis paused to shrug his shoulders. "Cissies don't get to the top of the evolutionary heap."

"Christ Admiral, you have a cynical mind," Callahan said in a tone of faint awe.

"Thank you, sir," Lewis replied calmly.

There was a sudden crackle as the PA system activated.

"Attention all guests. Attention all guests. Please make your way to the main observation lounge. The launch will begin in twenty minutes."

"Okay we're running out of time. Enough of the theorising. It's been... well it's been as disturbing as hell. What line are we going to take with the Council?" Callahan asked.

"There are three main possibilities. First, that there is no connection with the contact between these two races and the extermination of the Centaurs. That somehow the extermination was entirely internal. This seems unlikely but we can't yet rule it out," Wingate outlined. "The second is that the Centaurs somehow provoked the Nameless into destroying them. This seems at the moment the most likely scenario. The third is that the Nameless are inherently hostile. They perceived the Centaurs as a threat or liquidated them to provide living space. Not my favourite option, but a real possibility."

"That last one seems a bit unlikely. People generally need a good reason to go to war," Callahan said.

The three officers looked unconvinced.

"Well there are also a few things we can be starting on. First, send *Harbinger* back out, and see if we can release a second scout. Second, put in a request to Science Fleet to send one of their ships out there for a more in-depth investigation. Finally, I feel we now need to formalise war plans for combat against the Nameless," Wingate replied.

"That last point isn't going to be an easy sell to the Council," Callahan said dubiously.

"But a necessary one Daniel. We've been informally studying how we would fight them since *Mississippi*. But the time has come to formalise those arrangements," said Wingate with a slight shrug. "Equally, I have no intention of making the existence of those plans public."

"We will also want to examine our ship design contingency plans," Lewis added. "Simulations to date have indicated that the Luna class flak cruisers would fair best against the Nameless. But at present there are only six of them on strength. I'd like plans to be drawn up that would allow us to complete our stock cruiser hulls as flak ships."

"That will require a redirection of funds," Naismith warned.

"Well on that point Cody, if your office writes up the request I'll sign off on it."

The sound of voices came from the access way.

"Alright, we're out of time. Anyone have anything else?" Callahan asked.

"Just one small thing Paul. I want you to stick around this summer. The summer exercises will probably overlap with the Council meeting on this issue, so I want you to brief Han Fengzi on the planned manoeuvres."

Lewis started to object.

"I'm sorry Paul I'm going to need you around, not light years away."

"Can I at least keep my new flagship?" He asked sourly.

"She'll probably still be working up at that stage, so yes."

"Is this launch private, or can anyone come?"

They all turned towards the voice. It was Callahan's wife, drifting ungracefully towards them.

"Hello Suzie," Callahan replied as he fielded her. "I thought you were going to leave your grand entrance to the last moment?"

"Yes I was planning to," she replied cheerfully, "but after a long conversation with a nice young officer I was convinced this wasn't the time to be fashionably late."

"Not to mention you flounder like a beached whale in zero-G," Callahan replied with a big smile on his face.

"Oh you will pay for that one sunshine," she said punching his arm playfully, sending herself spiralling away.

Other guests were now pulling themselves into the lounge. The group took this as a signal to break up the meeting and drift apart.

Lewis pushed himself over to one of the view ports where he was able to watch the entire chamber and would have a good view of the launch. A few people nodded to him, but the tall serious Admiral tended not to be most people's first choice of conversation partner. For his part Lewis allowed his thoughts to drift.

'People generally need a good reason to go to war.' It was a line of reasoning he'd heard a lot in the last few months. Yet to Lewis it was a deeply flawed line of thought. It ignored that multiple human cultures had gone to war, simply because they could. In its first three decades in space, humanity had been lucky. Its galactic neighbours thus far encountered had either been friendly or weak enough in strength or spirit to face down. But to Lewis the Nameless already felt different. They were more dangerous and more implacable, like a people who wouldn't shy away from conflict and would willingly bleed to achieve their aims.

Lewis returned to reality as he belatedly realised that the speeches had not only started but were nearly over. A junior officer carefully guided Suzie Callahan forward to the podium and Lewis started paying attention again.

"...my privilege to launch this, the first of a new class of battleships," she as she pressed the button on the console in front of her. "I name this ship *Warspite*. God bless all who serve on her!"

The bottle fired from its launcher with a puff of gas and shattered against the battleship's side. A beautiful spray of glass and frozen champagne crystals glittered as right on cue the Sun came out from behind Earth to light up the dock and reveal the *Warspite* in all her formidable glory. In the crowded lounge there was a deafening cheer as astern the engines pulsed for a moment and the ship started to slide slowly forward out of the dock and into the waiting stars. As she cleared the dock there was a rippling flash as a waiting cruiser saluted Battle Fleet's newest ship.

Chapter Five

Baden

11th July 2066

By the standards of its kind the asteroid was vast, approximately the size of France. Its orbit, nearly nine light hours away from the local star, was such that one side was eternally, if weakly, sunlit, while the other remained in constant darkness. Mostly composed of heavy elements, the asteroid projected a mass shadow very nearly a light second deep. Had it been situated in Earth's solar system the harvesting of its mineral wealth would probably have been well advanced, but as it was it orbited at the very edge of the Landfall system. Even in this remote location commercial enterprise might have sought it out, and used it to support the various national colonies on the Earth-like planet located deeper inside the system. But another group had already staked its claim and put it to a very different use.

On the dark side of the asteroid there was a massive fifty kilometre wide crater. At some point, many millennia ago, something had struck the asteroid and nearly destroyed it. But what had been a symbol of its near brush with oblivion was now the asteroid's salvation.

Mounted in the dead centre of the crater, connected to the rocky surface by giant mountings was a three-and-half kilometre long cylinder style centrifuge. This formed the accommodation and administrative heart of the base. Surrounding the centrifuge was a mass of structures, storage bays and repair docks; both free standing and cut directly into the rock, plus weapon emplacements and communication arrays. The docks teemed with activity. Most of the vessels were military types of one sort or another but a few civilian ships also had places at the mooring points.

This was Baden Base, the largest and most important of Battle Fleet's installations outside Earth's solar system. It was also the home to the Third Fleet and in one quiet corner lay the *Harbinger*.

In his cabin Captain Flores sat in his chair sipping from a mug of coffee while staring out the window at the busy dockyard. The window wasn't real. It was a hologram image projected against the bulkhead. These 'window' holograms were a common feature on starships, useful for preventing cabin fever in ship crews. Normally Flores found the view relaxing, but on this occasion it wasn't helping and he knew why. Two interviews loomed in his immediate future, one good, one bad.

Three days ago, *Harbinger* had returned from her second tour out beyond Landfall. Unlike their first there had been no profound discovery, just a slow and tiring grind that wore them all down. Tempers had started to fray as the cramped confines started to get to people. Flores was almost grateful when an engineering problem forced them to head back a week earlier than originally planned. The civilian complement had immediately been packed off to Landfall for some R and R. None of the colonies were exactly tourist destinations but it gave them the opportunity to stretch their legs and breath air that hadn't been through the air recyclers a thousand times.

It had also brought forward a decision.

There was a tap at his door.

"Come in," he called out as he turned away from the window. "Commander Willis, please sit down."

A look of concern flashed across the Commander's face before she pulled up a chair. Flores hesitated as they looked across the desk at each other, wondering how to start. After a moment he decided on the formal approach.

"Commander, I regret to inform you that five days ago I sent a message via FTL transmission to Fleet Headquarters requesting a new commander. I received a reply this morning stating that they are granting my request and giving me permission to relieve you. Your replacement should arrive via courier within the week."

Shock was obvious on her face and for several second she made no reply.

"Am I to remain on duty for the next week?" There was a slight catch in her voice but on the whole it remained remarkably even.

"No. I don't believe it would be... useful, for either of us. Your duties here will be temporarily transferred with immediate effect to Lieutenant Humber. There is a personnel transport leaving Baden tomorrow morning. I have arranged with Dock Control that you will have a place on it."

"May I ask why I am being relieved?"

"Yes you can. I fact I want to answer that in detail." Flores sighed and leaned back in his chair. "As a technical officer you are beyond reproach, in fact you're probably the best I've had serve under me. As a tactical officer you're not quite as strong but still more than acceptable. The problem I am having is your ability to deal with your subordinates. You're cold with people. Worse, you're the source of friction, not the solution to it."

"You're referring to my disagreements with the civilian complement?" she asked. A month into their second tour there had been a raging argument between Willis and a member of the diplomatic team. Flores had never quite got to the bottom of what the row was about. He suspected the issue itself had been trivial but with tempers already short it had escalated into a major and very public shouting match.

"Only in part Commander. In truth I don't believe you work well even with fleet personnel."

"With respect sir, but I disagree."

"Really? What's Lieutenant Gleffen's hobby?"

Willis opened her mouth to reply, then hesitated, obviously wrong footed by the question.

Flores waited several seconds while Willis obviously racked her memory.

"It's restoring motorbikes. I can barely get her to shut up about it, but you've been aboard for the best part of six months and you don't know."

"I felt it was best to maintain professional distance."

"That works up to a point. But you don't know your fellow officers and they don't know you." He leaned forward resting his elbows on the desk. "Faith. When you accepted the rank of Commander, you reached a stage in your career where knowing the technology is less important than the ability to manage and know the people you command. This is something your previous superiors should have pulled you up on, and I'm sorry they didn't"

"I see." The Commander's voice was flat and unemotional. "Do I have permission to leave?"

Flores wished she hadn't asked that, it made it easy to be a coward.

"No, there is one final point Commander. I'm sorry I didn't send you back to Earth at the end of our first tour. You were brought in as a temporary replacement, so there would have been no questions asked if I had sought a permanent replacement after the first tour. Unfortunately by keeping you for a second tour I now have to provide a reason for relieving you."

Willis's face had been expressionless but now open concern became apparent.

"Commander Willis. I've made a recommendation to fleet that you remain in grade... for the foreseeable future."

"Sir... such a recommendation will... will mean I will probably never achieve command status."

"That is a possibility Commander. If it is I am sorry but I owe a duty to the fleet. If however can bring your personnel management skills up to standard, there is no reason why you might not achieve command. But not yet."

Chief Coxswain Benson waited outside the Captain's cabin waiting for his interview with the Skipper. The interview was mostly a formality but Benson was pleased to be seen off by an officer he respected. He stiffened as the cabin door opened and Commander Willis stepped out. Benson did a double take at the Commander. Normally so impassive, she looked shell shocked.

"Commander are you all right?" he asked hesitantly.

"Yes… yes. I'm fine," she said quietly. "The Captain will see you now." She looked around distractedly.

"Are you sure you're all right ma'am?"

"I'm fine," she snapped. For a moment her eyes flashed angrily. "It's just that you're not the only one being reassigned today," she added more calmly.

"Oh I hadn't heard. May I ask where to?"

Willis smiled bitterly.

"Oblivion Cox. Good luck." She turned and walked off without a further word.

There was another tap at his door.

"Come in," Flores called. Benson came in and stood to attention.

"At ease Cox. I know the petty officers' mess is planning to wave you off so I'll keep this brief," he said with a smile. "You've been aboard since our first commissioning. That's what… two years now?"

"Two years, three months, sir."

"Has it been so bad that you've been counting?"

"No, sir. I've enjoyed serving with you. I feel I've developed a lot under your command," Benson replied quickly.

Flores grinned with honest amusement.

"I was only joking Cox. I'm sure you're looking forward to the extra rank."

"And the extra pay, sir."

"I'm sure you are. I already have your next assignment. For once Fleet Personnel has been quick off the mark with a reassignment." Flores turned his computer screen to face Benson.

"You are to become the Bosun aboard the flak cruiser *Deimos*. She's attached to Third Fleet, so you should be able to join her in a day or two. Once the PO mess have finished with you, I've arranged for a temporary bunk on Baden. You can have a couple of days leave before the start of your new posting." Flores offered his hand. "Hope to see you again Coxswain. No... *Bosun* Benson."

17th July 2066

"With due respect, sir, you are seriously playing with fire," Commander Carol Berg warned her former captain. "Admiral Camile thinks Baden is safe and if you keep telling him he's wrong, you might find yourself on the next transport back to Earth."

Captain Ronan Crowe bit his tongue rather than snap at her. After a few seconds he let his breath out in an irritated hiss.

"Camile *is* wrong."

"Yes, but he has the slight advantage that he outranks both of us. I'm not senior enough to matter, but you? He is certainly able and, if you provoke him, willing to drop your career right down the toilet. If we're to be honest your reputation is already...."

"...less than great," Crowe finished for her.

Crowe stared down into the centre of the square. He and Berg were seated in one of the smaller cafÈs situated around the edge of Baden's recreation square. On the far side of the square was a McDonalds restaurant, proudly displaying a sign declaring it to be the furthest from Earth. With the square situated on the outer level of the centrifuge, a large section of the centre of the deck served as a massive viewing port. Every two hundred and twenty seconds the asteroid the base was built against rolled into view for fifty three seconds, then the view of the stars returned. The square teemed with off duty personnel, but you could always spot newcomers to Baden. They were the ones walking very carefully across the glass deck.

There had been a time when looking out across such a mass of Battle Fleet personnel would have filled him with a sense of belonging. But not any more. Crowe no longer felt that he really had a place here.

To say his reputation was damaged was probably one of history's great understatements. To all intents and purposes his career with Battle Fleet was already over. When he limped his battered command back into Baden, Crowe had hoped that he would be allowed to keep her until she could return to Earth. But to his utter lack of surprise, he was ordered to hand over command, get himself to Earth on a courier ship and explain his actions.

Yet despite his speedy return, news of the first encounter with the Nameless had reached Earth ahead of him. By the time he landed a thousand armchair tacticians, and perhaps ten times as many diplomatic and political types, had examined the *Mississippi* Incident in minute detail. There had been news reports, magazine articles and documentaries. Crowe found himself at the centre of this storm of attention. It had all quickly turned sour and Crowe soon found that in the public domain, he had been tried and found wanting.

This in itself might not have been fatal if he'd had the support of his brother officers, but this was not the case. Many made clear that they regarded him as the man who had fluffed a first contact situation and revived the image of the trigger-happy fleet officer. Others looked at the twisted and shattered hull of the *Mississippi* and saw a captain who had not reacted quickly or decisively enough. In short they saw failure.

There had been a few officers willing to publicly speak in his defence. The most prominent of these had been Admiral Lewis. Notwithstanding this, over recent months Crowe had occasionally wondered whether he would have been better off without the support of the Home Fleet's C-in-C. To his admirers Lewis was a pragmatist, but to his critics he was a cold-blooded butcher. As far as the Admiral was concerned, if a Battle Fleet ship found itself in combat the only important thing was that it won. Any political considerations came a poor second... at best.

Crowe had been mildly surprised when the posting orders giving him a new command had arrived. But he quickly perceived the touch of politics. There had been serious calls from both the media and the political establishments of the Command Council members to dismiss him or at least put him behind a desk. But instead he was given another ship. Not that this was any kind of ringing endorsement. If he was any judge, Admiral Wingate was once again reinforcing the operational independence of the fleet.

His new command was the Luna class flak cruiser *Deimos*; a relatively modern ship armed principally with rapid-firing small calibre railguns. On the *Mississippi* he had spent most of his time operating independently of the rest of the fleet but *Deimos's* role was very different. Her class had been designed to provide close escort for larger ships.

Or to put it another way, it kept Crowe within sight and reach of senior officers.

Berg had been luckier. As a junior officer she hadn't registered on the radar screen of public consciousness. So while Crowe's career when off the rails, hers remained on track. Six months after the incident Berg achieved sufficient time in grade to be offered a command of her own, in the form of the destroyer *Mantis*. A few months later *Mantis* was reassigned to Baden and the Third Fleet. It had been the first time Crowe had seen her since the last of the enquiries. Frankly he wouldn't have blamed her if she'd tried to distance herself from him but instead she had actively sought him out and offered her support. And support was something he badly needed.

By asteroid standards, Baden's mass shadow was tremendously deep. But compared to that of a planet it was very small. When he arrived Crowe had immediately made the judgement that Baden's defences were far from adequate.

Like damn near every ship and installation in the fleet, Baden had been built assuming that the Aéllr would be the most likely enemy. If an Aéllr force attacked Baden, even if they came out right on the Red Line, it would be over twenty minutes before they got into firing range of the base, enough time for the defenders to organise themselves. But the Nameless had their damn long-range missiles. If a fleet of their ships came out on the line and fired, those missiles would be arriving before the defences could respond or any moored ships could crash start their engines and get underway.

This assumed the Nameless were hostile, or even possessed a fleet.

When he first arrived at Baden he had kept his own counsel. But when the discovery of the dead world became public and he started to speak out.

He had started to argue forcefully that the base's defences should be reinforced, that more observation satellites be deployed outside the Mass Shadow and more ships kept on the outer picket.

The base commander, Admiral Azamat and the senior officer of the Third Fleet, Admiral Camile, listened but politely rejected most of his suggestions. Crowe persisted and the refusals got steadily less polite. Changing tack, he attempted to win the support of his fellow captains, but in most cases he was met with barely concealed derision. He was a captain who'd had his last command damn near shot out from under him and was now jumping at shadows, not to mention that *Mississippi* was old, borderline obsolete in fact. Yet she'd handled the Nameless. What did more modern ships have to fear?

Crowe belatedly realised he had settled into a brooding silence and gave Berg a wan smile.

"So, what's next for you?" she asked

"Back to the outer picket," Crowe replied tiredly.

"What? Again?"

"Yes again. Camile took on board the idea of strengthening the outer picket. The fact that it gets me out of the way is probably nothing to do with anything I expect." He replied with more than a note of sarcasm in his voice.

"How long have you been out there?"

"Twenty-six of the last thirty days. It isn't exactly making me popular with the crew. Where are you going?"

"Exercises off Landfall with the rest of the squadron and the *Antarctica*. Then showing the flag among the habitats in the Ice Teeth. We should be back by Friday."

"We should see you passing in that case."

"So what's the next step?"

Crowe leaned back in this chair and stared up at the deck head. For several minutes he didn't answer.

"I don't know if there is a next step, Carol," he eventually said. "I'm getting tired. I'm getting tired of wading through crap and achieving nothing."

Berg made no reply.

"*Deimos's* tour out here ends in three months," Crowe continued. "Once I get home, I think I'm going resign my commission."

Berg drew breath sharply.

"Sir I don't think…"

"I do."

"The fleet would be worse off without you, sir."

Crowe smiled slightly before finishing his coffee.

"Good of you to say Carol. Complete bollix of course but good of you anyway. I've got to go. New bosun turning up. I think the old one is glad to leave."

23rd July 2066

There was a flash as the small courier ship L12 completed its transfer from Jump Space. Within moments of arriving its radiator shields slid open and the radiators began glowing dimly as L12 started purging its heat sink. After a moment's pause the craft adjusted course, fired its engines and headed for Baden.

Although there were FTL transmitters on both Landfall and Baden, such devices were huge clumsy machines capable of delivering only very simple messages. Couriers represented the main means of communication across interstellar distance. Tiny ships, little more than an engine with the smallest possible hull wrapped around it, they constantly travelled the space lanes between Earth and her daughter worlds.

Back in the courier's engine room Petty Officer Chuong hummed to himself as he waited. His suit muted all sounds but he could feel the vibrations of the generator through the soles of his boots. The reactor status board was all green. It looked like another jump safely completed. After a few minutes there was a chime across the intercom signalling the all clear. With a sigh of relief he opened his visor. The other two members of the engineering crew also cracked their survival suits. Then the junior member of the team started to pull off his suit.

"No, leave it on Francis," Chuong advised. "We won't be staying long enough to make taking it off worthwhile."

Across the engine room Rating Stephens shook his head and muttered

"Yeah, right."

"We'll be dropping off the post to Baden, pick up whatever they want taken back, bounce back across the Red Line and make a quick jump over to Landfall. Do the same again there and then start back to Earth," Chuong continued ignoring Stephens.

"Well that's the theory anyway," Stephens added from the other side of the engine room. "It's a safe bet that someone will have dicked up and we'll be waiting around scratching our arses."

"You really are a glass half empty person, aren't you?" Chuong accused.

"Can't get used to the idea of crossing interstellar distance just to pop in. Seems kind of wrong to travel between stars just to deliver the mail," said Francis, trying to head off the argument.

"Joys of the courier service junior," replied Stephens.

The PA system cut off further conversation.

"All hands. This is the Skipper. We've just received a transmission from Baden. They're running late with their reports, so we're going to have to hold for a while. But it will give us time to purge the heat sink. Hopefully we won't lose more than an hour or two. Bridge out."

No one said anything for a moment. Then with a sigh Chuong started to pull off his suit.

"You ain't a cynic if you're right," Stephens remarked almost cheerfully.

"Oh shut up!"

"Contact bearing two, seven, three, dash, zero, one, three. Heading zero, nine, three, dash, three, five, three. They're on Alpha Baden approach."

Aside from the occasional nervous cough, the sensor rating's contact report was the first sound on the Bridge in ten minutes. The silence had coincided with the appearance of Crowe on his bridge.

"IFF confirms the contacts as the cruiser *Antarctica* and the destroyers *Rattlesnake*, *Scorpion* and *Mantis*."

Out of the corner of his eye the newly promoted Bosun Benson watched his captain. Crowe was slumped in his chair watching the tactical holo, taking little apparent interest in either it or the Identification Friend or Foe (IFF) report.

It hadn't taken Benson long to realise that the *Deimos* was not a happy ship. Its skipper was the man who, according to some, had so royally screwed up the first contact with the Nameless. He'd then followed that up by annoying the local commanders and now they were stuck on apparently indefinite picket duty. On the mess deck bets were being taken as to what the Skipper would do to complete his personal run of bad fortune. Although he'd been aboard the ship for less than a week, Benson was already aware that most of the officers and crew were counting the days until the end of the tour. He had a feeling the Skipper was too.

"Communications. Have you challenged the contacts?" Crowe asked without looking up.

"Err… no, sir," replied the Coms Officer.

Crowe looked up and glared at the unfortunate man.

"We challenge any contacts entering our area Mister Whedon. We do not blindly trust friend or foe."

"Emm… Captain. Engine profiles match three Predator class destroyers and a single Continental class cruiser, sir."

The Captain ignored the sensor operator as the Coms Officer sent out the challenge. A few seconds later, the officer reported with evident relief that the challenge had been correctly responded to. The Captain merely grunted and returned to his silent contemplation of the tactical holo.

Benson sighed inwardly. It was going to be a long tour.

Rating First Class Joe Keaveney swore softly as he glared at the monitor screen. All around him the Control Room's computer equipment hummed and buzzed. On the screen, menus appeared and disappeared as he ran through all the usual diagnostics without success. Finally he administered a dose of concussive maintenance to the top of the monitor, as much to relieve his own feelings as anything else.

"PO. Hey PO… PO Piper!" he shouted over his shoulder.

From outside a muttering started.

"What!" shouted an exasperated voice.

"There's a problem with one of the satellites."

"Well fix it!"

"I've tried fixing the sodding thing!"

"For the love of God! Can't a guy take a piss without having someone coming yapping?"

The Petty Officer walked in looking irritated.

"Alright what is it?"

"There's something up with the visual pick up on the sentry satellite A-fifty three."

"What the hell do you mean 'there's something up'? It either works or doesn't."

"Here look!" Keaveney slid out of the way.

The monitor was showing an unremarkable view of the stars, except for one small section. Here the stars twisted and shimmered as if being seen through the haze of a hot fire.

Piper examined it for a moment.

"You didn't clean the bloody dome, did you?" he said accusingly.

"Yes I did clean the fecking thing. Anyhow look!" Keaveney moved a small joystick on the control console. The camera panned back and forth. On the screen the disruption moved across the screen and back again.

"So what's that then? A mobile smear?"

Piper leaned closer.

"A jump in point forming?" he asked in a dubious voice.

"What, inside the Mass Shadow? I don't think so," Keaveney replied scornfully

"Where is it?"

"About twenty thousand clicks out, on route to a station beyond the Red Line. You want me to bring it back in?"

Piper stared at the screen and sighed. It was always the way of these things. They never showed up the glitches when they were in for maintenance and instead waited until they were back out again. This was definitely an odd one though. None of the other scanners on the probe were indicating anything outside normal parameters. He could bring it back in, but the brass had got a bee in its bonnet lately about having as many sentry sats on station as possible. If he brought it back in, the Lieutenant would probably moan and when you got right down to it the optical camera wasn't all that that important. It could wait for the next maintenance cycle.

"Just make a note of it in the maintenance logs. We'll check it out the next time we bring it in."

"All hands. Rig for ordinary, rig for ordinary," Flores ordered on the intercom.

Across the Bridge crewmen and officers cracked the seals on their survival suits. There was a low murmur of conversation as people started to stow their suits. After a few minutes the Day Watch started to take the place of the Combat Watch.

Like *Deimos* on the opposite side of Baden, *Harbinger* was patrolling back and forth about one hundred and fifty thousand kilometres inside the mass shadow. But unlike *Deimos*, the atmosphere on the Bridge was relaxed and comfortable. Flores scratched his stylus across his pad as he took notes while they were clear in his head.

With his ship's engine repairs complete he'd put in a request to spend a day on the outer picket. Sims were a useful way to train and exercise the crew, but they could never quite beat the real thing. Their spell in docks had seen a number of personnel being rotated out of the ship. Given the nature of their assignment the replacements had all been experienced hands, but new crew needed the opportunity to find their feet and picket duty gave *Harbinger* the room to work through some manoeuvres.

Given time Flores would have liked to have made use of the Fleet's live fire area but the civilians were already on their way back from their shore leave. Within a few hours they would be re-embarking and they would be on their way out to find the Nameless.

"Sir. Do you want to see the numbers from the exercise?"

Flores looked up. His new First Officer, Commander Weissensee, had been among those entering the Bridge from his action station in Damage Control. The Commander was a slightly portly Austrian of roughly average height, with a mop of brown hair and somewhat weak chin, creating an appearance that was far from the recruitment poster ideal. But with a record that included spells on almost every type of warship the fleet possessed and a series of excellent ratings, he was quite a catch. It seemed that Weissensee had caught the eye of someone senior and was likely being groomed for serious command. His previous commission had been in command of a destroyer and this would most likely be his final tour as a commander before being offered a captaincy with a cruiser of his own. Still for the time being he was a welcome addition to the *Harbinger*.

"In a moment Commander," Flores replied. "Helm set a course back to Baden. Navigation, how long until we berth?"

"About fifty minutes, sir," called out the Navigator.

"Right Lieutenant Siedl, you have the Bridge. Commander, if you'll join me in my office?"

"Yes sir," Weissensee replied as he fell into step beside Flores. "That looks reasonably good but I've spotted a few areas where improvement is possible."

"We'll compare notes and see what we ha..."

"Captain?"

Flores half turned.

The speaker was Lieutenant Siedl, who was leaning over the shoulder of one of the sensor operators. He glanced toward Flores.

"Sir, we've got something odd on visual off our starboard side," he said.

"Define odd for me please Lieutenant."

Siedl nodded to the sensor rating who put the image up of the main display. It was just stars, except for one small zone where the stars were rippling, dimming and then brightening. The picture shifted as the camera zoomed in.

"Okay that is odd," Flores commented to no one in particular.

"Hardware problem with the camera mount perhaps?" Weissensee suggested.

"No, sir," Siedl replied shaking his head. "We've looked at it with two separate cameras and they're both showing the same thing."

Flores walked back to the holo and watched the display. He wasn't sure if was imagining it but the rippling seemed to be slowly growing more intense. Weissensee joined him.

"Anything on radar or passives?" Flores asked.

"No, sir, both say nothing is there."

"You know, sir, this looks a little like the jump portal of a first generation drive," Weissensee suggested.

"Only a bit and we're well inside the Red Line." Flores turned on his heels. "Navigator, confirm our position."

"Yes, sir."

"Sensors any idea on range?"

Siedl shook his head again.

"No, sir. The computer can't make heads or tails of it."

"Do you want us to close up on stations, sir?" Weissensee asked

"Hold on just a mom…"

"Captain, confirmed position. One hundred and forty thousand clicks from Baden, one hundred and fifty inside the Red Line."

"Well it can't be a jump in." He drummed his fingers against the edge of the holo before turning away from it. "It must be a glitch somewhere."

"There must be a software corruption," Weissensee agreed. "I've never known dockyards to fix something without breaking something else. I'll get engineering to…"

"JESUS!"

The shout was enough to send both officers spinning back toward the holo. It wasn't like the hole in space a jump drive created. Instead a vessel seemed to almost extrude itself into reality. Ghost like at first but quickly becoming tangible.

The design was far cleaner looking than human ships, with little breaking its smooth lines. The ship was wedge-shaped, narrow at the bows and widening towards the stern. Half way along, a structure like a conning tower rose from the hull. Astern of that were a ring of small engine pods and finally something like a cowling surrounded the rear of the vessel. It wasn't the same type of ship that had attacked *Mississippi* but the resemblance was clear.

Seconds passed on *Harbinger's* bridge in stunned silence.

Flores abruptly broke the moment.

"RED ALERT! All hands to battle stations! All hands to battle stations! This is not a drill! This is not a drill!"

The crew exploded into action as officers and ratings dived for their stations and survival suits. Flores glanced desperately at the weapons status board. *Harbinger* needed just over three minutes to come to full combat readiness. Flores gave a desperate prayer that they had those minutes.

"Sensors give me range!" he shouted over the noise.

"Only *fifty* kilometres skipper."

"*Shit*! They're right on top of us!" exclaimed Weissensee.

"Engines all go ahead flank! Helm hard to starboard, bows down forty-five degrees!"

"Captain!" shouted a sensor operator. "The ports in their bows are opening!"

"Infra-red spike! They're preparing to fire!" shouted another.

The weapons board was still all red. Mere seconds had passed and few of the crew had yet reached their stations.

In a sudden moment of clarity Flores realised his command was already lost. They had been caught flatfooted by a foe capable of breaking the known laws of physics.

"Coms signal Baden. 'I am under attack by a Nameless ship.' NO, don't code it! Just send it!"

"Contact separation, we have four incoming!"

Flores spun back towards the holo: two pairs of missiles were streaking towards them.

"Guns?" he asked quietly. Weissensee shook his head, his face rigid with horror. Around him crewmen continued to rush onto the Bridge while those they were relieving sprinted off to their own stations.

On the display the four missiles came curving in like claws around *Harbinger*. Each one changed course slightly as they adjusted their final approach.

"Countermeasures on my mark. Point defence commence! Commence! Commence!" Flores ordered.

"We're being pinged!"

"Countermeasures full spread! Everyone brace for impact!"

Along *Harbinger's* flanks chaff rockets blasted out of their silos and detonated between the cruiser and incoming missiles. It was too little too late.

The chaff confused the guidance systems of two of the missiles. As a result the first missed completely and the second exploded fifty metres below. But the second pair scored direct hits. One struck the radar tower, demolishing the upper hull, while the other plunged through the starboard side radiator into the Engine Room. The missile detonated less than two metres from Reactor

Number One, ripping open the inner casing. Three tenths of a second later, the cruiser *Harbinger* was vaporised by a flash of nuclear fury

---

"PO. I'm picking up something odd around the base," said the only other person on the courier's bridge.

With cap perched carefully over his eyes, Chuong didn't budge in the command chair. The Skipper had gone below for a meal as their 'short' delay stretched into a second hour. As the courier's number two, Chuong took the Bridge whenever the Captain went off. It wasn't a duty he objected to. For one thing it got him out of the Engine Room and away from Stephens's moaning. With L12 well clear of Baden's transit lanes, it was really a one-man job, but the regs said two people should be on the Bridge, so Chuong rested his eyes while the bridge rating monitored the read outs.

"PO, are you even awake?"

"Yep, but unless you're reporting that Baden has finally given us our uplink, this is me not giving a monkey's."

"Yeah, but I think there's something serious up. There's a whole pile of radio chatter going out."

Chuong let out a sigh. With no gravity to hold it down his breath was enough to send his cap drifting away. Without opening his eyes he made a half-hearted swipe at it.

"You're not going to be happy until I've opened my eyes are you, you bastard."

"Hang on, we're getting a signal on the main command band. Oh, that's strange."

"What?"

"It's in the clear, no coding or encryption."

Chuong sat up and gave the rating a puzzled frown.

"Alright let's hear it."

"*This is Baden Command to all ships, we are under attack! All ships converge on Colossus. All ships are authorised to fire.*"

The two men exchanged a look of horror. Then Chuong lunged forward, flipped aside the plastic shield and slammed his fist down on the red button. Across the courier the alarms shrieked.

"Point us at the nearest edge of the Mass Shadow and get us out of here!" he shouted.

"On it!"

L12 slewed around as the engines slammed onto full power.

From behind them came a clatter as Lieutenant Malawati swam through the access way.

"Report!" she demanded.

"Skipper, we're in the middle of a goddam war zone! Baden is under attack," Chuong replied. "We're heading for the Red Line."

"How the hell did they sneak up on us?"

"I don't know ma'am and with respect I don't want to hang around in this flying eggshell..."

"Contact! Bearing one, eight, three, dash, two, six, three. Range *one hundred seventy four* clicks!"

"What! That's impossible. It's inside the Mass Shadow!" Malawati objected.

"Tell that to the radar Skip. Heading change: they're turning towards us!"

"Chuong, get below. Disconnect the engine and manoeuvring safeties," Malawati ordered. Chuong didn't waste time acknowledging and instead dived for the hatch.

"What the hell did you do up there?" Stephens shouted as Chuong came through. The reactor was roaring almost deafeningly and with the engines at one hundred percent they were pulling two G's, causing 'down' to be ninety degrees out from the usually accepted direction.

"Hostiles have just jumped in right next to us. We're getting out of there!"

"But how the hell..."

"Not now! Just lose the safeties, all of them!"

Stephens heard the fear in Chuong's voice. Turning, he yanked open an access panel, ripped off the plastic sheet with the label warning never to do what they were doing and started pulling inhibitors out of their sockets. On the opposite side of the Engine Room Chuong was doing the same at another panel.

"Done," Stephens called out.

Chuong flicked on his intercom.

"Skipper, the safeties are all off."

"Roger, hang on back there. We have incoming!" she replied.

Immediately the pitch of the reactor rose as it was pushed beyond its normal operating limits. At the same moment the ship went into a violent corkscrew. The three crew in the engine room could only hang on as they were thrown back and forth. The hull keened and groaned at the abuse it was being subjected to. Chuong knew full well there was a serious risk that the stress might be enough to open up the lightweight hull. But there weren't many options. Couriers didn't have any countermeasures or point defence and they sure as hell didn't have armour. That left acceleration as their only defence, but there was a limit to what that could achieve if someone popped up right in their lap.

"Hang on everyone, I'm going to have to dodge it!" Malawati shouted across the intercom.

The starboard engine abruptly went hard astern as the port continued to roar all ahead, sending the ship into a violent turn.

"It's miss…" Malawati started, but then there was a deafening bang that shook the entire ship and everything went black.

Keaveney studied the contents of his plate with suspicious expression. They hadn't managed to correct the problem with the sentry satellite before the end of their shift. Now off duty at last, their thoughts had turned to food.

Ironically dubbed 'the Chateau' by Baden's crew, it certainly wasn't the best canteen on the station but it ran twenty-four seven and always served breakfast, lunch and dinner. So no matter what meal your body clock felt you should be eating, the Chateau could supply it. The canteen was currently in one of its quiet periods, with only about a third of the tables occupied. With their trays filled, Piper and Keaveney had found themselves an empty table.

"Would you stop picking at that and just eat it." Piper said around a mouthful of food

"You're starting to sound like me mum," Keaveney replied as he continued to move his food around the plate. "What do you think this is?"

"Well what did you order?"

"Pork."

"Well it's pork then."

"Must have been a bloody funny looking kind of a pig. I think this has less real meat than a sausage."

Piper rolled his eyes and kept chewing.

Abruptly the alarms went off complete with flashing red lights.

"Crap it! Why is it always when we're off duty that they hold a drill?" Keaveney asked sourly.

Around them ratings and officers vaulted tables knocking aside food trays and drinks in the mass scramble for the exit.

"Just move it Joe!" Piper snapped as he jumped to his feet. Without looking back he ran for the exit. Grumbling Keaveney followed hard on his heels.

Piper and Keaveney's action station was at Primary Damage Control, situated deep inside the centrifuge. They were running down one of the main station corridors when the explosion threw them from their feet. For several seconds the entire structure lurched and heaved. Keaveney landed on his stomach and went sliding down the corridor. As everything around him rattled and shook, he clung to the deck waiting for it to stop. When it did he started to get up, but paused with both his hands pressed against the steel deck plating. There was always a slight vibration from the movement of the centrifuge but now he could feel a slight... inconsistency, like an unbalanced wheel. Looking over his shoulder he saw Piper on his knees, he'd gone pale even through his dark colouring.

"We've been hit," he said disbelievingly.

Then the world blew up in their faces. Fifty metres in front of them an explosion ripped open the structure. A wall of fire came surging up the corridor enveloping several men and women ahead of them. But before it reached them it slowed, stopped, and then went surging back. The air started to follow with increasing force back towards the explosion.

"Oh God! Hull breach!" Keaveney screamed as the howling wind started to drag him. Further up others were clinging grimly to the walls as the entire corridor became a giant wind tunnel. One of them lost his grip and flew past screaming. Keaveney didn't want to watch someone being pulled to his death but found his eyes followed the man of their own accord. Then an emergency bulkhead slammed down and abruptly sealed the corridor. The tumbling man hit it hard and slumped to the deck.

Only after several seconds did Keaveney let go of the wall and took several more to get to his feet. He tottered over the man, a rating, who was slumped against the bulkhead, from which came a faint hiss. The deck had buckled meaning the seal wasn't perfect. Probably good enough though. The man's leg was bent at an unnatural angle. Blood was seeping from his nose and ears, but his pulse was steady and strong.

"We can't help him."

Keaveney looked up at Piper.

"He needs a doctor PO. We can't leave him here!"

"Yes we can. We're in Damage Control, not stretcher-bearers. We need to get to our station so get on your feet and get moving."

Keaveney hesitated. Another explosion, further away shook the station again.

"If we pass a medical team we'll point them to him. Now *move*!"

Crowe slowly scrolled down through the file directory, wondering which set of pictures to look at next. Photography was a boyhood passion that had continued on and off into adulthood. A quarter century travelling with the fleet had given him plenty of opportunities to indulge his passion. Even the small part of the collection he kept on his personal computer included shots from planets otherwise untouched by man.

The other terminal in the cabin was also active. On the screen was a half complete letter, one that Crowe was struggling to finish. It wasn't his letter of resignation but it might as well have been. Once he'd informed Celine of his intention to quit there would be no going back. His wife had never taken kindly to him dithering over personal decisions. If he finished it quickly he could probably get it onto the weekly postal courier still hanging around somewhere out there. But really it didn't much matter whether it was this week or next that the news went home. Truth be told, even after what he'd said the Berg, he didn't want to admit that it was all over.

Switching off his own computer he considered for a moment returning to the Bridge, but rejected it. Every time he went up the entire bridge crew tensed. He couldn't really blame them; a captain taking heat from his own superiors could quickly take it out on his underlings. He only had himself to blame for that. Snapping at a number of personnel during the first month on board had created an atmosphere he hadn't managed to break since.

Crowe started violently as the intercom at his belt buzzed urgently.

"Captain here."

The lieutenant on the other end of the connection sounded nervous.

"Lieutenant Colwell, officer of the watch. Sorry to bother you, sir."

"It's all right Jason. What's the problem?"

"I wouldn't have disturbed you, but your standing order about anything unusual..."

"That's okay. So what's the problem?"

"We're seeing something strange on our close-up cameras, sir. It's some kind of distortion. We've been looking at it for the last five minutes."

"And it's not a fault?" Crowe asked.

"No, sir, the entire camera subsystem is showing all green."

"Can you direct the feed to my terminal Lieutenant?"

"Yes, sir, hold on a moment."

On his computer Crowe opened a programme to accept the uplink.

"Coming up now, sir."

Interference cut across the monitor for a moment before the image appeared. It panned and zoomed in on the area of the star field that was twisting and flickering. Immediately Crowe felt the hairs on the back of his neck rise. His mouth went dry and he felt short of breath.

"Do you have it, sir? Sir? Captain are you there?"

"Red alert." he whispered.

"I'm sorry, sir. I'd didn't catch that. If you..."

"RED ALERT! ALL HANDS BATTLE STATIONS!" he shouted as he leapt to his feet. His chair overbalanced and hit the deck with a clatter, but Crowe ignored it as he yanked open the cabin hatch. Out in the corridor crewmembers froze as the alarm screamed into life.

"MAKE A HOLE!" Officers and ratings flattened themselves against the bulkhead as he sprinted past. The Captain's cabin was deliberately positioned close to the Bridge and the ladder up barely slowed him, but for Crowe the dash was agonisingly slow.

This is madness, a small part of him was saying and it was hard to disagree. But instinct had screamed a warning overruling the rational part of his mind.

As he rushed in. the Bridge crew were pulling on their survival suits. With his survival suit half on, Colwell spun to face Crowe with a mixture of relief and dread on his face.

"I'm sorry sir, I don't understand..." he started before Crowe motioned him to be quiet. The display from the camera was on the secondary bridge display and to Crowe it seemed more urgent.

Deimos's weapons board was only starting to light up as the tactical systems were brought on line. The cruiser's plasma cannons were a couple of minutes away from being operational but the flak guns were much faster to power up.

"Sir what's happening?" Colwell almost demanded.

He didn't meet the Lieutenant's eye. *Christ, what have I done?* Crowe thought to himself. He'd sent the ship to battle stations on the strength of nothing more than a gut feeling.

He saw the Lieutenant exchange a look with the Bosun. It was obvious that both were thinking the same thing: *he's lost it*. If he was wrong this time there would be no coming back. His career wouldn't have to wait for the end of *Deimos's* tour. There could be no place on a warship for a captain who jumped at sensor ghosts.

"Sir." He looked up at Colwell. "You'll need to put on your suit for the drill."

The Lieutenant knew damn well that this was no drill. His suggestion was an attempt to protect his captain's reputation. It wouldn't work. All present had seen the way he'd entered the Bridge and it would be around the ship in less than an hour that the Skipper had flipped. Still he was grateful for the offer.

"Captain." the speaker was one of the communication petty officers. "We're receiving a voice transmission in the clear. Imbedded I.D. shows *Harbinger*."

"Play it please," Crowe replied as he started to pull his suit from under the seat.

"This is *Harbinger*. I am under attack by a Nameless ship!" The voice, a woman's voice, was filled with terror. Everyone on the Bridge froze in horror. "Repeat. This is *Harbinger*. I am under attack by a Nameless..." There was the start of a scream but then the transmission cut out leaving just the hiss of static.

"Oh my God. It's real," Colwell murmured.

"Captain... *CAPTAIN!*" shouted another crewmember. Crowe swung back towards the display. Where a second before the disruption had been, a wedge-shaped ship now erupted into real-space. He instantly recognised the design style. It was the Nameless.

"Contact bearing zero, seven, seven, dash, zero, eight, two. Range eight hundred clicks. Their missile ports are open! Repeat their missile ports are open!"

"Guns, reports!" Crowe demanded.

"Fire control and flak guns on line Skipper."

"Helm, roll to present starboard broadside. All guns, fire as you bear!"

As *Deimos* rolled her flak guns blazed into action. Two missiles blasted out of the Nameless ships' launchers and met a wall of metal coming the other way. *Deimos* carried eight quad flak mounts, each one capable of putting out nearly five hundred rounds per minute. Four batteries were able to come to bear and the storm of fire obliterated the two missiles almost before they cleared their launchers. Flak guns weren't generally considered to be an anti-ship weapons but at this short range, the effect was like a sandblaster. The front third of the Nameless ship simply dissolved under the hail of steel. Atmosphere gushed out of its shattered bows as riddled hull plating drifted away. The barrage continued, ripping mercilessly at the alien, working backwards. Secondary explosions added to the carnage. Then abruptly it proved too much and a huge explosion reduced what was left to fragments.

For several seconds there was silence on *Deimos's* bridge.

"We nailed them!" Colwell whooped.

A cheer went up from the entire bridge crew, fists punched the air, backs were slapped and hand shaken.

"Silence on deck!" Crowe's voice cut the cheering off abruptly. "Sensors give me a full sweep."

The main holo display switched over to tactical mode. Crowe's heart sank.

Half a light second away was Baden itself. The strength of the return from the great asteroid was drowning out the signals from most of the ships docked there. A few could be clearly seen as green blips on the display, but that wasn't what anyone was looking at. A mass of blue blips surrounded Baden and even as they watched more appeared.

"Tactical?" Crowe asked quietly.

"We're looking at fifty plus contacts, sir.

"How the hell..." Colwell murmured.

"Captain, we're receiving multiple transmissions on the combat frequencies."

"Put it up Coms."

The sound of dozens of voices filled the Bridge.

"*Where the hell did they come from... heavy fire we need back up... watch your six! Watch your si... ...abandon ship! All hands abandon ship...this is Baden Command to all ships, we are under attack! All ships converge on Colossus, all ships are authorised to fire.*"

"Coms, cut the feed."

Silence returned to the Bridge. Crowe felt the gaze of every crewmember there as they waited for a decision.

"Sir, what should we do?" Colwell asked quietly.

There was nothing within a hundred-thousand kilometres of *Deimos*, nothing to stop them from turning, going flat out for the Red Line and jumping the hell out of there. In all probability that would have been the wisest course. The situation around Baden was going to hell in a hand basket and in his heart Crowe knew that the base and the fleet, were probably beyond hope. How in the universe could anyone have planned to repel an attack that broke the known laws of physics? Right here, right now he could ensure the survival of his own ship, but to do so would mean living with the reputation of cowardice. He knew there was no decision to make. *Deimos* would charge in and probably share in a massacre.

"Helm lay in a course for the *Colossus*. Fire Control, don't engage any target with flak guns until range drops below one thousand clicks... we're going to need the ammunition. Engage with plasma cannons as I direct," Crowe ordered. He'd already been disgraced once and while this was almost certainly the wrong decision, he knew that to run away would require more strength than he had.

Five minutes into the attack and Baden already resembled a circle of hell. Most of the Nameless ships made real-space re-entry within a few seconds of one another and then fired without pause. Hundreds of personnel were killed as the opening salvo smashed into the base and the ships moored around it. One of the first missiles struck the recreation square in Baden, smashing through the great glass floor. Of the people in the square at that moment, those killed instantly by the explosion were the lucky ones, while the less fortunate were those who were drawn to their death as the area depressurised. On one side of the base the destroyers *Lancer* and *Samurai* vanished in a single flash as one ship's reactor breeched. At another mooring, the cruiser *Australia* vomited air and crew as the entire hull split in half. The *Balder* was driven back against the carrier *Yorktown*, trapping her. More and more chunks were ripped out of Baden's great centrifuge and finally the load imbalance forced the safeties to stop its spin.

Minutes passed and men and woman died as the Nameless continued to fire into the helpless fleet. Across the base, men and women, officers and crew started to fight back with both courage and desperation.

In Baden's Number Two Fighter Hangar, pilots and ground crew working side by side managed to get three fighters off the deck before a pair of missiles blew them away. The flak cruiser *Oberon*, her engines shattered, blazed away, swatting missiles and mauling one Nameless ship that dared venture too close. But in the end there were too many. Finding the airlock linking their ship to the base jammed, the crew of the heavy cruiser *Fenrir* fired her engines and ripped her clear. In the end it was the flagship of the fleet, the battleship *Colossus*, which took the most desperate action. Trapped by wreckage, she used her large calibre railguns to blast a clear path through a dying support ship. Around the battleship, those ships that had got under way started trying to fight their way to Colossus, but all the while the dying continued.

"Port fifteen, bows down five, guns target alpha five and engage," Crowe croaked out. Instantly the flak guns started to rattle and a second later an incoming missile disappeared from the display.

It had taken nearly twenty-five agonising minutes to close on the base. For most of the run in they had been left relatively unmolested, only having to swat aside the occasional missile. But now they had reached the fight proper.

But of course that was wrong word. Fight would have implied a two-way contest but this had been a massacre. Ships large and small lay either gutted or burning at their moorings. There was sporadic firing from a few of the base's defences but the great centrifuge was still and silent. Above the base a few ships were still fighting. On *Deimos's* tactical display each of the blue blips signified a human ship, while the brackets surrounding each one showed the ship's condition: green for fully combat worthy, orange for damaged, red for seriously damaged. Even as Crowe watched the brackets around one blip went from green through orange into red and then disappeared, all in a matter of seconds. There were now very few green brackets left and those that remained signified ships mounting hopeless individual last stands.

The Nameless had also suffered losses. A ring of wreckage surrounded *Colossus* but repeated hits were wearing the battleship down and her destruction could only be a matter of time. A few unarmed support ships were also still operational, each one trying to stay as near to a protector while not blocking its fire. The repair ship *Samaritan* had by some miracle remained undamaged and was now sticking as close to *Deimos* as possible.

"Captain. Fleet wide signal from Baden, audio only," called out the Coms Officer.

"Play it."

"This is Admir... ...amile on Baden... base lost... ships are to scatter ...ke your way to Earth at ...t speed."

Several individuals on *Deimos* groaned but Crowe was filled with a deep sense of relief. He could get his ship and his crew away without facing damnation. Searching the display he spotted a point where the victorious Nameless were weakest.

"Coms, instruct *Colossus* to come to heading three, two, zero, dash, zero, zero, zero and run for the Red Line. We'll cover their retreat. We're getting out of here."

In zero gravity small fires are of little danger. Without a clearly defined 'up', convection currents don't form and a fire tends to suffocate itself. By contrast major fires are terrible to behold. Up and down corridors, into cabins, barracks and work areas, fire rolled like golden orange syrup across every surface, consuming everything and everyone that got in its way.

"No use! This way's blocked as well!" Keaveney screamed over the roar of the fire as he strained to force the hatch closed again. The massive blaze had over-pressurised the section and Keaveney was forced to brace himself between the bulkhead and the uncomfortably warm hatch to close it. When it finally clicked shut he pushed himself back down the corridor towards the intersection. Down another corridor Piper was floating. When he saw Keaveney he shook his head.

"That way's no good, it's no good," he shouted.

"What now PO?"

Piper looked around him, uncertainty clear on his face. The pair had failed to make it to their station. Time and again they found their way blocked by fire, wreckage or hard vacuum. Since neither of them had their survival suits this offered the most impassable barrier. They were passed by scores of others all trying to reach their own stations. Finally they were stopped by an officer and told that Primary Damage Control was gone. He ordered them to follow him to the Secondary DC. All the while, Baden continued to take hits and the imbalance vibrations got worse. Then abruptly the centrifuge ground to a halt, hurling them against the bulkhead. Piper hurt his knee and Keaveney cut his face. The officer split his head open. They left his body drifting.

"What now PO?" Keaveney repeated in a defeated tone.

Piper hesitated. He knew what he wanted: to find an officer or anyone that could tell him what to do. Alternatively they could head for the nearest escape pod and get the hell out of there. But do that before the order was given and questions would be asked. The lights flickered badly now as the power system started to break down. They hadn't heard anything from the PA system in nearly ten minutes. For all they knew the order to evacuate had already been given. His eyes searched desperately for an answer on the wall-mounted map of the station beside him.

"We'll head down this way. That might get us to Secondary Damage …"

The scream cut Piper off. Both men automatically pushed themselves down the corridor. Just as they reached a junction a human figure tumbled past like a blazing meteor.

"Jesus! Put him out! Put him out!"

Keaveney ripped an extinguisher off its bracket and squeezed the handle. The blast of gas promptly sent him tumbling in the opposite direction.

"Damn it you bloody idiot! Brace yourself first," Piper snarled before grabbing another extinguisher and hosing down the burning figure.

"Is he still alive?" Keaveney asked.

"Just about. It's an officer," Piper replied turning the smoking figure. "And it's a woman. We need to get her to the infirmary." Her hair was mostly gone and face looked red and sticky. Going on what was left of her uniform she was a sub-lieutenant.

"If it's still there!"

Another explosion shook the station, but this one was different. A groaning sound continued long after the explosion report. It sounded like metal being pushed to breaking point and beyond. Piper's colour hadn't improved since the first weapon hit and now he went even paler.

"Oh Jesus! Cascade structural failure! This place is coming apart at the seams! We've got to get out of here!" he shouted.

"What about her?"

Piper hesitated. The officer was horribly burnt and probably already a goner, but you always tried to take your wounded. Not for heroics or any belief that a comrade should never be left behind but in the hope that if you got hit someone would do the same for you.

"Grab her, we're out of here!"

Grabbing an arm each the two men frantically used their arms and legs to pull themselves and the officer along the corridor towards the nearest set of escape pods. With every second the vibrations and the screams of tortured metal became more and more severe. With their lungs burning and hearts hammering they reached an escape pod silo. Even as they arrived a pod blasted out of its silo and away, leaving two still in their places. The Lieutenant was roughly shoved through the hatch before Keaveney and Piper followed. Piper turned to close the hatch. Shouting caused him to pause. Three more ratings were pulling themselves down the corridor.

"Move yourselves!" he shouted.

The bulkheads were visibly shaking now and the sound was almost deafening. Then suddenly it all came apart. The three ratings were sucked screaming into the void as the bulkheads around them just folded and tumbled away. For a split second there was nothing between Piper and open space. Then the drop in pressure caused the hatch to swing violently shut and the pod blasted clear as the silo came apart around it.

"Report!" Crowe shouted as he shook his head to clear it.

"It went into the port side reactor room. Number Two Reactor has gone down, both the generators are down!" Colwell reported. "The batteries have kicked in but we've lost damn near all the electrics!"

"Get one of those generators going again or we're dead!"

They'd managed to push through the Nameless warships, but as they broke the perimeter *Colossus* had taken several more hits. Three of the battleship's four reactors were knocked out and everything that last reactor could produce was being channelled to the engines. Ahead of *Colossus*, *Samaritan* was running at maximum acceleration ready to open a jump conduit the moment they crossed the Red Line. On either side of the battleship was a pair of supply ships ready to brace the conduit.

They had mostly encountered only light opposition on their way to the Red Line. With Battle Fleet ships in scattered flight, the Nameless were trying to cover a lot of different directions at once. Only as the five ships got within fifteen thousand kilometres did they seem to realise that that one of their plum targets was slipping their grasp. Missiles had started to home in on them in earnest. Dozens had been swatted aside by *Deimos's* flak and point defence guns. Others had been spoofed by the decoys and curtains of chaff the cruiser was laying down. But any defence could be saturated and if the hail of missiles was too much, one would get through.

They would have nailed it but when the turret assigned to deal with it brought its weapon to bear nothing happened. After nearly forty minutes of firing, the reloading system abruptly failed. On the Bridge Crowe didn't have time to react before the incoming missile struck.

Deimos was effectively unarmoured and the missile easily punched through the outer hull before detonating and sending out a spray of shrapnel inside the port reactor room. Several pieces of shrapnel struck the starboard reactor, cracking the outer casing. The reactor room crew were already dead but the safeties immediately activated the emergency purge, releasing a blanket of fire astern. Another metal fragment drilled its way through the bulkhead between the two reactor rooms and struck the second generator. All across the ship the electrical system died. The engines and plasma cannons ran directly off the plasma siphoned from the fusion reactors but the computers, radars and flak guns all needed the generators to convert plasma energy into electrical power. But without commands from Helm, the engines went to standby.

On the Bridge the main holo display winked out. Only the external optical camera system had power requirements low enough for the batteries to run.

"Skipper, main helm and internal communications are down!"

"Deploy Damage Control Teams Two and Three across the ship to act at message relays," Crowe barked back. "Order Engineering to take Helm and prepare to receive instructions."

"Skipper, runner from engineering. The Chief's dead!"

"We have incoming on visual," a sensor rating shouted.

"*Shit*!" Crowe looked frantically round his bridge for someone to send. "Bosun Benson, get your ass down to engineering and take over!"

Benson didn't wait to acknowledge his captain but was up and out of the hatch instantly.

As the hatch clanged shut behind Benson, Crowe turned back towards the display, his expression grim. The closing missiles looked to be a pair of the big ship killers. Just one of those things had damn near crippled *Mississippi*, a bigger and more sturdily built ship than *Deimos*. With them coming in from directly astern the closing speed was agonisingly slow but still enough to overhaul the starship.

With *Deimos* now only coasting, the other four ships were starting to pull away. With not a working gun among them there was no question of them waiting or coming back for *Deimos*. There were a couple sudden jerks as the engines came back on line, but without the main computers, there was no finesse in them. It was strictly a matter of on or off.

"Skipper. Damage control team's in position," said a voice on the intercom. "You have a piggy back connection to Engineering."

"Understood. Bridge to Bosun! Where the hell is my generator?"

"Five minutes sir!"

"We're going to be wreckage in two!"

"That's the best we can do. We're doing some major rewiring back here.

Crowe closed the connection and shouted across the Bridge.

"Does *Colossus* have anything left?"

"Negative! All their aft bearing weapons are gone and they've still only got one reactor."

"Bosun, stand by for evasive manoeuvres." Relaying evasion manoeuvres to Engineering would make them sluggish. The chances of dodging even one of the missiles were poor. Dodging both was one-in-a-million.

"Stand by."

"Skipper! Radio transmission. We're being ordered to hold course!"

Damn them! The *Colossus's* captain clearly wanted them to stand and take it rather than risk a missile missing *Deimos* and acquiring the battleship. Hell's teeth! *Deimos* and her crew had given enough.

"Signal *Colossus* to go to hell!" Crowe snarled.

The Coms Officer shrank back from his anger.

"Sir…. we don't have transmission capability… and the signal came from the *Mantis*," he stuttered.

Berg! Crowe automatically glanced towards the main radar display but it was still blank. He had no way of knowing where Berg was.

"Hold steady," Crowe ordered

"Sir!" Colwell objected.

"That's an order. Commander Berg has our back. We can trust her." *I hope.*

Seconds crawled past as the missiles bore down on them. Suddenly on the visual display a plasma bolt flashed past one of the missiles. She was attempting a crossing shot, the most difficult form of shooting. A second, then a third shot flashed harmlessly past the missiles. Crowe's jaw started to hurt from gritting his teeth. The fourth shot clipped the stern of one of the missiles. The missile's drive cut out and it started to fall away.

"Come on, come on," Crowe found himself muttering as seconds dragged by. Four shots in quick succession meant two destroyers. But now both ships were recharging their firing chambers, would they charge quickly enough? For sure it would be tight.

"Sir, we can still try to dodge."

If they started manoeuvring the missile would start making corrections and that would reduce Berg's chance of hitting to zero.

"No! Hold her steady."

"I think we have about twenty seconds to impact!"

Two shots sizzled past the missile. Someone on the Bridge let out a groan. Crowe closed his eyes.

"Thanks for trying Carol," he whispered to himself.

A sudden cheer deafened Crowe as every crewmember abandoned coms discipline. Crowe's eyes snapped open, just in time to see the fireball that was the missile's death being snuffed out by the vacuum. All round the Bridge officers and ratings embraced, slapped each other's backs and, as if the ship itself was celebrating, the electrics started to come back on.

"Navigator, start calculating our jump out. Communications signal *Mantis* to take position to brace the wormhole conduit around *Colossus*... and give our thanks."

On the radar display more missiles were visible, but they were far, too far astern to be any threat. They'd got out.

By its nature, space is always silent, but now in the aftermath of the slaughter it seemed even more still than usual. On some of the wrecks, now floating around the freshly cratered asteroid that had once been Baden Base, there was still life. Here and there, crewmembers that had managed to get into their survival suits were now trapped in shattered hulks that had once been starships.

It would be almost a day-and-a-half before the last of them died.

On L12 Chuong fought hard not to vomit as he looked around the Bridge of the courier. Everyone had a story of seeing someone hurl inside a space suit and no one wanted to be the subject of such stories. Chuong won the fight, just. There was now a metre-wide hole in the side of the courier's bridge. Outside the stars spun gently and the powerless vessel continued to slowly tumble. It was a far preferable to the view of the Bridge crew.

Lieutenant Malawati and the two Bridge ratings hadn't had time to put on their survival suits. None of them had died easily when the hole was blown in the hull. He brushed aside a lump of something organic and looked at the display. There was a single red light. That meant there was no choice on what must come next.

Chuong made his way back through the temporary airlock they had rigged between the Bridge and Engineering. Stephens and Francis waited anxiously in the latter.

"Well?" Stephens asked as they helped Chuong take his helmet off.

"The Bridge was opened up. The others are dead and the rad shield's gone. Looks like the hit went through the emitter, but other than that we haven't been damaged."

Francis let out a sign of relief.

"Well we can re-rig the control to down here in a day or two and then head for Landfall," he said in a voice shaky with emotion. "Even without the screen we can make that safely enough."

"Really thought we'd had it there," Stephens said.

"Did you?" Francis replied throwing a playful punch. "I didn't think an optimistic guy like you would be worried for a second."

"Nice to be wrong for once."

"We're not going to Landfall," Chuong said flatly, not looking at the two men. The two exchanged confused looks. "We're going to Earth, and we're leaving now."

"Err...PO there aren't any duplicate controls down here. We'd have to run the ship from the Bridge," Stephens said slowly. "We can't jump out with the Bridge open to space."

"Yeah, there's no need to head for Earth. We can make it to Landfall far easier," Francis added.

"This isn't about what's easy, it's about what has to be done."

"PO, what in God's name are you talking about?"

"We have to go to Earth and tell them what happened here. Tell them what is coming," Chuong said quietly.

The engine room suddenly seemed very quiet.

"PO. If we go to jump space anyone on the Bridge is going to take a massive radiation dose. No one would last three-and-a-half days of that!"

"You're right. No *one* person would last that long."

There was another long pause. Then both their expressions changed as they realised what Chuong was saying.

"Whoa! I did not sign up for that!" Stephens burst out. "You're talking goddam suicide!"

"Then what the hell *did* you sign up for?" Chuong roared back. "In case you haven't been paying attention the fleet has just been smoked by people who can make real-space re-entry inside the Mass Shadow! No one on Earth knows they can do that! That means they could do the same thing again over Earth. Do you understand what I am saying! The Home Fleet has to be warned!"

"The base will have sent a FTL transmission to tell Earth," Stephens replied weakly.

"Do you know that for sure? Are you absolutely sure of that?" Chuong demanded.

"There is the Landfall FTL..." Francis started to say.

"No, there isn't," Stephens said in a sick voice. "It's being overhauled this week. The thing's in bits. They won't get it working for days."

" That's it then, we have to go. The Home Fleet is all that's between whoever the hell these guys are and Earth, everyone on Earth."

Chuong knew damn well that was a low shot. Both Stephens and Francis had young families, and he was asking that they wouldn't see them again. But he couldn't do this without them both. Slowly both of them nodded.

"PO, I've got some letters to write first," Francis said quietly.

"I think we all have," Chuong replied equally quietly. "We may not be able to later on."

Twenty minutes later there was a brief flash as L12 left real-space.

Chapter Six

Storm Warning

25th July 2066

Despite a telephone warning, the marine guards manning the gate barely got it open in time as the staff car sped through. Its engine whined urgently as it continued to race towards the main building of Headquarters. Finally in a screech of rubber, it slid to a halt just in front of the building, forcing a number of personnel to scramble out of the way. Admiral Lewis was up and out of the car almost before it stopped. Taking steps two at a time, he was into the building within seconds.

Inside the main door Fleet Headquarters resembled a kicked ants' nest. Officers and ratings hurried back and forth carrying messages, conducting tasks with terrible urgency as if they could some how reverse what had happened. Lewis strode through the reception area, his expression thunderous. Even in the midst of such urgency and scarcely controlled panic, officers, ratings and even the marine guards were careful not to get in the admiral's way.

Staff Captain Sheehan joined his boss in the corridor beyond the main reception and automatically fell in step with the Admiral.

"Well?" Lewis demanded.

"Transmission's still coming in, sir. A lot of it's garbled but what we have at the moment is that Baden and the Third Fleet have taken a hammering," Sheehan replied.

"How in hell's name did they get into firing range of the damn base?" Lewis snapped half to himself.

"That we don't yet know, sir. Admiral Wingate is waiting for you in the main conference room. The Governing Council has been summoned but they haven't been informed why. Admiral Wingate is trying to keep this out of the press until at least the Council knows."

"Have you seen the chaos out there Tim? I'll be stunned if the press hasn't got a sniff already."

"Sir! Sir!"

A young lieutenant came running down the corridor towards them.

"Sir, latest signal from Baden!" she gasped, offering a signal pad.

Lewis frowned at the officer as he took the pad. She visibly wilted under his glare. Quickly he read across the message, his expression tightening as he did so.

"I see. That will be all Lieutenant. You are dismissed." Lewis half turned before snapping: "and this time Lieutenant, *walk*."

Fifteen minutes of walking took the two officers deep into the building. When Lewis walked into the conference chamber there were clumps of staff officers standing around the edge of the chamber speaking quietly. Unlike the chaos upstairs, the atmosphere in the conference room was that of a funeral. Admiral Wingate sat at the conference table alone, fingers steepled together, staring into space.

"Sir," Lewis acknowledged his senior as he took his seat beside Wingate.

"Paul," Wingate replied. "Have you seen the latest from Baden?"

"Yes, sir, I have. The odds are the bad news hasn't finished arriving yet either."

Wingate wearily rubbed his eyes. It was hard to believe that less than three-quarters on an hour ago it had just been a normal day. He'd been planning to spend it golfing, but then the first of the signals had arrived like a bolt from the blue and all hell had immediately broken loose.

"I pray to God you're wrong Paul, but really doubt you are," Wingate replied, running his hand through what was left of his hair.

A chime came from the ceiling.

"Please rise for the Command Council."

The officers standing around the edge of the room hurried to their places as the holograms on the other side of the table flickered into life.

No one who saw the Command Council at that moment could have doubted the seriousness of the situation. While US President Clifton was dressed in her usual business suit, the Chinese Premier was clothed in a dressing gown, the German Chancellor was in formal evening wear and the British Prime Minister was in t-shirt and casual trousers.

"All right Wingate. What the hell is this about?" Clifton snapped. "I've had to step out of a news conference, so this had better be *damn* good!"

"I apologise to you all that this meeting has had to be called so abruptly," Wingate replied matching the president's sharp tone. "Just over… forty minutes ago we started receiving an FTL transmission from Baden Station. We are still receiving the transmission at this time. It is stating that they are under attack, to the extent that the base itself is actively under fire."

The holographic Council collectively gasped as expressions of irritation and annoyance disappeared to be replaced by looks of shock and horror.

"The Aéllr have declared war?" Prime Minister Layland blurted out.

"No sir. The transmission has continued and identified the attackers as the Nameless. It has also gone on to report that the Third Fleet has been caught off guard, in effect, caught at anchor. In essence Council members, Baden and the Third Fleet have been subjected to a Pearl Harbour style attack.

There was a long moment of silence in the large chamber.

Layland cleared his throat nervously.

"Admiral, do we know the full extent of the losses yet?"

"Unfortunately no," Wingate replied. "Due to the thirty-nine hour communications lag we are only now receiving the transmissions sent in the opening minutes of the attack."

"What action can be taken?" the German Chancellor asked.

Wingate paused. On Earth, national leaders were used to being aware of, and capable of influencing, events minute by minute. But out in space, even with FTL transmitters and courier ships, it could be hours or even days before news of an event on the rim reached Earth.

"I am sorry Herr Chancellor. This attack started over a day-and-a-half ago. One way or the other it is doubtless already over," Wingate replied flatly.

"All right," Clifton said. "Let's approach this from another angle. How bad could this be?"

Wingate looked at Lewis. "Paul?" he prompted.

"The transmissions from Baden stated that the enemy has successfully achieved complete surprise. In the past we have wargamed a number of Pearl Harbour style scenarios. The basic premise is that a section of our fleet is effectively caught 'at anchor,' its weapons powered down and crews away from their battle stations."

"Admiral, will you be getting to the point anytime soon?" Clifton snapped.

"Yes Madam President, I will," Lewis replied evenly. "The point is very, very simple. Those wargames have indicated that the fleet would suffer the complete loss of *at least* fifty percent of those combat units present. Almost all units that did survive were judged to have sustained significant damage. Enough to require major dockyard time. I would like to emphasise, fifty percent was the minimum loss."

"Oh dear God," some one muttered.

"The deployment of the fleet at present, Council members," Lewis continued as if there had been no interruption, "is such that the Third Fleet possesses just over one quarter of our first line combat strength. In addition about a third of our support ships are based at Baden. Baden itself is the only significant dockyard facility in the region of Landfall. It is already certain that those facilities will have taken damage, although to what extent we can currently only guess…"

Lewis stopped as an officer crashed through the doors into the room and almost sprinted over to Wingate. He whispered urgently in Wingate's ear as he pressed a computer pad into the Admiral's hand. Wingate went visibly pale beneath his dark colouration. He glanced at the second sheet before passing them both sideways. Lewis's eye's flicked across the brief messages, his lips compressed into two bloodless lines.

"Gentlemen?" the President asked quietly.

"It's a signal from Admiral Camile, commander of Third Fleet. It reads; Base lost. Fleet ordered to scatter. Enemy…" Wingate said in a flat voice. "It cuts off there."

"What does this mean?"

"It means that the Third Fleet has been decisively defeated. Camile not only believes, well believed, that the Third Fleet couldn't defend Baden, but also that they couldn't retreat in good order. In essence a scatter order means that the Third Fleet has been routed and that the survivors are now fleeing back towards Earth."

There was a hushed silence in the room, broken only by someone coughing quietly.

"Oh, and the press have wind of this," Lewis added looking up from his pad.

President Clifton visibly composed herself. Aliens and space battles might be outside her control, but the press she understood.

"Alright everyone. We have a problem. The question is what action can we take?" Clifton said after a long moment's silence.

"After we received the first signal from Baden, we sent out an FTL transmission to Dryad where the Second and detached elements of the Home Fleet are currently exercising," Wingate replied. "They have been ordered to return from Dryad at best possible speed. I would like to remind the Council however that the distance to Dryad is such that the signal will not be received for almost another thirty-two hours. We can't know how long it will take Admiral Fengzi to gather the ships, but the very earliest we can expect those elements to reach Earth is one hundred and fifty hours *after* the receipt of that transmission."

"That would be..."

"The first of August Madam President."

"What do you need from us now Admiral?" Layland asked.

"We're already putting all Battle Fleet ships and installations in this solar system on full alert. What we now need is authorisation to go to full war footing, start calling up reservists and reactivate the red fleet. Also authorisation to inform and liaise with our counterparts in Planetary Defence."

President Clifton glanced left and right.

"You have it Admiral, don't wait for the paperwork. You'll have it within an hour."

"There's something else," Wingate said. "It goes outside our area of responsibility but I believe I must recommend that all nations mobilise their respective militaries."

"Admiral that would be a big step. The activation of so many troops would raise world tensions and..."

"I'm sure the world's diplomats can manage it, Madam President," Lewis interrupted abruptly. "The Centaurs were subject to orbital strikes. If we don't mobilise and disperse our ground forces we are vulnerable to command and control decapitation."

Clifton looked uncertain.

"Admiral, you can't be suggesting they'll get into a position to bombard the planet!"

"I believe in preparing for the worst."

"I would agree with Paul, Madam President. Battle Fleet will be activating its secondary command sites."

"Alright, we'll speak to the non-sitting Council members, but ultimately that decision is a matter for individual national policy."

Wingate nodded an acknowledgement.

"When can we expect to receive more information?" Clifton continued.

"If any courier ships got clear they will be arriving within the next twenty to thirty hours. Emergency Message Drones don't have the range to make it to Earth from Baden so they'd have to route through a junction station. That means they could reach us in maybe two days from now. As for ships, again we can't expect to see any surviving combat or support elements of the Third Fleet reach us earlier than the first of August. Hopefully Council members the situation will clarify over the next few days."

———————————

"…official sources have neither confirmed nor denied the complete destruction of the Battle Fleet forces based close to the Landfall colony. However a spokesman for Battle Fleet has requested all media outlet to publish a complete recall of all off duty and reserve fleet personnel. Sources inside the fleet have also suggested that Landfall may have been subject to nuclear strikes, but this remains unconfirmed. Experts are saying…"

The old 2D television set clicked off. David Guinness walked around the small crowded living room, his brow knotted in thought. He came to a halt in front of the mantelpiece. There were many pictures on the crowded surface, but one monopolised his attention. It was a picture of the crew of the *Mississippi*, digitally manipulated to look like they were all lined up on the cruiser's outer hull. Rating Mary Pelikan had been a bit of whiz with photo manipulation and loved crew photos. Before and after every tour she'd managed to chivvy everyone into position for a group shot. Once a suitable background had been inserted she sent a copy to every member of the crew. They were something of a joke to many since the layout was the same each time but Guinness found them interesting. With each one a few faces would change, sometimes a change in position due to promotion, or new crewmembers joined. But in all of them Guinness was there, sitting two places to the right of the Skipper. Pelikan and Guinness had both served under Captain Crowe for nearly four years, so he had several photos. He stared at the picture for several minutes with a slight smile on his face. Those had been good times all right, pushing back the frontiers of known space. At least they'd been good until the day the frontier pushed back. There was no photograph of the *Mississippi's* crew after their last tour. Pelikan was one of the ones who came back in a body bag.

Even now, nearly a year on, it sickened him how the Skipper had been treated. Crowe had been hung out to dry by both the ignorant and those who should have known better. In his own case, with only two months left to run until mandatory retirement, the fleet hadn't been willing to give him a ship posting. Instead he was given a temporary training post dirtside, which put him in an excellent position to watch his plans for life after retirement disintegrate.

Guinness turned sharply on his heels and walked into the bedroom. Quickly he packed a small rucksack of bare essentials. Then he pulled out a uniform, protected inside a dust cover. Taking it out with almost reverent care, he admired it for a moment before pulling it on. It was a bit tight across the chest, well stomach really, if he wanted to be honest with himself. A bit of service would soon sort that out, he thought with a slight smile.

Hitching the rucksack over his shoulder he headed for the front door. In the hall he paused. There on the wall was a picture frame. It contained half a dozen separate pictures, Christmases, birthdays and other happy times. Carefully Lewis took the back off the frame and removed a picture of a middle-aged woman smiling into the camera. He put it inside his wallet before putting the frame back together and returning it to its place.

"I don't know what the old fool is thinking now," Mrs Phillips said over her shoulder to her husband as she watched Guinness walk in the direction of the train station. "They're hardly going to take him back. He's over sixty for heaven's sake!"

"It's hard to see this coming at a worse time," Wingate admitted to Lewis as they both gazed down into the fleet's main control room. "I wonder how much they know?"

Below them was a huge holographic display of human space. Also displayed was the position or estimated position of every Battle Fleet ship. The icons for the Third Fleet were slowly blinking on and off.

"What I would kill to know is how in hell's name they got into firing range without warning," Lewis replied. "I know Camile's a bit conservative but he is… well perhaps was, no idiot. I just hope more information turns up. I can feel that there is something we haven't heard yet."

In August of each year the fleet conducted its main annual exercises in the Dryad system. The purpose of these exercises was twofold, for aside from the training and wargames, they were an active reminder to the Tample Star Nations that Dryad was a human world, and was going to remain that way. But now that show of strength might have fatal repercussions. The Home Fleet was now facing the prospect of action while seriously reduced, since much of its usual strength was now nearly a week away.

A modern military plans constantly. Each new technique or technology is incorporated into the plans, as is each new analysis of the military, economic and political strengths and weaknesses of possible enemies and allies. But at their heart any military's plans rest upon certain assumptions.

For over three decades Battle Fleet's core premise had been that the Aéllr would be the enemy in the next war, as they had been in the last. While some of the Star Nations of the Tample were undoubtedly more hostile than the Aéllr, their relatively primitive warships kept their ambitions in check. The expectation in most of the fleet's thinking had been based around the idea of the Aéllr fleet making a direct drive from the frontier towards Earth. The forces based at Dryad and Landfall would have been able to harass the Aéllr flanks and supply lines, or if required, get back to Earth quicker than the Aéllr could get there from the frontier.

With the attack on Baden, thirty years worth of planning had suddenly gone out the window. To be replaced by… what?

Eight hours after the transmission from Baden had ceased, Headquarters was only starting to recover its composure. Up in orbit the Home Fleet had spent much of the day at battle stations. With everyone's nerves frayed, they'd damn near blown away a transport ship when it made real-space re-entry. The only thing the day had clarified was that their right flank was too far away to assist and their left was now swinging in the breeze.

"If we're really lucky the objective of their campaign is the seizure of Landfall," Wingate said quietly.

"That would certainly be the preferred option," Lewis agreed. "If they make a drive for Earth it's going to be a race between the Second Fleet or the Nameless. It'll be too close to call who arrives first. Christ, I wish Landfall's FTL wasn't down"

"The answers will come Paul."

"Yes but what will they tell us?" Lewis replied. "Do we know if *Illustrious* and her escort had left Landfall before the attack began?" he asked a nearby staff officer without looking around.

"No sir, we've not heard anything," the officer replied. "If they stuck to the timetable they should have dropped their fighters and started back before the attack."

Lewis's fist slammed down on the desk with a force and suddenness than made everyone present jump.

"Damn it Lieutenant! I didn't ask what's supposed to have happened! I need to know what has!" Lewis roared at the startled officer before forcing himself to stop and take a deep breath. It was no use blaming staff officers for being unable to achieve the impossible.

"What about the *Dauntless*?"

"She jumped for Alpha Centauri only an hour before we got the first signal from Baden," the staff officer replied nervously. "Given the age of *Dauntless's* engines they'll be taking it very gently. They won't make real-space re-entry for another two days."

"Damn it," Lewis said, but quietly this time. "All right, thank you Lieutenant. That will be all."

Faster Than Light transmissions were one of the great miracles of modern science. Unlike so much of humanity's interstellar technology, they had not simply inherited FTL transmitters from the Aéllr ship that had force landed on the west coast of Ireland. The captured ship had indicated that FTL transmissions were possible but not how. Humanity had only finally figured out the secret eight years ago, but they were still constrained in certain regards.

Once a ship made the transit into jumpspace it was effectively severed from the universe. It could neither send nor receive radio or FTL transmissions from anyone other than ships sharing the same jump conduit. Communications would only be regained once the ship or ships returned to real-space. As the Flag Lieutenant had said *Dauntless* was old, a Contact War veteran in fact, and to be brutally honest clapped out. The only way she could make even the short hop to the Sun's closest neighbour was by running at low thrust. Any faster and she'd simply slag her small heat sink long before reaching her destination. It all raised the question of whether they could make *Dauntless* and the various other isolated ships aware they were at war, before the war found them.

Wingate hadn't moved during Lewis's outburst. He now stood up and flexed his back, wincing as various muscles complained. He eyed his subordinate with some concern.

"I think we've reached the limit of what we can hope to achieve this evening," he said. "I think we both need sleep. We might not get much opportunity later on."

Lewis nodded. "With your permission, sir, I'd like to return to the *Warspite*." He gave a weak smile. "To sleep, not to bite the heads off my own staff officers."

"Do you intend to remain there?"

"Yes sir. I think from now on I should remain at my post."

Wingate nodded his agreement.

"I'll need you for the Council but you can attend by hologram. Now go! Get some sleep."

"The car should be around in a minute, sir," Sheehan said.

Lewis nodded without replying. After a day spent inside, the cool night air was like balm. Then out of the corner of his eye he saw an officer in a captain's uniform approach and salute. With a sigh he turned and started to acknowledge.

Then stopped.

"Tim, could you give us a moment please," he said over his shoulder.

Sheehan nodded to the other captain and withdrew back into the shadows without a word.

The captain was of average height and build. She looked to be in her late forties but Lewis knew she was ten years older. Her uniform was also nearly ten years out of date. She hadn't had any reason to wear it in a long time.

"I didn't think we'd actually got as far as reservists turning up," he said quietly.

"I didn't see any reason to wait. Don't think I'm the first to arrive either. Although I have to admit this jacket has got a bit tight since the last time I wore it," she replied running her hands down her sides.

"It still looks good on you Laura." Lewis smiled sadly as he stepped into her embrace.

They stood together without speaking for a while.

"I've never understood how someone so willing to charge into the breach could join Science Fleet," Lewis finally said.

"Mystery keeps a marriage interesting," Laura replied.

Lewis smiled with amusement as his chin rested on the top of her head.

"Besides, you lot are already requisitioning all of our ships. What am I supposed to do?"

"Laura. Dublin will probably be the first target for any strikes on Earth. You..."

"No Paul." Laura cut him off. "You're going to be on the Bridge of *Warspite*, so don't talk to me about danger."

Lewis sighed and nodded.

"Sir, the car's here," Sheehan called from the shadows.

Laura sighed and stepped back. Lewis reluctantly let her go.

"Go. And look after yourself out there."

Lewis didn't have an answer. As the car pulled away he looked back to see his wife wave once, then turn and walk into Headquarters.

David Guinness straightened his uniform jacket as he paused outside Fleet Headquarters. He had taken the first train to Dublin and from there caught a taxi to the fleet complex to the north of the city. Now standing outside the concrete monstrosity that housed the fleet personnel bureau, he hesitated. The called up reservists hadn't started arriving yet and in any case many of them would never come here, but would instead head for the Battle Fleet offices in their own countries. That meant there wasn't a crowd for him to blend in with, which probably meant that the only place he wanted to be would turn him away.

As he approached the steps, a staff car pulled away and disappeared into the night. A captain on the steps waved once before turning back towards the building. Guinness took a deep breath and followed her in.

Despite the late hour, inside there were still dozens of people rushing about.

"Yes? Can I help you?" The young female Petty Officer at the reception looked tired and harassed.

"Reservist reporting for duty," Guinness replied with as much confidence as he could muster.

The woman gave him an uncertain look.

"Second floor room two five seven. Do you need directions?"

"No thank you, I've been here before," Guinness replied, firmly this time.

Twenty minutes later, after once seeking directions, he found the correct room. Another young woman, this time in a lieutenant's uniform, was typing at a computer. She looked up as Guinness knocked on the door. He entered and stood at ease.

"Yes?"

"Chief Engineer David Guinness reporting for call up, ma'am."

"Ah... right..." She typed at her computer for a moment. "Do you have your serial number?"

"Alpha, two, seven, nine, eight, four, two," he recited. He'd always had a good memory for numbers, handy for remembering the setting of an intermix chamber rather than having to look it up every time.

The Lieutenant typed the serial number into her computer and waited for it to spit out the data. Once it did, she examined the read out, then frowned and shook her head.

"I'm sorry Chief. You're listed as retired."

"That's right ma'am, six months ago under the thirty-five year rule. I wish to re-enlist."

"You're over fifty eight. We can't..."

Guinness did something he hadn't done in thirty years: interrupt an officer.

"Error in my record, ma'am. They entered a wrong date of birth. Put an extra couple of years on to me. Never did manage to get it cleared up. I'm only fifty-seven."

"Chief, we don't make those kinds of errors," she objected.

Guinness didn't reply but a subtle change in his stance suggested he's seen personnel make a lot of mistakes.

"Alright, I'll correct the file." Guinness started to relax. "If you have your birth certificate with you," she added with a malicious glint in her eye.

"Oh..."

"Until you provide that there's nothing we can do since we can't enlist some one over..." The Lieutenant was interrupted again. This time an inner office door opened and a captain put his head out.

"Claire can you..."

Guinness snapped the Captain a smart salute. Technically this wasn't a situation in which a salute was required, but it did serve to get the Captain's attention.

"Chief Engineer David Guinness, retired. Reporting for re-enlistment. Sir!"

The Lieutenant frowned at the blatant attempt to go over her head.

"Sir, this man's attempting to re-enlist despite being over age."

"Wrongly recorded date of birth, sir."

The Captain walked over to the Lieutenant's computer and tilted the screen so that he could read it. After a minute or so he scrolled down.

"I'm sure the Chief knows his own birthday Claire. No point in refusing a man of his experience over an obvious clerical error," the Captain remarked distantly. "Re-enlist the Chief, subject to a successful medical." The Captain offered a hand. "Welcome back to the fleet, Chief Engineer Guinness."

26th July 2066

The buzzer over the bunk trilled angrily.

Lewis fumbled for it and groaned: "yes."

"Sorry to wake you, Admiral. A signal has been received from FTL Relay Station Alpha Four. A force consisting of at least forty vessels has been detected by a sensor satellite transiting through System A, two, eight, seven, dash, two, eight, zero."

Lewis rubbed his eyes as he tried to get his brain into gear.

"Am I right in thinking that system is nearly half way between Baden and Earth?" he eventually asked.

"That's correct Admiral," the voice at the other end of the intercom confirmed unhappily.

"Wake my staff please. I'll be up directly."

"Our original projections were based on the assumption that the earliest the Nameless could reach Earth would the morning of the first of August. Perhaps as little as two hours ahead of the leading elements of the Second Fleet" Admiral Wingate told the Council. "This new information shows that assumption was wrong."

"What does this mean in practical terms, Admiral?" President Clifton asked with a worried frown on her face.

"There are two plausible explanations. The first is that another Nameless fleet got in behind Baden before the attack. The second is they are moving faster than we anticipated. If it is the former then we can expect them at least one day ahead of the Second Fleet, if the latter, at least two days. I stress the words at least."

"So what are we saying? Their jump technology is better than ours?"

"We know so little about the Nameless that we're basically guessing," Lewis said. His holo image shimmered for a moment as the signal from *Warspite* shifted from one satellite to another. "We have no idea what their design philosophy is. A speed advantage could be attributed to more internal volume being dedicated to the propulsion system. However the most likely scenario at this point is that a second Nameless force did get in behind Baden before the attack."

"How can there be this uncertainty? Do we not have means of tracking their progress?" the German Chancellor demanded.

"With respect, sir, space is very big. In every system the Nameless have so far passed through the only human presence has been observation satellites. Those satellites have no FTL, only EMDs. It takes time for those message drones to reach an FTL relay station. The fact that we aren't receiving follow-up messages from those observation satellites probably means they've been taken out or forced to self- destruct."

"How could they even have found out so much about us? And enough to launch an attack. How is that even possible?" the Chinese Premier asked.

"If they found our home world and then listened long enough and sifted hard enough, there is very little that radio intercepts couldn't have told them," Wingate replied.

"Does this change things?" Clifton asked.

Lewis and Wingate exchanged unhappy looks.

"Yes Madam President, it changes things a great deal," Wingate said. "The situation has just become far more serious. Paul can you run the Council through it?"

"Yes, sir. Our core problem is that it now appears likely that the Home Fleet will have to hold out for an extended period, at the very least twenty-four hours. That forces us to change our tactical plans drastically. Our original plan was to wait until the enemy made real-space re-entry, then move to engage them as far away from Earth as possible. If we could force a fleet engagement it would have hurt, a lot. But even if they destroyed the Home Fleet in detail, the enemy would have been forced to pause to refuel and rearm. That would have bought the time for our detached forces to arrive. However, while this approach would have bought us hours there is no possibility of it buying days."

"Then what's the alternative Admiral?"

"I need all Council member to understand the situation I am facing. I have at my disposal one new battleship, one old battleship, twelve cruisers and eighteen destroyers. I may be able to add some older decommissioned ships to that, but to all intends and purposes those ships will be meat-shields at best. It is my intention to shift the orbits of our major orbital construction facilities to bring them closer together," Lewis replied. "Once that's done, it's my intention to form up with the orbital fortresses of Planetary Defence over the top of them, until the rest of the fleet arrives.

"Erm... perhaps I'm missing something, but I don't see how that protects the planet Admiral," Prime Minister Layland asked hesitatingly.

Lewis turned slightly to look the Prime Minister directly in the eye.

"It doesn't, sir," he replied emotionlessly.

There was silence. The eyes of the Council members darted between the two admirals. Several looked as if they were wondering whether the commanders of the fleet had gone mad. Even the military personnel at the table looked shocked.

"Council members, you must be entirely clear that we are facing a potential disaster. The Nameless are essentially mounting a blitzkrieg style attack, in effect, an attempt to land a single knockout blow. I do not have the numbers to defend the surface. That fact would not change if I had twice the ships I have. I could spread forces out in upper orbit, but if I do so the Home Fleet will be destroyed one ship at a time." Lewis's voice remained calm and even.

"Admiral how..." Clifton started

"Council members. More importantly there are the construction platforms themselves. They are the product of over thirty years of investment. They could not be replaced in less than two decades. I cannot overstate the importance of those platforms. Without them we cannot build ships, we cannot repair ships and even resupplying them becomes more difficult. If they are destroyed, this war will be lost in a single stroke."

"But Admiral that will leave most of the planet exposed."

"That's true Madam President. But we must be cold-blooded and accept that we, we as the human race, can survive without a number of our major cities. But if we lose our orbital facilities we lose... everything."

The room reverted to shocked silence. Even a number of fleet officers looked shaken by the pronouncement.

"Surely admiral... " the German Chancellor started.

"I'm afraid not Herr Chancellor." This time it was Wingate interrupting. "We've run this through every simulator and used every tactical officer we have. Admiral Lewis's resources are simply not equal to the tasks he faces. If we try to defend orbit we'll be weak everywhere and strong nowhere. This proposal is in effect the best of a bad set of options. We've deployed a number of couriers across their presumed route to Earth in an attempt to open a dialogue. But I am not hopeful. Nothing we have seen so far indicates that they lack resolve. I believe direct attack on Earth isn't just possible but now probable. Planetary Defence's ground-based missile batteries and fighter squadrons should be able to soften the blow but we must still brace ourselves because we are going to be hit hard."

The courier ship L12 made real-space re-entry right at the edge of Earth's mass shadow. The little ship didn't respond to radio challenges and a squadron of fighters was ordered to intercept. Three quarters of an hour later Admiral Lewis walked into the sickbay of the cruiser *Io*.

"Well?"

"His name is Petty Officer Van Chuong. The other two were already dead from radiation poisoning," the cruiser's captain told him. "Going by the state of the engines they must have run red hot with barely any cool down time."

"What about the computer core?"

"The data storage units have been corrupted by radiation, sir. Given time we should be able to recover the data."

"Time, Captain, is now at too high a premium for us spend it carelessly," Lewis replied in voice so emotionless it caused the Captain to wince. "What is the condition of the survivor?"

Io's doctor stepped forward.

"He isn't a survivor Admiral. He simply hasn't died yet," the ship's doctor replied quietly. "He is in the final stages of radiation sickness. I can keep the pain down, but that's all I can do for him."

"Can he talk?"

"No, sir, he's heavily sedated."

"Wake him up."

"Sir. That's quite impossible," the doctor objected.

"That wasn't a request doctor," Lewis replied in a low, dangerous voice.

"Admiral, medical matters are not subject to the usual..."

"Doctor you will obey orders or I will have you arrested. And then I will find someone *who can do as they're told*!" Lewis snarled. "Now do it!"

The doctor visibly flinched, then looked to his captain but found no support there.

"This is against my advice," he said nervously.

"Noted," Lewis snapped. "Now get on with it."

The doctor walked over to the patient and turned off a medication dispenser before filling a syringe.

"This will quite likely kill him," he warned again as brought the syringe to the patient's arm.

"You've already said he's dying anyway," Lewis replied flatly. With an unhappy expression the doctor pushed the syringe in.

"I've given him a stimulant. If he's going to come round at all, it will be in the next few minutes."

"Very well, leave me with him. Both of you."

As the doctor and Captain left, Lewis pulled up a chair next to the dying man. For nearly ten minutes there was no change, then Chuong's breath began to quicken. His crusted eyes began to open and after a few moments focused on Lewis.

"Petty Officer Chuong do you understand me?" Lewis asked.

Chuong opened his mouth, his lips cracked and bled, and his voice came out as a weak croak. Lewis poured a glass of water and helped Chuong to lean forward to drink.

"Where am I?" Chuong whispered as Lewis helped him back.

"On board the *Io*, Earth orbit."

"Thank God," Chuong replied painfully. "My crew?"

Lewis shook his head.

"What happened at Baden PO, tell me what happened," Lewis asked in a low voice.

Chuong's breathing quickened and his hand clamped painfully around Lewis's arm as he half levered himself up.

"The Nameless ships," he gasped. "They made a jump inside the mass shadow! They took the fleet totally by surprise."

Lewis went white as a sheet.

"Are you certain! Are you sure?" he demanded.

"Yes." Chuong breathed as he sank back, his brief energy exhausted. "With my own eyes. One dropped in less than a hundred clicks from us. We were thousands of kilometres inside the Red Line."

Lewis jumped to his feet and paced back and forth across the sick bay with nervous energy.

"Did any of our ships get clear?"

"A few," Chuong replied his voice fading.

Lewis started towards the hatch then paused and returned to the cot.

"Can I do anything for you PO?"

Chuong's eyes flickered towards the pain killer dispenser. Lewis flicked the switch and the medication started to pump into the dying man's veins. As Lewis turned away Chuong whispered.

"My crew's families, tell them I'm sorry."

Admiral Lewis felt old. For over thirty years he had done everything in his power to be ready for another war. Now the starter's pistol had been fired and suddenly all the rules had been changed. He was standing on the Flag Bridge of the *Warspite*, humanity's newest and most powerful starship, and yet she could already be as obsolete as the nautical battleships of the early twentieth century.

Every one of the past few days had brought new information. With each new revelation he had adjusted his plans to compensate, but he could not see a way past this final one. He had simply never considered the possibility of the Nameless willingly seeking combat inside plasma cannon range. The encounter with *Mississippi* had shown that once in range, plasma cannons could quickly take their ships apart. But you couldn't keep ships at red alert indefinitely. Neither the crews nor even the ships would be able to take it. The Nameless would be able to choose their moment and simply drop in around his fleet like they had at Baden, guaranteeing that they would get the first shot. Half the Home Fleet would be obliterated before they realised they were under attack.

Certainly the plan to hold station above the orbital construction facilities was now out. He could pull the fleet out of Earth orbit and keep them moving. That would give them space and headway to take evasive manoeuvres. But leave Earth uncovered? There was no point in saving the fleet if Earth didn't survive.

No, the best way to buy Earth the time and space they needed would be bring the Nameless to action in a time and place of his own choosing. His lips twisted in a bitter smile. Time and place of his choosing? Merely the desire of every military leader ever. The Nameless Fleet was making re-entry in every system between Baden and Earth. The point of entry was roughly in the same place relative to the local star. Three couriers that had been on route to or from Landfall had been ordered into those locations in an attempt to make diplomatic contact. But Lewis had no more faith in anything coming of that than his boss did.

He had considered taking the Home Fleet to one of these locations to intercept. And rejected it. There was enough variation in the Nameless's re-entries to make a guarantee of interception impossible. If they failed to force contact they would have left Earth exposed.

Lewis pushed himself over to the Bridge view port and pressed himself down. Once they came into contact with the deck plating, the small magnets in his boots held him down. Below him was Earth. Even after thirty years in space he still found it a breathtakingly beautiful view. But in his mind's eye, he could see Earth burning beneath nuclear fire.

He turned abruptly back to the Bridge display holo. There had to be a solution. If only he could…. an icon blinked at the edge of the display. The *Dauntless*, plus tender, plus two escort destroyers, all about to arrive in Alpha Centauri. The Nameless force would pass through Alpha Centauri within the next fifty hours. There was an FTL transmitter on Alpha Centauri Three, an old one dating from when they were being developed. It wasn't manned but it was still serviceable. Transmission lag time would be short, less than thirty minutes over such a distance.

"Tim, what is the shortest transit the Home Fleet can make to Alpha Centauri?"

Sheehan was the only other person on the Flag Bridge. Well accustomed to his admiral's moods, he had been waiting quietly at the rear of the Bridge. He now started to type instructions into his pad.

"Least time transit, two-and-a-half hours, sir. That will require the cruisers *Hood, Hurricane, Tempest,* and *Whirlwind* to be towed, assuming they get any of them going in the first place. Without them we can shave off fifteen minutes."

Lewis nodded slowly as he considered the possibilities.

Each time the Nameless dropped into real-space it was outside any planetary mass shadow, probably to save on wear and tear to their drives. In theory that made them vulnerable to an enemy jumping directly into contact, just as they had done to Baden. But without knowledge of position, the chance of actually forcing contact would be damn near negligible.

On the other hand, if the Nameless could be held in place for three hours that would give the fleet time to make the passage and then drop into real-space inside energy range. If *Dauntless* failed to make contact or land a strike, the fleet would still be close enough to Earth to offer battle in the planet's defence.

"Tim. Contact Admiral Wingate, I'm going to need to speak to both him and the Council."

———————————

"Thank you Admiral Lewis," Wingate said.

The Council chamber was silent, apart from the tap of Lewis's shoes as he returned to his seat. The atmosphere in the chamber had been tense when the meeting started. Now, there was an edge of real panic in the air.

Wingate studied the faces of the Council members. A week ago their biggest worries had been the state of the economy, their opinion poll ratings and other assorted political concerns. Now they were facing a threat on a global scale and a pair of fleet officers who were offering no real solutions.

"Admiral, this plan… it seems to have weaknesses," Clifton said eventually.

The Indian Prime Minister Faisal Farooqui slammed his fist down.

"Weak? Weak! This isn't weak, this is madness!" He pointed an accusing finger at Wingate. "You told us that the fleet would hold and protect us. Now you want to run away, to run away and to leave us!" A restraining hand appeared on the Farooqui's shoulder, then a ghostly form appeared as an adviser stepped into the pick up for the hologram system. The figure whispered urgently in Farooqui's ear and the Prime Minister visibly controlled himself.

The room went utterly silent.

"Admiral Wingate, this seems like a very drastic course, based on the reports of a dying man," Layland said.

"That is true. We cannot discount the chance that the man was raving."

"No."

All eyes shifted to Lewis.

"Those men knew the consequences of their actions. They could have chosen to make for Landfall. They could have chosen to take the time to reconfigure their ship and fly it from the engine room." Lewis's voice was flat, without any inflection at all. "Instead they chose to make for Earth without the protection of a radiation screen. They chose, Council members, to subject themselves to a lethal dose of radiation. They chose to die in a particularly lingering and painful manner, to bring us that information. That, Council members, is why I am treating the information provided by the courier crew as gospel, unless or until such time as information that directly contradicts it turns up."

"I'd still like independent debriefing of the survivor Cody," said Clifton. "I can have specialists there in about an hour."

"I'm afraid that isn't possible," Wingate replied grimly. "I received word just before the start of this meeting, that the last survivor of the courier has died."

"The Pentagon has made a number of…"

"Yes Madam President, I've read the document. We welcome the contribution the United States military and of course those of the various national militaries. However there are sufficient problems with all the proposals to make them impractical," Wingate said diplomatically.

"Such as they would require us to rewrite the laws of physics," Lewis added. "Council members, we need an answer now, yes or no. If no, the Home Fleet will remain in upper orbit. When the time comes we will fight to defend this planet, but in my opinion we will probably fail. If yes, we will move beyond the Red Line in preparation for a jump to Alpha Centauri."

"Admiral as I understand it, this plan hinges on the Starship *Dauntless*," Layland asked.

"That is correct Mister Prime Minister."

"A ship that is over thirty years old."

"That is also correct," Lewis confirmed. "But that ship is currently under the command of Rear Admiral Emily Brian, our foremost advocate of carrier warfare. It is her presence that will make the difference."

"Council members, what is your decision?" Wingate asked.

Clifton looked up and down the table.

"Members in favour?" she asked quietly.

Three came out against, five in favour.

"Admiral Lewis, you have a green light. God help us if you're wrong," Clifton said.

Chapter Seven

The Geriatrics

26th July 2066

Chris was scared, really, really scared. The rest of the crew probably were as well, but at least they had jobs to do. All Chris had was his fear. He wasn't supposed to be here, he should have been at home, with his wife, enjoying the comforts of both. Not in some arse-end of nowhere star system, smack in the path of an alien war fleet.

This wasn't the job he had come out here to do. In actual fact he had already done his job. He'd been sent out mediate a small dispute between the Chinese and American colonies on Landfall. Chris, along with the H Class courier that was his transport, had been on the way back to Earth when the message came through. Baden had been destroyed and the fleet scattered. They were ordered to make their way to an FTL relay station and await instructions. The Captain had been confident that the order to hold position was just an instinctive reaction by Fleet Headquarters and they would soon be ordered to get to Earth as fast as possible.

It was a good theory. Problem was someone back on Earth wanted to try the diplomatic option. So instead they'd been ordered into the path of the alien fleet, to make contact, to open a dialogue, to stretch out the hand of friendship, etc, etc.

These aliens were predictable if nothing else. For some reason they'd touched base at every system between Landfall and Earth. They'd also made real-space re-entry in the same position relative to the local star. So that made getting into roughly the right position easier. Okay, good, focus on the positive. The alien would drop into the system and he, Chris Byrne, would extend the hand of friendship. If he pulled this off it would definitely be promotion time. Hell it would be Nobel Peace Prize time.

On the other hand it could all go horribly runny and he would be right in the middle of it. If he'd wanted to get shot at by aliens for a living, he'd have joined Battle Fleet, not the diplomatic service!

"Contact!"

Chris jumped and in the zero gravity environment of the courier bounced off the ceiling.

"Oh crap! I'm reading dozens of contacts all dead ahead! Range about two-and- a-half light seconds."

"Any sign they've spotted us?" The Captain sounded cool, calm and collected. Chris immediately started to hate him.

"No, I'm getting nothing Skipper."

"Okay then, time to wake them up. Mister Byrne, you're up."

"Show time," Chris muttered in a voice that sounded far calmer than he felt. He leaned over the communication console and typed in a set of commands. "Sending greeting message now."

The Captain gave a terse nod before addressing the helmsman quietly.

"Frankie, if they ain't feeling chatty we're going to have to get our arse out of here sharpish." The courier's jump drive had been kept spun up as they waited. Bad for the drive but Chris wasn't about to complain.

Time crawled as they waited for a reply, any reply, as the alien fleet moved slowly towards them. Ten minutes passed, then twenty, twenty-five, thirty. Chris checked the communications console that it was definitely sending.

"Range now crossing through the one-and-a-half light seconds," the sensor operator reported.

"We can't go in much closer," the Captain muttered. "Byrne, once we hit the one light second mark I'm going to fire the thrusters and hold range."

Chris nodded.

"Do I look as if I'm about to start arguing? Do what you think best to protect the ship, Captain. How long do you think that will it be?"

"If they hold velocity, about fifteen min..."

"Captain, I'm reading two new contacts from the fleet. They're small and they're turning towards... oh Jesus! We have incoming!"

"Hell's teeth! Helm execute jump out manoeuvres," the Captain bellowed.

"Two missiles inbound, three minutes to impact!" the sensor operator screamed.

Chris clung to a support beam as the courier started to swing round. Behind him the engines began to rumble and in the bows the whine of the jump drive climbed in pitch. Astern the engines slammed into life. They had to build up enough forward motion before they could open a jump conduit, otherwise the portal would fatally close on the stern of the courier.

"Thirty seconds to impact!"

There were no orders being given on the Bridge of the courier. No point now, it was a race between the accelerating courier and the approaching missiles.

"Ten seconds!"

"*Five!*"

A light on the helmsman console lit.

"Jump!" the Captain roared, even as the helmsman's finger stabbed down.

A hole in the face of the universe opened, consumed the ship and vanished even as the missiles flashed through the space the courier had occupied.

On the Bridge of the courier there were nervous laughs and much patting of backs. For his own part Chris let out his breath explosively and released his death grip on the support beam. After a couple of minutes the captain called the Bridge to order.

"Alright everyone, settle down. Helm, make best speed. Communications, the second we make real-space re-entry signal the relay station 'have made contact, peace proposals have not, repeat not, been reciprocated, send instructions.'" The Captain turned to Chris. "Do you have any objections Mister Byrne?"

"No Captain. I think diplomatic channels have been exhausted."

"Is Commander Faith Willis in here?"

Willis looked up from the book she was failing to read. A petty officer was leaning in the hatch looking around the tiny compartment. She poked her head out from under the bunk above.

"Down here PO."

"Ma'am," the petty officer squatted down beside her floor level bunk, "a signal has come up from Headquarters. You're to report to Admiral Clarence on the StarForge III platform."

"When?"

"Right now ma'am. We're prepping a shuttle to get you over there."

Willis rolled out of the bunk pulled on her jacket and picked up her pack.

"Alright, I'm ready."

The *Crimson Star* was a civilian transport chartered to carry personnel between Earth, Landfall and Baden. They had arrived at Earth only a few hours after the FTL transmission from Baden. Willis had already been roused from Deep Sleep and had been on *Crimson Star's* bridge when they made real-space re-entry. Almost instantly they were pinged by radar. Even looking over someone's shoulder, Willis recognised the profile of a Type Twenty-three radar array. The targeting radar of a Myth Class heavy cruiser, locked onto them. She could only hold her breath waiting for the crash of plasma bolts striking the hull, but nothing happened. Thousands of kilometres away someone realised the blip on their screen wasn't a threat and held their fire. The civilian crew of *Crimson Star* remained oblivious to the near miss as the ship trundled into Earth orbit.

It was only then that they finally heard what had happened at Baden. *Crimson Star* was ordered to take up an orbit out of the way, awake all the personnel from deep sleep and wait. With all the confusion down below, Headquarters wasn't willing to bring people down that it might instead want to keep in orbit. Now it would appear that after a full day of cooling their heels, the fleet was finally starting to get its act together. Not that Willis was really looking forward to the next posting. The most she hoped for was a distraction. *Harbinger* had been her first failure. Before that it had been an unbroken series of successes, leaving her unaccustomed to anything else. The period in deep sleep had merely delayed a lot of brooding.

StarForge III was an early construction platform. Its small size had rendered it obsolete for ship building decades ago and it now served as an orbital administrative centre. When her shuttle docked at the platform, a staff lieutenant and a rating were waiting for her.

"Commander if you want to follow me. Gemayel, take the Commander's belongings." The staff officer looked back to Willis. "There is a Luna shuttle waiting for you once you're done with the Admiral. If you'd like to follow me ma'am, he's waiting for you."

Willis passed her pack over and followed the officer without comment. A number of other officers were already waiting outside the Admiral's office, but Willis was led straight in.

"Ah, Commander Willis, you're here." Vice Admiral Clarence waved her towards a chair. "No, no, don't bother with the saluting crap, just park yourself."

The Admiral fiddled with his computer. Clarence was one of the fleet's more distinctive flag officers. With a huge ginger moustache and an upper class English accent, the Vice Admiral looked and sounded like an escapee from the nineteen-forties.

"Ah! Here we are," he declared pulling out a computer pad from the middle of the pile. "Right this is going to have to be quick since I'm up to my eyeballs trying to juggle crewing list. Headquarters, in its infinite wisdom and mercy, has ordered that we activate anything that even resembles a warship and make them combat worthy yesterday. Naturally that leaves yours truly trying to find crews to put in them. You're getting command of the *Hood*." Clarence tossed the pad across the desk to land in her lap. Willis started to open the file then her brain caught up with her ears.

"I'm sorry sir, did you say *the Hood*."

"Yes I did."

"Are you serious… sir?"

"Yes I am and yes I know. There's a few hands already aboard trying to get her started but at this point I honestly don't know what kind of shape she's in," Clarence replied with a shrug. "All the Red ships are to be recommissioned. We're currently hunting around for tech manuals and spare parts, but frankly don't hold your breath waiting for either. I'm sorry I have to rush you, but look on the bright side Commander. Your first command, it's always a big step forward. Just get it moving in some shape or form. Although I advise you to make sure the escape capsules are working. We're not asking for miracles, just near miracles. So if there's nothing else?"

For a moment Willis considered taking here leave but the impulse to speak was too strong.

"Sir, my last captain didn't feel I was ready for command." She wasn't even sure herself why she raised the point. Was she honestly pointing out something her superiors had perhaps missed, trying to avoid an undesirable posting or did she no longer feel she was capable? In all honesty she didn't know.

"Yes, I noticed that. I know Captain Flores personally. He's usually pretty restrained in his report writing. You must have seriously made a balls of things out there. My problem Commander is with so much of the fleet's out on the summer manoeuvres that there aren't many line officers with enough experience kicking around. So even if Marko had said you were a blithering idiot, you'd still be getting this posting. There is a shuttle standing by to take you out to her. Now unless you have something really interesting to say, you're dismissed Commander."

"Yes, sir." Willis moved to leave but as she reached the hatch the Admiral spoke again.

"Oh Commander, good luck."

The shuttle was already half full of junior officers, petty officers and ratings. A staff officer was waiting at the airlock with a clipboard. He ticked her off his list as she showed him her orders.

"Are any of these mine?" Willis asked waving her hand toward the shuttle seating.

"No" he said, shaking his head, "we put the first lot onto *Hood* this morning. I think the old man is still trying to figure out the rest of your roster. Unfortunately, the Amber ships have swallowed most of the available reservists. Basically you're going to be getting whatever's left."

"Thank you. I really needed to hear that," she replied sourly.

"Sorry. You'll be getting underway in a minute. We're just waiting for someone else who's just received a surprise posting so you'd better take a seat."

Willis took a seat near the front where she could see into the cockpit and out through its view port. Astern there was a clatter from the airlock as someone scrambled through and the hatch was closed behind them.

"Faith?"

Willis looked up, into a familiar face.

"Vincent? Where did you come from?"

"I was going to ask you the same thing. Move up."

She pulled herself into the next seat. Commander Vincent Espey was an improbable looking officer. With his dyed blond hair and permanent tan, he looked more like a surfer dude than anything else.

"Last I heard you were still on *Harbinger*," he said as he clipped in.

"I left," Willis replied shortly. "I wasn't expecting to see you either."

"Two days ago I was working on my tan on a Florida beach. Next thing I'm being lobbed onto a shuttle and told that I'm the new CO of the fusion powered antique *Hurricane*!"

"The *Hood*," Willis replied.

"Ouch," Espey said. "Gone from one of the newest ships to damn near the oldest."

"Thanks for the reminder Vince," she replied sourly.

Unnoticed the shuttle had pushed itself with thrusters far enough from StarForge III to fire the main engines. The passenger seats all rolled through ninety degrees to make the G forces more comfortable.

Their conversation continued but every time it strayed towards her most recent posting, Willis changed the subject. Most people wouldn't have noticed but there weren't many people who knew her better than Vincent. They had entered the fleet in the same academy intake, and with similar interests found themselves in a lot of the same classes. Slowly they became friends, and later, a couple. They made for an odd partnership, the socially uncomfortable Willis and Espey, the life and soul of the party. Their first ship postings though had brought it to an end. They found themselves on ships going in opposite directions. They tried to keep the relationship going, but finally Willis sat down and worked out that in two years they had spent less than a full week in the same solar system together. By mutual consent they ended it but Willis always looked forward to the occasions when their paths crossed.

"Faithie, why are you avoiding talking about *Harbinger*?" he eventually said.

Willis gave a half laugh.

"I'm not avoiding it, just not a lot to say."

"Not a lot to say?" Espey looked sceptical. "Faithie, you were there when they found a depopulated planet. The biggest story in, what? Ten years? And you're trying to tell me there isn't a lot to say? What happened really?"

Willis stared fixedly in front of her.

"I got given the boot Vince," she said quietly. "I blew it, I really blew it out there."

"How?"

"According to the skipper I was the cause of friction." She gave a short bitter laugh. "For all I know he saved my life. I've been recommended as not yet suitable for command status. Yet here I am about to take command of a ship. At least they're not wasting a good one on me," she finished bitterly. She glanced sideways. Espey was watching her with a worried expression.

"Faithie..."

"I honestly thought... I thought... I thought I was doing a good job. Well I obviously thought wrong."

"Faith, don't do this to yourself," Espey asked gently.

"Why not Vince? Do I really have what it takes to be a captain?"

"Faith, I'm talking to you as a friend here," he said. "You've never been that good with people for as long as I've known you. You're always a bit too sharp. If people aren't doing things your way then they're doing it wrong. The tech stuff, the tactical stuff, they came to you pretty easy, but people you're gonna have to work on. It's a bummer but that's life. *Hood* might be a relic, hell it *is* a relic, but it's a chance to show you can handle the big chair. So chin up and just remember: think, don't snap."

"You've always been a good shoulder to cry on," she said eventually.

"Uniform cut from special absorbent material, it gives me the edge for shoulder duties," he replied, his face returning to its usual grin. "Now if you want to talk sob stories we can talk about our commands. I know sure as hell I'm not going aboard *Hurricane* without my survival suit on."

The ships of the fleet were divided into three status categories. Green ships were those vessels commissioned and active. Amber ships were decommissioned but still manned by small maintenance crews. Finally there were the Red ships, decommissioned, pushed into lunar orbit and basically left to gather dust. Given that the fleet was barely thirty years old there wasn't much in the Red fleet and currently its ranks were made up exclusively of first generation ships.

Those ships had been built at a time when humanity could barely construct starships at all. With the underlying science simply not understood, they were obliged to blindly copy most of the key systems from the Aéllr ship that had force landed in Ireland. The resulting ships had been inefficient, unreliable and clumsy. But it had been enough.

Hood was the oldest of the Red ships, an Admiral class cruiser and the only one of that class to survive the Contact War. The design had been something of a failure even back then, but now, thirty years on, the small elderly cruiser might be about to reclaim her place in the battle line.

It took three hours to reach the moon from Earth orbit. At first the parked ships were merely spots against the face of the lunar surface. Slowly, details came into view, seven ships all orbiting in a line. *Hood* was second in the row.

Size was always tricky to judge in space. The lack of any external reference points really messed up a person's judgement of distance and size. However from the flight deck of the shuttle, *Hood* looked pitifully small and, with her flush bows and high conning tower, desperately outdated.

During the trip Willis had managed to read through the file the Admiral had given her. Unlike most of her contemporaries, *Hood* had a centrifuge, making her suitable for extended duration operations. This, in turn, had given her a longer and more varied career. Her last duty before her final decommissioning had been customs duties. Fortunately, at some point after she'd been decommissioned, she'd been returned to the fleet's standard blue grey, but there was still the odd flash of bright yellow here and there. The ship had also been through other modifications. The two bow missile launchers, which had caused much of the class's problems, had been removed and plated over decades ago. Plus her two plasma cannon sponsors had been replaced by four shuttle bays, two on each side, another left over from her customs days.

The end result of these changes was that the *Hood* barely had the firepower of a modern destroyer.

There was no one waiting at the airlock when Willis pulled herself through. Most of the lights were on, but the air still had that edge that comes from the deep cold of space.

"Hello? Anyone?" she called out. Her voice echoed down empty passageways. Then a rating stuck his head round a hatchway.

"Ma'am?" he asked in a puzzled voice.

Inwardly she took a deep breath to ready herself.

"Commander Willis. Who's senior here?" she demanded.

"That would be the Chief, ma'am. He's on the Day Bridge. Do you need me to show you the way ma'am?"

"I'm sure I'll manage," Willis replied coolly, then consciously corrected herself. "Finding my own way will be a good chance to get to know the ship. You can go back to what you were doing."

"Yes ma'am," he replied before disappearing again.

"Faith?" Espey's voice echoed through the docking hatch.

Willis looked back down the airlock.

"Have we got the right ship?" he asked.

"Looks like it, I'll talk to you later Vince."

Espey flipped her a salute.

"Look after yourself Faithie, and remember, I'm only a radio transmission away."

Hood might have been small compared to modern cruisers but Willis still ended up going round in circles trying to find her way into the ship's centrifuge. Nothing she saw filled her with optimism. Although she could feel the vibrations of a generator, the ship didn't feel like it had come alive. When she finally got to the Day Bridge it initially appeared deserted. A small noise made her look around the back of a control console. A pair of buttocks protruded from underneath.

"Chief?"

With a grunt a white haired man levered himself out and up. Willis wondered briefly whether her new Chief Engineer had been kept in deep freeze somewhere on the ship, only to be thawed out when the ship was taken out of mothballs. He was a short man, slightly overweight. But while his hair was white his round friendly face was almost unlined; like most old space hands he clearly hadn't had the chance to absorb much UV light.

"Commander Willis?" he asked in a soft Welsh accent.

Willis nodded.

The engineer came sharply to attention and saluted.

"Welcome aboard ma'am. I apologise for not having a side party ready to greet you. We weren't expecting you for another couple of hours. I'm afraid there's only about six of us aboard at the moment."

"That's all right. Under the circumstances I wouldn't have expected one. Now who are you Chief?"

"Chief Engineer David Guinness ma'am."

"You obviously knew I was coming before I did."

"Well, I was told that someone would be turning up."

Willis nodded.

"Well Chief. I Commander Faith Willis, on the date of twenty-sixth of July Two thousand and sixty six, am formally taking command of the Battle Fleet cruiser *Hood*." Words she'd dreamed of saying and now… it seemed like a let down. She stifled the emotion.

She looked around the Bridge, her Bridge now, and felt a deep sense of gloom settle over her. Everywhere she looked there was signs of age and long use; cracked and discoloured plastic seats, metal handholds worn shiny by a thousand grips. And she hadn't seen anything like the equipment outside the fleet museum. In her opinion *Hood* was a casualty of war looking for somewhere to happen.

Belatedly she realised she had allowed a silence to develop between them.

"Alright chief, what have we got?"

Guinness studied her for a moment before answering.

"Not as bad as you might think ma'am," he said. "Me and the lads have only been aboard since oh seven hundred but we've got most of the major systems going including the reactor and the generator. Haven't had a chance to look at the tactical systems yet. Main problem at the moment is in the command lines. Since we repressurised and powered up, we've had some condensation problems. The Lazarus systems would get us moving right now if we had to, but of course that would leave us without any slack and we'd soon conk out. Lucky for us when they converted this old girl to customs duties some of her electronics got updated. A bit anyway, it's still gen-two stuff. No, it's the lads trying to get those old Storm class ships going I feel sorry for."

"I think we'll have ourselves to feel sorry for if we have to take any of these buckets into action." Willis mentally bit her lip. That one had slipped out. To show uncertainty in front of a subordinate was one of the cardinal sins of command.

Guinness folded his hands behind his back and shifted to an at ease stance.

"Permission to speak frankly, ma'am."

Willis nodded.

"I know what you're thinking ma'am; that she's an old rust bucket that will likely shake herself to pieces the first time we roll the engines. But you're wrong, ma'am. She is old and she is worn out but she's an Admiral and the Admirals never let the side down." Guinness patted a support beam fondly. "I know the history book say they were failures, but neither of the ones we lost gave up easily. The *Nimitz* was still firing even as she broke up. Even with her forward third gone and not a working gun left, the *Scheer* still held her place in the line. As for the *Icarus*, well she wasn't a proper Admiral but she had the spirit of one."

"You've served on this class before haven't you?"

"Not just the class." He looked around with a smile. "This ship, she was the first one I ever served on. I know her of old Commander. Trust me I can get her going."

"You're a veteran?" she asked.

"Yes ma'am. Battle of the Rings under Admiral Lewis, back when he was a commander. I was on her for the Second Battle of Pluto as well."

"What was your last appointment?"

Some of the enthusiasm drained from his face to be replaced with hardness.

"*Mississippi*."

"Oh. You were…"

"Yes ma'am under Captain Crowe. And with all respect I don't give a damn what the political gobshites say, he saved our bacon out there. If any ship has got out of Baden I'd say it'll be his."

Willis blinked, surprised by his passion. He truly was glad to be here. For a moment the sheer power of his will and belief in the ship penetrated Willis's gloom, but then she looked around and sank deeper into depression.

Guinness sensed that his words had failed to reach her as the uncomfortable silence between them returned.

"StarForge III sent up a crewing list while you were on route," he said, as much to break the silence as anything.

"Then I think I'll leave you to it Chief. If you need me I'll be in my cabin working out where we're going to put people."

Without waiting for a reply she turned and walked out of the Bridge, her footsteps sounding leaden against the deck plating.

Guinness watched her go, face creased into a worried frown. There were a lot of dangerous things out in space, but few could match a skipper who didn't have faith in their command. He wasn't surprised though. He'd heard much the same from the petty officers and ratings he'd come aboard with. Compared to the fleet's current workhorse, the Myth class cruisers, with their thick armour and heavy guns, *Hood* was a toy. But *Hood* had something they lacked: history. It was in every plate and weld, in the very air. Her bridge had known the shout of orders as broadsides crashed into her hull. And the crews, they'd been giants, undismayed even when their ship threatened to come apart around them. These youngsters however, they seemed to go to pieces without their modern toys. Guinness sighed and shook his head. Then he did what he always did when presented with problems he couldn't solve, shrugged his shoulders and went to do something else.

Chapter Eight

The Dubious

28th July 2066

The jump conduit walls glowed and shimmered, bathing the four ships travelling down it in a soft blue light. At the head of the column was the destroyer *Piranha*, next the fighter carrier *Dauntless*, followed by *Piranha's* sister ship *Hammerhead* and finally the supply ship *Samuel Clemens*. All four were only firing their engines very occasionally, merely to compensate for the gravitational turbulence within the conduit. Most of the time, they were allowing momentum to carry them. While the support ship and the two destroyers were of modern design, the carrier they escorted was of a much older vintage.

Dauntless was a venerable ship, the last veteran of the Contact War still in service, although long since relegated to a training role. Mounted on her flanks were the fighter hangars, resembling twelve great shipping containers bolted onto her. Nestled between each pair of engines were the radiators, which immediately made obvious why the small squadron was travelling at such a slow pace. Unlike her more modern compatriot's radiators, which remained black, that of the *Dauntless* glowed a dark orange as they attempted to purge the ship's waste heat.

Deep inside the carrier Rear Admiral Emily Brian sat in her cabin brooding, her round, usually expressive face, blank. On the computer screen in front of her, the mission outline remained forgotten. Every few seconds the hull of the old ship would gently groan or keen, as it was buffeted by the gravitational forces of jump space. But like the computer screen, this was ignored. Above her desk, the public address system speaker came to life, or at least tried to. The first few words were unintelligible. Like everything else on the ship the PA system was worn out. On the Bridge someone tried again.

"Attention all hands. Attention all hands. All hands close on jump in positions. Real-space re-entry in five minutes," it squawked.

Brian glanced across the tiny cabin at her survival suit, still in its canister. Regulations said all personnel should have their suits on for real-space re-entry. She considered getting up and putting it on but then shrugged her shoulders. Regulations said many things. In all likelihood they said Rear Admirals should be on the Bridge of their flagships for the start of an operation, but she wasn't going to do that either. Captain O'Malley was more than capable of running the whole operation without her assistance. He had no reason not to be. Having previously managed to run dozens of these kinds of missions without a flag officer, he didn't need one now. Leaning back she continued to think back on the choices that had brought her here.

"Good morning Admiral Brian, you can go right in. He's already waiting for you," the Staff Captain informed her as she entered the outer office. Never the less she tapped on the door before opening it.

"Come in."

The office was almost completely bare. There was a desk, a computer terminal and a couple of chairs, but no personal touches anywhere in the room. Even signs of work were few and far between. The office's owner preferred to keep most of his files elsewhere and only brought in what he expected to use that very day. Brian knew a lot of visitors found the stark office somewhat intimidating and suspected he knew that too.

Admiral Lewis rose from his desk as she limped into the room and they exchanged salutes.

"Sit down Emily," he said, waving her towards the room's other chair.

Immediately there was an uncomfortable silence between them.

"You certainly know how to choose your words," he said in a weary voice. "What was it you called Vice Admiral Sudell... a backward looking inbred cretin?"

"Yes, something to that effect," she replied evenly.

"And you really had to do it in front of a group of ratings?" he continued.

Brian made no reply.

"You do know that he has made an official complaint of insubordination to Admiral Wingate? Had you blown off at Sudell in private, I think this would have been laughed off by all concerned, but you did it in public and Wingate can't ignore that."

"I wouldn't ask him to," she replied woodenly.

"You could publicly apologise to Sudell. It might stand some small chance of heading this off."

"Yes, sir, but with respect, I'm not going to." Her voice remained as flat as ever.

Lewis drummed his fingers on the top of the desk, but otherwise he remained calm.

"Emily, is there any particular reason I'm getting the silent treatment here?" he eventually asked.

"Sir?"

"I know you weren't happy about the decision to cancel the project, but that was months ago."

"Permission to speak frankly."

"Of course."

"The committee didn't come out against the carrier due to its findings. They were looking for an excuse to cancel it from the very start. That report was a whitewash designed to 'prove' that another class of battleships would do the job better than a pair of carriers. That's why I told that cretin to go to hell when he told me I had to sign off on the report."

Lewis sighed and leaned forward.

"I agree with you, for what it's worth. Much as I would like to strengthen the battle line, I believe we need at least one extra carrier to cover maintenance cycles. Especially now that it's agreed Illustrious will become a drop fighter carrier," Lewis replied quietly. "But unfortunately what you've said and where you said it means I cannot bail you out this time."

"As I've said, sir, I'm not asking anyone to." She looked past him out through the windows. "I don't think we'll have any space fighter carriers ten years from now. Not if those idiots in planning get their way."

"This was just one battle Emily. That particular war goes on. I've already put on the record that I reject the committee's findings, but now I have to take action against you."

Brian made no reply.

"I've persuaded Wingate and Sudell that a court martial isn't necessary or desirable. In six weeks time, when you reach sixty, you will be given a full discharge." He glanced toward her weak leg. "On medical grounds. The fleet owes you that much at least."

"Am I to keep Akagi until then?"

"I'm sorry but no. On that point I couldn't sway them. You're being transferred to the Dauntless, nominally to provide a review of the training regime."

"In other words, a posting that will keep me out of the way." She replied bitterly.

"Yes, that's basically it."

The whoop of the alarm once again broke her reverie. The pitch of the deck plating vibrations had changed now and without conscious thought she used her good leg to brace herself. There was a moment of silence then *Dauntless* lurched violently back into real-space on the outer limits of the Alpha Centauri system. With the transit complete, the rumble of the engines dropped away. Now that they had arrived the first order of business would be purging the carrier's heat sink before they moved deeper into the system.

She should probably go up to the Bridge now that the jump in had been complete and perhaps she would in a few minutes. Or perhaps not.

"ALL FIGHTERS SCRAMBLE! ALL FIGHTERS SCRAMBLE! THIS IS NOT A DRILL!" the PA abruptly screamed.

Brian automatically leapt to her feet and staggered as her weak leg sent pain shooting through her, threatening to collapse. Frantically shaking her walking stick into the open position, she half limped, half hopped out of the cabin. As she got into the passageway her intercom started to buzz.

"Brian here," she snapped as she shoved the earpiece into place.

"Admiral, you're needed on the Bridge immediately."

Trainee Flying Officer Alanna Shermer ran her fingers around the back of the connection between the helmet and body of her suit, checking for any stray hairs that might weaken the seal. Only when she was satisfied that all was in order did she pull on the thin 'skin' gloves over her hands. The gloves were only a very thin layer of a semi-permeable material, lightly reinforced across the back of the hands and fingers. They would keep air in but allow sweat to pass through. They were inadequate against hard vacuum, but the protection they did grant would give enough time for the wearer to don heavier gloves. Unlike starships, fighters didn't depressurise their cockpits, so flight crews used special light gloves that didn't limit the sense of touch to the same extent as heavier ones. The rest of the squadron were also putting on their suits. Around them *Dauntless* trembled and groaned as the carrier prepared for the jump back into real-space.

At the head of the room Squadron Commander Moscoe continued to outline the exercises planned for the next ten days. Alanna was only half listening to him really, more a case of making sure there was no last minute changes being sprung on them, as the fleet sometimes liked to do. The next ten days represented the last phase in their training as fighter pilots. Not quite a formality, but it was unusual for anyone to fluff it at this stage.

Sitting near the back of the briefing room, she glanced around at the other nine trainee pilot officers, plus the ten weapons operators. There had been three times as many when they started but at each stage a few failed to make the cut. The ones that had made it through had been a together for just over two years now. Soon however the training squadron would be breaking up and their graduation would be accompanied by posting orders. Each crew would go its own way. The luckiest ones would go to carriers and others to space bases, but the majority would find themselves on bases dirtside somewhere. She would be sorry to see them all go; they'd been a good group to come through with.

An elbow dug her into her the side, bringing her back to reality. It belonged to Flying Officer Simon Scammell.

"…in a change from the earlier plan, on day three…" Moscoe continued.

Alanna gave Scammell a quick smile of thanks, which he immediately returned. Like all good wingmen you had to look out for each other.

A second whoop from the PA cut across the Squadron Commander, warning that the jump in was imminent. Everyone braced themselves. *Dauntless* didn't use her own jump drive and instead relied on their escorts to generate the jump conduit and the interface points. This meant however that the carrier's transfer from jump space to real-space was rougher than that of most ships, which reinforced her unflattering nickname, 'the Dubious.'

There was thump accompanied by a few groans from the hull and they were down. Moscoe continued his briefing but then the main alarm suddenly screamed into life.

"ALL FIGHTERS SCRAMBLE! ALL FIGHTERS SCRAMBLE! THIS IS NOT A DRILL!"

For a moment Alanna thought it must be a surprise, to test the trainees' reactions. But she was looking directly at Moscoe when the alarm sounded and therefore saw the expression of surprise appear on his face. It was matched by one of shock on the face of his deputy Wing Commander Devane.

Moscoe recovered his composure fast.

"MOVE! Move yourselves!" he bellowed. There was no time for thought as the entire squadron made a rush for the hatch.

"Captain, *Piranha* and *Hammerhead* report they are closed up and at action stations," Commander Ferrara reported as Brian limped onto the Bridge. "The duty fighters are launching now and the rest of the squadron is fuelling and arming. It's going to be at least twenty minutes before they're all ready, sir."

"Order flight control to launch each one as it comes ready," Captain O'Malley replied. With his back to the hatch the Captain didn't see Brian come in.

"Captain, what in God's name is this about?" she demanded irritably, rubbing her aching knee. O'Malley turned around and Brian stopped dead in her tracks. The Captain was a large ruddy-faced man, but now he looked rattled.

"Admiral, we received a transmission from the FTL relay satellite near the jump in point. On the strength of that transmission I have ordered the entire squadron to battle stations." He sounded as shaken as he looked as he held out a signal pad to her. "It was G fifty-one encoded."

Brian hesitated, drew a sharp breath and then paused before reaching for the pad. G fifty-one was a coding protocol that the fleet had developed and trained its communications personnel on, but never ever actually used. Its purpose was as a contingency measure. In the event of war the fleet would immediately switch over to G fifty-one, thereby hopefully rendering void an enemy's pre-war code-breaking efforts. To receive a message so encoded was therefore a declaration of war in its own right.

She took it out of O'Malley's unresisting fingers and ran her eyes across the short message.

Message start: ++*Baden destroyed – Third Fleet scattered – at war with Nameless – authorisation to commence hostilities granted – proceed to Alpha Centauri Three – reactivate FTL transmitter – confirm receipt of message – await further instructions.* ++ Message End. Coding: G FIFTY-ONE, CORRECT Frequency: CORRECT Authorisation code: CORRECT. Conclusion: MESSAGE CONFIRMED AUTHENTIC.

She slipped the pad into her pocket, and walked slowly over the command chair at the centre of the Bridge. It was almost silent. Only the hum of machines was audible and she could feel the eyes of the crew follow her. At the front of the Bridge, the main holographic display was set for navigation mode. The four ships of her command were represented by a single green blip, tiny against the vastness of the solar system. She folded her stick up again and pocketed it, as much to give herself a moment to think.

"Captain O'Malley, what is our jump status?" she asked quietly.

"The destroyers are showing green across all systems. Our heat sink is saturated however. We need at least twenty minutes before we came make even an in-system jump."

"That's to be expected," she said quietly to herself. "Tell engineering to do whatever it takes to shave a few minutes off that."

"Admiral, we could send *Samuel Clemens* on ahead now and follow when we're able," Commander Ferrara suggested.

Brian considered it and shook her head.

"No. I'm not splitting ships up," she said firmly. "We'll take the opportunity to refuel. In fact, we'll make use of this time. First, order flight control to form the fighters that are up into as good a perimeter as they can manage with the numbers. Captain O'Malley, I want this ship stripped for action. If it can burn and we don't need it, lose it. Order *Piranha* to make calculations for a jump to Alpha Centauri Three. I want the jump in as tight to the Red Line as their navigator can make it. While we're docked with *Samuel Clemens*, I want our munitions magazines filled with all the fighter missiles they have. If you have to dump dummy missiles, so be it. Once we've made the jump I want all but the duty fighters kept on board, and a complete systems check performed. Tell the flight deck engineers that if I start losing sorties to breakdowns, the Nameless will be the least of their problems. Oh, and can someone get my survival suit from my cabin."

O'Malley nodded in agreement and waved his people into action, before approaching her chair.

"I'm sorry ma'am, I should have thought of most of that myself," he said in a lowered voice, so only she could hear.

"That's all right Denis, you got the ships to battle stations. That was the immediate priority," she patted him lightly on the arm. "Flag officers don't like subordinates that do everything. It leaves us feeling surplus to requirements."

"Thank you Admiral. On that note, there is one thing which I think you missed," he replied. "The crews will need to be told."

The pilots' mess was almost silent. A few people were having conversations, but in voices so quiet as to be barely audible. The ship wide announcement from the Admiral had finished ten minutes ago, but people were still trying to take in what they had heard. Alanna had visited Baden during her year as a rating and could remember marvelling at the great station, built so quickly, so far from home. She could remember watching the massed ranks of the Third Fleet, from battleships to fighters and it had been a breath taking show of force. How could such a fleet have been defeated? The Admiral didn't know. All she said was that they were awaiting orders from home. They'd been in jump space a mere two days, but instead of travelling between solar systems it felt like they'd travelled to a different reality entirely.

Alanna suspected that a lot of people aboard the ship were considering their own immediate future. She certainly was. If, as the saying went, truth is the first casualty of war, then training was generally the second. There was no doubt in her mind that her own was now over. The training period of next intake would be pared back to months, possibly even weeks once front line squadrons started crying out for fresh blood. She wished that her fighter had been on the duty roster. Flying picket duties would have given her something beside the future to think about. But her plane, C for Caesar, was currently in its hangar, with its machinery opened up.

"Attention on deck!" Moscoe barked as he stepped through the hatch. Everyone scrambled to their feet as the Admiral came in.

"At ease," she said waving them back into their seats.

A few people shifted their chairs to get a better view of the Admiral. Alanna had last seen Brian when she'd first come aboard and was now struck by the change. The Admiral, when she pulled herself through the airlock on that first day, had looked tired and more than a little depressed.

If her presence on *Dauntless* had been a surprise, and it had, then her behaviour was even more so. Rarely leaving her cabin and showing no interest in the running of the ship, she had left the ship's regular officers baffled as to what she was even doing with them. The ship's gossipmongers hinted that she had somehow fallen foul of Headquarters, and certainly her behaviour and demeanour had done nothing to disprove that theory. But now she looked and sounded like a completely different person. While the rest of the crew were shocked by what had happened to Baden, the Admiral, it seemed, saw the situation very differently. Certainly she seemed to be throwing herself into the crisis.

"Now I know you've all heard my address," she began briskly, "but I want to speak to you separately. Firstly, by my own authority, I am promoting you all to full operational status, so you can all lose your trainee stripes. I'm also changing the designation of your fighter squadron from training to a line unit. Now at this very moment, the *Samuel Clemens* is launching an engineering party, who will shortly make the FTL transmitter on Alpha Centauri Three operational. Once we have confirmed we are in position, I expect Command to tell us why they want us out here."

"Admiral?"

Brian's head immediately snapped round towards the raised hand and her eyes focused on Alanna.

"Err… Trainee Fly… I mean Flying Officer Alanna Shermer ma'am," she stuttered.

"Yes?" The Admiral's tone was businesslike, but not unkind.

"Ma'am, may I ask what kind of missions we're expected to fly?"

"As I said, we are waiting for Command to contact us," the Admiral replied. Alanna felt her face heat up. "However since you're asking," Brian continued, "I believe that our most likely mission will be to support retreating elements of the Third Fleet. Strike missions, are however, a possibility."

The gathered crews stirred uncomfortably. The Admiral sensed their unease, and its source.

"I know what you're all are thinking: the Vampire Three is old. In fact several of you are younger than your planes," Brian shrugged. "Not perfect I admit, but I remind you all that while you know it as a training fighter, I have flown them into action. The Vampire is combat proven design and it won't let you down."

A lieutenant appeared at the hatchway and tried to catch the Admirals eye. Brian glanced towards him and then looked back at the assembled fighter crews.

"Duty calls," she remarked. "I want you all to get some rest. One way or the other, we're going to be earning our pay in the next few days."

Once the Admiral left, the squadron flight crews broke up. Some gathered into small groups, others wandered off. A few did as the Admiral suggested and headed for their bunks.

Rest was the one thing Alanna definitely didn't feel in the mood for. Scammell looked like he wanted to talk, but she didn't feel in the mood for that either. Instead she slipped out of the pilots' mess and down to the second hangar on the port side upper row.

The engineering crew were just finishing up on C for Caesar when she entered the hangar. The flight chief nodded to her as he left, but didn't stop to talk. Too many fighters to service and not enough hours to do it in, she guessed. Within a minute of entering, she was alone with her fighter.

The Mark III Vampire strike fighter would never be considered a thing of beauty. With engine pods on each side and plasma guns in ventral and dorsal turrets, unlike its successor the Raven, it made no concession to aerodynamics. With its blocky appearance, it well deserved its nickname, 'the Flying Brick.'

She wasn't sure how long she'd been there when she heard the main hatch open behind her.

"So, this is where you are, Skipper," said a familiar voice.

"Were you looking for me?"

"Not really. I think half the pilots are with their planes at the moment, but of course you pilots do so love your planes."

"I think... I think, Wasim, most of us are wondering if we're really as good as we thought we were yesterday," she replied as she turned around.

Wasim Dhoni, her weapons and systems operator, regarded her seriously. A short but heavyset man of Indian origin, among the frequently boisterous trainees, Dhoni's seriousness and reserve stood out. Unlike the rest of them, he had already served with the fleet for a decade before he decided to transfer to the Fleet Fighter Corp. They'd been crewing together for over year but even now Alanna didn't feel she knew him well.

"There is no good purpose served by worrying. We cannot affect events Skipper. We just have to try to be ready."

"Admiral?"

Brian looked up into the worried face of Staff Lieutenant Gore. Brian was sitting in her cabin studying charts of the solar system. She'd left her cabin hatch open, an old habit from her days as a captain. She'd always felt that being able to see the crew passing helped her to sense the mood of the ship. The Lieutenant's mood was an easy one to judge. He was standing as far back from his Admiral as he could politely manage. As the only staff officer she'd brought to the *Dauntless*, Gore had, unfortunately for him, borne the brunt of her anger.

"Yes William, what is it?" she asked in what she hoped sounded like a friendly voice.

"Captain O'Malley reports that two military couriers have made real-space re-entry on opposite sides of the planet. They've both signalled that their orders are to only transmit our instructions once they are in laser transmission range," Gore reported nervously.

"Hmm... that's interesting," she commented to herself. "Does the Captain have an estimate on when they will be close enough for coms lasers?"

"Approximately one hundred and thirty minutes ma'am."

"Good. What's Captain DuBois's latest estimate on the FTL being operational?"

"Erm..." Gore flicked through a notebook. "The last estimate was about an hour, that was twenty minutes ago, ma'am."

"Good."

Brian nodded to herself with satisfaction. Once they had got over their initial shock the officers and crews of the four ships had snapped to it and *Dauntless* had rapidly transformed into a hive of activity. She suspected that many were glad of the work since it didn't leave time to brood. And there was much to brood about.

"Alright, thank you William. Can you instruct the Bridge to send the transmission down to me as soon as we get it."

"Yes, ma'am," Gore replied before gratefully retreating.

Brian smiled with amusement and returned to her reading.

"The couriers should be reaching them about now," Admiral Lewis said quietly, his voice breaking the long silence.

Admiral Wingate nodded. The room was silent except for the buzz of the hologram projector. With orders given, the two officers could now only await developments. This forced period of inactivity sat uncomfortably with both men.

"What do you think is the chance of her pulling this off?" Wingate asked quietly.

"With the element of surprise," Lewis paused, "she has perhaps a ten to fifteen percent chance of landing a strike. What chance there is of her pinning them in-system, I can't even guess."

Wingate leaned back and shook his head.

"That assumes that Brian presses home that attack. We're sending her in with a training ship for Christ's sake. I wouldn't blame her for showing a degree of caution."

Lewis gave an amused snort.

"If there is one thing we can be sure of, it's that Emily will press home the attack, if for no other reason than to ram her after action report down Sudell's throat. She doesn't work in half measures, she never has."

"Well I wish it was Rear Admiral Heyerdahl we had out there," Wingate replied distantly.

"With respect, sir, I'd only want him out there if I needed the *Dauntless* kept in one piece," Lewis said, his tone blunt.

"What do you think the chances of *Dauntless* surviving are?"

"If they make contact, ten percent," Lewis replied flatly. "At absolute best. I'd happily trade *Dauntless* for a chance to get the Home Fleet into weapons range. I just wish we weren't going to lose Emily as well… she would have been very useful in the future."

The briefing download was the biggest Brian had seen in her entire career, literally hundreds of files, plus a video briefing from Admiral Lewis. That in itself was unusual. Paul Lewis had never liked the informality of video briefings and within the fleet was renowned for issuing almost every order in writing. As the video file was marked as the first item she was to look at, she clicked on the icon. Lewis's face came up on her screen and she was immediately struck by how tired and harassed he looked. His expression was the same as it had been the last time they met and she sensed that what she was about to hear wasn't going to be good.

"Emily, on the twenty-third the Third Fleet and Baden Base were attacked by the Nameless," he said without preamble. "The Fleet was defeated and Baden has been destroyed. The full extent of our losses are currently unknown but the indications at this point are that they have been severe… possibly even total. Unfortunately this isn't our biggest problem. We've also had indications, which I regard as reliable, that Nameless ships can make real-space re-entry *inside* a mass shadow."

"Oh *crap*!" Brian muttered.

"In addition to this, they are now making passage from Baden to Earth faster than we thought possible. By our calculations they are going to reach Earth before any surviving elements of the Third fleet or the forces coming from Dryad. It is the opinion here, that the Home Fleet cannot withstand an assault on their terms. If we are to stand any chance, we have to force an engagement with them. According to our estimations, by the time you receive this message, the Nameless will be forty to fifty-five hours away from passing through Alpha Centauri. It is your mission to hold the Nameless inside the Alpha Centauri system, by whatever means at your disposal. Transmission to Earth from the Alpha Centauri FTL will take thirty minutes, passage of the Home Fleet another two and half hours. I need you to hold them in the system long enough for me to arrive and engage. You should find everything we know about the tactical situation at time of sending in the download. The two couriers are now under your direct command and hopefully they will give you some limited standoff strike capability. However you are ordered to take whatever measures are necessary to land a strike... I'm sorry Emily, but I have to consider both you and the *Dauntless* expendable." Lewis gave a wan smile. "Good luck Admiral."

    Brian laced her fingers together behind her head and leaned back in her chair. She was glad now that she had decided to listen to the briefing in the privacy of her own cabin. The senior officers would have to be told, but for the crew at large to know that they had been written off would be disastrous for morale. *'You and Dauntless are considered expendable.'* How typical of the man. Where others would have hinted Lewis just came right out and said it. They'd met during training for the old Phoenix fighters just before the start of the Contact War. But now, the best part of forty years later, that hadn't stopped him from throwing her into the fire. Frankly she would have been disappointed had it been any other way. Reaching down to her belt she activated her intercom.

    "Captain O'Malley."

    "Yes ma'am?"

    "Gather all the senior officers to the briefing room. We have a lot to do."

Chapter Nine

Scorched Earth

31st July 2066

Deimos hung dark and silent at the edge of the system, her passive sensors probing, searching for any sign of activity. On his bridge Crowe sat silently in his command chair, while around him the sensor ratings slowly worked their way through the various frequencies. Anything that seemed out of place was checked against the ship's records, but every time they found it to be a natural occurrence. They had been holding position for three hours already. The time to make a decision had arrived.

Crowe looked across the Bridge at Commander Hockley. His second-in-command was standing behind the sensor ratings, looking over their shoulders. Hockley turned and shook his head.

"We're picking up no sign of enemy activity, sir."

Crowe felt a sense of disappointment. It looked they were going to have to do it.

"What about Junction Station? Anything?"

"Negative sir, no beacons, no chatter, no sign of in-system communications. It's plausible, that they could have heard the war warning, in which case they could have gone dark sir."

"That's the best case scenario Commander," Crowe replied before shaking his head. "Alright. Navigation, make the jump calculations as close to Junction as you can get it," he ordered. "Sensors, I want a passive drone dropped to monitor our entry/exit point. Commander Hockley, I want the ship closed up at action stations for the jump in. Then assuming nothing happens we'll open up, except the gun crews. They stay at their stations. Alright people, we're going in."

29th July 2066

In the starboard engine room of *Deimos*, Bosun Wallace Benson and Commander Hockley examined the electrical generator. Both men were in their survival suits with their helmets sealed.

"Do you see what I mean, sir?" Benson asked.

"Yes I do," Hockley answered as he pulled himself out from under the generator. "Let's go outside."

A temporary airlock had been fixed over the hatch into the engine room, which Benson closed behind them, muting much of the noise of the machinery beyond.

"That's a serious botch job under there, Bosun," Hockley said as he pushed back his visor.

"Not lost on me, sir," Benson agreed. "Sorry about that, sir, but we were seriously pushed for time. With respect however, it was a crappy design to begin with."

The one hit they had taken during the escape from Baden had wrecked the portside reactor room and also driven missile fragments into the centreline bulkhead that separated the two reactor rooms. While most of the fragments had failed to penetrate, one had punched through and clipped the starboard side generator. It hadn't damaged the generator itself and instead had struck the power distribution box, which, unlike on most human ships, was integrated onto the generator rather than a separate component. It was a space saving design feature that Benson had spent much of the past four days cursing.

The problem was that the box was the point at which the power from the generator was split into the ship's various electrical circuits. The damage to the distribution box had severed the power flow to those circuits. Combined with the write off of the generator in the port engine room, *Deimos* had suffered a complete loss of electrical power. In the rush to restore it, the repair had been very rough and ready, not helped by the fact that so many of the engineering crew had been killed.

"The problem is, sir, it's going to fall over again. That's a cast iron guarantee. The whole repair job is just a mess of potential short circuits. Any kind of physical shock will do it, particularly since we had to bypass most of the breakers."

"Any chance of fixing it on the fly?" Hockley asked.

Benson shook his head.

"I'm not a good enough electrician, sir and neither is anyone else that's still standing. It doesn't help, that we have to wear suits in there."

"Still haven't pinned down that slow leak?"

"Oh we know where it is, sir," Benson replied sourly. "The bloody hole is somewhere behind the number two power line, but its too small to pull in a sealant. So we're going to have to stay in suits in there, which makes everything that bit harder."

"What are we talking to fix this?"

"Complete shutdown of the electrics for at least six hours," Benson said in an uncompromising tone. "It might well be longer, depends on how well it goes."

"Bosun, that's not going to go down well with the Skipper."

"I know, sir. I can talk to him..."

"No," Hockley interrupted sharply.

Benson looked surprised at the reply.

"Sorry Boss," Hockley added apologetically. "We only got the Skipper off the Bridge about an hour ago. He needs sleep."

"How long had he been..."

"At least thirty hours." Hockley sighed and rubbed his eyes tiredly "There's nothing we can do about this until we drop back into real-space. I'll talk to him then. We're going to need the Skipper's personal radar to be sharp when we stop for our next cool down."

"Amen to that, sir. When will we be jumping in?"

"About four hours. I'll talk to him then," Hockley replied after glancing at his watch. "Hell, I should be off duty myself. Look,

I'm going to hit the bunk for a few hours, I suggest you do the same."

Crowe lay on his bunk, watching the holo display that was being projected against the bulkhead. He felt desperately tired, but sleep eluded him. The stimulant he'd taken a few hours ago hadn't done a damn thing to take away the tiredness and had instead just left him feeling slightly numb. Yet hours more had trailed by and he remained on the Bridge. Finally the Commander summoned the ship's surgeon, who politely but firmly threatened to remove him from duty on medical grounds unless he rested.

He rolled out of his bunk and walked back and forth across the cabin, before throwing himself back onto the bunk. He felt edgy, like he needed to do something. He picked up a book but then tossed it back onto the shelf. He had a fair idea of the cause of his disquiet. At Baden he'd reacted on instinct, overreacted really, but his almost panicked response had at least meant that while the rest of the fleet was being butchered, *Deimos* was closed up and ready to fight. Now he couldn't drop out of that mental state of red alert, and it was wearing him out.

Not that there weren't some positive points. Before the attack neither his officers nor crew had faith in him as their captain, but now even the most junior rating knew that their skipper had saved them. The 'Skippers Radar' was what they were calling it. After a year of accusation and criticism, it was almost exhilarating to find himself promoted to the position of a walking, talking good luck charm.

He gave up on sleep, for the time being at least, and sat up in his bunk to watch the holo. The image was being sourced from one of the ship's rear facing cameras. The closest ship was clear, but the furthest was little more than a glimmer in the blue-lit distance. *Deimos* was at the head of a column of seven ships. Astern was the repair ship, two merchant vessels, two destroyers, and last but by no means least, the battleship *Colossus*, the other source of Crowe's concerns.

While *Deimos* had got away with relatively light damage, *Colossus* had been battered terribly. Her entire armament was knocked out, her electronics package mostly shattered and her engines barely running. Worst of all was the loss of crew. Over half had been on Baden when the attack began and few had made it back to the battleship before she disengaged from the station. All told, the once powerful flagship was now little more than a millstone, slowing the progress of the rest of the squadron.

Third Fleet C-in-C Admiral Camile had been aboard Baden for a meeting and among those left behind. Captain Lukeman, his Flag Captain, had remained on the ship however and was now the senior officer of what remained of his command.

For the moment Crowe was prepared to accept that the state of the *Colossus* was one problem he couldn't solve. The gentle blue light of the conduit walls finally began to lull him towards sleep and his eyes finally started to flicker closed. But then they snapped open again and frowning, he rolled off the bunk and walked over to the bulkhead. He reached through the projection and scratched curiously at the metal, before stepping back again. He picked up his intercom set and clicked it on.

"Bridge, this is the Captain."

"Bridge here, sir."

"Bridge, is there a problem with *Colossus*?" Crowe asked.

There was a pause before the Bridge responded.

"Jeez Skipper, how did you know?"

Crowe stood in the middle of the Bridge, his arms crossed and his face set hard as he watched the display. Most of the ship's senior officers were also there, to see for themselves the latest problem. The destroyer *Mantis* had closed up on *Colossus*, holding a position less than two hundred metres clear of the battleship's hull. The images were being taken by the destroyer's cameras, then transmitted to *Deimos*. They focused inside a massive rip in the battleship's hull, caused by one of the half dozen or so big missiles *Colossus* had stopped the hard way.

"Thank you Carol, we're getting the pictures now," Crowe said looking down at a smaller screen. "Have you managed to contact Colossus?"

"To a certain extent, sir," Commander Berg replied cross the radio link up. "Their radio and laser coms seem to have gone down again. We had someone try to talk to us with a signal lamp."

"Try?" he asked

"They weren't very good at Morse, sir. I'm reasonably sure that they know their fuel tank has ruptured."

"Does anyone have any idea on how much fuel they had or lost?"

"No, sir," Commander Hockley replied. "We did ask *Colossus* yesterday but we were basically told to mind our own business. 'Fuel levels are the concern of the flagship' was the precise answer." Disgust was obvious in the Commander's voice.

"From where I was standing, it looked like a lot of fuel sir," Berg said.

"Captain," said Benson.

"Yes Bosun?"

"Sir, if you look at this," Benson's finger ran across the screen, "the fuel tank must have taken a glancing hit. You can see the scoring here and here, it gave under the pressure."

"Which means it was full," Crowe said flatly.

"Or nearly full sir," Benson agreed.

"And those idiots over there didn't think to check the tank's integrity, even after taking a hit so close to it?" Hockley exclaimed. "How the hell could they miss something like that?"

"There aren't enough of them left, Commander," Crowe replied quietly. "Most of Lukeman's officers were on Baden station and so were a lot of the crew. I think he only got about one third of his people out. I honestly hate to think what the inside of that ship is like."

"What do you want to do now, sir?" Hockley asked after a few moments.

"Unfortunately we don't have any real choice. We have to continue to our intended cool down point and hope Colossus has enough fuel to make it."

"That's more than three hours, sir," Hockley objected.

"I know Commander," Crowe said.

"Sir, the next fold is twenty minutes away. We could drop out into interstellar space and try to affect repairs."

Crowe considered the option before replying.

The pre-contact theories had come up with the idea of folded space, a single fold joining two points in the universe. The reality was somewhat more complicated. Instead of a single fold there were many folds, more like corrugated space, with the jump conduit tunnelling through the middle of the corrugation. Jump drives didn't bring the two points together, but it did bring them a lot closer. The compression of reality meant that the distance between two points actually travelled by a ship in the conduit, was far shorter than the distance travelled between the same two points by a ship in real-space. However each time the ship passed from one fold to another, it had an opportunity to break back into real-space early.

As a general rule however, it was more of a theoretical option than a practical choice. Early real-space re-entry would usually put a ship somewhere in interstellar space, which brought dangers of its own.

All navigation boiled down to knowing your position, relative to the local spatial bodies. In interstellar space the nearest points of reference would be light years away, making the exact location of a ship impossible to determine. If a ship in interstellar space suffered a jump drive failure, then even in peacetime, when a beacon could be activated, the chances of anyone finding the ship again would be insanely remote.

"No, we won't do that Commander," Crowe eventually said. "With their communications down we can't tell them what we're doing and if they miss the jump out… " He shook his head. "Well, that would be bad. No we continue as planned."

"And hope we're lucky?" Hockley suggested.

"Well that would be a break from form," Crowe replied shaking his head. "Who's watch is it?"

"Mine sir," Lieutenant Colwell replied.

"Lieutenant, keep an eye on *Colossus*. Conform to her speed but if it starts dropping drastically wake me."

"You're going below, sir?" Hockley asked.

"The other shoe has dropped Commander," Crowe replied as he walked towards the back of the Bridge. "Nothing we can do for the moment but wait and see how things pan out. I had a feeling we were going to have more trouble before we reached home."

"Looks like the Skipper's radar is still on line," Colwell muttered as the hatch clanged shut behind Crowe.

The solar system had first been charted in twenty forty-eight, by the Japanese exploration ship *Yubari*. They had found little of interest, not even enough to justify naming the system. For nearly twenty years it had been nothing more than a dot on star charts. Now humanity had once again returned.

Colossus had made it, but only by the most slender of margins. Shortly after achieving orbit the battleship's engines were shut down completely. She now hung over an unnamed Mars-like planet, broken and silent. Well, nearly silent. Shortly after returning to real-space, Lukeman had ordered Crowe aboard, along with the captains of *Scorpion, Mantis* and the repair ship *Samaritan*. It seemed that their senior officer felt that a conference was in order, and on that point Crowe agreed. He was now back in his cabin, changing into a clean uniform for the meeting. Under the circumstances it probably wasn't necessary, but Crowe also wanted to have a word with Hockley, out of earshot from anyone else.

"Have you ever served with Captain Lukeman, Commander?" he asked, as he pulled on a clean shirt. Crowe's eyes didn't leave the holo, with the mauled battleship in the middle of the image.

"Yes, sir," Hockley replied. "On board the *Nile*. He was the gunnery officer during my first ensign cruise." The Commander was sitting on the only chair in the cabin, the only way both of them could both fit in.

"Know him well?"

"No, sir," Hockley said shaking his head. "We were only on the *Nile* together for a few weeks, then he was promoted off the ship. Do you know him?"

"We were in the same intake year and went through the Academy together. I don't think I spoke to him more than a dozen times though. I do know that tactically he was very good, top three in my year. He's not married, extremely career-orientated, definitely aiming for flag rank." Crowe added to himself, "I was always happy to top out at captain."

"I see, sir." Hockley respond in a noncommittal tone.

Crowe turned towards Hockley as he pulled on his jacket.

"I'm worried Commander. I'm worried about Lukeman's plans."

"Sir?"

Crowe waved towards the holo.

"If that ship simply ground to a halt through system failure, that would at least make the situation simple. We'd take the crew off, scuttle her and carry on. Instead that bloody fuel tank ruptured and that makes things less simple."

"You think he'll..."

"Take fuel from other ships, yes," Crowe finished.

"There isn't any real slack in our fuel reserves, sir. The numbers I got yesterday said no one else is running with more than half tanks. *Samaritan* in particular is going to be flying on fumes and memories by the time we reach Earth."

"Yet she is the biggest ship after *Colossus*. She doesn't have any *spare* fuel, but she does have the most fuel."

"I don't think he'll do that, sir. We could drain and abandon the two transports."

"Their fuel would be like a daisy in a bull's mouth, even if *Colossus's* engines are running at normal efficiency, which I guarantee they aren't. Plus to give himself any kind of meaningful reserve he'd have to take our fuel."

"Sir, I think you're being... erm... a bit..." Hockley visibly searched for the right words.

"Paranoid?" Crowe suggested calmly. "Possibly Commander, possibly. But I would make a couple of points to you. I've had personal experience of bringing back a smashed up ship. In that personal experience, Headquarters doesn't look kindly upon skippers in such situations. So failing to bring ships back at all is not a career-advancing move. Secondly that battleship is a wreck. Assuming she's even repairable at all, she won't be fit for service again in less than a year."

"I accept those points, sir, but this is speculation."

"Yes it is. I may be slandering Captain Lukeman, but I can't shake the feeling, that he is about to make a bad decision."

Hockley's face was expressionless, but behind his eyes Crowe could see wheels turning.

"Sir, am I correct in thinking that you are suggesting that any order to abandon *Deimos* be disobeyed?"

"Nearly Commander. Can you open the top draw in my desk and take out the envelope on top." Crowe waited for the Commander to remove the envelope. "Those are written orders to get this ship back to Earth. Any other considerations are secondary. Any orders by any other officer to the contrary are to be ignored. This is by my authority."

Hockley looked shocked

"Sir if this result in a..."

"Court martial? Yes, that's why I'm giving orders on paper." Crowe waved towards the envelope. "If I'm wrong about this, that can be destroyed."

Hockley made no reply, but simply sat there staring at the envelope. The Commander could choose to arrest him. To give an instruction to disobey lawful orders was mutiny, there was no other word for it. Certainly he wasn't going to try to hide from that fact, not inside the privacy of his own skull.

"Sir," Hockley said quietly, his eyes still lowered, "if you believe this, why are we not leaving now?"

Crowe sat down on his bunk, studied the holo again for a long moment before replying.

"Because when you get right down to it, James," he paused, realising that after four months of serving together it was the first time he had addressed his second-in-command by his first name, "I have a duty to protect the men and women on those ships. But at the same time *Deimos* fought her way into Baden, and fought her way back out. There's a new kind of war being fought out there and this ship is better at fighting it than any other we have. That means we owe a greater responsibility, to preserve this ship for the next battle."

"What about you, sir?"

"I'm not important James, the ship comes first."

There was a tap at the hatch.

"Yes?" Crowe called out.

"Skipper, the shuttle is ready."

"All right."

Behind him there was a faint rustle of paper, he turned and saw Hockley tucking the envelope into his jacket pocket.

"Good luck over there, sir," he said, "Try not to get arrested; the crew need their good luck charm."

―――――――――――

"Welcome on board, sir." The petty officer saluted sharply, as Crowe pulled himself through the entry hatch. By the book, there should have been a side party to greet him. Instead there was one man in a uniform that looked like it had been slept in. Its wearer however, looked like sleep was but a distant memory. There were dark circles under his eyes and a grubby bandage was wrapped around the knuckles of his left hand.

The PO closed the hatch behind Crowe, followed by the sound of pumps removing the air from inside the lock.

"I'm afraid I have to ask you to wait sir, until the Captains of *Mantis*, *Scorpion* and *Samaritan* have come aboard," the petty officer told him. "Then I will take you all to the Captain. On behalf of Captain Lukeman, I apologise for this."

"That's all right PO, I've served on this class. I can find my own way," Crowe replied. The ship was obviously so short-handed they couldn't even spare a couple of crewmembers to escort the arrivals. The one man they assigned to the job looked like he would have been swaying on his feet if they had been in gravity.

"I'd advise you wait sir. A lot of access ways are blocked off or open to space."

There was a further series of clunks from outside as another shuttle connected to the outside of the lock. The pumps went into action again and after a minute the light above the lock switched to green, the hatch opened and Berg pulled herself through. Crowe waited as Berg accepted the Petty Officer's salute before pushing himself forward.

"Carol," he greeted her with a smile. "Good you see you in the flesh again." He embraced her for a moment.

"Oof. What was that for?" Berg looked somewhat surprised at the friendliness of the greeting.

"For shooting those missiles off our ass," Crowe replied. "Thanks for that."

"You're welcome, sir. We won't cut it so fine next time."

Crowe gave a half laugh and turned as the airlock's pumps started to sound yet again. After a minute Captain Agostini of *Samaritan* came through. Last to arrive was Commander Baird of the *Scorpion*.

"Thank you for your patience," said the Petty Officer. "I'll now take you to the Captain."

The journey through *Colossus* was a sobering experience. In their clean uniforms, the three visitors looked completely out of place among the battleship's ragged crew. Everywhere Crowe looked, he could see tired and defeated men and women, working to keep what was left of their ship going. It was hideously battered, with power cables and communication runs dangling from their mounts, steel bulkheads crumpled like tinfoil and burnt-out circuit boards scattered everywhere. Worst of all, time after time they passed sealed hatches with red lights glowing above them, indicating that the sections beyond were now open to space.

"Thank you for coming, all of you, thank you," Lukeman said as they entered *Colossus's* wardroom. If he'd felt out of place before it was nothing to what Crowe felt now. Lukeman was wearing a scorched Captain's jacket over an engineer's uniform that was slightly too large for him. His left hand was visibly trembling before he moved it out of sight behind his back. He knew that Lukeman was somewhere in his forties, but right then he looked at least twenty years older.

"I apologise for my app… appearance. I'm afraid officers' row took a direct hit, so I've had to make do with whatever was to hand. Please take a seat, all of you. Time is pres… pressing and we have much to decide."

Crowe chose a seat opposite Lukeman. Out of the corner of his eye he noticed Berg studying him carefully. He waited for Lukeman to start telling them how important it was to make sacrifices to save his battleship.

"As you all know, *Colossus* suffered a major fuel leak during our last jump, which forces us to make some difficult decisions," Lukeman began.

"How much fuel does *Colossus* have?" Crowe's voice was flat and without any emotion, but his eyes didn't leave Lukeman's face.

"I will come to that," Lukeman replied with a frown. "It's important for us all to understand the overall situation and the options that are open to us at… at this time."

Crowe rested his chin on hands, but otherwise remained silent.

"As you all know, *Colossus* suffered very serious damage at Baden. That damage has now been compounded by the rupture of our number two fuel tank." Lukeman look embarrassed. "I must admit that errors were made aboard this ship. My engineers didn't balance our fuel across the undamaged tanks, so almost all we had was in the tank that burst. In answer to your question Captain Crowe, we now have only three percent of capacity."

"That's not enough to reach Earth," Captain Agostini said.

"Not even close," Lukeman agreed. "We need fuel and worse, we need a lot of it."

"Do you have a proposal?" Crowe asked.

"My first instinct was to drain the tanks of the other ships. Unfortunately this falls far short of operational realities."

Crowe sat back in his seat, Berg continued to watch him carefully.

"You don't intend to take fuel from other ships, sir," he said.

"No," Lukeman replied with a shake of his head. "Or at least not from our ships. The two merchant ships could be drained and scuttled without any great rep... repercussions, but that would not provide nearly enough and they are the only expendable ships."

"We could abandon *Colossus*," Crowe said in a neutral voice.

"Yes, but we're not going to. This ship took four years to build, meaning she could not be replaced in less than another four," Lukeman replied, his voice growing in strength.

"*Colossus* may already be beyond practical repair," Crowe commented. "I've see what those big missiles can do to a ship structure."

"My engineers do not believe that our core structural strength has been compromised," Lukeman replied, his voice betraying his growing annoyance.

"Are they qualified or experienced enough make that determination?"

"That doesn't matter!" Lukeman shouted. "We are not aban... abandoning this ship!"

"We may not have a choice," Crowe snapped back. "In the past few days we have lost so many ships that we can not afford to sacrifice more. Any ship that can be saved must be!"

"Sir, could we not leave her here, for later recovery?" Commander Baird asked.

"No!" Crowe and Lukeman replied sharply as one, before looking at each other. Crowe sat back, surrendering the floor.

"That isn't a possibility Commander. On that point it would appear that Captain Crowe and I are agreed. If the Nameless came across her, the amount of military intelligence they'd gain would be catastrophic. Abandoning the ship would mean scuttling her."

"What about leaving a small crew aboard?"

"It would have to be a couple of dozen just to keep life support going. If the Nameless came across them, they would be left with a choice between self-immolation and falling into the hands of an alien race."

"Or slow death, if the fleet couldn't send a recovery force," Berg added.

"Then what do you intend?" Crowe asked.

"I believe there is only one course of action open to us," Lukeman said. "We need to send a ship to fetch fuel and return here. *Deimos* is the only one of our ships that is both big enough to carry enough fuel, and armed."

"What!" Crowe's chair hit the deck. "You want to send my ship, out its own! Where in hell's name are you planning on sending my ship?"

"Captain you are out of line!" Lukeman protested.

"Am I! Am I? Well tell me, where am I supposed to be going?"

"Junction Station."

Crowe turned away from the table and walked back and forth across the wardroom, his fists clenching and unclenching.

"The reason, the whole bloody point, of us going so far off the commercial track, was to avoid contact with the Nameless. Now you want to send my ship, on its own, with depleted ammunition, *directly* onto the main route between Baden and Earth," he said through gritted teeth.

"Captain Crowe, the Nameless cannot possibly have reached Junction…"

"Says who?" Crowe cut him off. "Would that be the same people who said it was impossible to make real-space re-entry inside a mass shadow? Or the same people who said Baden was totally safe? Or the ones who said the Nameless are no threat," he finished bitterly.

"Captain, I still have authority here. Sending *Deimos* is a risk yes, but an acceptable one."

"Acceptable to who? The ones who are going, or the ones who are staying here?" Crowe snarled.

"Captain I do not have to stand for this! I am sen...senior officer present and this is my order!"

"It's an idiotic order!" Crowe snarled back. "My ship is one of only six..."

"Five, sir," Berg cut in. "*Oberon* didn't make it. Sir, for the record, I agree with Captain Lukeman. We must at least attempt to salvage *Colossus*."

Crowe looked at her with an expression of betrayal.

"Your ship's big advantage is that it has flak guns," she didn't look happy to be siding against him but continued. "*Deimos* is a brittle ship though, the first solid hit will at least disable you. If we can retrofit ships like *Colossus* with flak guns..."

"We'll become more than a target," Lukeman finished.

"I'm sorry Skipper, but we have to think long term, not just what we're facing right now. This ship is useless in the short term, but perhaps important in the future."

Crowe's face went expressionless. If Berg was siding against him he wasn't going to win this one.

"Captain Lukeman, are there any other alternatives to Junction?" Agostini asked. "I would share Captain Crowe's reservations about this mission. Heading for Junction would be a serious case of asking for it."

"There aren't any alternatives to Jun... Junction, closer than Earth," Lukeman replied.

"What about taking spare fuel from the rest of our ships," said Commander Baird, "it wouldn't get *Colossus* all the way but it would get us closer to Earth."

"It would also mean that none of the ships would have any fuel reserve," replied Crowe as he righted his chair and sat down heavily. "We'd have no safety net. Any contact with the enemy would be fatal, we wouldn't have the fuel to run or fight."

"In that case, sir, I have to agree with Captain Lukeman," Baird said carefully to Crowe.

"I'm not a combat officer," Agostini said quietly. "It seems like a very dangerous course to me," he shrugged. "I don't… don't have experience of this."

"Which is why we need the fuel from Junction," Lukeman said. "I know there are risks, Cap… Captain Crowe, but we are getting this ship back to Earth. While you are away *Samaritan* will carry out repairs to *Colossus*. I am wi… willing to over look your insubordination Captain Crowe, we've all had a tough time, but that is an order."

"*Deimos* will have to retreat, if they contact the enemy," Berg added.

"Yes," Lukeman replied reluctantly. "If you sight the Nameless, you have permission to retreat."

"Alright, *Deimos* will go. But this is a mistake Matthew," Crowe replied, his anger still obvious. He hadn't even glanced at Berg when she spoke. "I will tell you this. If I pick up even a trace of the Nameless on passives, I will be out of there in a flash. I will not piss away a working warship to save this collection of spare parts."

Crowe didn't pause to acknowledge Hockley and the side party's salute at the airlock and instead brusquely motioned for the Commander to follow. Once out of sight and sound of anyone else, he turned on Hockley.

"Lukeman never had any intention of taking fuel from us," he said.

"That's good n…" Hockley started to reply.

"No it isn't !" Crowe cut him off sharply. " He's made a worse decision Instead. We're going to Junction."

"The squadron?"

"No. Just us."

"Oh," Hockley said. Then after a pause added: "what are your intentions, sir?"

"To go to Junction and get fuel, if we can," Crowe replied tersely. "Refusing to abandon your ship is one thing Commander, but refusing to take that ship into action…" Crowe shook his head. "That we can't do."

"But, sir, we still haven't fixed the electrical problem. We can't take a hit in our current condition."

"One more reason to bug out at the first sign of trouble," Crowe replied flatly.

"Sir, what about the population of Junction?" Hockley asked.

Crowe put his hand over his face.

"*Bugger*! I hadn't even thought of that," he muttered. "We'll have to see what the situation is. One thing's for sure, we can't take them all off."

The jolt ran through *Deimos* as they emerged back into real-space, right at the edge of the Planet Phyose's mass shadow. Crowe watched the main holo intently as the first radar returns came in but nothing unexpected appeared. Even so he felt extremely exposed. If there were hostile forces in the area, the spike of radiation released by the jump portal would have announced their arrival. Their engines immediately went to one hundred percent normal. Even so it would still be eleven very long hours before they reached Junction.

Humanity's expansion into space following the end of the Contact War had mostly been organised by the various national governments. But part of human nature is a tendency for some to want to strike out on their own and be beholden to none. Most of these independent groups had been religious, either seeking to get closer to God or further away from the unbelievers. The rest were a collection of rebels, idealists and misfits. Each one with their own scheme and intended destination. Most never got off the ground, both metaphorically and literally, and the rest came a cropper one way or another, with Battle Fleet usually obliged to bail out the survivors. But amidst this litany of failure, Junction was the one successful independent.

The Planet Phyose was a gas giant, roughly two-thirds the size of Saturn. It had two notable features: firstly a thick series of rings with a high concentration of water bearing asteroids; and secondly and far more importantly, an upper atmosphere composed largely of hydrogen isotopes, which used as fuel by fusion reactors. It was possible for specially fitted ships to skim the upper atmosphere to gather hydrogen, which with a minimum of purifying, was then ready for use. Initially, this wasn't of much more than scientific interest. The transport costs of moving the fuel back to Earth made it uneconomic. Then Landfall was discovered and as a result Phyose was very close to the most direct route from Earth.

Junction Station was the brainchild of a Canadian called Alex Gibbons. A highly successful corporate banker before he caught the space bug, he spotted the planet's potential as soon as the discovery of Landfall was announced. He'd sunk his entire fortune into pulling together both the equipment and people required to set up an outpost.

Other independent outposts had failed, because many attempted to live largely separate from the rest of humanity, while others could not attract a second wave of capital and people to sustain growth. Junction on the other hand, existed to serve the traffic between Earth and Landfall. Despite a huge profit margin on their fuel, Junction was still the cheapest place in Human space for commercial starships to fill their bunkers. Plus with so many ships coming and going, Junction had no problem getting the materials and people it needed. Now fifteen years after its foundation, Junction Station was the home to over three hundred people.

Crowe stayed on the Bridge for the first two hours after their jump in. When nothing happened he forced himself to go below for rest. He didn't expect to be able to sleep. His body had different ideas however and he went out like a light as soon as his head hit the pillow.

He'd ordered Hockley to wake him after a couple of hours, but the good Commander creatively misinterpreted this as 'let me sleep for at least seven hours.' He would have been annoyed about it, but for the fact he did feel a hell of a lot better for it and nothing had been detected. But that in itself was worrying. Junction was usually a hive of activity, but even this close, the passive sensors were still registering nothing. If the station had gone dark, shutting down everything short of basic life support, it was possible, even this close, that any emissions were below *Deimos's* detection threshold. But such a course of action and the discomfort that would come with it would be an impressive display of discipline for a civilian crew.

Deimos decelerated and started to thread her way in among the great drifting lumps of ice and rock that made up the planet's thirty kilometre thick rings. There was still no sign of any other human activity in the system. By now, the hairs on the back of Crowe's neck were standing on end. He wasn't the only one who found the sensor silence unnerving, with the other officers on the Bridge looking equally concerned. Finally, as they rounded the last asteroid, there was Junction Station. The Bridge went completely silent.

"Oh Christ," Hockley said quietly

"Bridge to all hands. Battle Stations, Battle Stations," Crowe said flatly without taking his eyes off the display.

Before, them lay the shattered ruins of Junction Station. The main ring of the centrifuge was dark and motionless. An entire section had been blown away, while great gashes had been torn in the storage and work areas, exposing the interior. Out beyond the station, one of Junction's harvesters lay smashed against an asteroid.

"Skipper, all sections report closed up and ready," Hockley reported.

"Understood. Helm can we come around?" Crowe asked.

"Negative, Skipper," the helmsman replied. "We haven't got enough room to make a turn here. We need to move forward at least twelve kilometres."

"You're planning to leave, sir?" Hockley asked.

"I think it's fair to say the Nameless have been here Commander, would you not agree? This zone is hot," Crowe replied.

"Been sir, past tense," Hockley said. "We've seen no sign of them, even if they are here, we're safe in here. We can complete our mission, a couple of the fuel tanks look to be okay."

Crowe's fingers drummed on the armrest of his chair.

"There may still be survivors in there, sir. Not all sections appear to be breached," Hockley added. "This can't have happen more than a day or two ago. Anyone that got into a survival suit may be still alive."

Crowe flicked on the intercom.

"Bridge to Fire Control."

"Fire Control here," came the gunnery officer's voice.

"Guns, how do you fancy our chances if we're engaged in here?" he asked.

"Respectfully, sir, if they take us on in here, we'll kick seven kinds of snot out of them," the gunner replied confidently. "Maximum engagement range in any direction is barely twenty clicks. The first alien that sticks its nose out into the open is gonna get it ripped off."

Crowe suppressed a sigh. It wasn't that long ago his officers barely spoke to him. Somehow that seemed better now than it had then.

"It'll be out in the open they'd want to take us on, when we're heading for the Red Line," Hockley added.

"And we have to do that to get out of here, no matter what we do. Damn that bloody fool Lukeman," Crowe said half to himself. "Damn it. Alright, Helm take us in, put us in the middle of this open area, and turn us around. Commander, I want two teams, one to sweep Junction, the other to check the contents of the undamaged tanks. Issue both teams with side arms."

The thrusters in the nose fired in a series of controlled bursts, slowing the shuttle's velocity to less than one metre per second. A slow roll brought the docking port into alignment with one of Junction's main airlocks. Gently, it settled into place.

"We have hard lock, seal is showing green Bosun," the shuttle
co-pilot reported.

"Do you know if there's pressure behind that lock?" Benson asked.

"No reading, nothing at all. Station mainframe must be down."

Benson nodded, before turning and pulling himself back into the passenger compartment. The other four members of his search party were suited up and ready.

"We have no readings beyond the lock folks, so visors down," he told them. "You can load your guns, but if anyone blows a hole in a survivor, I will not be happy and I will share that unhappiness. Are we clear?"

They all murmured affirmatives. He looked back into the shuttle cockpit.

"We're going to use a password. If anyone tries to get in without it, break contact and head back to the ship for instructions."

"Stand off from the lock until we call you back."

"Understood."

The passageway beyond the airlock was almost completely dark. Only the occasional glow tab provided any illumination at all. Benson tapped his external pressure gauge. He then looked down the passageway. Fifty metres away a pressure hatch hung half torn from its hinges and beyond it asteroids were visible through a rip in the hull. Everywhere shattered equipment hung from mounts or drifted free.

"Shuttle, we've got hard vacuum in here. We're carrying on. Over," he reported

"Roger that, shore party. Shuttle over and out."

He bounced back and forth, from wall to wall, making steady progress down the corridor, with the rest of the party strung out behind him.

They headed for the station command centre in the centrifuge. En route, they passed through the station accommodation block and there found their first body.

The section was unpressurised, in a state of deep cold. The body was that of a young woman, barely into her twenties. She was drifting in the middle of the passageway, barring their path. Her clothes were the bright colours favoured by the residents of Junction and now drifted around her. She had been quite an attractive girl, but her face was horribly twisted by pain and terror. There was no visible wound, nothing to indicate that she had died easily. Crystals of frozen blood floated in front of her like tears.

Benson brought himself to a halt in front of her. After a minute one of the others tapped him on the shoulder.

"Bos, you all right?"

"You know something," Benson replied quietly, "the last time I saw a body like this, it was a centaur. Now it's a girl. What the hell did they even come here for? This isn't a military base, just families that we didn't protect. Oh God… I wonder will they give the bastard who did this, a medal for his 'victory.'"

"We couldn't protect them. Bos, we have to move on."

"Yeah, nothing to see here," Benson replied bitterly, before gripping her gently round the waist and moving her to one side.

"I'm sorry," he mouthed to the corpse.

In turn each one of them pulled themselves round the body and carried on. Benson lingered for a moment, looking back at what had been a human, before turning his back on her.

Several times they were forced to backtrack when they found their route blocked by wreckage. Finally, they successfully worked their way to the command centre, but there were no answers there. The entire chamber had been gutted and every piece of equipment had been unbolted and removed. There was a gaping hole where a piece of the outer hull had been sliced away. In the distance Benson could see *Deimos*.

"This place must have been pay dirt for them," one of the men said. "A chance to get a look at our tech, without anyone shooting at them."

"Yeah, and a chance to look at us," someone else said. "Poor bastards, they're probably being dissec..."

"Shut your mouth. *Now!*" Benson snarled. "We're going to sweep this place, one deck at a time." His voice shook with emotion. "If there is even one person still alive here, we're going to find them. Find them and save them."

So, slowly, they made their way down, deck-by-deck, shining their torches down each passageway. Every so often they came across a floating corpse, like the first killed by depressurisation. But even at a rough count, hundreds of Junction's population were missing. Finally, they reached the lowest storage level of the station.

The chamber was large, mostly filled with mag-clamped storage containers. By this stage, Benson was tired. More than tired, he was heartsick. Despite the lack of air, the station had a stench, one of bad death and failure.

"Bosun." Benson looked towards the speaker. The rating tapped the air gauge of his suit. "Coming up on turn back."

It was something he should have been keeping an eye on.

"We'll finish this section," Benson replied as he pulled himself round another set of boxes. "How many did we find? Anyone keep a count?"

"Thirty-three."

"Thirty-five," someone else said.

"They were mostly in out-of-the-way places," a third voice offered.

"They were the ones that hid," Benson said, half to himself. "Then the Nameless blew holes in the station and out went the air."

He turned another corner and his torch lit up another four floating bodies. By this stage the ghostly forms had long since lost their power to shock. But, nonetheless, Benson's curiosity was stirred. It was the first group of bodies they had come across and he realised it was a family: Mum, Dad and two nearly grown children. He stopped, unable to go forward. He looked around to one of the others.

"Check them," he said in a tired voice.

The two adults were dead. There was still a tiny amount of air in their tanks, but the carbon dioxide scrubbers of their suits had been removed. They'd chosen their own way out. The bodies of the two teenagers were equally still. Sickened, Benson turned back towards the exit hatch, motioning one of the others to check them. He rested his head against a storage crate and closed his eyes. In one day he'd seen enough bodies to last a lifetime.

"Bosun! One of them is still alive!"

―――――――――――

The last survivor of Junction Station lay in *Deimos's* sickbay, breathing slowly.

"How is she even still alive?" Crowe asked from the foot of the cot.

The ship's surgeon fussed with the monitoring equipment hooked up to his patient before answering.

"She was drugged to the eyeballs, Captain," he replied without taking his eyes off his patient. "I don't know whether it was deliberate, but she was put into a very rough chemical hibernation, without the benefit of an escape pod's support systems."

"Is that even possible?" Crowe asked surprised.

"Not really, but what they did manage was to drop her respiration rate right down. That stretched out her air long enough for the Bosun to find her."

Crowe glanced towards Benson, who was also in sickbay, standing in one corner. He'd barely allowed the child out of his sight since they brought her aboard. The man looked haunted and barely blinked as he watched her. All of the boarding party had looked shaken when they came back on board, but the Bosun was clearly the worst affected. When he'd asked for a report, he'd simply shaken his head and said it was 'bad'. Crowe didn't press the matter. For the time being it could wait.

"What's her prognosis?" Crowe asked.

"Not so good. Chemical hibernation is a hell of an assault on the body, even at the best of times. This was a strictly amateur hour affair. Best I can do is to keep her stable until we can hand her over to specialists." The surgeon glanced towards the Bosun, and lowered his voice. "She might never recover consciousness and even if she does, she'll suffer major health problems, probably for the rest of her life."

"Alright, we'll leave you to it doctor." Crowe headed for the hatch and paused beside Benson. "You did well to find her, but now I need you in engineering."

"Yes sir," Benson whispered without taking his eyes off the patient.

Back on the Bridge, Crowe watched as Junction Station receded into the distance and finally disappeared behind an asteroid. He considered opening fire on it to destroy what the Nameless had left. There were good solid military reasons to do, but just as many to leave it. None of them mattered a jot. This was a place of the dead and needed to be respected.

As *Deimos* cleared the planet's rings and started to make her way towards the Red Line, the mood aboard ship was sombre. The boarding party had talked about what they had seen on Junction. Crowe knew that he would have to make a statement to his crew and try to channel what his people were feeling into anger, something that would sustain them the next time they went into action.

Crowe and Hockley were talking quietly at the rear of the Bridge.

"Well sir, at least we got the fuel," Hockley commented after a moment of silence.

"Yes." Crowe replied staring into the middle distance.

"What are you thinking, sir?"

"Nothing good Commander." Crowe shook his head. "They've overhauled us and passed us out. I just wonder how far ahead they've got."

"It can't be that far. We lost days moving off and on the commercial corridor. They're perhaps only a day or two ahead of us."

"Maybe. But we're going to lose another couple of days getting back to *Colossus*," Crowe replied. "Damn it James, they're making a drive for Earth and we're out of the loop. If we'd carried on, *Deimos* might have got back in time to join the Home Fleet. Instead we're still pratting around out here."

"No saying we would have got back in time, sir, and we have salvaged Colossus," Hockley objected mildly.

"I'm sure the breakers yard…"

"Captain!" The sensors operator's shout cut across the Bridge. "We're getting a download from the sensor drone we dropped! It's detected ships re-entering real-space. They've done it inside the mass shadow, sir. Bearing zero, two, one, dash, zero, three, three. They're moving to intercept us."

"Sensors, put the feed on the main holo!" Hockley called out, "What's the transmission time lag?"

"Six-and-a-half seconds, sir. "

"Battle stations." Crowe snapped as he threw himself into his chair.

"Skipper! Thermal spike, they're preparing to fire!"

"All sections report closed up for action," Hockley called out.

On the main display six contacts appeared, all arrayed in a line.

"Navigation, can we outrun them?" Crowe asked, his voice even.

"Negative that, sir. They have too much velocity on us. They're going to overhaul us, even on full burn."

"Sensors, do you have an estimation of strength?" Crowe continued in the same calm voice.

"I'm calling it four escorts, two cruisers and one cap ship, sir."

We're out of our weight class, we're outgunned and deep inside a mass shadow, Crowe thought. *Even if we could outrun them, they can use their Jump Drives to cut us off. We're trapped.*

Chapter Ten

On the Eve of Battle

30th July 2066

The sheet of armour slowly drifted across the silence of interplanetary space. For the briefest of moments, four quick flashes of light lit its surface. Then the darkness returned as the metal continued its destinationless journey

On the Bridge of the *Hood*, Commander Faith Willis vented her frustration, pounding the armrests of her command chair.

"God damn it! For Christ's sake, Chief! The safest place is in front of the damn target!" she snapped down the intercom as the latest salvo of plasma bolts whizzed harmlessly past their indifferent target.

"I know ma'am. I'm sorry. We'll try another set of adjustments," came back Guinness's unhappy voice.

"Captain, signal from *Hurricane*. They're asking how much longer we're going to be," the signal officer nervously called out.

Willis let out a hiss of irritation. All around her officers and ratings suddenly became incredibly focused on their duties as they attempted to avoid the attention of their fuming CO.

Two days previously the cruisers *Hood, Hurricane, Tempest, Whirlwind* and *Onslaught* had been officially put on fleet strength and designated Cruiser Squadron Eighteen. Their crews had immediately nicknamed their ships 'the Geriatrics.' However despite her age, *Hood's* first set of engine tests had gone surprisingly well. All the engines fired on the first attempt and nothing fell off. For a few heady hours, Willis actually started feeling good about her elderly command. Guinness had been almost swollen with pride as *Hood* broke Luna orbit and headed for the rendezvous with the rest of the Home Fleet. There were a lot of systems they still hadn't checked, but with the engines running so well Willis had been hopeful that everything else would just as easily fall into place. Which made the current live fire exercise an all the more frightening wake-up call.

The target was a six by six-metre section of metal plate, moving along a fixed trajectory at a velocity of twenty metres per second, currently at a range of twenty thousand kilometres. By space combat standards, it should have been like shooting fish in a barrel, but so far *Hood* had racked up a one hundred percent record of inaccuracy.

The guns themselves weren't the problem. Twelve years previously, much of the *Hood's* electronics package had been upgraded. Since even at that stage it was already inconceivable that she would see action again, that upgrade had unfortunately not been extended to her fire control computer. What Willis and Guinness had belatedly come to realise was that this meant their weapon controls had never been properly integrated with the ship's newer systems, such as her radar. Guinness was now frantically attempting to marry two systems that belonged to entirely separate electronic generations. All the while the rest of the Geriatrics waited impatiently for *Hood* to finish so they could take their turn.

"Chief, how long until our next salvo?" said Willis, fighting to keep her voice level.

"I need another twenty minutes Captain. There're a few things I can try. I'm going to try to disable some of our electronics advanced features, see..."

"Alright go for it Chief, I'm going to come down to give you a hand."

"That probably isn't..."

Willis cut him off again.

"I spent last night reading the manuals they sent up. I'd guess I've a better understanding of our computer than anyone, bar yourself."

There was pause on the other end of the line. Guinness was smart enough to realise that she was making a statement of intent, not a suggestion.

"Alright ma'am. Chief out."

"Helm, come about to starboard. Take us down the line and bring us in astern of *Onslaught*. Guns go fore and aft, open gun crews from stations," Willis ordered. Standing up she tried to rub the tension out of the back of her neck. "We'll have to hope the rest of them leave us enough of a target, to come round and try again. Commander... Commander, what's your name again?"

"Horan, Captain."

"Right. Sorry, Horan. You have the Bridge. I'll be down in Fire Control."

"Yes ma'am," her second-in-command replied.

As Willis left her bridge, she heard Horan mutter to the communications officer.

"They can't send us in, not if this bucket can't shoot straight!"

Closing the hatch behind her, Willis leaned against it and close her eyes. That was wishful thinking if ever she heard it. The reality that she had come to accept, but not shared with her fellow officers, was that *Hood* and the rest of the Geriatrics were cannon fodder. In the cold-blooded mathematics of war, the missile that blew the *Hood* away would be a missile that didn't hit something more important. They were all expendable, that was the unavoidable fact. Willis brushed the back of her hand angrily across her stinging eyes before starting towards Fire Control.

"What have you got for me Tim?" Lewis asked without raising his eyes from the work in front of him. For man of his age, the Admiral still had excellent peripheral vision and saw his staff captain hovering at the hatch.

"Sir, Cruiser Squadron Eighteen has completed its gunnery exercises."

"What's the damage?"

"To be honest, sir, that's the problem. There wasn't much," Sheehan replied, offering a pad. Lewis accepted and put it down.

"Give me the highlights."

"The skipper of the *Hood* reports they have all four guns and both missile launchers working, but she's admitting that they can't hit anything past fifteen thousand clicks. *Onslaught* also has all guns, but no launchers. *Tempest* has only *three* of her six guns working, plus three of her four launchers. *Whirlwind* has five guns and three launchers. *Hurricane* is the only one reporting all primary weapon systems working."

Lewis nodded slowly as he signed yet another document.

"Better than I expected," he eventually replied. "Order the four that have to be towed to dock with their tugs."

"You're still planning to take them, sir?" Sheehan asked, obviously unhappy.

"You still think I shouldn't?" Lewis replied.

"Sir, those ships are old. Their gun barrels are worn. They're using such early models of missiles that we can't fill their magazines and their machinery is clapped out. In any kind of sustained engagement, they'll start losing systems just to breakdowns."

"If they're lucky, Tim," Lewis replied quietly.

"Sir?"

"We... I have given them less than five days to get those relics going again." Lewis shook his head. "Five weeks would have been too little time. But I *need* those ships." Lewis looked across at his Staff Captain. "If I thought their engines would take it, I'd put them in the vanguard, to absorb the first incoming salvo."

"That's tough for the crews, sir." There was more than hint of reproach in Sheehan's voice.

"It's what we signed up for Tim, each and every one of us. We can dress it up any way we like but ultimately we gave the fleet the right to put us in harm's way." Lewis's voice hardened. "And I'm about to exercise that right. Has Headquarters found us a Rear Admiral for Squadron Eighteen yet?"

"No, sir." Sheehan shook his head." They're trying to find Rear Admiral Tan, sir. He's hiking with his partner in the Australian outback. Unfortunately he hasn't taken a phone or radio with him. The Australian government is assisting, but it's a big country."

"That's unfortunate. It looks like they're going to have to go in without a section commander. Do you have anything else?"

Sheehan offered another pad.

"The situation dirtside is getting worse, sir. People are poring out of the major cities. There have been protests outside Headquarters. Dublin, London, Washington, Moscow... they've all experienced riots and looting." He shook his head. "What the hell are they thinking? Do they think that there's anywhere they can hide if the Nameless do get into firing position?"

"Fear doesn't think Captain, it simply reacts. It's fight or flight and they can't fight," Lewis replied, staring into space. "When the system seems to be failing, people look to their own."

"Sir... was it... was it like this the last time?"

"Yes it was. People prefer to remember themselves shaking a defiant fist at the stars, rather than cowering in a refugee camp somewhere," Lewis replied quietly, before looking up sharply. "Put fighters into them."

Sheehan looked baffled by the non-sequencer.

"I'm sorry, sir, I don't..."

"Pick a squadron of fighters and put them into Squadron Eighteen's shuttle hangars. That's ten units, which means those old ships will achieve something before they're eliminated."

"Do you want fighters to replace all the shuttles in the fleet?"

"No," Lewis replied after a moment of thought. "With the red ships we can afford to risk it, but not with the amber and green fleets. Is there anything else Tim?"

"No, sir."

"Alright, see to it. And try to get some sleep yourself, if you can."

"Yes, sir." Sheehan saluted and left.

When the hatch closed behind the captain, Lewis picked up his pen again and paused over his paperwork. Then he put it down again and rose from his chair. Crossing his cabin he sat down on his bunk. Opening a drawer in his bedside cabinet, he carefully removed a framed photograph. It was a picture that had travelled with him for over thirty years, through every posting and command. But in all that time, it had never once been hung up. The photo had faded somewhat with age, giving it a slightly washed out appearance, but still clearly showed a group of young men and women dressed in old-fashioned British Royal Air Force uniforms. Automatically Lewis's eye went to one of the laughing faces, a face that was younger and far more innocent.

Lewis could still remember the day clearly. The squadron had just been certified operational on the Phoenix fighter, the first squadron of space fighters in the RAF. The CO had wanted a squadron photo to mark the occasion, another notable moment in the history of Number Seven Squadron of His Majesty's Royal Air Force. But the photo Lewis stared at wasn't that formal picture. Instead it was a picture taken by one of the squadron's aircraft fitters as the pilots headed for the photo shoot, pushing and shoving at one another like children let out of school early. Frozen in that moment of time they laughed, oblivious to what they would soon be heading into. Four months after the photograph was taken, only one of the twelve was still alive: Flying Officer Paul Lewis.

By the time of the First Battle of Earth, Lewis had served with Number Seven Squadron for three years. It had been a good place to serve in, at least during peacetime. But in wartime he had buried every one of them.

The Home Fleet was now holding position on the edge of the Earth's mass shadow, ready to jump for Alpha Centauri or race back to their home planet. Two battleships, seventeen cruisers, twenty-one destroyers and well over three thousand men and women. Even if things went as planned, many of them would soon be dead.

The price of service.

Lewis put the photograph away, lay back on his bunk and closed his eyes.

Forgive me Lord, for those I lead into your embrace.

Positioned at the rear of the Home Fleet, were four tugs, short, squat, ugly vessels, with heavy hulls and for their size, a massive engine. Under each one, almost like an afterthought, was a member of the Geriatrics. A small ship-to-ship shuttle homed in on the tug locked onto the *Hood*.

When the intercom buzzed, Willis was touring her ship, trying to become more familiar with her command and also give her people the opportunity to see her, and hopefully, know they could trust her. There was certainly no point staying on the Bridge. With the *Hood* locked beneath the tug, Willis was not in control. And that was grating on her nerves.

"Captain, this is officer of the watch. A staff officer has arrived from the flagship with orders," the duty officer reported. "Says he needs to speak with yourself and the Chief Engineer."

"Put him in my cabin and tell the Chief to come up," Willis replied.

"Yes ma'am."

"Ravens?" Willis asked

"Yes ma'am. You're to drop your shuttles and take aboard four Raven fighters," said the flag lieutenant. "They should be arriving at oh six hundred hours tomorrow."

Willis, Horan, Guinness and the flag lieutenant were all squeezed into Willis's tiny cabin. The daily visit by a staff officer had become necessary. With no flag officer assigned to the Geriatrics, there was no one responsible for channelling information about the squadron to the flagship. Neither was there someone there to make sure that the instructions coming from *Warspite* had been received and acted upon. So a junior staff officer had been sent out to Willis and the other skippers of Squadron Eighteen, to deliver orders and pick up reports.

"We only have one shuttle anyway, which I think they forgot about when *Hood* was mothballed. But we have no capacity or personnel to rearm and service fighters. Not to mention that the docking cradles we have are different from those the Raven uses," Willis objected.

"You'll need to alter the launch arms. Headquarters engineering department has included specs for the conversion," the flag lieutenant replied. "It's crude but will allow you to get them away."

Guinness looked up from the computer pad he was reading.

"Crude? That's one way of putting it. You're talking about more or less, welding a cage around the fighter. Christ, as if I don't have enough to do," Guinness muttered wearily.

"And arming?" Willis prompted. "How in hell's name are we supposed to arm them?"

"Erm… That's on the second page of your orders, ma'am. They'll be arriving armed," the Lieutenant replied, before adding helpfully, "you'll just have to launch as you go in."

Horan had been looking over Guinness's shoulder at the pad. Willis was flicking through the orders as one the three looked up sharply.

"Did you say launch as we go in?" Willis demanded.

"Yes ma'am…"

"And hope to God that we manage to launch before we get hit, with fuelled and armed fighters in our hangars… our unarmoured hangars," Commander Horan muttered.

"You should be able to launch them a minute or two before jump in," said the Lieutenant, now wilting under their combined glare.

"No we bloody well won't!" Guinness replied hotly. "The main armatures in our bays aren't strong enough to take the gravitational sheer inside a jump conduit. If we take fighters, we can only launch 'em in real-space. Whose brain fart was this anyway?"

"Chief," Willis said with a note of warning in her voice, before turning back to the staff officer. "Lieutenant, this plan is an unacceptable risk to my ship."

"Erm… Err… last paragraph Commander."

Willis turned to the last page and read.

I am aware that to jump into a live fire situation with fuelled and armed fighter craft embarked presents a significant risk to the launch vessel. However given our lack of a dedicated carrier and the otherwise limited combat potential of Cruiser Squadron Eighteen, that risk must be taken. Your squadron will be deployed at the rear of the fleet to minimise the risk, but I still expect Cruiser Squadron Eighteen to have fighters embarked before the end of the day. No alternatives will be accepted.

She read out loud, before looking at the uncomfortable Lieutenant. You didn't have to be very good at reading between lines to get the message. The C-in-C was willing to lose an obsolete cruiser or two to get a handful of fighters into action.

"Well, now we know how much the Admiral values us. Do you have anything else?" she asked coldly.

"No ma'am."

"Then you are dismissed."

The Flag Lieutenant gratefully left.

Guinness sighed and sat down heavily on Willis's bunk and rubbed his eyes tiredly.

"At this rate we won't need any bloody aliens to shoot at us," he muttered. "We'll have collapsed of exhaustion."

"Will you be able to do it?"

"It's nothing complicated, just welding really. Well, a lot of welding," Guinness shrugged.

"What about the fire control computer?"

Guinness shook his head.

"Sorry Skipper, I've done my best with it but fifteen thousand clicks is about our limit for accurate shooting. Beyond that it's pretty much fire and hope. There's just nothing more I can do, not without pulling the hardware apart. With your permission, I'll start on the docking cradles.

"No," Willis replied, looking up sharply. "You need a couple of hours in your bunk. Hand it over to your number two and hit the hay."

"I'm all right Skipper, I'm starting to get my second wind."

"That was an order David, not a suggestion." Willis turned to Horan. "Make sure he gets some sleep, at gun point if necessary."

"All right, all right ma'am, I know when rank is being pulled," Guinness muttered as he pulled himself to his feet. "You need sleep too, you know."

"Alright, go, and good night Chief."

When the others were gone, she stretched out on her bunk and closed her eyes. Undoubtedly there were many more men and women, here on the eve of battle, struggling to sleep, on what might be their last day. But after days of frantic activity, Commander Faith Willis wasn't one of them.

Chapter Eleven

Silent Running

"Bridge to Fire Control, Guns, how much flak ammunition do we have?" Crowe snapped out. Around him the crew were scrambling into their survival suits. Crowe took his time pulling his own suit on, so that he wouldn't miss anything. On the main holo, the uplink from their sensor drone was showing seven blue blips arrayed across their path.

"Bridge, we have thirty-four percent of capacity balanced across all magazines," the Gunner called back across the intercom.

"That's not enough to shoot our way out," Crowe muttered to himself.

"Skipper, our electrics haven't been fixed. If we take a hit they're probably going to fail again," Hockley warned.

"All right, Helm, reverse course to port. Engines hard burn," Crowe snapped out. "Head for the planetary rings, we'll have to try to lose them in there."

Deimos immediately slewed round.

"Contact separation! We have ten plus incoming!" called out a sensor operator. "Time to convergence, three minutes fifty."

"Guns, hold fire until incoming pass through the four thousand clicks mark, short controlled bursts," Crowe ordered.

"Roger that bridge," the intercom squawked back.

"Navigator, how long until we re-enter the rings?"

"On hard burn, forty minutes Captain," the officer shouted back. From the rear of bridge came the sound of air being drawn out as the Bridge started to decompress.

"Looks like we're in for a long three quarters of an hour, sir," said Hockley just before he snapped closed his suit visor.

Time crawled by with agonising slowness. Every few minutes another wave of missiles curved in, only to be blasted away or miss the weaving cruiser. It had taken ten minutes on full burn just to arrest their forward motion and now, thirty minutes after the arrival of the Nameless, they were breaking again to enter the rings. Instinct was screaming inside Crowe's head to keep running as fast as possible, but they had to come in slow and steady to make the orbital insertion safely. This made them more vulnerable than ever. As each wave of missiles curved in towards them Crowe's entire body tensed, preparing for the blow. Ahead of them the rings, and the safety they offered, seemed as far away as ever. Every few minutes he glanced across toward the Bridge's weapons status board. The ammunition for the flak guns was steadily draining away. Already the loader crews were frantically transferring rounds from the forward magazines to the aft.

The holo flashed red as a pair of missiles breached the five hundred kilometres perimeter. Crowe's knuckles went white as the pair charged in. The weapons board buzzed urgently, as two of the upper aft flak guns magazines abruptly ran dry. The two mounts continued to track the missiles, their feed systems clicking uselessly.

"Helm roll to Port! Roll to Port!" Crowe shouted. "Ventral guns engage!"

As the lower guns came to bear they blazed away at the missiles. At three hundred kilometres one was vaporised as it took a direct hit. The other was now so close in that the turrets were struggling to track it. Without waiting for the order the helmsman swung the ship port, dragging round the guns' aiming point. A single flak round went in and the missile detonated only thirty kilometres short of the hull. The shockwave rattled the ship and fragments of missile casing peppered the hull.

On the Bridge the lights dimmed for a moment and the tactical holo flickered. Crowe's stomach gave a lurch, inspired by pure fear. Then the lights brightened again and the holo stabilised.

"Half the electric primary ring main just lost power, Skipper," Hockley reported. "Lazarus systems are rerouting power from secondary life-support to tactical systems. Number Three engine is off line and venting coolant."

"Helm, compensate with the remaining engines," Crowe ordered.

"Confirmed, sir, ten minutes from the rings."

"Captain, the enemy contacts are accelerating, range to contacts decreasing."

On the holo the enemy ships started to edge forward. Also visible was a trail of engine coolant.

"I think we just put blood in the water, Captain!" Hockley called out between shouted instructions to his damage control parties. Crowe didn't have time to reply as another wave of missiles closed, twisting and turning trying to find a way into their currently defenceless upper rear arc. In turn *Deimos* kept rolling and weaving, doing everything possible to make the approach vector difficult. The bursts from the flak guns were getting shorter and shorter as the gunnery officer tried to conserve his ammunition.

Several more missiles burst close enough to rattle the hull. Each time the lights wavered and Hockley reported loss of power somewhere in the ship, but each time the electrics failed to make good their threat to collapse completely.

Another five desperate minutes inched past and two more guns briefly fell silent and then restarted. But now the rings were starting to offer protection. The mass of asteroids beyond *Deimos* was clearly starting to confuse many of the missiles terminal guidance radars. Crowe watched with relief as, increasingly, missiles ignored *Deimos* and instead passed them out to home in on an asteroid.

"Captain, what do you want me to do?" the helmsman called over her shoulder.

"Take us into the middle of the rings. Use as much cover as you can," Crowe ordered.

"Yes Skipper."

On the holo, behind the Nameless warships, another three blips appeared. To Crowe it looked to be in the same position as the first seven, which ruled out friendlies.

"Captain…"

"I see them. Tactical, what do you estimate?" Crowe asked.

"Our probe isn't getting an IFF return, sir. Getting data from the drone's passive sensors… Captain, additional contacts are hostiles. I make it two escorts and what looks like a support ship."

"Are you sure of that, tactical?" Crowe demanded.

"Of the escorts yes, not so sure on the support ship, sir."

"Important?" Hockley asked.

"Maybe," Crowe replied, without taking his eyes off the holo.

"Captain, we're now entering the rings."

"Understood helm, carry on as instructed. Tactical, shut down active sensors and weapons as soon as we enter the rings."

Crowe leaned back in his chair and let out a sigh of relief as *Deimos* slid into the protective embrace of the asteroids.

"Commander, I'm going to need a full damage and status report, then…" Crowe trailed off as he studied his bridge.

"Then, sir?" Hockley prompted.

"Then Commander, we're going to have to figure out, how the hell we're going to get out of here."

"I've got another burn-out here Bosun," called out an engineering rating.

Benson nodded and turned back to Hockley.

"Every time we took a jolt, we got a power surge. Result, I've got burnt out circuit boards all over the place, Commander," Benson reported. "The Lazarus systems have so far managed to keep up, but they're running out of ways to reroute signals."

"I just spoke to the Gunnery Officer," Hockley replied. "He told me that he's noticing a lag from the dorsal radar hook up."

"I'm not surprised, sir," Benson said with a sigh. "The signal from that radar array is currently being routed via an environmental control node on Deck Three. It's gonna take us a couple of hours to fix the burn-outs but that doesn't fix the core problem."

"I know, but shutting down the electrics right now isn't a runner," Hockley replied.

"Yeah I know, sir, but them's the facts," Benson said.

"Alright, let the Bridge know when you're done." Hockley turned to leave, when Benson spoke again.

"Sir, the survivor. Have you heard anything from the doctor?"

"Mind on the job Bos," Hockley replied. "I've heard nothing and I haven't asked either. Her best hope is for us to get her back to Earth."

"Yes, sir," Benson agreed in a sombre voice.

Crowe was standing in front of the main holo, his arms crossed. He had chosen to remain on the main bridge, rather than move to the combat centre outside the centrifuge. The combat centre was better protected, but if they took a direct hit from one of those big missiles, it wouldn't make any bloody difference.

"Sir, I have the reports from engineering. The Bosun needs at least two solid hours to effect temporary repairs," Hockley reported. "The hull has been pretty much riddled on the port side by missile fragments. Everywhere on that side aft of frame D is no longer capable of being pressurised. We also took three casualties, two fatal."

"Who?"

"Ratings Donaldson and Root. They were hit by fragments, sir."

"I can't think what either of those men looks like," Crowe admitted.

"That would be Alison Donaldson, sir."

"Damn it," Crowe turned back to the holo.

"What about the enemy, sir?"

"Look for yourself," Crowe shifted himself sideways. "We've shut down radar and minimised emissions, but we're revealing our position every time we fire the engines." He gestured at the holo. "We're picking them up on the passive sensors. We have two ships, the cruisers I think, holding position, ten K above us. The cap ship is another ten K below us, with two of the escorts."

"What about the other four escorts? Where have they got to?" Hockley asked.

"I don't know." Crowe shook his head. "These asteroids might be protecting us, but they're also muffling the passives. I don't know where either they or the support ship are. But if I had to guess, I'd say they're well out of harm's way, rearming from the support ship."

"Ten ships, just to hunt us, one straggler," Hockley asked, in dubious tone.

"Yeah, worrying."

"Sir?"

"Three possibilities. One, this is just a detached element of their fleet we've been unlucky enough to run into. Two, it's a group left behind to deal with any stragglers. Three, they I.D'd us, or at least our class, at Baden. They saw what we did and they're now specifically hunting any Luna class cruisers they come across, particularly as we're now on our own."

"I don't like that last one, sir," Hockley admitted.

"Hmm… They've already been sitting above and below us for fifty minutes. Don't look like they're in any kind of hurry. That's pretty much ruling out option one," Crowe replied. "Personally I think it's option two. They're here to eliminate stragglers and because of Captain bloody Lukeman, we've blundered into them."

"The only thing is, sir, as far as they know, we could sit in here for weeks," Hockley pointed out.

"Fair point, Commander," Crowe admitted. "I doubt they're willing to wait weeks. Once they've rearmed their escorts… then they'll be ready to make their move."

"They aren't going to want to fight in here, not with our flak guns."

"Yeah well, there's a problem there James." Crowe waved towards the weapons board. "The flak guns are about to leave the equation. We have about... six percent of capacity. I'm not sure whether or not to move it all to the aft magazines."

"They don't know that, sir."

"No, but they'd have to be stupid not to suspect it."

The two officers studied the holo.

"Captain."

Crowe turned toward to new speaker.

"Yes Colwell, do you have something?"

"An observation, sir," said the Lieutenant. "The groups above and below us are isolated from one another by the rings. We could exit the upper or lower surface of the rings and try to force our way past. As soon as we clear the rings they're in range of our plasma cannons. The other group would have to work their way round, or through the ring to support the one we were attacking."

"Except their jump drives don't have a problem with Mass Shadows. They could jump away from us," Hockley objected, "or the group on the other side, could do a short jump to reinforce them. We'd find ourselves fighting the lot."

"I don't think so, sir," Colwell replied. "Can I show you something?"

Crowe and Hockley followed him over to the tactical sensor console. Colwell typed in commands.

"This is the record of the enemy ships jumping in," Colwell said. "They all dropped in over six light seconds away from us."

"The last one of their ships that jumped in right on top of us didn't enjoy the experience," Hockley pointed out.

"Yes, sir. But that's not my point. If you look here, the second group arrives in at almost exactly the same distance out from the planet. I think sir that the Nameless have their own Red Line for their jump drives. If we break through one group, the second group would have to chase us in real-space, where we could outrun them." Colwell looked up with a pleased smile.

"I think you're reading too much into a few passive readings," Hockley said repressively. "Remember they dropped in within a few thousand kilometres of Baden."

"They dropped out six full light seconds away from us. None of our weapons can reach beyond half a light second. Why give us so much room, sir?" Colwell replied. "Plus Baden's mass shadow is pretty shallow. A planet has a much deeper and stronger mass shadow. They might not be able to drop as close to, say Earth, as they could to Baden."

"You're assuming they know the maximum range of our weapons. They could have been playing it cautious. With those damn missiles of theirs, they have no need to get in close anyway," Hockley replied.

"Then, sir, why did the support ship come in at the same distance? Why not further in or out?"

"It's an interesting theory, Lieutenant," Crowe said finally. "It matches the observed facts, but that's all it does at the moment. It's not something we would want rely on." He patted Colwell on the back, "Not yet anyway. Might be worth exploring though."

"You have a plan, sir?" Hockley asked.

"More a thought than a plan," Crowe replied as he turned back to the main holo. "The Lieutenant is right about one thing, they've got very close to us. If we could stick our noses out of cover, we should be able to nail at least one of them with the plasma cannons."

"If we see a redeployment by jump drive, that will disprove the Lieutenant's theory," Hockley added.

"Thank you, sir," Colwell said behind them

"But if we don't, it adds weight to it," Crowe replied. "Plus we'll get to take a look around and hopefully find out where those other escorts have got to."

"We'll have to wait for the Boson to finish the repairs to the engines, otherwise, sir, that coolant leak will pretty much advertise that we're coming," Hockley said.

Crowe nodded slowly.

"We'll make our move in two-and-a-half hours. Assuming the Nameless don't take the initiative."

The *Deimos* slid silently through the asteroids of the ring, her engines only occasionally firing. Once again the ship was closed up for action. With the lights dimmed, the almost silent bridge was dominated by the main holo. Crowe's attention was fixed on the two hazy dots, showing the approximate position of the Nameless ships they were closing on.

"Keep it gentle Helm," Crowe ordered, "let's not give them too much to spot us by."

"Yes, sir," the helmsman replied quietly.

"Helm, no need to whisper. I don't think those sensors of theirs can *hear* us," Crowe said, a grin appearing briefly on his face. There was a brief burst of quiet laughter.

"Alright Helm, roll ninety degrees to port. Bridge, Fire Control, prepare to engage to starboard."

"Roger that bridge," Crackled back the intercom. "Powering primary armament now."

"Sensors, any sign of those missing ships?"

"Negative Skipper. We're starting to lose the ships on the other side of the rings."

"Jumping out?"

"No, just so much material between us I can barely make them out."

"Understood."

Deimos continued to crawl slowly upwards, wending its way through the asteroids.

"Sensors, Bridge. We're now two thousand metres from the perimeter of the rings," Colwell reported from his side of the Bridge.

"Understood sensors," Crowe replied, "just watch those cruisers."

"Roger."

Deimos's turrets swivelled smoothly round to starboard, already tracking the enemy cruisers above them, beyond the asteroids. The covers of the four cannons slid aside, plasma pumped into the firing chambers and the barrels started to glow gently.

"Captain," called out the helmsman, "we clear the rings in thirty seconds."

"Thank you helm," Crowe replied. "Bridge, fire control."

"Fire control here."

"Guns, we're about to get clear," Crowe instructed, "once you have line of sight take..."

"*Captain*! The cruisers are firing! We have incoming!" Colwell shouted across the command frequency.

On the holo, several blips appeared out of the two icons for the enemy ships and lanced down towards them.

"Helm! Down! Take us down hard burn!" Crowe shouted.

But at such short range, there was no time to react in. *Deimos* was still moving forward when the four missiles arrived.

Miscalculation by the Nameless was the only thing that saved *Deimos* from immediate destruction. The four missiles plunged into the asteroid *Deimos* was passing beneath, the last one before she cleared the rings. The great mountain of ice and rock shuddered under the bombardment, then split sending multi-mega tonne boulders lumbering down towards *Deimos*.

The collision detection system let out a shrill buzz. The helmsman flipped the controls onto manual and twisted them violently.

"Helm, turn us away from them!" Crowe shouted, "Then find a way through!"

The helmsman, hunched over his console, didn't waste his breath replying.

A boulder, bigger than several battleships, tumbled slowly towards them. Even with the engines going full burn it was overtaking them, other lumps, big and small, closed down all escape routes. Then two fragments collided and ricocheted off one another, opening a tiny gap in the tumbling wall of rock. Crowe opened his mouth to shout the order, but the helmsman had already seen the opening. It was more than tight and the manoeuvring engine on the starboard wingtip brushed against the passing rock. The wing was a lightweight structure. Usually the first thing to get hit in action, they only existed to support the manoeuvring engines. As it was designed to, the connection point to the hull failed immediately. Bent and twisted, the wing tumbled away. But the danger was past. The shattered asteroid continued to smash its way deeper into the rings. A few fragments would eventually exit from the opposite face of the rings, knocked into a new orbit, but in the meantime *Deimos* disappeared back into the safety of the asteroids.

The officers' mess was silent, the only illumination an emergency lamp placed in the middle of the table. Leaving Lieutenant Colwell on the Bridge, Crowe had called the meeting, hoping that between them they might manage to hammer out a plan. Not that it was looking too hopeful at this point. *Deimos* was now at rest relative to the surrounding asteroids. The ship's surviving reactor was operating at the lowest power possible and nothing bar the passive sensors was switched on. Yet the five Nameless ships were all holding position above and below them, giving every impression they could afford to wait forever.

So far the meeting had lasted twenty minutes and produced precisely zero ideas. The thought that kept going round in Crowe's head was just how close they'd come. If the gunner up there in the Nameless ship had just held his fire for another few seconds, *Deimos* would have been out in the open with no hope of either dodging or stopping all of the missiles.

There was certainly no doubt about it. Even through the asteroids, the Nameless had been able to track them accurately enough for a weapons lock. The asteroids might be muffling the signal, which might explain why they were so close to the rings. Alternatively, it might be to reduce the flight time of the missiles. There just wasn't the information to make an estimate one way or the other. Meanwhile time was ticking away for *Colossus* and Crowe wanted to have a long, long discussion with Lukeman about reasonable risk, possibly using one of the missile fragments that had come to rest inside *Deimos* after penetrating the hull, to hammer home his point.

"So, does anyone have anything to offer beyond 'wait them out'?" Crowe asked, as much to break the silence than in any real hope of a solution.

"Just one thing, sir," Hockley said. "If we're here for the long haul, there is Junction Station. There are probably extra food supplies available there."

"Just how long are you planning on us staying in here?" Lieutenant Mohsin asked. "We already have, what, two months worth on board."

"It might be necessary. These guys don't seem to be in any hurry. If we've ended up behind the front line they might feel they have no choice but to bottle us up," Hockley replied with a shrug.

"Sir, I can't see how that..," the gunner started to reply.

"We're getting off topic," Crowe said cutting off the gunner. "Bosun, what did you see in the way of supplies on Junction?"

At the far end of the table, Benson stirred.

"I'm sorry, sir, I didn't hear you there."

"Supplies on Junction?" Crowe repeated.

"The cargo spaces seemed to be intact, sir," Benson replied. "We didn't look very carefully, so I couldn't say what's actually there, sir." He paused for a moment before adding: "with respect, sir, I don't want to go aboard that station again."

Everyone in the room knew what he was referring to but no one made any comment.

"Well I am not resigning myself to long term residence," Crowe stated firmly. As he stood up and his officers hastily got to their feet, he added: "We are going to make a break out, how I don't yet know, but it will happen. You're all dismissed."

Brave words. Crowe thought to himself in his darkened cabin as he stretched out on the bunk, staring up at the deckhead. But at the academy he'd read enough to know that in naval history, warships frequently got pinned in a port or waterway by a superior enemy, and when it happened the final outcome was rarely good for the blockaded ship. He also doubted they would have to worry about running out of food. *Deimos* was in terrible shape, with the damage from their various engagements now taking its toll. While individually minor, hits were now adding up and reducing the ship's effectiveness, and all the while their supply of spare parts was being steadily diminished. The problem with the damaged electrics in particular, had eaten through the spares at speed. Although that, at least, was now being dealt with, their forced stop had finally given the engineering crew time to do a proper repair to the power distribution box.

There was a polite tap at the cabin door.

"Come in."

The door swung inwards, and one of the ship's ratings peered cautiously into the unlit cabin.

"Sorry to disturb you Captain. The Commander ordered all the carbon dioxide scrubbers on this deck be checked," she said nervously, waving toward the block hanging from the deckhead. "With the life support shut down, he's concerned we might get foul spots."

"It's all right, carry on," Crowe replied in a friendly voice. He recognised the cause of her nervousness. In the normal cause of events, a rating would never have a reason to step into officer country. Hurriedly she waved the wand of the chemical analyser around, and checked the scrubber.

"All done, sir," she announced with relief.

"So I'm not going to turn up red in the face and dead then?" he asked with a slight smile.

She gave quick shake of her head.

"Alright, you're dismissed."

She started for the door then paused and looked back at him.

"Captain, are we going to get out of here?"

Crowe raised his head off the pillow and looked her in the eye.

"Yes we will."

The cabin was still dark when a rough hand shook him awake.

"Nrk?"

"Sorry to wake you, sir." Commander Hockley was leaning over him.

"It's all right," Crowe replied rubbing his eyes. "What is it?"

"Sir, it's the Nameless. They're making their move."

When Crowe reached the Bridge, he immediately studied the main holo. The familiar groups above and below the rings were still holding position, but now a new group of contacts had appeared below them, beyond the capital ship.

"Sensors?"

"Its four escorts, sir," Colwell replied. "Probably the missing four."

"But you're not sure?"

"No, sir, we haven't had a good enough look at their engine profiles to be certain this isn't a totally separate group of ships."

"It doesn't look like they're planning on joining the capital ship's group," Crowe replied after a few moments.

"Yes, sir. They are decelerating sir, but unless they go hard burn in the next few minutes they're going to overshoot. Also their formation is opening up." Colwell typed a command into his console. "This is their projected course, if they hold their heading."

On the display lines flowed out from the four approaching ships, terminating at the rings. If they held course, each of the Nameless ships would form the corner of a square, centred round *Deimos*.

"Looks like they've got bored and decided to come in after us," Hockley commented.

"Or they're sending in the beaters to flush us out," Crowe replied. "Sensors, how long until they reach the rings?"

"Twenty minutes, sir," Colwell replied.

"What's the status of the repairs to the electrics?"

"Complete, sir," said Hockley, "we've done circuit tests, it's all good to go."

"Good, that's good."

Now what? He thought to himself. The issue was about to be forced, but he couldn't see a path.

"We should be able to take them in here," Hockley said. "At this range, even with the scrag-ends of the ammo we'll tear them a new one."

"Problem is, I think they're willing to lose a ship or two to take us out," Crowe said shaking his head. "If they can, they're going to engage us from all angles, throw out more missiles than we can cope with."

"So we're going to…?"

"This is dangerous for them," Crowe replied, his voice distant, "they have to close on us in force. If we manage to jump one on its own, then as you say, we should be able to nail them. If they manage to engage us in force, or drive us out of the rings, then we'll be smothered with fire. Those damn sensors of theirs are going to make closing difficult, but I think we can match them in real-space."

"Assuming sir, they don't simply jump away if we get line of sight on them," Hockley pointed out.

"Well if that happens, we'll know there's nothing to Lieutenant Colwell's theory." Crowe turned and seated himself. "First however, we have to wait for them to enter the rings. Then we'll see how this pans out."

Crowe's hand bumped against his helmet visor. Without conscious thought he had tried to rub his eyes. Instead he rubbed at his neck, trying to push away some of the stress that was sending pain shooting down his back. Looking round his bridge, weariness was clear in the body language of every man and woman present.

For five hours *Deimos* and the Nameless ships, had jostled for position without any kind of result. The Nameless were being careful now, clearly mindful of the power *Deimos* could bring to bear as such short range. Twice, the human ship had nearly got close enough to take a shot but on both occasions the Nameless had climbed away, out of the top of the belt, where *Deimos* could not follow. Once they'd got too close to the surface, a barrage of missiles from the two cruisers outside the rings had sent them scrambling for cover. On the other side of the balance sheet, several times the Nameless succeeded in forming a ring around *Deimos*, but each time their prey had managed to slip or force a way out.

But Crowe was certain this game of cats and mouse couldn't last much longer. His people were getting tired and the ship's heat sink was slowly approaching saturation. Once that happened, they would have to keep the radiators open and then they wouldn't be able to hide any more.

Not that they hadn't learned a few things. On silent running, with radiators closed and everything bar manoeuvring thrusters shut down, they clearly dropped below the detection threshold of the Nameless sensors. When that happened the aliens stopped and in doing so, they in turn dropped below Deimos's threshold. Those were the times Crowe really sweated at the fear that they might round an asteroid and find themselves nose to nose with a Nameless ship. It was like sneaking around inside a large darkened room, where everyone was armed with rocket launchers.

"We've lost Alpha and Charlie again, sir;" Colwell called out, his voice sounding as weary as Crowe felt. "They're somewhere off to port, probably trying to ghost in. The other two are holding position high and low."

"I see them," Crowe rubbed his neck again. "I'm nearly ready to let them come. Let them take their best shot," he said quietly, before adding in a firm voice, "helm take us up two kilometres, engines ahead ten percent, and open all the radiators."

"Still no sign that they can jump this deep into a mass shadow. Sir, we could still make a break for the Red Line, if we can just get an opening," said Crowley.

On the other side of the Bridge Hockley spun on him.

"And how in *fuck's* name are we supposed to get an opening!" he shouted. Most of those on the Bridge weren't on the command frequency so they couldn't hear his outburst, but several heads turned towards the movement.

"*Commander*!" Crowe snapped.

Hockley stopped, his hands, clenching and unclenching.

"This is not the time to lose it James."

"Yes, sir, I'm sorry, sir," Hockley replied his voice now even more tired. "I'm sorry Lieutenant."

"We're all tired Commander. We've tried conventional means and it isn't working. We're going to have to get more... Helm turn us five degrees to port then shut down main engines, close all radiators, all section go to silent running." Crowe paused, "Where was I?"

"Something more creative," Hockley replied. "If we could only give them something else to..." He turned sharply. "What about one of the shuttles, on remote?"

"No. Sir," Colwell said flatly. "Any data uplink will give us away, plus the engine profile is totally different. To get the output to look like ours, even at low power, the shuttle engine would have to be going full burn, but that means the shuttle would simply rocket away."

"Captain, we've regained contact with Alpha and Charlie. They've fallen behind. It looks like they're breaching the rings. They're going underneath us to get ahead of us again," called out a sensor rating.

"Understood, sensors," Crowe replied. "We'll probably get a few minutes peace while they redeploy."

He chewed thoughtfully at his lip for a few moments, considering what his two bridge officers had said.

"Captain to Bosun."

"Bosun here Skipper," Benson replied.

"Bosun, it's being suggested up here that a shuttle could be used as a decoy. Any thoughts?" Crowe asked.

"Won't work Skipper, engine profile is much too small," Benson replied flatly.

"Lieutenant Colwell just said much the same thing. Can anything be done to alter the profile Bos, something to make it look like ours?"

"No, there is… is… erm…" The connection went silent. It hadn't been cut off though as Crowe could still hear the Bosun breathing.

"Bosun, have you got something?"

"Err… I might have. If we rig the engines so they're running both fore and aft together, that would keep the acceleration right down and still give us a big enough engine flare."

"Won't that mean that the shuttle doesn't move? Equal and opposing forces you know?" Crowe asked.

"No…" Benson replied slowly. "I should be able to get it so that the thrust pushing back is slightly weaker than thrust pushing forward."

"Right get on it Bo'. We'll work out the rest of the details up here."

Hockley and Colwell had both been listening to his conversation with the Bosun. Now they both turned towards him.

"Okay that's the engine profile question. Now we have to come up with a solution to the matter of control," he said to them both.

"Well we can't use a radio signal. It would be like putting up a big neon sign saying 'we're here,'" Colwell said.

"And no way can we keep the line of sight for a coms laser," Hockley added.

"So that leaves autopilot," Crowe said.

"There's a problem there too, sir," Colwell said. "I've checked the navigation database and the only bit of the rings that we have really accurate charts for are the parts around Junction Station."

Crowe turned towards the main holo. For five hours they'd been slowly moving away from Junction, zigzagging cross the rings. Two of the Nameless ships, were directly between them and Junction.

"Could we use the data from our own readings?"

"Not accurate enough, sir," Colwell replied with a shake of his head. "Not if we're really counting on it. The shuttle would probably run into the first asteroid, especially if we've monkeyed around with the engines."

"Okay, so we've got to force our way back to Junction," Crowe said, his voice resigned. "Bugger!"

"Try to sneak past them, sir?" Hockley asked.

"No, this time we're going to drive our way through, with brute force and unreasoning violence."

"Are you sure about that, sir?"

Crowe beckon him closer.

"We're all getting tired Commander, we're going to make a mistake sooner rather than later. We can't afford to play the long game, not anymore. If we run at the highest speed possible in here, it will take maybe an hour to get close to Junction, that should also keep our four friends off our back as well."

"I don't like to be the one to throw cold water on this idea, but even if it works its not going to get us far enough away from them," Hockley said flatly. "If they get a visual on the shuttle, the jig is up. To keep them at a distance the shuttle will have to run fairly straight and it will cross through Junction's neighbourhood in short order. Once it gets to the other side we have no data at all to feed into the shuttle's autopilot."

"Damn, there's always a fly in the ointment," Crowe muttered to himself. "On the other hand, we might be able to get them to help us." He pointed at the holo. "Those two cruisers above us, they haven't been shy about taking a pop when we've got close to the surface."

"But why would we or the shuttle want to get close to the surface. Without wanting to sound theatrical, what's our motivation?"

Crowe didn't have an answer for that, but Colwell came to his rescue."

"If we programme the shuttle to head for the opposite side of the Junction area, there is a region, here, where there is an almost solid barrier. The shuttle would have to dive or climb to get round it," Colwell said, his finger pointing to the relevant areas of the navigation display. "It could look like we'd found our way blocked and were trying to quickly nip over it."

"Not give them time to analyse," Crowe said, half to himself. "Force them to take a quick shot or lose the opportunity. Yes, that sounds good."

"Question is, sir, high or low?" Colwell said

"No question, high. Those two cruisers have already fired a few times with those big capital ship missiles and they can't be carrying that many. If we have to make a break out it would be better if they're running low on ammunition."

"All right," Hockley cut in, "so we've programmed the shuttle to get close to the surface, we've provoked them into firing. A shuttle won't stand much in the way of even near misses. It's still not going to leave much in the way of debris though."

"Tell engineering to heave in all those burnt-out electrics the Bosun replaced, plus any other broken components into the shuttle. That should give a debris field." Crowe hesitated, sickened by the thought that had just crossed his mind, but it was too good an idea to ignore. "How many bodies do we have on board?"

"Err, eight, sir. What… sir, you're not thinking..." Hockley looked disgusted.

"Yes I am," Crowe looked up at his second command, "the living come first Commander. Bodies in the debris field will make it look more real. Set their survival suit beacons to transmit when the shuttle loses atmosphere."

"Yes, sir," Hockley replied still obviously unhappy.

"You oversee arrangements with the Bosun. We'll have to manage without you for a moment."

As Hockley closed the Bridge hatch behind him, Crowe turned back to the holo. The Navigator had highlighted the section of the ring around Junction that they had charts for. He took a deep breath to steady his own nerves.

"Helm, reverse course to starboard, then go to one third ahead together on engines. Bridge to Fire Control, activate all weapons, be ready to fire on my mark."

"Understood Bridge," Fire Control replied.

"Sensors, go active on radar." Crowe paused to examine the monitor screen in his chair armrest. Using a stylus he sketched a brief line on the screen and transmitted it to the helm. "Helmsman, follow this course through the rings."

Watching the display, Crowe allowed himself a brief smile. The two ships that had cleared the rings to get ahead of them, had been wrong footed by their sudden about face. They'd gone full burn to get ahead of *Deimos*, but were now carrying too much velocity. Both had turned and gone full burn within seconds of *Deimos's* course change, but it was going to take time for them decelerate to stop, then accelerate back towards them. If Crowe was any judge, they were off the board for at least twenty minutes. That just left the two they'd dubbed Bravo and Delta, which were now closing on *Deimos* from either side. They could go to silent running again and try to ghost past, but that would give Alpha and Charlie the time to catch up. No, straight through it was.

Deimos continued to slalom through the asteroids. On the holo, the emissions from Bravo and Delta faded and disappeared. Going on their last known position, Crowe had a pretty good idea where both were. They were both holding position behind separate asteroids, ones that *Deimos* would have to pass. The Nameless would have the advantage of knowing exact *Deimos's* position and they would already have firing solutions ready for the moment when they got a clear shot. *Deimos* would need a second or two to localise the enemy before she could fire, time that they definitely wouldn't get. It was too late to adjust course around. They had to force the Nameless back and not give them the space in which to fire.

"Guns, fire, just past the starboard side of the asteroid at bearing three, zero, nine," Crowe barked out.

"Bridge, I have no target! Repeat, no target!" the gunner shouted back.

"Its suppressive fire, shoot, god damn it!" Crowe shouted back.

"Got it, firing."

The ship's plasma cannons, flak guns and point defence batteries, all blazed into action, sketching a line of firepower from *Deimos* to the edge of the asteroid. Rock and ice shattered as plasma bolts and projectiles hammered in and the stream of fire curved round the asteroid as Deimos began to pass it. The enemy ship suddenly reappeared on the passive sensors, as its engines fired. Frantically, it went hard astern, to avoid the hail of fire now curving towards it. For the briefest of moments, there was a clear line between the two vessels. Holes were punched into the hull of the Nameless ship and in return, a volley missiles streaked back, one punching through *Deimos's* dorsal wing while the rest hammered into another asteroid as the human ship disappeared from view.

"Delta has just got active!" Colwell shouted out." They're climbing!"

Ahead the second Nameless ship didn't wait for *Deimos* to do the same thing and instead climbed until it cleared the top of the asteroid, then fired.

One big missile and four small blasted out of their silos and surged towards *Deimos*, which once again opened fire. With the likely direction of approach known, by the time the missiles cleared their launchers, the flak rounds that would stop them were already on their way. The large missile and two of the smaller ones were cut down short of their target. The other two went in. One knocked a matching hole in the ventral wing and the other struck the main hull, level with the centrifuge, just as the Bridge inside swung level.

In the near vacuum of the Bridge, there was no sound of the explosion, just sparks as steel splinters punched up through the deck. The main holo disintegrated into a spray of fragments and at the front of the Bridge, the Helmsman slumped soundlessly over his controls, the back of his head sheered neatly off. In his chair at the centre of the Bridge, Crowe sensed rather than saw fragments punch through the deck all round him. Then something jolted him hard and his left arm went numb. Looking down he saw a dagger-like splinter of steel embedded in the meat of his upper arm. Sealant around the edges of the tear bubbled for a moment, then hardened. *Where's the pain?* he thought to himself as he studied it with mild curiosity. Colwell was shouting on the command channel and the dead Helmsman was thrown out of his chair as a rating replaced him. There was a lot of noise and excitement, but for the moment for Crowe, it all seemed very distant and unimportant.

But while the Bridge was temporarily thrown into havoc, Fire Control was hitting back. The two turrets that housed the ship's plasma cannons had been traversing round when the missiles struck them. With no other targets available, they now took their revenge on the Nameless ship. With the range so short, there would have been no excuse for missing. All four bolts punched into, and through the alien. Now trailing fuel and atmosphere, the ship dived back behind the asteroid.

None of the three ships had suffered mortal wounds but all needed time to recover from the shock of contact. On the Bridge of *Deimos*, Crowe was recovering his wits as the shock and the endorphins wore off. The surgeon had been summoned, but to remove the splinter would mean leaving the Bridge and going to a pressurised chamber where he could remove his suit. With the suit's sealant also sealing the wound for the time being, after a shot of painkillers the surgeon was sent back below.

Crowe was standing on one side of his bridge, watching the remaining sensor displays over the shoulders of the sensor crew. He was to having stand with one arm held away from his body, so he didn't nudge the protruding splinter. The two ships they'd exchanged fire with, were now following Deimos but remaining at a respectful distance. The two that had dropped below the rings were overhauling them, but at their current rate of acceleration, it would still be another forty minutes before they would get ahead of *Deimos*, by which stage they would be back in the charted region of the rings around Junction.

However that still left the decoy.

"Bridge to Commander Hockley, how are we doing on the decoy?" Crowe asked.

"We've got it loaded with the… cargo. The Bosun is still working on the engines. We're starting to programme a route into the shuttle autopilot, but we're going to need a start point," Hockley replied.

"We're working on it Commander, but we took a hit up here. We're still sorting ourselves out."

There was a pause on the line.

"Do you need me up there, sir?"

"Negative on that Commander. I need you back there; you have thirty minutes to be ready."

"Roger that bridge."

The *Deimos* continued to make her way through the rings, above and below. Crowe had to force himself not to call the shuttle bay. He briefly examined his command chair, but quickly looked away. The left armrest had been sheered off and was now resting on the deck. If it hadn't taken the worst of the hit, it would probably have been his arm, rather than the armrest, lying on the deck.

Almost everything was ready now. The shuttle with its tricked out engines and cargo bay filled with rubbish, broken parts and broken bodies. Most of the programming for the autopilot was complete. Now they just needed somewhere to launch the shuttle from, somewhere that the following Nameless ships would go around, rather than through as they chased after the decoy. Time wasn't on their side. If they lingered the Nameless would probably close on them and definitely sense that something was up. They might already have realised that something was being planned. There was simply no way to know.

"Captain, I think I have something," called out Colwell.

"Show me," Crowe told him as he hurried over to the navigation centre.

"It's here," Colwell replied, pointing at the relevant part of the screen, "Junction's records called them 'The Lovers.'"

"I can see why," Crowe muttered to himself. The Lovers were a pair of mid-size asteroids, perhaps five kilometres long each. Wide and thin slabs of rock, some quirk of nature had brought the tops of the two together, in the most gentle of contact, forming an arch underneath them. If *Deimos* were to hide underneath that arch, no one would be able to get line of sight on them from port, starboard or above. That would still leave fore, aft and below wide open. Not perfect but time was running out, and they could reach The Lovers without having to make the kind of major course correction, which would give them away. As an added plus, the current starting point of the shuttle's programmed course was off to the port from The Lovers. A turn would have to be added to the instructions, to allow the shuttle to get to where it needed to go. That would give the following Nameless a chance to gain on the shuttle, by cutting inside that turn, which would keep them clear of The Lovers.

"Alright Navigation, give helm the course. Also send it down to the shuttle bay," Crowe ordered after a few moments of thought. "We're going to have to come to a halt under them, but we can't do a major breaking burn, that would give us away. So we need to start losing velocity now. We'll launch the shuttle as we do our final deceleration. Having the two sets of engines firing together should hide the hand off."

"Yes, sir," Colwell replied.

"This has to be done right the first time Lieutenant. If we overshoot, we can't fire the engines again without giving ourselves away. Close down all tactical and radar systems now."

"No radar, sir?" Colwell objected. "If we're going to be accura..."

"No radar Lieutenant," Crowe cut him off, "there's already a good chance they'll spot a change in the engine profile. If they see us switch off the radar at the same time they'd have to be idiots not to suspect something. You'll have to manage with visuals only."

"Yes, sir," Colwell replied, additional worry now on his face. "With your permission I need to speak to helm."

Crowe nodded and turned back to the sensor displays.

Deimos was now barely crawling along, all running lights were off and aside from the engines, now firing only occasionally to make small course corrections, the only sign of life was the shuttle that was being lifted up and out of its bay. Hockley and the Bosun had both returned to the Bridge.

"All ready?" Crowe asked Hockley quietly.

"Yes," Hockley replied. "We have it all set to accept the launch command from navigation. After that we can't affect it in anyway. We did make a couple of late additions, we've added a scuttling charge on a ten-hour timer."

"Good idea," Crowe agreed. "What else?"

"If their top ships don't take a shot at it as it goes up, it's set to shut down just as it leaves the area round Junction. If they're still following it at that stage it will hopefully look like we've gone to silent running."

"Your idea?"

"No, sir, the Bosun's," Hockley nodded to Benson. "Sorry, we were getting too pushed for time to run it past you."

"Don't worry about it." Crowe looked up from the sensor display. "What do you think the chances are?"

"Of the shuttle actually following the right course and not running into anything," Benson replied in a flat voice, "fifty, fifty. As for whether it will fool them, who knows?"

"The whole plan has too many unknowns to say," Hockley said. "We don't know how their sensors work and that adds a whole pile questions on its own."

"We're now ten minutes from launch point," Colwell announced.

"Thank you Lieutenant." He turned to Hockley and Benson. "Whether or not this works you both did well to a get such a complicated plan ready on the fly. Alright, to your posts gentlemen."

The Lovers loomed only ten kilometres ahead of *Deimos*. Its engines were all on standby, ready for the final thrust that would bring the cruiser to a halt. On the Bridge, Crowe was standing next to the helm station. With the main holo gone, the helmsman's display offered the best overall view, even if it did lack detail.

"Thirty seconds to burn and hand off."

"Putting shuttle engines into standby."

"Docking clamp released."

"All radiators closed down."

"Helm, shift our vector eighty metres to port."

Crowe allowed the stream of orders and reports flow over him, taking it in at a subconscious level.

"Captain, fifteen seconds, everything is ready," Colwell called out.

"Understood, Colwell. Countdown from ten. Helm and Navigation, break and launch on my mark," Crowe ordered, as he took a firm grip of one of the handhold in the deckhead.

"Ten," Colwell started the count.

"Nine... Eight... Seven... Six... Five... Four... Three... Two... One..."

"Mark," Crowe ordered bringing his hand down on the helmsman's shoulder.

Deimos shuddered. From the rear of the ship came a deep rumble as the engines went full reverse burn, which lasted less than two seconds before cutting off. Immediately the firing elements dimmed as all power was cut to the engines. The burn had been enough to slow their forward motion to only a few metres per second. A few quick bursts from the docking thrusters were enough to complete the job and bring them to a halt. With the halt complete even the cruiser's reactor went into shut down, leaving the ship dark and silent. But as *Deimos's* engines were winding down, the shuttle's were starting to fire. With its forward and rear facing engine nozzles both firing, it slid only slowly off the launch rail. As it passed out from under The Lovers, it turned to port and disappeared from view.

The Bridge was dark and silent, the only source of light coming the screen of the passive sensor displays. Most of the crew had to simply wait in the darkness, not knowing whether the

Nameless were still coming for them. Not that Crowe was much wiser. Only now had they belatedly discovered why the ill-fated residents of Junction had made a special note of The Lovers: its high heavy metal content. The petty officer responsible for passives flicked through the equipment's various settings, before looking up at Crowe and shaking his head. They'd lost contact with almost all of the alien ships.

The only ones still detectable were the cap ship and its escort, holding position below the rings. The all-important group, the ones inside the rings with *Deimos*, the ones that would kill them if they were found, were now lost to their sensors. The cap ship was now the only indication where those ships might be. Crowe watched the small collection of blips, barely daring to breathe. With so much material between them, the passive sensors could only provide a very rough position, certainly not enough to say whether the ships were stationary below them or moving slowly, tracking the shuttle.

"If they come up behind us, we aren't going to be able to restart fast enough," Hockley said quietly.

Crowe didn't reply. There wasn't much that could be said.

Was that movement on the screen? Had the cap ship moved? Crowe wasn't sure, but he wasn't the only one who thought he saw something, as the petty officer burst into another frenzy of activity.

Then another movement, more definite this time. They were following the shuttle!

There were no cheers, or shouts of joy. Everyone on the Bridge knew that fooling the more distant ships was no guarantee that the ship inside the rings had been equally deceived. There would be no way of knowing that they had been fooled and were chasing the shuttle, or, if it had been programmed correctly, that it would not lead them across the arcs of visibility left open by The Lovers.

Minutes passed with glacial slowness. Crowe stood motionless, watching as the cap ship's group disappeared from view. Not a word was spoken for nearly twenty minutes. Nothing appeared on any of their screens. Finally Crowe broke the silence.

"How long before the shuttle reaches the point where it has to climb?"

"Another... twenty-five minutes. It will reach the apex two minutes later."

"We'll slide out on thrusters just as it starts the climb. See what's there to see."

Twenty-five minutes later thrusters at the rear of the ship briefly fired. Advancing at less than fifty kilometres per hour, *Deimos* edged out from underneath the Lovers. Once again all the Bridge officers were clustered around the sensor consoles.

"Contact."

Only now were there sighs of relief. There on the passive display, the shuttle and all of the Nameless ships were visible, far away.

"Hope to God we haven't given ourselves away by moving," Hockley said quietly.

"Captain," Colwell said, "the Nameless ship Alpha has nearly caught up with the shuttle."

"How close?"

"Less than fifty clicks."

"They can't have eyeballed it yet," Hockley replied, "They wouldn't be still chasing it if they had; how long till it start to cli... There it goes."

The shuttle started to climb, far above the two enemy cruisers were in position.

"Come on you devils, fall for it."

Crowe didn't realise he had spoken out loud until Hockley half turned toward him.

"Contact separation! The cruisers are firing," shouted a sensor rating.

There was no time for any reaction or comment before the missiles hammered into the asteroids above and around the shuttle. The warhead discharge blotted out the shuttle for a moment, but when the screen cleared it was still gamely rising. Then another wave of missiles, large and small plunged down. This time the shuttle's signal didn't reappear.

"Sensors?" Crowe asked.

"I'm not sure, sir, but we might have seen a radiation spike. It could be the shuttles reactor rupturing; it definitely wasn't catastrophic failure though," the sensor's petty officer reported.

"Bridge, Communications."

"Bridge here, report," Crowe replied.

"Captain, we're picking up at least one survival suit beacon, possibly two."

"So the shuttle was destroyed, but not vaporised," Hockley said. "Looks like we've had the best case scenario so far."

The four Nameless ships inside the belt had been sent scrambling back when the two cruisers started firing. Now they were almost stationary with their engines powered down. They'd have been invisible to *Deimos's* sensors except for the FTL transmissions they were making.

"I guess they're waiting for the dust to settle, before they go in and see if they got us," Crowe said.

This time it was Hockley's turn to nod without replying.

It took time for the asteroids to settle themselves, for those knocked out of their orbits to either be brought to a relative halt by their neighbours, or smash their way clear of the area. Only then did the four start to nose their way forward in a wide picket line. It didn't take long for one of them to stop and start transmitting again. The other three started to converge. So intent was he on the four that had hunted them, he didn't register the second movement.

"Sir, the cruisers, they're closing on the rings."

Crowe whipped round towards the sensor console watching the cruisers. It was no mistake, their main engines were firing and they were heading straight for where the shuttle had been.

"Damn, they're going to do a serious search. They're going to realise that isn't enough debris." Hockley shook his head.

"No Commander, this is an opportunity," Crowe replied slowly but with growing excitement. "Their top cover is moving out of position, if it gets close or into the rings we can make a break for it without having to fight past them. Helm, take us up, thrusters only, make our heading for exit of rings but be subtle."

"Roger."

"This is our best chance James. We just need to be in the right position to take advantage. Bridge, Engineering."

"Engineering here," Benson replied across the intercom.

"Bosun, the shuttle might have bought us an opening. We may be making a break for the Red Line in the next fifteen or twenty. I need the reactor and engines ready for a crash start."

"Understood Bridge. Engineering's waiting for the word." There was a note of hope and optimism in the Bosun's voice that hadn't been there since Junction.

"Sensors, are the cruisers both still closing on the rings?"

"Confirmed Captain, their velocity is holding steady."

"Alright, as soon as we breach the rings we make a high power run for the nearest point of the Red Line."

"I'd advise against that, sir." Hockley cut him off mid flow. "In line with Lieutenant Colwell's theory about their Jump Drives, I suggest we go directly up. That keeps us in the Mass Shadow for longer, but the Rings will provide a barrier between the cap ship's group and us. They'll have to go around or through the rings and we'll be long gone before they do."

"Assuming the Lieutenant is right," Crowe pointed out.

"If he is it makes getting out that bit easier. If he's wrong then no route we can take is going to make any difference," Hockley replied.

"Good point James."

For the next ten minutes Crowe waited impatiently, well aware that if they acted prematurely they'd blow their big chance. Every time any one of the searching ships turned towards them, even for a moment, Crowe felt his blood freeze. The two cruisers started to break and at first Crowe was afraid they were going to stop, still clear of the rings, but they were slowing, not stopping.

Deimos was now holding position at a right angle to the plane of the rings. Her bow pointed up at a gap in the asteroids, through which the waiting stars were visible.

"They're going to enter the rings," Hockley observed. "Are we going to let them get comfortable before we start?"

"No. As soon as they drop below the line of the rings we make our move," Crowe replied before switching his intercom onto a different channel. "Bridge, Fire Control."

"Fire Control here."

"Guns, we're about to make our move. As soon as you're able I want suppressive fire on the enemy cruisers' positions."

"Understood. Be advised Captain, all remaining flak gun ammunition has been moved to the aft magazines."

"How much is that Guns?"

"Less that a hundred rounds per mount, Captain."

"Thank you Guns. Stand by."

With all possible orders now given, the only thing left for Crowe to do was walk over to his command chair and buckle himself in. It was uncomfortable without the left armrest, the absence of which reminded him of his own injury. The metal splinter was still there, but the adrenaline must have been pumping because he couldn't feel a thing.

"Captain. They're entering the rings."

"Engineering, crash start now. Tactical and sensors, power up. Helm, all ahead. Emergency power as soon as the engines come on line."

From astern came the familiar rumble of power as, slowly at first, *Deimos* started to move. Had there been an observer standing on the upper surface of the asteroids, they would have seen the cruiser breach the rings, like a missile blasting clear of its silo, slow at first, but gathering pace. The plasma cannon turrets swung towards the distant enemy and within seconds their first salvo flashed out.

On the Bridge Crowe was being pushed back into his chair, muscles in his head and neck complaining as he turned to watch the sensor displays. The six ships inside the rings had been thrown into confusion. The two cruisers were braking hard, trying not to go further in. But now their entry point was under fire. The Gunner wasn't firing full salvos, instead of which the four guns were firing one at a time, keeping the point under an almost continuous barrage.

The cap ship and its escort underneath the rings had disappeared from the passive displays. It was impossible to say whether they had jumped or *Deimos's* engines were simply blotting out their signals. With the rings between them there was no way the radar could hope to pick them up.

Three minutes after their exit from the rings, the Nameless were starting to get organised. Their ships were spreading out as they started to climb, having all emerged simultaneously. But they were losing time, distance and most important of all, velocity.

Deimos was out-accelerating them by many, many multiples. Still inside the rings, it was going to be at least ten minutes before they could go full burn and even begin to pursue. Then there were their missiles. With the launching ships going so slowly, those weapons would have to accelerate hard to start to gain on *Deimos* and their closing speed would be slow. The last few flak gun rounds would probably be enough.

It was nearly fifteen minutes before the Nameless once again breached the rings. The moment they did they all fired, but by now *Deimos* was more than forty thousand kilometres away and still accelerating. The big cap ship missiles could barely pull more acceleration than their target, which had such a head start that they were never going to catch up. The smaller missiles did have the acceleration required, but the overtake speed was still so low that they presented no problems to *Deimos's* point defence. The only question mark was the Nameless cap, ship but then a new set of contacts appeared, rounding the inner edge of the rings. It was the missing ships, now even further behind than the ships that had entered the rings.

Nine hours separated *Deimos* from the Red Line. The Nameless didn't let up the chase, but even on only three engines *Deimos* continued to open the range. There was little that could be said or done on the Bridge. Colwell had marked two lines on the navigation display: the Red Line, where Deimos could slip into the safety of Jump Space, and a blue line showing a distance from Phyose that corresponded to the Nameless's Jump In. Six hours after breaching the rings, *Deimos* passed through the blue line, putting them nearly two light seconds ahead of Nameless. The Red Line was nearly a half as much again beyond however. Navigation had run the numbers and the answer was not comforting. Whether the Nameless reached the blue line first or *Deimos* the Red, it was too close to call.

It had been hard for Crowe to sit there and do nothing. He'd called for more power only to be told that everything that could be done was being done, and that the engines were already showing signs of overheating. But now they were less than two minutes away from the Red Line and already the jump drive was spinning up.

"Bridge, Sensors! Four contacts have just jumped out.

Crowe and Hockley exchanged looks.

"Guns stand ready," Crowe warned.

"Bridge, Sensors. Distortion pattern, dead ahead."

"Range?" Crowe barked.

"Uncertain... They've completed the jump, range one point five light seconds. They're facing away from us. They're coming about. They're firing!"

As the missiles closed on them, Crowe turned to Hockley with a grim smile on his face.

"Sir?" Hockley said.

"Now that, Commander, was a mistake," he said. "They should have let us go. Instead they've told us *exactly* how close to a planet they can jump. Their 'magic' jump drives have limitations."

"Crossing the Red Line now, sir," Colwell announced, "we are free and clear to jump."

"Make the jump. Commander." Crowe paused as with a jolt, *Deimos* left real-space. "I guess I can't murder Captain Lukeman after all. Commander, the Bridge is yours, I'm going to sickbay."

"Yes, sir."

Crowe paused again, his hand on the Bridge hatch.

"Hopefully Commander, this will be the last time we run away from these bastards."

Chapter Twelve

Contact

31st July 2066, 21.30 hours Fleet Time, Alpha Centauri system

Dauntless hung motionless in the space between planets, nine-and-a-half light minutes out from the Alpha Centauri star. With the engines powered down and running lights off, the old carrier looked more like a derelict than a functioning warship. Fifty kilometres off either beam, the carrier's two escort destroyers *Piranha* and *Hammerhead*, were equally silent. Astern, the two couriers that would provide them with a stand off strike capacity waited in *Dauntless's* shadow.

On the carrier's bridge, Vice Admiral Emily Brian prowled back and forth like a caged tiger. Her walking stick tapped on the deck plating with every step. At each pass she paused at the Bridge communications console and the increasingly nervous rating manning it. As she turned to make another lap up the Bridge, her flag lieutenant opened his mouth to speak.

"Lieutenant Gore, if you're about to suggest I go below and rest, *I* suggest you don't," Brian snapped at him.

The Lieutenant's jaw closed with a click. Once the Admiral's back was turned again he caught the eye of the ship's first officer and shrugged.

The last two days had been ones of intense activity, preparing for the arrival of the Nameless. With the ships cleared for action, the destroyers and couriers had proceeded to deploy observation satellites across the solar system. Back on *Dauntless* there had been much discussion about where to deploy the carrier to launch against the Nameless. It was a complicated issue, with no clear right answer. Headquarters had estimated that the Nameless would jump into an area of the Alpha Centauri solar system, which while relatively small was still huge in practical terms. The first and most obvious position was suggested by the most aggressive senior officers, who argued for taking up station smack in the middle of the likely jump in point, ready to strike within minutes of the Nameless arrival.

That idea was quickly shot down by the more cautious officer, who countered that this would run a major risk that the Nameless would jump in right on top of them, a scenario *Dauntless* wouldn't survive. Brian was forced to agree with them. There was no point making contact if they got obliterated within seconds. Emboldened, the caution lobby advocated a position at the edge of the solar system, well out of harm's way.

That a fleet officer would make such a suggestion in time of war, and that others would publicly agree, took Brian's breath away. If the objective was to protect *Dauntless*, then the outer edge of the system was the place to be. But even if the Nameless arrived where Headquarters thought they would, if *Dauntless* were at the edge of the system it would take the transmissions from the observation satellites, travelling at only light speed, nearly eight hours to reach them. If they came out somewhere else, like the opposite side of the system, it could be anything up to *twenty* hours. The Nameless would be long gone before *Dauntless* even knew they'd arrived.

"I will say this once and only once." Her snarl had been enough to silence the room. "We are not here to play it safe, to be cautious, to avoid contact or keep out of harm. We are here to fight, we are here to show them what the fleet fighter wing can do!"

Who 'them' was she didn't spell out. Aliens, Headquarters, it didn't really much matter. Either way the caution lobby became more cautious toward her. The captain of the *Samuel Clemens* then mentioned that during their work on the FTL transmitter, they had noticed that the base inventory included a consignment of space mines, sitting in an orbital store. He had then gone on to suggest that *Samuel Clemens* jump in just in front of the Nameless fleet and lay a minefield in their path. As plans went, it merited ten out of ten for gutsy but scored rather less for practicality. However they loaded about a hundred of the mines onto the *Samuel Clemens* anyway, for self-defence. If the support ship found herself engaged by the Nameless, they could drop a minefield astern as they made a run for it.

It took hours of throwing ideas back and forth, but eventually they found a workable compromise. Compromise… even the word caught in her craw. The compromise position settled on was twenty light seconds clear of the edge of the estimated jump in position. If the Nameless came out where expected, then the observation satellite's signal would reach them in less than a minute. Furthermore, *Dauntless* would also have one of the Alpha Centauri stars at their back. No one knew whether that would have any effect on their sensors, but it couldn't hurt.

Her big fear wasn't losses to the fighters, or even *Dauntless* herself coming under fire. It was that they might fail to make contact at all. With nearly a dozen observation satellites deployed across the system and no other ships to foul the sensor plot, there was little prospect of the Nameless entering the system without being detected. But if they came out somewhere unexpected, it would take longer for the report to reach *Dauntless* and longer for the fighters to get into position to make their strike. With every second that passed, the chance that the Nameless would jump away rose. If she had to report to headquarters that they had swung and missed, that would be the end for fighters in the fleet. Better for the fighters to beat themselves bloody, than miss completely.

It had been easy to ignore such concerns while they were rushing about trying to get organised, but now with everything in readiness, the hours were dragging past. And with each uneventful hour, the probability that the Nameless had simply bypassed Alpha Centauri increased. Then what? They could set course for Earth, but it had taken *Dauntless* the best part of three days to make the transit, and it would take another three to get back. But at what point could they assume they had been bypassed and turn for Earth? The worse of all scenarios was for them to jump for Earth before the Nameless arrived at all. But already they were well beyond the time Headquarters had estimated the Nameless would arrive. Was it time to head for Earth? She could send the destroyers back on their own. Without *Dauntless* to slow them down they could make the passage in a matter of hours. But that would leave the carrier stranded. Her old jump drive was only ever capable of in system work, and hadn't been powered up in years anyway, making it a doubtful proposition.

Her brow creased in thought, Brian turned on her good leg and started another circuit of the Bridge.

Down in the pilots' mess, Alanna Shermer stirred from her sleep as she started to overheat. Sleeping in your flight suit wasn't technically a skill the fleet taught its personnel, but it was something every pilot learned. Throwing back her thin blanket she rolled onto her side towards the barracks hatch and opened a single sleepy eye. The duty pilot was sitting beside the operations phone, thumbing through a dog-eared magazine. Reassured she started to sink back into her slumber. A drilling noise threatened to drag her back to consciousness, prompting her to automatically kick one foot out and up against the underside of Scammell's bunk. From above there was a snort, a grunt and some movement before the return to heavy breathing. Alanna returned to her dreamless rest.

The satellite designated Anton Five orbited Alpha Centauri, sixteen light minutes from the twin stars. Five times each second it took readings from its three big passive sensor arrays. Five times each second it compared its readings to its list of programmed responses. Five times a second, for countless seconds, the array took no action.

23.23 hours Fleet Time

The small region of space was still. In all probably it had been still since the foundation of the universe, but then there was movement. The stars started to ripple, like a pond after a stone has been thrown in. A starship blinked into existence. After a moment another appeared, then a third, then a fourth and then within thirty seconds dozens of ships were present. Immediately lean and deadly looking warships started to form up around the large ships at the centre of their formation.

Anton Five registered the arrival of the first alien ship at a range of four and half light seconds. As it had each previous time, the satellite compared its reading to its programmed responses. This time however a different set of responses came into play, power flowed to the radio transmitter and more processor capacity was dedicated to the passive array facing the alien ships. It waited for half a minute, then sent a two-second burst transmission. Twelve minutes later the satellite registered a small object approaching it at high velocity. Again it transmitted this information. Thirty three seconds later, Anton Five ceased to exist.

23.40 hours Fleet Time

"Admiral. Admiral!" An insistent hand shook Brian's shoulder.
"Hmm?"
"We've had a signal from Anton Five."
Brian's eyes snapped open. She jumped out of the Bridge command chair, in the same motion snatching the signal slip out of her flag lieutenant's hand. The satellite had provided her with everything they needed to know to launch the strike, but the clock was ticking. With every passing moment the information was sliding towards obsolete. The message had taken fifty seconds to reach them and jumping the fighters to a position six-and-a-half light seconds from the enemy's projected position would take sixteen minutes. Finally it would take the fighters forty to fifty minutes to

coast from the jump in point to weapons range. Against all of this there were no guarantees that the Nameless would stay in the system that long.

"Captain O'Malley!"

"We're already scrambling the fighters, ma'am. We'll have the bays clear in thirty seconds," he shouted back.

With no orders to give, Brian could only stand impotent as the ship went to action stations around her.

When the operations phone rang Alanna was up and out of her bunk in less than a second. She was up one ladder and halfway along the corridor before she really woke up. Second in the line of pilots, she climbed up the ladder to the hub of the centrifuge. Once in the micro gravity of the main hull, she pushed herself down the corridor headfirst.

"Make a hole!" bellowed Squadron Commander Moscoe, at the head of the line of flight crews.

Crewmen flattened themselves again the bulkheads, as flight crews shot past them like human torpedoes. Grabbing the hand bar, Alanna swung herself into the access tube to her fighter.

"Good luck Alanna!" Scammell shouted as he passed the top of her access tube. He was gone before she could reply.

Swinging herself round in the tube, Alanna landed in her seat with a thump. Grabbing the handholds on either side of her cockpit, she stopped herself from bouncing back up the tube. Wasim Dhoni landed beside her in his own seat with a matching thump, then Alanna slapped the controls and above them the cockpit canopy slid shut.

Automatically her hands went through the routine of belting herself and running through the pre-flight checks.

"Flight board is green. Reactor at standby," she called out. "Disconnecting from starter."

"Weapons board is green. Communications at standby. Sensors, passive and active are green," Dhoni called back.

"Launch control, this is Caesar, we are good to go," Alanna announced as the boarding tube withdrew.

"Roger that Caesar, opening bay doors now," the launch control office's voice crackled.

The big bay doors on their port side swung open. The launch bay had already been depressurised, so barely a puff of atmosphere escaped into the void. Then another voice came up on the connection to the Bridge.

"All fighters, this is Admiral Brian. Remember, command and capital ships are your targets, so make sure to distribute your fire. We're only going to get one shot at this. Good luck all of you, *Dauntless* out."

Immediately the fighter slid sideways and out. Directly in front of Alanna was A for Anton, Moscoe's fighter. The nose of the fighter was lifted slightly, so the fighter following wouldn't be flying through the engine plume. Then the docking arm's coilgun launcher hurled the commander's fighter forward, before snapping back into its bay. Alanna pushed her head back against her headrest. In her ear three sharp beeps sounded as a countdown. Then Caesar was away.

On the Bridge, Brian watched the fighters launch in four smooth ripples. The twelve fighters formed into two lines and took position between the two courier ships. Three minutes later they all disappeared into jump space. Brian sighed and rubbed her eyes tiredly, before turning and heading back to the plotting table.

"If we get even half of them back, I'll be surprised," she murmured to Captain O'Malley as she passed him.

After the mad rush of a combat scramble, the actual transit to a target usually seemed like a bit of an anti-climax. But that had been training and this was the real thing. It was also the first time she'd done a jump in a Vampire. The jump conduit walls glimmered around them, bathing the fighters in a soft blue light, but Alanna wasn't getting much of a chance to look at it. Unlike the modern Raven fighters, Vampires didn't have an in system jump drive, so they also didn't have an autopilot capable of dealing with the gravitational turbulence experienced within conduits. In front and astern of her, the two lines of fighters wiggled like a pair of snakes, each pilot working hard to keep on station. Ahead, the radiators on the back of Moscoe's fighter were glowing red hot, venting what little heat jump space would accept. There was little communication between Dhoni and Alanna as both of them concentrated intently on Caesar's engine read outs. The flight deck chief had signed off the engines as good, but the Chief wasn't here now and Moscoe had spelt it out in the briefing. Any fighter that fell behind due to engine problems would be left behind, a death sentence for a vessel lacking its own jump drive. So both of them watched for any sign, of any variances outside normal operating parameters.

They were only due to be in jump space for sixteen minutes, but they were busy ones. Except in combat, flying a fighter usually involved programming in a route, then taking your hands off the controls. Alanna didn't remove her hand from Caesar's control column and not a moment passed where she wasn't correcting their heading or making a subtle change to their engine output. As the minutes edged past the two lines became noticeably more ragged. Alanna could feel the back of her survival suit becoming slick with sweat as she worked the controls.

"Ninety seconds from jump in," Dhoni said. "Begin burn in thirty."

"Roger, breaking for jump in."

Jets of plasma burned past the cockpit as they reduced velocity to get below the safe re-entry speed.

"Fifteen seconds, brace for re-entry."

Then with a violent jolt they were back into real-space. The couriers immediately angled off. As soon as they had spun their jump drives back up, they would be making a jump to the far side of the alien fleet. There they would wait to take any survivors of the strike back to *Dauntless*. If there were any. The squadron formed back into two neat lines in a formation right out of the fighter playbook. If each fighter could hide in the radar shadow of the one in front, the squadron's radar profile would be little more than that of the two lead craft. They burned their engines for six minutes to build up velocity again, before, at Moscoe's command, they all cut their engines and began to coast in on silent running.

The term 'silent running' was of course scientific nonsense, a left over from the wet navy. But for those who had not experienced it, the stillness of space was unimaginable. The only noise in the fighter was the quiet sound of Alanna's and Dhoni's breathing. Beyond that there was nothing, no hum of equipment, no light from instrumentation. They sat there in the darkness waiting. They were travelling at several hundred kilometres per second, but without external references it didn't feel as if they were moving at all. The only thing to do, was watch the clock count down to the estimated time they would make contact with the enemy.

Captain O'Malley studied the watch set into the wrist of his survival suit.

"They should be making contact about now," he remarked to no one in particular.

Brian nodded without speaking.

"Contact," Commander Moscoe's voice sounded quietly in Alanna's ear. "Twelve by one. Looks like we're coming in slightly below them. Transmitting visual back at you. Prepare for targeting data people." Alanna swallowed hard as her mouth suddenly went very dry. She hadn't realised it but she must have been half hoping that they wouldn't make contact. But they had and now there was no avoiding it. They were going in.

Alanna and Dhoni both turned on their targeting monitors. They might only be useable when in tight formation but one thing to be said for short-range coms lasers was that they were undetectable by anyone not in the transmission beam and totally unjammable... bar blowing the sender or receiver out of the stars of course.

Alanna studied the image of the alien ships on her screen. The ships of the Nameless were certainly very different from those of Battle Fleet or any of the other known races. She couldn't see any weapons turrets, not even for point defence guns. The ship that had fought the *Mississippi* had relied totally on missiles. For the Nameless that was clearly the norm rather than the exception. It gave their ships a sleek and clean look compared to the blocky warships of humanity.

There was no sign of any fighters among their fleet and she couldn't identify any ship that looked like a carrier, but that didn't mean there wasn't one in there somewhere. There were too many ships too close together, their overlapping silhouettes confusing the Vampire's computer, which couldn't decide where one ship stopped and another began. Perversely, the human eye was better able to interpret what they were seeing. For her part, Alanna concentrated on reading the mood of the fleet and gauging what state of alert the aliens were at. They certainly hadn't been spotted yet, but how alert were they? There was an outer picket of escorts, deployed in a loose sphere, but the majority were clustered in the centre around several large ships.

It was irritating not to have direct control over what she was seeing, Moscoe kept moving the camera when she would have liked to have studied individual ships for a moment. The camera in Moscoe's fighter focused on one of the big ships in the centre of the formation for a moment, then moved on, but it was long enough for something to twig Alanna's interest.

"Wasim, are you recording this?" she asked.

"Of course, Skip," he replied.

"Wind back a few seconds, to that big ship."

"What are you looking at?" he asked as he worked.

"This," she replied pointing at the screen. "This big ship here. These things along the side of its hull look very like hydrogen tanks and they run all the way down the length. I think it's a fuel tanker."

"Hang on a moment," Dhoni murmured as he fiddled with the controls. The recording wound back again for several seconds, then stopped and zoomed in. "Here look at this." The screen showed two enemy ships close together, a thin boom connected them. "Those are without doubt tankers, they're refuelling from them."

"Hell if we put missiles into them…"

"Yes, definitely," Dhoni agreed. "We might well get some very good damage from secondary explosions before the other ships could pull away. It looks to me like most of them are still waiting to fuel. If they don't have enough reaction mass to go anywhere that will keep them still. I'm seeing four of them."

As he was speaking, Alanna reached over and switched the display back to the live feed.

"Oh…" she said. "Moscoe hasn't noticed the tankers, he's looking at warships."

"That is our objective skipper, target warships."

"Yeah, but a fleet of that size. Even if we nail one each, there's nothing stopping the rest going on without them and still having a decent sized fleet." She paused. "Wasim, give me a laser link to Moscoe."

Dhoni looked at her sharply.

"Skipper, sending a coms laser forward is risky, it could give us away if any of the beam leaks past Moscoe and hits one of them," he said.

"Yeah. Do it anyway."

"Okay."

"Anton, this is Caesar, over."

The response was lightning fast."

"Caesar! Cut transmission!" Moscoe barked.

"Negative Anton, have identified four enemy ships as fuel tankers, sending forward targeting information. Recommend tankers as primary targets. Caesar, over and out."

Alanna cut the transmission.

"That's going to cost us," she said. Dhoni nodded without reply.

The com link came to life again.

"Listen up people," said Moscoe. "I can see four tankers, we're going to target three of them, put a wing onto each one. I'm designating them A, B and C." On Alanna's screen a note blinked up showing which was which. "First wing with me, we're taking A, second wing B and third C. I'm going to coast us in as far as I think we can go. Be ready to spark up your drives. Leader out."

"Well, perhaps he won't shoot us after all," Dhoni said dryly.

"He'll have to wait his turn," Alanna replied as she rested one finger of her left hand on the button for start up and closed her right hand around the control stick. "Look, there they are."

Dhoni glanced up in the direction she was looking and there they were, just the engine flares at this point, but you still had to be very close to see anything with the naked eye.

"Are we all set there?" she asked.

"Yes, I've just tested the missiles. They're all registering okay."

They coasted for another five minutes. Now Alanna could make out the light of the local star glinting off their hulls. Every ship looked confident and deadly. Alanna noticed her right hand was shaking slightly. She closed it into a fist until it stopped. Finally came the welcome sound of Moscoe's voice.

"Okay people on my mark. Single pass, no fancy stuff," he ordered. "Three, two, one, mark."

Alanna pushed down the button and heard the *thunk* of the chemical catalyst dropping into the reactor. There was that agonising second of uncertainly before the reactor roared into life. The control panel in front of her lit up as Caesar's systems came back on line. Alanna slammed the engines into plus ten override and Caesar leapt forward like a spurred horse. With a smooth motion to her control column, she swung out from behind Moscoe's fighter, giving her own targeting radar a clear view of the ships ahead. As her search radar came on, she saw Scammell's fighter swing out onto her port wing. All around them was the hot glow of plasma engines going full burn as the squadron thundered in.

"Come on! Come on!" Alanna muttered to herself, as the seconds crawled by and every nut and bolt holding Caesar together started to vibrate. All the alien sensors must have been screaming by now, so what the hell were they waiting for?

Caesar's threat detection system finally sounded, sharp and shrill, just as the squadron flashed past the ships of the aliens' outer picket. Several of these fired but the fighters now had so much velocity that the missiles floundered harmlessly in their wake.

Ahead of them, the knot of Nameless starships was only starting to react to the squadron's appearance. The formation was opening up as individual ships sought to clear their fields of fire. As Alanna watched, there was a bloom of fire and sparkle of ripped metal as two ships grazed one another. Then they began to fire.

At first it was only single missiles but then the barrage gained strength as every ship that could fire did so in earnest. Scores of missiles surged across space towards them. With the squadron going straight for the launchers, the closing speed was incredible. Dhoni fired off a spray of decoy rockets directly to their front. The rockets detonated five kilometres in front of Caesar, putting down a wall of chaff between them and the approaching missiles. All down the line the other fighters were doing the same thing. Caesar had two turrets, below and above the fuselage, from which their computer guided plasma guns now opened up, launching a stream of plasma bolts at the approaching missiles. Alanna pressed the trigger on her control column, causing a stream of plasma bolts to pipe out of the fighter's third, fixed gun. She didn't expect to hit them, but anything that added to the confusion couldn't hurt. Dozens of the approaching missiles were destroyed or decoyed, but they were being fired by the score.

The threat detection alarm increased in tone and before Alanna could react, a missile missed them by less than ten metres and detonated half a kilometre behind Caesar. Alanna realised that the closing velocity was so high, that the missile's proximity fuse hadn't triggered fast enough. Not everyone was as lucky. There was a flash from behind them.

"Just lost our wing man," Dhoni announced bleakly.

Simon, Alanna thought briefly, but she had no time to grieve for a friend.

Off to their port side, another fighter had one of its engine pods ripped away and went into a flat spin before another two missiles smeared it out of existence. Caesar gave a jolt as something clipped them without hitting anything vital. The squadron's loose formation had disintegrated, as the pilots desperately sought to find their own safe course. Alanna worked the controls of Caesar, sending the fighter twisting and turning, but the space all around them was filled with missiles, making the survival of any individual fighter little more than a matter of blind luck.

"Skipper I can't get missile lock! They're jamming our frequency!"

"Goddamn it! Switch missiles to manual!" Alanna shouted. "We're going to have to fire open sight!" Above them another Vampire was obliterated.

Now that they were in amongst the enemy fleet their fire slackened slightly as the aliens tried to avoid hitting each other. Out of the corner of her eye Alanna saw a Vampire, its port engine aflame and cockpit ripped away, continue straight and level into a maelstrom of fire, until it slammed into the side of an enemy starship.

"Target five hundred clicks!"

"Roger!"

"Two hundred!"

"Fifty!" The tanker loomed large ahead of Caesar.

"Missiles away!" she shouted.

Four deep thumps rang through Caesar, as the missiles blasted out of the rotary launcher. An enemy missile intercepted the first, the second corkscrewed away as its guidance system malfunctioned, but the last two ran straight and true. The two speared into separate fuel cells and detonated. Both cells were ripped open. Hydrogen fuel spilled out and ignited. In turn the fires triggered secondary detonations in the neighbouring tanks. Explosion after explosion wracked the tanker, as each fuel cell was ripped open and detonated in turn.

"Direct hit! Direct hit!" Dhoni screamed. "Scratch one tanker!"

Alanna didn't have time to celebrate, as they now needed to find an exit. To turn away would mean losing speed and that would be fatal. They had to find a way directly through. She opted to dive under the tanker she'd just hit. A few seconds later she realised she'd made the wrong decision. Relative to their position, the explosions were pushing the tanker towards them from above. Below lay an enemy warship, its manoeuvring jets firing frantically as it tried to get out of the path of the dying behemoth. The gap between the two hulls was narrowing by the second, but she and Caesar were already committed. She found herself trying to push forward the throttle lever, even though it was already fully open. The gap was hair thin now.

"Don't breath in Wasim! This is going to be tight!" Alanna shouted.

The hull of the warship passed as a blue blur, as Caesar flashed through a gap scarcely big enough to contain her. Behind, fresh explosions lit space as the two hulls ground together.

And then they were clear

"Holy… I think we took off some of their paint," Dhoni gasped.

"Stay focused, we're not out yet!"

But the response from the outer picket on the far side of the fleet was feeble compared to the holocaust of fire they had come through. Perhaps the aliens realised the damage had already been done and within a few minutes they were clear.

Caesar disappeared into the cold dark safety of deep space. Astern space was briefly lit by two pinpricks of fire.

After several minutes Alanna belatedly realised her engines were still running at plus ten and throttled back sharply. The sudden drop in the tone of the engines caused a cry of alarm from Dhoni.

"Sorry about that Wasim," she apologised, "if I left us on plus ten, we'd have used all of our reaction mass before we got to the rendezvous."

"Yeah, that would be bad," Dhoni agreed.

There was a silence between them for several minutes before Alanna forced herself to ask the question.

"Any of the others on radar?"

"Err... hang on." Dhoni's wits were clearly still back there with the Nameless. "Not at the moment skipper," Dhoni replied unhappily. "I know I saw three go down."

Against such fire, it didn't seem possible that anyone could have survived. Alanna could barely believe she was herself still alive. Perhaps they were the only survivors out of the entire squadron...

"Contact!"

Alanna jerked out of her reverie.

"Friendlies?"

"It's two of ours!" Dhoni replied with open relief.

By the time they reached the waiting couriers, another two vampires had caught up and formed a loose formation. The attack had taken under three minutes, and cost the lives of fourteen crewmen.

1st August 2066, 01.20 hours Fleet Time

"That one there, see it? That's definitely a second reactor going up."

"Yeah, not so sure about that one though. It might be a reactor being scrammed."

Brian rapped her stick on the deck plating.

"Gentlemen, we're on a time limit here. What is your conclusion?" she asked.

Captain O'Malley, Commander Moscoe and the ship's intelligence officers all stepped aside to allow her to see the main screen.

"We're seeing two clear reactor explosions, here and here," O'Malley said, pointing to the appropriate areas of the holo. "They are definitely two of the tankers going up and judging by the size of the explosions, they must have been close to full load. This here is the third tanker, clearly well ablaze. We lose track of it from here. Now here, there's a flash, which might be it going up or it could be a reactor purge. We're not sure. Either way though, if they've saved the ship, they've had to dump the fuel to do it."

"So you're saying three of their four tankers are off the board?"

"Well ma'am, two are for sure but the third is more of a judgement call. With only five fighters surviving there are gaps in the records, so we can't be one hundred percent."

"All right. Anything else?"

"They sent an FTL transmission after the strike," O'Malley replied. "It was short but it was complex, so they could have sent a lot of data."

"Have we heard any reply?"

"No, ma'am. There is something else though. Over the last twenty minutes we've received transmissions from four separate observation satellites. They report groups, we think two, of perhaps half a dozen ships, jumping in, taking a look around and then jumping out."

"They've sent out hunting groups, looking for us."

"That's our thinking."

"Anything else?"

O'Malley shook his head.

Brian walked around the plotting table to the main communications console. The Bridge was silent, except for the hum of equipment. The officers on the Bridge turned to watch her. Whatever message she sent would decide the actions of the Home Fleet. On paper Admiral Lewis might be the C-in-C, but here and now she was its real commander. Make the wrong choice and the war might be over very, very quickly. Was the loss of the three tankers, enough to hold the Nameless in position for three hours? They didn't have time or for that matter the capacity to carry out a follow up recon. A few seconds of poor quality digital imagery wasn't much to base a decision that could affect everything.

"Communications," she said after a long pause, "send the following message to the FTL on Alpha Centauri Three for relay to Earth: Have made contact with enemy, stop. Estimate three of four enemy tankers destroyed, stop. Recommend Home Fleet attack, stop. Enemy position, ten point four minutes from hub, bearing zero, four, three, dash, zero, zero, three, message end. Send it now please."

Turning back to the Bridge, Brian saw a range of emotions on the faces of her crew, fear, worry and relief.

"What now, Admiral?" O'Malley asked.

"Assuming they make contact, Captain O'Malley, once the Home Fleet arrives, we are going to move into position to carry out supporting strikes with what's left of the squadron."

The executor was an old tradition among military pilots. Each member of a flight crew would nominate someone from another fighter as their executor. If someone was killed, whether on operations or dirtside, the executor went through their stuff. Anything that might tarnish the memory of the deceased, like say... any sign of a second girlfriend, was quietly removed before it was sent back to parents or spouses. It wasn't something mentioned in any of the fleet's manuals and wasn't really talked about, even in private, but even in a training outfit like *Dauntless's* squadron, executors had been nominated.

In the case of Flying Officer Simon Scammell, there was nothing sordid. Among his personal possessions, there were a few changes of clothing and a post card from the Armstrong Lunar station. Alanna could remember him cursing when he realised that he had forgotten to post it. His emails were mostly to and from his sisters and parents. The rest were from old college friends. One in particular caught Alanna's eye, someone called Clare, planning a party to celebrate his successful commissioning as a fighter pilot.

Alanna set the email account to download to Fleet Headquarters upon their return and logged out. His physical belongings she packed up and took to storage. With more casualties than survivors, some of the designated executors were themselves among the dead. That had meant that some of them had to go through two sets of belongings. Alanna was grateful that she wasn't one of the ones who had drawn that short straw. She honestly wasn't sure she could have stomached doing it twice.

When she got back from storage, she immediately noticed that someone had moved her stuff onto one of the vacated bunks. She opened her mouth to object, Dhoni saw her come in and gave a very slight shake of his head. Realising why it had been done she closed her mouth without speaking. It was a drawing together, easier for the survivors to ignore the empty bunks and what they represented when they were packed away into the bulkheads.

01.55 hours Fleet Time, Earth

Message start. ++ *Have made contact with enemy – estimate three of four enemy tankers destroyed – recommend home fleet attack* – enemy position, ten point four minutes from hub, bearing zero, four, three, dash, zero, zero, three, plus, plus. Message End. Coding: G FIFTY-ONE, CORRECT Frequency: CORRECT Authorisation code: CORRECT. Conclusion: MESSAGE CONFIRMED AUTHENTIC.

Lewis handed the paper slip back to Staff Captain Sheehan.

"So, Rear Admiral Brian has managed to land a punch," Captain Holfe, the *Warspite's* captain, said, "and survived long enough to tell us about it." There was a note of respect in the Captain's voice.

Lewis grunted in reply. Indeed, Emily had managed to get a strike in. Now if she had any sense, she'd find a hole to hide in until the shooting stopped. Three tankers destroyed could stop a fleet for days, but only assuming no replacements were close to hand. That was the gift and the curse of the FTL transmitters. They granted the ability to send simple messages winging between the stars but nothing more, he couldn't be given the data Emily had based her conclusion on. Had she overstated the achievements of her beloved fighters? It all boiled down to trust. Did he trust her judgement?

Yes he did.

"Captain Sheehan, signal Headquarters that we are leaving for Alpha Centauri as planned. Captain Holfe, signal the fleet to form up for jump out."

Ten minutes later there was a flash as the Home Fleet left Earth astern.

Brian rubbed her eyes tiredly as she sat down on her bunk. Her knee was aching fiercely, but she'd lived with that for long enough to know how to ignore it. With the message now on its way to Earth, there hadn't seemed much point in staying on the Bridge. That wasn't quite true. Unquestionably they had alerted the Nameless to their presence in the system, but she needed to see her pilots with her own eyes, to judge whether they had anything left.

It had been a mistake.

The executors had finished packing away the gear of the fallen by the time she arrived. Squadron Commander Moscoe looked okay. Wing Commander Devane on the other hand was clearly shaken, while the rest of them were plainly shell-shocked. Oh they snapped to attention smart enough when she came in, but the glazed looks in their eyes told her everything she needed to know.

Militaries had long known that few people had endless reserves of courage. For most courage was more like a bank account they could draw from for a while, then replenish during periods away from the fighting. But if there was a run on the bank that went on too long or was too severe, there were few people who wouldn't crack. Rookie fighter pilots were, if anything, more vulnerable. Brian knew from experience, that in their case they had a sense of invulnerability that they were too good, too fast or even simply too lucky to die. Today had shattered that illusion for the survivors. They'd pitted youthful confidence against bloody reality and in the process learned the harshest lesson of all: just how easily human beings broke. Given time people developed defence mechanisms, most of which revolved around not thinking about it. But the pil... no, trainees hadn't had a chance to develop those.

Unfortunately, the *Dauntless* was the worse possible place to come to that realisation. The small carrier had never been designed for long-term habitation, so had no recreation facilities. That left people with plenty of time to dwell on what had happened... and what it would be like the next time.

Some people simply never recovered. Paul Lewis, an officer most people considered to have ice water for blood, had never been able to climb back into a cockpit after the First Battle of Earth. Neither had she of course, Brian reflected as she started to massage her knee. But her reasons were physical rather than psychological.

The survivors of *Dauntless's* squadron weren't going to have that luxury because they would have to go in again. Brian glanced at the clock mounted on the bulkhead. The Home Fleet would be receiving their message any minute now, if they hadn't already. That would put their arrival, if they had stuck to the plan, in roughly two hours and forty minutes. She'd have to send one of the couriers to shadow the Nameless and provide the Home Fleet with a homing beacon. As for them, as an operational unit, it was *Dauntless's* duty to get into combat, but perhaps it would be enough for them to hover at the edge of the combat zone and use their fighters to pick off enemy lame ducks. Try to salvage something of the squadron.

"Admiral Brian to the Bridge! Admiral Brian to the Bridge!" screamed the PA system cutting savagely across her thoughts.

Christ, they've found us!

Brian leapt to her feet, and nearly fell as her weak leg buckled under her. Violently yanking her stick open she scrambled to the Bridge. As she burst in her eyes immediately sought out the main display holo. Only five blips were visible, *Dauntless*, her destroyers and couriers.

O'Malley was standing next to the communications console. The man was looking physically sick.

"Captain what is it!" she asked urgently

"Ma'am we've received a signal from the observation satellite Anton Eight. It's on the far side of the system from us, so it's already nearly thirty minutes old."

"Norman what the hell is it!"

O'Malley took a deep breath.

"A second enemy force has just jumped into the system."

"What? You mean a supporting elem..." she began.

"Ma'am, it's three times the size of the one we attacked! We've just aimed the Home Fleet at the wrong target!"

Chapter Thirteen

Blooding the Guns

Brian stood frozen, her mind unable to comprehend what she was hearing. She walked slowly over to the main holo, to see the data for herself.

She activated the playback herself and the holo sprang to life. The second alien fleet had dropped back into real-space less than a light second away from one of their sensor satellites and come out close enough so that even the satellite's optics could see them. There on the holo, were orderly ranks of starships, composed of the same types that *Dauntless's* fighters had already attacked, but far more of them. After several seconds a missile detached from one of the alien ships and accelerated towards the satellite. A few seconds later and the image was replaced by 'SIGNAL TERMINATED.'

She leaned on the holo's casing, her head lowered. How the hell could they have been so stupid? They'd assumed the enemy had only committed one fleet and that the methodical destruction of the sensor satellites from Baden to Alpha Centauri had been an instinctive reaction to deprive them of information. But now it was revealed that the Nameless had been playing a deeper and more cunning game. The ships they'd attacked hadn't been the main force, but a sweeper group, there to distract and eliminate their reconnaissance and trip any defences, leaving their main force to advance undetected.

The second Nameless fleet was close enough to the first to offer support, but far enough away that it could choose not to engage. The Home Fleet could either find itself fighting a force four times bigger than the one it expected, or be bypassed completely.

Brian slammed her fist down on the side of display causing the holo to flicker and buzz for a moment.

"God damn it!"

The Bridge was deathly silent. Every man and woman present was aware that they had a grandstand view of an impending catastrophe.

"Suggestions?" Brian asked without raising her head or turning around.

"Signal the Home Fleet when it makes real-space re-entry," Captain O'Malley said in a subdued voice. "It's all we can do."

"Not good enough Captain. It will take the Home Fleet at least three hours, to purge their heat sinks sufficiently to allow transit back to Earth. Even then, I doubt more than half of them will be mechanically in any condition to do another high-speed run. That means it will be at least twenty hours before they can return to Earth, which assumes they don't make contact. If they do, it will be days before the Home Fleet, complete with damaged ships and depleted fuel and ammunition, returns to Earth. We have to hold that second fleet here."

"*Us*! Ma'am we punched above our weight once! We're not going to be able to do that again. I'm sorry ma'am but we've blown it."

02.15 hours Fleet Time

The page made absolutely no noise as it was turned. With *Warspite's* flag bridge decompressed, there wasn't any air to carry the sound. The book was a cheap novel Lewis had picked up the last time he was passing through Washington DC. It wasn't very good but he stuck with it. It was all about keeping up appearances. As well as the usual command frequency, he had his intercom set to pick up everything being said on the Bridge. He could hear orders being given and reports made. Beneath his feet, he could feel the deck-plating tremble slightly as the battleship rammed her way through jump space. Out of the corner of his eye, he could see the occasional looks both the officers and ratings were giving him. It was all an act of course and every man and woman on the Bridge knew it. But equally, they all were prepared to pretend it wasn't. Here they were, about to go into action, but things must be going to plan if the old man felt he could catch up on his reading.

Lewis's eyes flicked to the other side of the Bridge, to the navigation repeater display. In the centre of the display, in big red numbers, was the countdown to their arrival in Alpha Centauri showing their ETA. The digits flicked to one hundred and eighteen minutes. A long time to wait and find out if he'd made the right or wrong decision.

On the Bridge of the *Hood*, Commander Willis resisted the urge to fidget in her command chair. Modern warships would decompress most of their fighting chambers ahead of action. It reduced the likelihood of secondary damage from fires and made life easier for the ship's damage control teams. Like all ships of her generation *Hood* didn't have that capacity however, as the lesson had only been learned during the Contact War, subsequent to her construction. It was a fact that was starting to get on Willis's nerves. Decompression would have meant that her survival suit would have expanded very slightly. But on *Hood* it hadn't and as a result was now rubbing in places it had never rubbed before. That wasn't the only thing irritating her however.

Heat, or to be precise, waste heat was the big limiting factor that decided how far a ship could travel in a single jump. The radiators, which vented that excess heat in real-space, were much less efficient in jump space. So instead starships stored this heat in heat sinks, to be radiated off once the ship made real-space re-entry. However heat sinks were volume and mass intensive, and the size of the sink determined how much heat it could absorb. The fastest ships, couriers, were little more than a heat-sink with a ship wrapped round it, but most ships had to balance the volume given to the sinks against everything else. *Hood* had been designed to serve and fight inside Earth's solar system. Consequently, her heat sink was far too small to allow the little cruiser to make an interstellar passage. All of this meant that *Hood*, rather than being under her own power, was hanging as deadweight beneath a tug ship.

It was like being on a leash. To all intents and purposes she was cargo. She could just as convincingly command her ship lying in her bunk! Her first jump in command of her first ship, and she effectively wasn't in control of the vessel's movements.

She knew this was an irrational line of thinking, but even so she'd feel better when they undocked from the tug for the final approach. Then, and only then, Faith Willis would find out whether she measured up as a captain.

02.35 hours Fleet Time

It was a question of firepower, or a lack thereof. O'Malley was right: there was no doubt they had got lucky the first time. The tankers had been pretty much the only things they could hit that would reliably throw a spanner in the works. And as the Captain said, a repeat performance was not on the cards. Over half *Dauntless's* fighter group was gone, and Brian sincerely doubted she could count on the survivors to press home any second attack.

That was a moot point anyway as much of her stand off launch capability was gone. The destruction of the sensor satellites had forced her to dispatch one of the couriers to shadow the second Nameless fleet and report its movements. Its first report had been that the Nameless had learned, as the escort around the six tankers present was far stronger and tighter. The other courier had been despatched to the first alien fleet, to both shadow it and alert the Home Fleet to their findings as soon as it arrived. It was a lot to ask of unarmed eggshells and both couriers were already reporting that the Nameless were taking pot-shots at them. She couldn't send a message back to them to acknowledge their efforts as to do so would risk compromising *Dauntless's* position. They could still use the two destroyers to get the fighters close enough and they could even join the attack themselves, but against such a force that would definitely count as pissing into the wind.

Brian rubbed her tired eyes and took a sip of stone cold coffee. The conference room was utterly silent. Each of the officers present avoided the eyes of their neighbours, as if they were trying to distance themselves from the approaching disaster. The minutes were trickling away and nobody had any ideas.

No sane ones anyway.

There was one option: a zero range combat drop. Like the first, the second Nameless fleet was not inside any mass shadow. That meant *Dauntless*, plus escort, could make a jump straight into the middle of their fleet, dropping her fighters directly into the fray. As with the first time, the warships were fuelling from the tankers, which would suggest they needed that fuel.

Having the human ships appear in their lap, would cause absolute havoc… for a few minutes. Then *Dauntless* would either have to jump out, or more likely be destroyed. It was a risk only worth running if there was at least half a chance that they could inflict some serious damage. But with only five fighters and two destroyers, there was a pretty limited amount of hurt they could dish out in the short window of opportunity they would have. And by a roundabout route that brought them back to the original problem: firepower.

"The Home Fleet might make real-space re-entry close enough to the second fleet to engage," *Dauntless's* second-in-command ventured cautiously.

"That's only going to happen if they royally screw up their jump calculations," O'Malley replied flatly. "If they come out where they should, they will immediately be in contact with the first fleet."

"We can't afford to ignore either of their fleets anyway," Brian added. "The first fleet is much smaller than the second, but it's still big enough to pack one hell of a punch, if we allow it do what it likes. We have to engage both fleets!"

Silence returned to the table.

"The *Samuel Clemens* still has those anti-ship mines ma'am," said Captain Beevor of the *Hammerhead,* breaking the silence of despair.

"So what," O'Malley replied, "even if we had a proper minelayer, we couldn't get them into position. To deploy the mines safely, we'd have to be so far ahead of them that they wouldn't reach the minefield for hours, assuming they reached them at all."

"If we can be sure of one thing, it's that they will react to the Home Fleet turning up. It doesn't matter whether it's changing course or jumping out, they will miss the minefield," Moscoe added.

"Well what about putting them onto fighters and use them to drop the mines directly into their path?" Beevor said.

"Vampires could probably only carry one each. We'd have more firepower with our missiles," Moscoe replied. "If we could dump a hundred in front of them, then yeah, but we can't do that."

"What kind of mines are they?" Brian asked quietly.

"Medium anti-ship mines, ma'am. Only old Mark Threes but the *Samuel Clemens* does have a couple of hundred of them."

"Yeah but we still don't have a minelayer. There is no way we can put them across the path of a fleet in open space," O'Malley objected. "We can't use mines, that's the top and bottom of it."

Beevor shrugged.

"I only mention it as an option," he replied defensively.

Brian leaned back in her chair as silence returned to the table and stared up at the deckhead. Anti-ship mines? The words had prodded a brain cell into action. She could feel an idea forming in her head and listened to it grow and gain substance. She considered how it could work. She considered the much longer list of how it could go wrong. It could possibly do the job, but it really needed several weeks of work on simulators to figure out all the variables. To even consider doing it on the fly, you'd have to be mad… or desperate. She glanced at her watch; the Home Fleet was about one hundred minutes away. Madness? Well time would tell, but desperate? Certainly.

Ten years previously there had been a proposal to build a class of dedicated high-speed minelayer cruisers. The design was ultimately shelved for budgetary reasons, but before it was, Brian had been on a committee involved in working out the ways such a ship could be used. The vastness of space made strategic min laying a bit of a non-starter, but on a tactical scale there were more possibilities. The idea of discouraging pursuit by dropping mines astern had been obvious, but the most junior member of the committee, a lieutenant commander, had suggested the idea of using a minelayer offensively.

As a rule of thumb, fleets would spend much of their time inside a planet's mass shadow. However if a fleet wanted to travel from one planet to another it had to leave the mass shadow before it could activate the jump drives. This, the lieutenant commander suggested, offered a brief window of opportunity. Assuming friendly shadowing or screening elements were present to report the enemy's position, the minelayer could make a jump directly in front of the opposing fleet and drop its mines in front of enemy, too close for them to take evasive action. The lieutenant commander himself had admitted that such a scheme would be dangerous in the extreme, since the minelayer would have to spin its jump drive back up before it could make its escape. Because of this and other flaws, the committee decided against including the scenario in its report.

The idea however had struck a chord in Brian and in the years since she had from time to time re-examined it in her own time. Always though, the weak point had been the sheer unlikelihood of the minelayer surviving the hail of short-range fire that would be directed at it. But what if the minelayers survival wasn't a consideration? Would mines pack enough of a punch?

The Mark Three anti-ship mine had been designed primarily to defend deep space installations. Despite its name, the weapon was basically an autonomous single shot missile launcher. Heavily stealthed and equipped with passive sensors, the mine would wait until a starship came within range, then it would rotate to face the contact and fire its missile. The range was likely to be extremely short, offering the target vessel almost no time in which to react. The mine's small size and, unlike ship missiles, its requirement to hold station for years if necessary, precluded the use of any sort of fusion power derivative to provide propellant or explosive. Instead the designers had used chemical rockets and shaped charges large enough, it was hoped, to penetrate the armoured hulls of Aéllr ships. Certainly against the unarmoured hulls of the Nameless, the mines could inflict catastrophic damage. More importantly, no fleet finding itself in a minefield would hold formation. And that would offer them a chance at the tankers.

"Actually we do have a minelayer," she said out loud, still staring at the deckhead. "We have seven empty fighter bays."

03.53 hours Fleet Time

The whole squadron was seated in the briefing room. Several of the *Dauntless's* officers and petty officers were also present. Yet there were still a lot of empty seats.

Unnoticed, Brian slipped into the briefing room from the back. To take the weight off her bad leg, she was now leaning against a bulkhead. Captain O'Malley stood silently beside her. Moscoe was at the head of the room and had just finished outlining what they were facing. It wasn't the fleet's usual practice. As a rule pilots were sent on missions without knowing the wider situation. Where they were going and what they were to shoot at was all flight crews normally needed to know. But not this time. 'Tell them everything,' she had ordered Moscoe, 'make sure they know why we are doing this.'

"Currently your fighters are being fitted with the standard load for an anti-ship strike, that is to say four Long Lance light anti-ship missiles plus the usual countermeasures. Within the next forty minutes, *Dauntless* will be jumping to these co-ordinates here," Moscoe indicated on the display. "This will place us approximately six light minutes ahead of the second enemy fleet's outer screen, assuming they hold their current speed and heading. There, we'll receive a final update on their position from the shadowing courier on their position. We'll then make a second jump... to *here*."

For a moment there was silence in the briefing room, then shocked whispers raced around the room.

"Christ! They only asked the Light Brigade to go once!" someone at the back muttered audibly.

Beside Brian, O'Malley stirred.

"Silence on deck!" he snapped. "This is a briefing, not a discussion!"

Heads turned and faces showed surprise at finding the two senior officers behind them.

"Eyes front," Brian said calmly. "Squadron Commander, please continue your briefing."

"Yes ma'am. As I was saying, we will make a second jump. This should place us inside the outer screen of their fleet," Moscoe continued once silence had returned. "At this point, *Dauntless* will make a two-stage launch. First, all fighters will launch simultaneously. Our primary targets, will once again be fuel tankers. Large warships are your secondary targets.

"Sir, you said two stage launch. How can there be two stages if we all launch with the first one?" a pilot asked.

"If you had waited, Duggen, you would have found out without interrupting me. You'll probably all have noticed that the *Samuel Clemens* is currently along side us. At the moment we are loading mines into our empty hangars. Fifteen seconds after we clear the bays, the hatches on the remaining hangars will be blown. We will deploy a minefield directly across the path of the enemy fleet. It is expected that this will cause major disruption to the enemy's formation. So you see, this time round, everyone is going to get shot at..."

Out of the corner of her eye, Brian saw the ship's armoury officer wave to get her attention. She limped out of the briefing room. Behind her Moscoe was starting to go into the fine detail of the attack

"Well?" she asked.

"All mines are on board ma'am. Eight to each of the fighter hangars and ten to each of the shuttle hangars," he replied. "The hatches have been rigged with cutting charges. We put delay coils on the fuses to the main hinges, so they'll blow a split second after the connections at the bottom of the hatch. If it works each hatch will flip up and away rather than straight out and possibly in the way of the mines," he explained.

"Only seventy-six mines though? I thought we'd get in more than that."

"Physically ma'am, we could get twelve into each bay, but we're relying on the explosive decompression to throw them clear. We've run the pressure in the hangar up to twice normal but still, more mines means less air in there to push them out. Not to mention it would raise the chance of mines crashing into one another as they exit." The Lieutenant looked tired and more than a little scared, and not without good cause. They'd only found out when the *Samuel Clemens* arrived with the mines, that the weapons were a good fifteen years old, plus they'd spent much of that time going from extreme heat to extreme cold as they orbited around Alpha Centauri Three. Chemical explosives generally did not age well and often became... unpredictable. In a well-organised universe, all of the variables would have been simulated and tested well ahead of time, rather than worked out as they went along. They certainly wouldn't be trying to fit explosive bolts next to large piles of explosives of uncertain stability. There was more than a passing chance that they would arrive in front of the Nameless and blow themselves up before the aliens could react. In a moment of dark humour, Brian had found herself wondering whether the Nameless would be puzzled by a counter attack that apparently involved self-immolation.

"Ma'am? Admiral?"

"I'm sorry Lieutenant," Brian replied, realising she'd hadn't been listening. "Please carry on."

"Admiral, I was saying I still can't guarantee that none of those mines will hang up in the bays. If we get hit with a mine still on board..."

"If we get hit, the odds are we'll be blown away Lieutenant. If we are hit with a mine or mines aboard, the only difference is we'll be blown away that little bit faster. Either way, it will be a closed casket funeral for the lot of us."

"I just want you to know that I can't guarantee it will work right."

"Welcome to real combat Lieutenant," Brian replied with a sigh. "Guarantees never come attached. Anything else?"

"No ma'am."

"You're dismissed then."

The armourer's departure offered no respite though. The sound voices from the briefing room signalled that the meeting was apparently over. The ship's engineering officer emerged, looked around, spotted Brian and approached.

The armourer saluted the engineer as they passed, but the latter was so intent on Brian that he didn't notice the Lieutenant. His face was set into a frown.

The engineer opened his mouth but then paused as Brian held up a hand.

"Close the hatch commander," she ordered and waited impassively as the engineer obeyed.

"Alright, what is it?" she asked once he was facing her again.

"Ma'am, I've just heard the briefing and I must tell you that, with all respect, this idea is not going to work," the engineer burst out.

"Really? Please explain, Mister Varadkar."

"Ma'am, if we jump into the middle of their fleet, we won't have time to wait for the destroyers to spin their jump drives back up. We'll have to use *Dauntless's* drive to make our escape."

"That's correct," Brian agreed.

"Admiral, *Dauntless* hasn't jumped using her own drive in a *decade*," Varadkar exclaimed.

"But I know it has been maintained," she replied calmly.

"Maintained yes, but we haven't run current through it in years. Ma'am it's a first generation drive. You don't seem to understand it needs careful calibration before it can open a jump conduit. We can't do that under fire!"

"Two points Commander Varadkar, first I remind you I am nearly sixty years old. I served in the fleet when Gen One drives were all we had. No matter what the manuals say, those drives can be used under fire. Paul Lewis managed it with *Hood*..."

"He blew out most of her power grid!"

"Secondly," Brian continued, ignoring the interruption, "we are doing this regardless of usual considerations. As I said before, we are not here to be safe, we're here to kill aliens, and if it turns out to be a one-way trip then *so fucking be it!*" Brian shouted the last few words, causing the Commander to take an instinctive step back. "This is war Commander and the possibility of getting killed is par for the course. Now instead of complaining, get down to the drive room and make sure it *is* working. You are dismissed."

Varadkar saluted stiffly and began to walk away.

"Oh and Commander Varadkar," Brian called after him, then adding as he turned back, "if you step outside the chain of command again, I will cut you off at the knees."

The engineer stalked away, his shoulders stiff with fear and anger. Once he was out of sight, she let out a heartfelt sigh and leaned back against the bulkhead. It wasn't really Varadkar's fault. With the exception of the instructors, training ships weren't the first choice assignment of top flight officers, so invariably they didn't get them. Since she had first outlined her plan, damn near everyone one of *Dauntless's* senior officers had forwarded to her some sort of quiet or not so quiet reservation. Every one of them had raised valid points, but each time Brian heard those words of Admiral Lewis: *'I'm sorry Emily, but I have to consider both you and Dauntless expendable'* and dismissed their concerns.

Beside her the hatch opened again and O'Malley ducked through. He saw her and closed the hatch behind him.

"As ready as they're ever going to be," he replied to her unasked question. Of all her officers O'Malley was the only one who hadn't attempted to dissuade her from the attack. "They might be wet behind the ears Admiral, but they aren't stupid. They know what this is going to be like."

"I know Norman. Not that we have much choice, do we?"

"Not that I can see, ma'am."

O'Malley, in truth, wasn't that good an officer, which wasn't to say he was a bad one. It was just that his career had been undistinguished. So although he was only three years younger than her, he was several grades below her in rank and commanding a ship that had represented a career dead-end. But unlike his subordinates, he was a father and hoping to soon become a grandfather, a fact that may or may not have explained his willingness to seize upon Brian's plan and see it through. Whatever the reason was, without him running interference Brian doubted she could have forced through the scheme.

"Ma'am, do you think this will work?" There wasn't any fear or reluctance in the Captain's voice. It was simply one professional officer asking another.

"Depends on what you mean by works," Brian admitted. "If they have itchy trigger fingers, there is a good chance we'll be destroyed before the mines deploy. If we catch them by surprise we'll get the mines out, but the odds of us getting clear…" Brian shook her head for adding. "But you and I both know that isn't important."

O'Malley nodded soberly.

Just then several deep clunks echoed through the ship's hull.

"*Samuel Clemens* is casting off," Brian commented. "We're all set."

"Yes ma'am let's not keep them waiting."

04.10 hours Fleet Time

The beams supporting the deckhead of the Bridge keened and groaned. Every surface was vibrating madly, making most of the Bridge displays damn near unreadable. The entire ship was straining at the seams, trying to match the Home Fleet's punishing pace. Sitting in her command chair, only twenty minutes after undocking from the tug, Willis was seriously wondering whether her ship would even survive long enough to make it to the battle. The

Geriatrics were already one ship down. Unlike the rest of the squadron, the old raiding cruiser *Onslaught* had a heat sink big enough to allow interstellar passage unassisted. But the mad charge had proved too much for her clapped out machinery and after four of her six engines blew, she was forced to drop away astern. If she arrived at all, it would be hours after the rest of the Home Fleet.

Hood might have only been under her own power for twenty minutes, but already the temperature of the heat sink was crossing through the forty percent mark. In all her years in the service, Willis had never seen a temperature gauge go up so fast. If it hit saturation point, then they would have to cut power or watch the heat sink, and with it the rest of engineering, start to melt.

Behind her an alarm started to buzz urgently at the engineering repeater display.

Now what? Willis thought to herself as she twisted in her seat. The master engine alarm light was glowing.

Willis flicked on her intercom.

"Chief, what's going on back there?"

Across the intercom came the sound of a fire extinguisher being let off.

"Just a bit of an overheat problem in the grid Skipper. We're on top of it." Guinness's voice sounded totally calm.

Willis snapped her visor down, so that her bridge crew couldn't overhear her.

"Chief, we're still twenty-five minutes from re-entry. Can the engines take it?"

"They should do ma'am, but don't worry. If they do pack up I'll get out and push."

"It's slowing down to re-enter that concerns me, Chief. Over the last few days I've appreciated the faith you have in this ship, but right now I need you to be objective. We're soon going to be slamming from all ahead to all astern. Can she take it?"

"She'll hold Skipper. Trust me she'll hold."

Guinness clicked off the intercom. The Skipper had sounded shaken and he was glad none of his people had heard her. Captains were supposed to be god-like beings, beyond petty concerns such as their ship coming apart around them. But the Skipper hadn't got the 'feel' for *Hood*, didn't know her, didn't trust her, didn't like her. Still she had been quick enough to take offence at the C-in-C's flat dismissal of their combat value, that was a positive sign. But then she was a pretty prickly individual, if he was any judge, so that didn't prove much. He shrugged inwardly, nothing he could do about it for now. The engineering room ratings had managed to put out the junction box fire, but the stink of burnt plastic still filled the place.

"Check the other boxes," he instructed his deputy. "If they're starting to overheat, cut them out of the load until they cool down again."

Guinness looked back down the bay. The petty officers and ratings were all at their stations, watching the computer readouts and ready to head off the next crisis. A deep groan shuddered through the ship and several ratings looked up as if expecting to see the ship disintegrate around them. The nearest looked at Guinness. He looked very young and very frightened. Guinness gave him an encouraging smile.

"Don't worry lads. She can take it."

There was a sullen silence in the briefing room, most of them were too shell shocked by what they had just heard to talk. Rumours had gone round the pilots' mess about what was being planned, but the reality was far worse than anything any of them had imagined. At the front of the room Wing Commander Devane started rocking back and forth in his chair, muttering quietly to himself. After a few minutes the four members of the other two trainee crews, gathered together in a corner and started to talk quietly but intensely among themselves.

Alanna didn't join them and instead remained slumped in her chair. She felt drained of all energy and it was all she could do not to burst into tears. It was so unfair. They'd done their bit and lost all those people for *nothing*. She thought she'd survived and earned the right to go home and see her family again, but no. They were going to be sent in again, and this time right into the middle of the firestorm.

"So... now we know," muttered Dhoni as he sat down next to her.

Alanna wanted to snap at him but couldn't find the energy. They sat in silence.

"Serves me right really," he eventually commented, without looking round at her.

She looked at him.

"What do you mean?"

" Before I transferred to fighters, my last assignment was in the missile magazine of Titan. I would have gone into action behind nearly half a metre of composite armour."

"Why did you transfer anyway? You've never said."

"You've never asked Skipper," Dhoni replied. "I was tired of being cooped up inside armoured hulls. I wanted to be able to see what was happening and experience a bit of excitement. "

She gave him a wan smile.

"One of those 'be careful what you wish for' situations."

Alanna looked round at her navigator. They'd been flying together over a year, yet only now did she realise how little she actually knew about him.

"Yes, I believe you're right Skipper. I don't think the old lady is any happier about this than us, but that's the nature of the job. No point in moping."

There was another long silence.

"Is that your idea of cheering someone up?" Alanna asked. "Because if it is, you really suck at pep talks."

"It doesn't mean I'm wrong though," Dhoni replied unperturbed. "Besides, in your fighter, I think I'm in a good place to survive this."

"Thanks," she said.

Someone stopped in front of them. Alanna looked up and snapped to her feet.

"Flying Officer Shermer," Moscoe said, "you'll be flying as Wing Commander Devane's wingman."

Alanna glanced briefly towards Devane. He had stopped rocking, but was still muttering to himself.

Oh hell no. Alanna thought to herself, before her eyes snapped back to Devane. For a split second she saw a look of distaste in the Squadron Commander's eyes, directed towards Devane.

"Understood?"

Bugger that for a game of soldiers! She might have to go into action again, but she certainly wasn't going to lumber herself with someone who'd clearly gone off his head. As soon as the shooting started Devane was going to be on his own.

But what she said was:

"Yes, sir, understood."

"Good."

Moscoe slapped his hand on the briefing pedestal to get everyone's attention.

"Alright enough chitter-chatter, everyone to your fighters, good luck and give them hell."

04.27 hours Fleet Time

"The shadowing courier reports that the enemy is still on the anticipated vector and holding speed. All ship sections report as ready ma'am. The other courier has confirmed receipt of the message, to be forwarded to the *Warspite*," O'Malley said in a very formal voice.

Brian nodded as she checked her restraint harness and settled her survival suit's helmet into position.

"Thank you Captain O'Malley," she replied with equal formality, "you may start countdown for jump out. Coms, give me a laser link up to all ships, open intercom." Brian waited until the communications officer gave her the thumbs up.

"All hands, this is Vice Admiral Brian. In a few moments we will be jumping directly into the lions' den. Be assured however that this is not a display of futile defiance. The enemy thinks that we have shot our bolt. They think that their plan has all but succeeded. They think we will stand impotently by, unable to prevent them attacking our homes and families. They are about to find out that they are very much mistaken. I will not lie you. It is probable that many of us, possibly all of us, will die today. But, God willing, we will take hundreds of those bastards with us and stop them cold. Good luck, Brian out."

"Very stirring, ma'am," O'Malley said with a straight face. "Brought a tear to my eye."

"Mocking your commanding officer on the eve of battle?" Brian replied equally gravely. "Remind me to have you court-martialled when we get home."

"Jump out in ten seconds, nine, eight…"

"Yes of course ma'am. I'm sure when Hollywood turns your life into a film, they'll come up with something better."

Brian gave him a quick grin.

"On second thoughts let's not bother with a court martial. I'll just shove you out the airlock," she replied before turning to the ship's tactical officer. "Make sure we're on target before we drop the mines. We only have one shot." The officer nodded, his gloved finger in position above the button.

From the bows of the ship a whining noise started to gain volume as *Dauntless's* long unused jump drive started to slowly spin up. Not for this jump but for the jump that would hopefully get them out of the middle of an enemy fleet. Ahead there was a crackle of energy as the destroyer *Hammerhead* opened the jump conduit, astern *Piranha* braced it open.

"…three, two one. Jumping!" the navigator called out.

With a rippling flash the three ships disappeared from the face of the universe.

04.34 hours Fleet Time

Warspite trembled as her engines, now running full astern, attempted to force the ship below safe jump in speed. Every ship was doing the same and the arrowhead formation of the Home Fleet, was now decidedly ragged. This was predictable in a fleet where barely two ships had the same performance and there had been several heart stopping near misses. The *Hood* had damn near ploughed into the back of the heavy cruiser *Cerberus* when one of her engines suddenly blew out. On *Warspite's* flag bridge, Lewis had only been able to watch with horror when the *Hood's* engine failed and suddenly the rate at which the old cruiser was decelerating was a lot lower than the *Cerberus* directly ahead. *Hood* had plunged forwards like a lance. Blinded by her own engine emissions, *Cerberus* hadn't seen the disaster looming from astern. Fortunately *Hood's* skipper had their wits about them and managed to avoid collision by the thinnest of margins.

"Thirty seconds to jump in, Admiral," someone called out.

Lewis nodded without taking his eyes off the screen link to his subordinates.

"Gentlemen, I believe that this briefing is about to come to an end. Remember, hold your squadrons together. I don't want to see ships isolated and picked off piecemeal... and good luck."

Lewis closed the com link, folded away the screen and tightened the straps on his harness. He would have liked have been able to offer some suitably Nelsonian words to his crews, but that wasn't the kind of person he was. Sometimes it was better to simply accept one's personal limitations.

"Re-entry in five, four, three, two, one. Brace, Brace, Brace!"

On the *Hood's* Bridge, Willis's heart was still hammering madly. She wasn't sure exactly how close they had got to *Cerberus*. The collision detection system was only sensitive to about thirty meters, but it had sure as hell been too close. The remaining three engines were now making some distinctly expensive noises and the entire engineering display was lit up like a Christmas tree. She'd stopped getting engineering reports shortly after the engine failed. Guinness was clearly running from one crisis to another and only just keeping up. Plus, the heat sink was only a few minutes from saturation.

"Skipper! Signal from flag. Thirty seconds to jump in."

Willis had to work hard to keep the relief from showing on her face.

"Okay everyone. We've done the really dangerous bit by actually getting here." It was a weak pun but nonetheless it raised a few relieved laughs, both on the Bridge and across the intercom from the senior officers spread across the ship.

"Fire Control, be ready to start shooting but keep the guns shut down until we need them. We have to shed some heat, but you're going to have to make choices fast, so don't wait for my orders. And for the love of God though, watch for friendly fire. Last thing, save our missiles for their big cap ship missiles. Point defence is little bloody use against those things. Long Lance missiles are our best hope."

"Jumping in five."

"All hands brace for jump in, this is where it gets fun!"

Warspite lurched violently into real-space. Immediately the battleship's radar and passive sensors started to sweep the surrounding space. Seconds crawled by as they waited for the light speed returns to reach them. Had they made contact or had they left Earth exposed to destruction?

"Contact! We have multiple contacts! Bearing three, five, three, dash, zero, two, one. Range one hundred thousand kilometres, checking profiles... Bridge, confirmed enemy in sight!" shouted out a sensor rating. "Sir we have them!"

Admiral Lewis gave no outward show of emotion, but inside he felt relief rise off him like steam. The mad charge through jump space with the prospect of finding nothing but an empty solar system had been a waking nightmare. But now they were in contact and even more important, in range. The greatest gamble of his life had paid off. Now they just had to hurt the Nameless, before they made a dive for jump space. On the *Warspite's* Flag Bridge reports continued to flow in.

"Enemy's bringing radio and targeting jammers on line. They're also blanketing the FTL bands, they must have a transmitter on every damn ship," Sheehan reported. "Oh…" Sheehan paused and looked up from his console towards Lewis. "Admiral, one of squadron eighteen didn't survive jump in."

"Do we still have laser hook up?" Lewis replied ignoring that fact that they'd suffered their first loss. It certainly wouldn't be the last but he couldn't afford to think about it.

"Yes, sir, all ships are on grid."

"There's something else, a courier ship, one of ours. It's on the far side of the alien fleet. We got its friend or foe code. It tried to send us a transmission, but the jamming blotted it out."

"Probably doesn't matter," Lewis grunted.

"All ships now report ready for action, sir," Sheehan said

"Coms make signal to all ships, 'you may engage at your discretion.' Captain Holfe, work your ship."

"Yes, sir," the captain replied.

Even as he spoke the great battleship rolled and turned slightly, while the four forward turrets and the secondary mounts smoothly swung to bear. Then the *Warspite* vented her fury in a single rippling salvo.

The target was an escort ship, part of their outer screen. When the Battle Fleet ships arrived, it desperately tried to retire back towards their main fleet. But the Home Fleet's arrival had been too sudden, too close. She was only starting to make her turn as the leading elements of Warspite's broadside arrived. The Nameless jamming had been partly effective. *Warspite's* fire control couldn't confirm exactly where the alien was, but it could know roughly and spread the salvo to cover all the places the target might be by the time the plasma bolts arrived. Of the eight bolts fired, two struck home. Designed to defeat heavy armour, they carved effortlessly through the small vessel, severing power lines, cutting control runs and wrecking equipment. The ship staggered sideways as fuel and atmosphere gushed from its wounds. But the carnage had barely started. The jammers that had offered some measure of protection died as the plasma bolts tore through. Following hard on the heels of the plasma cannon salvo, a pair of Slammer anti-ship missiles locked on. The wounded ship tried frantically to defend itself, succeeding in blasting one aside, but the second smashed home, reducing its target to little more than a hulk. Finally, nearly seventy-three seconds after the missiles, a single twenty-eight centimetre railgun round arrived and reduced the hulk to very small pieces.

No other Home Fleet ship could match *Warspite's* firepower, but they claimed several other escorts before the rest of Nameless perimeter force fled before the thundering juggernaut.

"Admiral. The enemy is transmitting in FTL on band D."

"Understood Coms. Sensors, any sign of them charging their jump drives?" Lewis responded.

"Negative, sir, we're not seeing anything resembling a power build up," replied the lieutenant at the sensor repeater display.

"Good."

On the tactical holo all the individual signals for every ship in the Nameless fleet shifted, as they turned to face. Then a mass of new radar signals emerged as, hundreds of missiles bore down on the Home Fleet.

"Here comes the whirlwind," someone muttered.

As he watched the rain of missiles plunge towards them, Lewis felt the old mad urge to jump out of his seat and flee aft as if he could outrun the death coming towards him. To his left someone started counting down the seconds until the missiles arrived.

"Lieutenant Preston, would you kindly *shut up*!" Lewis snapped at him without taking his eyes off the display. "Coms, order all railguns to switch to canister."

Within seconds, all ships so armed, were firing projectiles that once clear of the gun barrel split open and unleashed thousands of ball bearings. A wall of steel formed between the approaching missiles. Dozens, then scores of missiles were shattered as they were struck by projectiles travelling at many times the speed of sound, but dozens more found ways through. Point defence guns started to blaze away at the missiles, shooting down many more small ones, but the big resistant Nameless cap ship missiles could soak up repeated hits before succumbing. The handful of fighters present, used their small anti-fighter missiles to further thin the incoming, but still the missiles closed, the salvo massively reduced but still formidable. The fire from the railguns was slackening now as individual ships kept one up the spout to fire at any missiles that might make a terminal approach. Chaff rockets were fired by every ship, laying down glittering curtains of foil. The tight formation didn't allow much room for evasive manoeuvres but each ship started to make small course corrections, anything to make the missiles' firing task more complicated.

Finally they arrived.

———————————————

On board the *Hood*, the re-entry had been brutal and right at the borderline of what the old ship's structure could take. In her command chair, Willis wondered whether she'd received whiplash, but even as the thought crossed her mind she was bellowing orders.

"All fighters launch! Clear the bays!"

"Thirty seconds," Horan shouted back. He glanced left out of the Bridge view port, then did a double take. "Oh God! Skipper. Look at *Tempest*!"

Only a kilometre off *Hood's* port quarter, *Tempest* hadn't exited into real-space exactly parallel to the vector of the jump conduit, but had instead come out slightly side on. For a newer ship, it would have been merely a matter of embarrassment on the command deck, but decades of exposure to solar radiation had weakened her hull and the sheering forces were too much. The cruiser snapped clean in half between the turrets and the Bridge structure. From the Bridge of *Hood*, the flash of escaping atmosphere was clearly visible. The engines fired wildly out of control, before a pillar of fire erupted from the engineering section as the reactor scrammed. Then *Tempest* was nothing more than a hulk.

"Captain..." Horan began.

"We can't," Willis shook her head. "We can't stop. We haven't got shuttles. We might be able to go back for survivors afterwards. Concentrate on launching the fighters."

Horan didn't object. He just nodded.

Willis's fingers drummed on her armrest as on either side of the hull Raven fighters were pushed clear of the four hangars with stately slowness. Finally in the fully deployed position, the four fighters blasted clear and away towards the flagship, leaving the Geriatrics far behind. Willis relaxed very slightly. There was now one less thing that could kill them. Positioned at the back of the fleet *Hood's* own radar couldn't see anything, but the data feed from the leading ships showed the Nameless fleet in all its terrible glory.

Willis felt her throat tighten as the Nameless fired.

"Captain, shall we fire?" The gunner asked nervously over the intercom

It took a moment before she could speak.

"No, hold fire. Let's wait until we have something close enough to hit. Select a target and start running a targeting plot."

There was silence on the Bridge as the missiles bore down. With her guns masked, *Hood* was merely an observer to this first exchange of fire. They were close enough to see the flashes as the forward ships opened up. It was hard to sit there but there was simply no point in firing just for the sake of it. No point in wasting the ammunition.

Thus impotent, *Hood* had a grandstand view as the missiles arrived and the dying began.

The *Warspite* lurched violently sideways as a missile slammed in. The two starboard side shuttle bays were flattened like tinfoil and bits of hull plating spiralled away. For the most part however, the ship's armour absorbed or redirected the force of the blow away from it vitals. But no other human ship had an armour scheme as massive as *Warspite's*.

The destroyer *Dragoon* staggered out of line, shattered as a missile blew away everything forward of the Bridge. Only one escape pod got clear before another missile streaked in and reduced her to atoms. The crew of *Cuckoo* was luckier with nearly half getting out before she was gutted. The heavy cruiser *Anubis* gushed atmosphere as her portside railgun sponson was ripped clean off. The cruiser *Nile* lurched out of formation as her bridge was wiped away, and her fourth lieutenant abruptly found herself in command. One cap ship missile, its guidance system perhaps damaged or confused by the mass of interference, missed the leading elements of the fleet and plunged down through the formation, still seeking a target.

"We're being pinged!" the senior sensor operator shouted.

Willis let out her breath in a hiss as the display revealed a red blip with brackets bearing down on the Geriatrics.

"Bringing guns on line!" called out the gunner.

"Negative! Negative! We cannot fire up through the fleet!" Willis shouted back. "Point defence only, commence! Commence! Commence! Countermeasures full spread on my mark!"

Willis caught the petty officer at the countermeasures board casting desperate looks at her, as his hand hovered over the launch key. They couldn't afford to launch too soon though.

"Steady people! Steady!" Willis ordered almost impressed how even her voice sounded.

Off to starboard, their fellow Geriatric *Whirlwind* let off her chaff rockets, concealing herself behind a glittering curtain of foil. *Too soon!* A little voice in her head said. The missile was now close enough to see on the visual display. Hits from the point defence guns were striking sparks off the missile casing, but not biting deep. On the Bridge tactical display, the green blip at the centre started to blink urgently as the system registered that the missile was now locked onto *Hood*.

"Countermeasures, now!"

Four rockets blasted out of their launchers and exploded thirteen kilometres in front of Hood's bow. The missile hesitated as its chosen prey was blotted out. To their portside, *Hurricane* fired her rockets, depriving the missile of that option. But now *Whirlwind's* chaff screen had dispersed leaving the little cruiser denuded. The missile turned away from *Hood* and roared in. Desperately *Whirlwind* fired off another volley of chaff rockets but it was too late. The missile burned past the rockets before they burst and hammered squarely into the cruiser. There was a flash, then a second much larger, eye-watering flash as *Whirlwind's* reactor breached.

When the vacuum of space snuffed out the fury of nuclear fire there was nothing left.

"Sensors?" Willis asked quietly. It was more like a plea than an order.

The petty officer at sensors shook his head.

"Negative escape pods. No one got out, skipper."

"*Oh God! Oh God...*" someone muttered in the background.

Back in the engine room, Guinness instinctively glanced towards the forward bulkhead. The blank steel wall told him nothing. The old adage that 'the waiting is the worst part' didn't apply to engineer crews. The worst was not knowing. On starships there wasn't any boom of gunfire or concussion from near misses, only the hum of the reactor and generators. Oh he knew that *Hood* was firing because the guns were now drawing power but other than that, nothing. Some skippers he'd served under had given a running commentary when they got a chance, but it would seem Commander Willis wasn't one of those. Which, given that this was her first time out on her own, wasn't such a bad idea. Still it would have been good to know how they were doing.

He looked back down at his people and felt a swell of pride. They might be a scratch crew thrown together but they were performing magnificently.

"We're giving them what for lads!" he shouted down the bay, adding *I hope* in the privacy of his own head.

Lewis grimly read through the damage reports. Ten minutes into the action and already the damage was appalling. Big as the Nameless cap ship missiles were, they were still bloody small targets for the plasma cannons and railguns. The status indicators of several ships were showing serious damage. In particular the *Nile* was now outside the main control grid and struggling to keep up. If only he'd been able to put squadron eighteen out in front to absorb the first salvo. It would have been pure murder for the crews, but it might have left the rest of the fleet in better condition. At a hundred thousand kilometres, the Nameless were right at the edge of the effective range of his cruisers' guns and beyond the destroyers'. They'd come out close to the Nameless, but not quite close enough. Any moment now, the aliens would come about and start to move away from them. *Warspite* and the other modern ships would have the acceleration to close range in a stern chase, but the older vessels and the damaged ships would struggle. Within the next few minutes he would have to choose between keeping his fleet together and failing to close, or pursue at best speed and see the Home Fleet string out, leaving individual ships vulnerable.

"Sensors, Command!" rang out across the command frequency, "Profile change, they're turning."

"Coms, prepare to order the fleet to pursue," Lewis called out.

"Hang on, sir," Sheehan said, "sir, they're turning *towards us*!"

"What the hell?" Lewis said out loud. "Sensors, confirm the enemy is closing."

"Confirmed command, range is dropping. Their formation is opening up, but all combat vessels are closing on us. We're seeing two large contacts moving away, we're assuming they are the tankers."

Lewis shook his head in open puzzlement; why in hell's name would the Nameless close on them? Range was their big advantage and yet they seemed to be intent on throwing it away. With every kilometre they closed, the killing potential of the Home Fleet increased. Lewis tried to get into the mind of his opposite number. What the hell was the alien thinking? Had seeing scores of missiles fall short of their target convinced him that he needed to be close? Or did he believe that their first salvo had been so devastating that the Home Fleet was already severely mauled. Certainly the humans' combat capability was reduced, but the casualties had mostly been suffered by smaller and older ships. Most of Lewis's command was still very much combat worthy.

Even as Lewis considered these points, *Warspite's* guns were stabbing out and an alien cruiser died beneath the battleship's guns. It didn't make sense, he couldn't believe they were that stupid. There had to be something he was missing.

"Sensors, are we picking up anything other than ourselves and the enemy?

"Command, the only other thing we have is that courier on the other side of their fleet."

"It's still there?" He asked with some surprise. What the hell was a courier still doing running around in a combat zone?

"Yes, sir."

"Can we put a laser onto it?"

"No, sir. Too much traffic between us."

"Any sign of *Dauntless* herself?"

"Negative to that, sir."

Lewis nodded. Alright, he thought to himself, the courier had probably been sent to act as beacon if necessary. They were sticking around through a misplaced sense of duty or lack of wit. There was no sign of *Dauntless* but hopefully Emily had survived and had the good sense to head for cover. The Nameless had broken into four uneven groups. The largest was moving across the Home Fleet's bows, the second and third groups were going high and low, the fourth looked like it was working its way round the back. Within the next twenty minutes, the Home Fleet was going to be surrounded. Not good but not automatically fatal. The bulk of the Nameless ships seemed to be committing themselves to forming a conventional battle line though. This was a gift horse he'd looked in the mouth long enough.

"Captain Sheehan, I want Cruiser Squadron Seventeen to form top cover, Squadron Seven to take bottom, Third and Fourteenth form up around *Warspite* and *Fortitude*. What's left of Eighteen will cover the rear. Destroyers take up screening positions. Once we've reformed, we will turn in succession at these co-ordinates. If they want to trade punches, I'm more than willing to oblige them."

———————————

Hood's guns fell silent as the leading elements of the fleet crossed through her firing lane. As rearguard elements, the surviving Geriatrics would be the last ships to make the turn. In her command chair, Willis was gritting her teeth. The gunner was doing his best, but with the range to the closest Nameless still fifty thousand, Willis doubted that *Hood* had hit anything yet. There was no point in shouting at the gunner as he could only work within the limitations of his equipment and there was certainly no point distracting him with worthless instructions. That just left her to worry and there was plenty to worry about. Once the turn was complete, *Hood* and *Hurricane* would be playing tail end Charlie. With the turn complete, a dozen or so Nameless ships would be behind them. With no gun bearing aft, plus the difficulty of seeing through their own engine inference, the Geriatrics would have to zigzag across the rear of the rest of the Fleet. She'd run the numbers quickly on her own console. The shallowest zigzag they could run and cover their own rear would increase the distance they had to travel by at least a third compared to if they ran straight. The problem was holding a steady course. *Hood* could just about pull enough acceleration to keep up with the fleet, but if they were required to start steering back and forth across the Home Fleet's wake, that ability to maintain contact would start to become more than a little suspect.

Willis flicked on her intercom.

"Chief, I need an update on the engines. Any progress on getting Number Two engine back on line?"

There was a pause on the line then Guinness replied.

"Number Two is a no go. I'm sorry Skipper but it's a dockyard job. We've isolated it from the rest of the grid so we don't get plasma bleed, but that's as much as we can do. The rest of the engines are holding up all right at the moment Skipper, but I recommend easing off a bit."

"Where do we stand on increasing power?"

She heard a sharp drawing of breath at the other end of the line.

"Skipper, we've already redlined the engines for over half-an-hour. We're just about keeping ahead of the breakdowns at the moment, but if we don't throttle back..."

"If we throttle back Chief, we'll fall behind the rest of the fleet and I don't think the flagship is going to wait for us."

There was another long silence.

"I'll do what I can, Skipper. Engine Room out."

As the connection closed they started to make their turn. *Hood's* bows swung around and the guns once again went into action.

For forty minutes the two fleets had burned through space, tearing at one another. The crew on *Warspite's* Flag Bridge remained as professional as ever, but there was an atmosphere, one of jubilation. Even the greenest rating could see that the Home Fleet was giving a lot better than it was getting. They'd lost ships certainly, but over twenty Nameless warships were now wreckage drifting astern.

At odds with the atmosphere on his bridge Lewis studied his tactical display, his face locked in an intense frown. There was no doubting the battle was going well, so well in fact Lewis could feel his hackles rising. *Warspite* alone had destroyed or severely damaged ten plus enemy ships. The rest of the Home Fleet was dealing out equally horrific punishment. But why were the Nameless standing and taking it?

In the clash against *Mississippi* the Nameless had fired from outside radar range and only closed after it appeared the human ship was destroyed. But here, they had accepted action inside plasma cannon range from the outset, a range bracket in which they were at a clear disadvantage against the heavily armoured human ships.

Why? Any halfway competent Admiral, facing combat at such a disadvantage would cut his losses and attempt to break off. He would only stand and fight if the loss in ships could be justified by something else. But nothing Lewis could see looked like a reason for the Nameless to stand. They were killing a Nameless ship every few minutes, yet his instincts were screaming that something was wrong. What was it that he didn't know?

The only possible clue was the courier ship. Shadowing the Nameless when they arrived, the little ship was still visible on *Warspite's* radar. It had been fired upon several times, forcing it to jump away, usually from one side of the battle zone to the other. But each time it started to sidle back in. Even military courier skippers were a cautious lot. With ships no sturdier than eggshells, they had good reason to be. But this one had remained. Why? It was unarmed, unarmoured and could not assist the fleet. So why had it remained? The more Lewis watched the more he saw a pattern. Whenever it started to get close, Nameless ships would disengage from the battle and run it off. Very strange. What the hell did that courier know that it was so desperate to pass on and the Nameless, were equally desperate for him not to know?

"Tim, have we had any luck putting a coms laser onto that courier yet?" he asked knowing what the likely answer would be.

"No, sir," Sheehan replied. "We've tried and they've tried. There's so much rubbish floating around us all, we can't get a solid lock. All we've got has been corrupted to hell."

"Send general signal all ships, ordering them to laser that courier if they can. Pass on anything they get to Flag."

———————————————

"I'm making it four cap ship missiles, two pairs, plus light missiles out in front. I think they're trying to confuse our radar by getting them so close together the contacts merge."

"Understood, sensors. Time to effective range?" Willis called back. After three quarters of an hour of action her voice was becoming hoarse. She was desperate for a drink but the action had been so intense, that she'd barely had time to blink let alone anything else.

"Twenty seconds, skipper. *Hurricane* is firing ma'am," sensors replied.

"Signal from *Hurricane*, they'll take the ones on the right" called out the signals man.

"Roger! Guns target the ones on the left. Countermeasures stand by," Willis ordered.

"Roger!" the Gunner confirmed.

"Skipper, signal from Flag. If possible we're to make laser hook up with courier at the edge of the combat zone and forward to Flag," the Coms Officer shouted across the Bridge.

"Jesus, we have better things to be doing!" Willis snapped. "Signal confirmed. Keep an eye on it but first priority to the tactical coms net."

Willis looked back at the display holo with a worried frown. As she had feared, the two remaining members of the Geriatrics were falling behind the rest of the fleet. Keeping up meant pushing the engines and the old machinery just couldn't take it. Every few minutes one of the engines broke down, *Hood's* acceleration dropped and they lost another few thousand kilometres on the rest of the fleet. Each time Guinness managed to bandage the machinery back into operation, but Willis didn't need to ask him to know he could not keep that up indefinitely. When the engines started to fail, she had reported to the flagship that they couldn't continue to match the fleet's acceleration. To her profound lack of surprise the pace hadn't slackened. *Hurricane* was also struggling and the best the two stragglers could do was stick together for mutual protection.

"Missiles crossing into range."

"Designator locked on."

"Fire."

The calls came across the Bridge from different locations as they went through the firing procedure. It had been ragged at the start of the action as *Hood's* hotchpotch crew learned on the job, but now it was as smooth as silk. Willis tried to find comfort in that, but instead worried that it would all fall apart if they took a hit and people suddenly had to think rather than react.

A Long Lance missile blasted out of *Hood's* portside launcher. Her idea of using their missiles to knock down the Nameless's big cap ship missiles had worked surprisingly well. She hadn't realised just how it would strain her nerves through. Coming in from nearly directly astern, the overtake speed of the missiles was slow. But *Hoods'* radar problems meant they still had to nail a missile the first time. They wouldn't get a second shot. The Long Lance missiles *Hood* carried relied on a laser being kept focused on the target. To do that the *Hood* had to fly straight and level. And when an enemy missile was bearing down on you and your every instinct was screaming for evasive action that was easier said than done.

Two missiles blew as both *Hood* and *Hurricane* claimed a kill. A wave of small missiles was mostly destroyed by point defence, while the ones that got through failed to inflict significant damage. As one the two ships rolled to present their starboard launchers. After an agonising pause the designators locked on and both ships fired again.

On her holo display, Willis watched as the two pairs of blips converged. The pair on the left came together, then blinked out. The second pair merged… then separated again.

"Oh *shit!* Hurricane's missed! Countermeasures full spread. Bows down twenty degrees. Engines, all ahead emergency!" Willis snapped out.

The missile curved in as the two cruisers started to weave and swerve. Plasma bolts burned around it, but even at short range, the cruiser's elderly fire control systems couldn't cope with such a small target.

"It's going for *Hurricane*," Willis muttered to herself.

No one on the Bridge responded. There was nothing to say.

They obviously realised the same thing on the *Hurricane's* bridge and the cruiser started to throw itself about in increasingly violent manoeuvres. The missile went full burn for its final approach and *Hurricane* lurched downwards, in a last desperate attempt to dodge.

It nearly succeeded.

The missile contacted the dorsal wing and detonated, *Hurricane* was enveloped by a sphere of fire. Willis felt her blood freeze as the ship disappeared then the fire burnt out and *Hurricane* staggered back into view.

The damage was horrific. Almost all the upper surface fitting were blown away or flattened, one engine had been ripped almost clean off its mounting. Debris cascaded away from the shattered cruiser like metal confetti as atmosphere gushed from multiple hull breaches.

"Give me a com link up to Commander Espey, *right now*!" she screamed at her communications officer. She could hear an edge hysteria in her voice, yet didn't care. It only took a minute or so to get the link up, but it felt like a lot longer. Since the start of the battle she hadn't had a chance to communicate directly with Vincent. Now as she looked at what was left of *Hurricane*, she wondered whether she had already spoken to her friend for the last time.

Espey's face appeared on the small screen in her chair's armrest beside her. He appeared at an odd angle on the screen and the visor on his survival suit was closed. He was pale and there were spots of blood on the inside of his visor, but otherwise he seemed unhurt. Static blotted him out for a moment before the image stabilised. The Bridge that was visible behind him was a wreck, a motionless body rested against the rear bulkhead.

"Oh thank God. Vince, how bad?" she hadn't realised she'd been holding her breath and the words came out in an explosive burst.

Espey shook his head.

"I think the power of prayer is the only thing holding this old girl together. The hull's severely damaged and only two engines are still working. I think everyone in fire control is dead, which is a moot point as we don't have a working gun left. I don't know how many of my people are still alive," he said flatly. He shook his head again and added more quietly. "I think we're going to be walking home Faithie. I can feel her dying under me."

"We'll take you off..."

"Not in the middle of a firefight you won't. Make a break for the fleet, we've had it."

This time it was Willis's turn to shake her head.

"No, I won't do that. Tuck in I'll cover you as best I can."

"Faith this isn't the time..."

"I won't catch the rest of the fleet," Willis cut him off. "Tuck in. That's an order."

"We're the same rank Faith."

"I've seniority by ten days... and the less banjaxed ship. Just hold her together Vince, we'll get you home."

The courier was getting ever more determined, or perhaps desperate, to reach them. It kept pushing forward. It nearly pushed too hard. One of the Nameless ships got tricky, cut its drive and coasted towards the courier on a ballistic run, before suddenly powering up its systems and opening fire. For a horrible moment Lewis thought the courier had been destroyed. After a minute *Warspite's* computer dispassionately stated that it had jumped out. Twelve minutes later it appeared once again at the edge of radar range and started to move in.

Lewis had read enough history to know that many military leaders of the past had lost battles by becoming obsessed with some small and unimportant aspect of the conflict. There were scores of Nameless ships still around them, space was still thick with their missiles and almost all of his surviving ships were carrying damage to a greater or lesser extent. But the courier didn't *feel* unimportant. Far from it in fact, it felt like something vital.

"How many fighters do we have still out there?" he asked without looking around.

"There're none left, sir," Staff Captain Sheehan replied immediately.

Lewis's eyes fell upon the two small blips of Cruiser Squadron Eighteen, the Geriatrics. The two ships were far astern of the fleet, but also the closest to the courier. They might be able to get close enough to put a com laser on it, yet still be able to laser the rest of the fleet. It would however unquestionably be a suicide mission. Lewis opened his mouth to give the order that would send them to their doom. The courier blinked out.

The courier burst back into real-space right in the middle of the Home Fleet! Two cruisers had to make violent turns to avoid running it down. Seconds stretched out as the courier turned towards *Warspite*. A cap ship missile changed course towards the little ship. A communication laser speared out at *Warspite*. The courier must have seen the missile, barely smaller than itself, burning in. But it held a steady course, it couldn't deliver its message and dodge at the same time. It opted to take the hit.

"We've been lasered," Sheehan called out.

The missile went into the courier. The little ship folded around it then disappeared as its reactor detonated.

"Did we get their signal?" Lewis shouted. Men and women had died to deliver the message. There couldn't be greater proof that something was terribly wrong.

"Going to your screen, sir!"

Lewis yanked his screen into position. The message scrolled down.

"Oh dear God," He murmured.

"Sir! The enemy is changing course!"

Lewis glanced up. Like a flight of starlings the Nameless ships suddenly turned and came curving in towards the Home Fleet. Every one of them burning towards the human ships at maximum acceleration.

On Lewis's screen, momentarily forgotten, lay the message.

++ Message Start. From Vice Admiral Emily Brian – Dauntless to C-in-C Home Fleet – Warspite. Have encountered second, repeat second enemy fleet at ten point two from hub, bearing zero, three, nine, dash zero, zero two. Estimate enemy strength two hundred plus, I am moving to engage. Message End ++

Chapter Fourteen

Wing and a Prayer

The Nameless Fleet glided serenely through the unimaginable vastness of space. Lean and deadly warships queued patiently for the attention of lumbering fuel tankers. Around the massive and terrible fleet the stars shone indifferently. Then far ahead, a new pinprick of light appeared and just as quickly disappeared. More flashes followed, some points of light, others rippling pulses. The Nameless ships did not react. All was going to plan.

On his bridge, Lewis sat in his command chair, locked in uncharacteristic indecision. At his elbow, the screen still showed the short but terrible message.
… From Vice Admiral Emily Brian – Dauntless to C-in-C Home Fleet – Warspite. Have encountered second, repeat second enemy fleet at ten point two from hub, bearing zero, three, nine, dash, zero, zero, two. Estimate enemy strength two hundred plus, I am moving to engage.…
They were fighting a decoy, a bloody decoy! The main fleet was elsewhere in the system refuelling unmolested while they fought a decoy. As he sat there almost paralysed by shock, Lewis knew he needed to be giving orders, sending signals, *reacting!* But his mind was stalled, unable to comprehend the information it was being presented with. Instead a single thought jammed in his mind like a stuck record. They were fighting a decoy!
Dimly he heard Staff Captain Sheehan shouting as if from very far away.

"Sir, your orders!... Admiral, we need orders!"

Behind Sheehan, on the tactical display the Nameless fleet burned in and Lewis's personal reality suddenly snapped back together.

"We have to break contact! Signal all ships of the fleet to prepare to jump out to the second fleet," Lewis snapped out.

"Roger! Transmitting."

The Home Fleet's fire began to slacken as its ships channelled power to their jump drives. The range between the two fleets was dropping rapidly as the Nameless charged. Their missiles were still coming thick and fast but now the defensive fire was heavily diminished, more and more missiles were finding their mark.

"Admiral, *Cerberus* reports her jump drive as been knocked out," Sheehan reported as *Warspite* was rocked by missile hits.

"Pair her up with someone who still has a drive," Lewis called back. He paused as another missile hammered into *Warspite* and the ship rocked wildly. "Order the destroyers to lay down chaff to screen the main fleet."

"Bridge to Flag," Captain Holfe's voice crackled across the intercom.

"What is it Captain?" Lewis replied instantly.

"Sir. The enemy's firing pattern has shifted. They're targeting our bows. Sir, they're going for our nodes!"

"How many have we lost?"

"Three already and we're still ten minutes from jump out."

"God damn it."

The nodes were part of the jump drive that channelled the massive energy necessary to open a jump conduit. Inherently delicate components, they spent most of the time protected behind a ship's heaviest armour. But to be used they had to jacked out from behind that protection and heated up to operating temperature. A process that would take at least fifteen minutes.

On *Warspite's* tactical display, the status codes for the cruisers *Isis* and *Vali* changed as they took node damage. In doing so they joined the four ships that had already lost their jump capability. Lewis didn't need anyone to tell him that the Home Fleet was being steadily stripped of the ability to enter jump space. Few if any ships would be jump capable if they kept their nodes out.

"General signal. Cancel jump command." Lewis turned towards Sheehan. "We're pinned," he admitted. They'd blown it. At short range the Home Fleet would beat the hell out of this Nameless Force. But the time that took, would allow their second fleet to move unmolested into position to strike against Earth. *I am moving to engage.* Emily had never lacked backbone, but to pit a single overage carrier and a pair of destroyers against an entire fleet, was an act of madness.

But what else could they do? They, no, he, had blown it.

On *Hood's* Bridge, Willis cursed beneath her breath as the Nameless ships charged in from all angles. Even the handful of enemy ships astern, which had so far been content to snipe at them, were now going full burn and overhauling them fast.

"The rest of the fleet is decelerating ma'am," reported her senior sensor operator.

"That's something at least," she muttered.

"Bridge, Coms. We caught the edge of a laser transmission, skipper."

"What was it?"

"I only caught a bit of it, something about jumping out."

Willis and Horan exchanged a look of alarm. *Hood* had needed the assistance of a tug to get to Alpha Centauri. That tug had dropped back into real-space short of the battle zone and was now waiting somewhere beyond the limits of the solar system. Under her own power, jumps within the solar system were as much as *Hood* could manage. Willis doubted that *Hurricane* would be able to get into *Hood's* jump conduit and even if she did, the gravitational turbulence would probably shake her apart.

"Sensors! Any sign that the fleet is jumping out?"

"Err... no ma'am I thought I saw one of the ship deploy its nodes but they seem to have been retracted."

Willis let out a small sigh of relief.

"Okay it must have been just garbled communications," she said.

"Or wishful thinking by someone," Horan added.

Willis didn't reply to him though, her attention had shifted back to the main holo. The formation of the Home Fleet was tightening up. By eye she measured the distance between the remains of the Geriatrics and the rest of the fleet. Much as she willed it, it remained very wide, far too wide. Even if they'd been on their own, there was no way, given the state of Hood's clapped out engines, that they could close on the fleet before being overrun. Of course they weren't on their own. The mortally wounded *Hurricane* was still tucked in under *Hood's* starboard wing. Vincent had made clear that his ship was dying on her feet. If *Hood* stood and fought it would probably make little difference to *Hurricane's* ultimate fate, except that *Hood* would share it. As a professional officer, Willis forced herself to consider the possibility of breaking for the fleet and leaving a friend behind.

And rejected it.

Hurricane was so beat up she wouldn't even serve as a speed bump. The Nameless would simply mow her down as they passed and then proceed to overhaul the *Hood*.

"Helm prepare rotate one-eighty and go all astern on engines. Communications inform *Hurricane* of my intentions."

"Ready ma'am," the helmsman called back.

"Execute."

The steady pull of acceleration disappeared as the engines cut out. Then the wingtip motors fired and the ship swung round. The gunner didn't wait for the order from Willis. As soon as his weapons came to bear he cut loose at the approaching targets. *Hurricane* didn't attempt to match Willis's manoeuvre, instead she swung in directly behind *Hood*. To protect her comrades stern with her own battered hull. Thus, back-to-back, the two cruisers braced themselves.

———————————

The walls of the jump conduit sparkled around the *Dauntless* and her escort, as the three ships rushed down it. On the carrier's bridge, Brian found herself dry washing her hands. She glanced around the Bridge almost guiltily, but no one had noticed their commander's temporary lapse. For such a short jump, little more than nine million kilometres, they would only be in the conduit for a few seconds. Then things would get exciting.

"Five seconds to real-space re-entry," the navigator called out.

"All hands brace for jump in," O'Malley called out across the intercom.

Brian clicked her helmet into position but left the visor open. She glanced towards the young lieutenant at the launch console. His gloved finger now rested lightly on the button that would unleash their cargo.

"Not before I give the word Mister Kelly," she warned him. "We don't want to drop our mines in the middle of some inoffensive bit of space."

The Lieutenant nodded tersely, his finger raised a millimetre above the button.

The navigation console buzzed urgently as the countdown reached zero.

"This is it! Brace! Brace! Brace!" O'Malley called out.

Dauntless lurched violently as she burst back into real-space.

The tactical holo blanked out as it waited for the first radar returns. Brian's hands tighten around the armrests of her chair, as she prayed to God that the first returns wouldn't show a missile bearing down on them.

"Contact... No! Multiple contacts!" Everyone on the Bridge jumped as a rating shouted out. "IFF confirms enemy ships!"

"Launch control, run out and launch all fighters," O'Malley snapped out. "Tactical, bring ECM on line, point defence to standby."

On the main tactical holo, red icons started to appear all around the blips at the centre of the display. Surrounded by red, the three green icons of the human ships seemed lost and alone.

Brian found the sight was almost mesmerising, so many enemy ships so close. When you were used to fighting across astronomical units, the idea of the enemy being mere thousands or even hundreds of kilometres away was startling. Then abruptly the spell was broken.

At the front of the Bridge the helmsman muttered,
"Oh sweet Jesus!" Before screaming: "contact *dead ahead*!"

C for Caesar was the first of *Dauntless's* fighters to slide smoothly sideways out of its hangar, in preparation for launching into the stars. Alanna's control board was green but the docking lock indicator glowed a sullen red.

"Skip… What's that?" Dhoni asked.
"What?"
He tapped the screen displaying the visual feed from the nose-mounted camera. There was a bright dot near the centre. Dhoni zoomed in. It was a Nameless warship and it was on a collision course.

"Oh crap," Dhoni said in a perfectly level voice. It was the first time Alanna had ever heard him swear.

The human and alien ships were thundering towards each other, with a closing speed in excess of several hundred metres per second. No matter how glancing, at such a velocity impact would be mutually catastrophic. In the van, *Hammerhead* jinked to port and fired a salvo into the enemy ship. Next in line, *Dauntless* was much slower to respond as the helm thrusters along her flanks fired frantically in an attempt to overcome the carrier's momentum. In her cockpit Alanna hammered uselessly at the launch button. But with the docking lock still activated, the safeties refused to allow their engines to fire.

On the Bridge, Brian found herself holding her breath as the two ships hurtled towards one another. They saw *Hammerhead's* salvo connect, sending atmosphere and pieces of shattered hull plate tumbling away from the alien. Stunned, it took no evasive action.

"This is going to be close!" someone muttered unnecessarily.

Alanna pointlessly braced herself for the impact as the alien ship reached them. One moment it was a dot in the distance, the next it was right on top of them.

Alanna knew instantly that she would always remember the sandy blur as the alien, moving too fast for details to be discerned, flashed past them. It got so close it seemed as if she could touch it by just reaching out her hand. Then just as suddenly it was a receding dot far astern.

"Skipper?" Dhoni said quietly

"Yeah?"

"Please get us off this ship would you?"

The intercom crackled into life. The voice at the other end sounded as shaken as she felt.

"All fighters stand by to launch. Launching!"

The docking lock light went green and Alanna slammed her finger down on the launch button. To her immense relief, Caesar blasted clear. Once again she had some control over her own fate.

"All fighters are clear, ma'am."

Brian nodded without comment as she studied the tactical holo. Out of the corner of her eye, she was aware of the crew casting her desperate looks, each willing her to give the order to drop the mines and allow them to get the hell out. Aside from the near collision, the jump in had been perfect. They were inside the outer screen with the main formation of the fleet a mere five thousand kilometres ahead.

"Dump the mines."

Lieutenant Kelly's finger stabbed downwards. Small flashes rippled down *Dauntless's* flanks as shaped charges severed the load bearing pins for the hangar hatches. Unsupported against the pressure pushing behind them, the hatches blasted out of their housings like corks from champagne bottles, to be followed by the mines, tumbling almost gently in a cross formation with *Dauntless* at its centre. Brian held her breath as she watched. If a mine collided with either a hatch or one of its fellows, it could detonate. And with them bunched so close together, a single explosion would take out half the mines, and probably *Dauntless* too.

But fate continued to smile on them as all the mines safely cleared the bays and Brian let out a huge sigh of relief. On the display at the head of the Bridge, a red LCD lit up displaying three minutes and started to count down. She turned to O'Malley.

"Alright captain, you can now get us out of here."

O'Malley gave a terse nod, before barking out orders.

"Engines, all ahead emergency. Signals, order the destroyers to form up on us. Counter measures full spread. Point defence, commence, commence, commence."

The three ships charged straight into the teeth of the Nameless Fleet. They couldn't turn away, to do so, they would expose the flank of the carrier to the minefield cascading after them; *Dauntless* would be almost guaranteed to be taken out by one of her own mines. If they braked and allowed the mines to go ahead, *Dauntless* would be near stationary and a sitting duck. There was only one option, all ahead full, and race ahead of the mines like a surfer before a tidal wave. Plus hope to god that the IFF recognition systems in the mines worked properly, and that the hell that was about to break loose would distract the Nameless.

Succeed or fail, the matter was now out of Brian's hands. As Julius Caesar had so eloquently put it all those centuries ago '*The die is cast*'. Her ability to influence proceedings was now over. She had to sit back and allow Captain O'Malley to work his ship. Instead, she kept her attention focused on the tactical display and watched with disappointment, but not much surprise, as her fighter strike unravelled.

By any standards the squadron had performed well. By the standards of raw trainees, they had done miracles. But the near miss was the straw that broke the camel's back. Two fighters immediately discharged their ordinance at the nearest enemy ship and bugged out. One started to run without even firing. Only two kept their heads and started weaving their way into the enemy fleet, seeking tankers

A glance at the long-range display, told Brian that the three who had panicked had almost certainly sealed their own fates. The Nameless outer picket was in good order. Approaching as three individuals they would be easy targets. As if to confirm her thoughts one of them abruptly blinked out.

Also on the display, the alien fleet was starting to react to their arrival. The Nameless first swerved to avoid the ships charging into their midst, then to dodge each other as their tight formation disintegrated. The formation of the human ships was also shifting; *Hammerhead* and *Piranha* were drawing along side *Dauntless* to interpose their hulls between the enemy and the carrier.

"Navigator – Engineering, prepare jump out sequence," O'Malley ordered.

From the bows of the ship came a slowly rising whine as the drive started to spin up.

"Nodes are hot, charge building. Jump out in four minutes and counting!" The Navigator called out.

If we're still alive! Brian thought to herself as she tightened her harness. The countdown for the mines was now nearly two minutes.

Alanna found herself flying alone among groups of enemy ships. Countless jammers and ECMs so close together were playing hell with Caesar's radar, to the point that she couldn't see any of the other fighters and could barely make out the carrier she'd just left.

"Dhoni, where the hell's Devane?" she demanded

"Bugged out," he replied sourly. "We're on our own Skip."

"Well, we all saw that one comin..." The threat alarm screamed out and without conscious thought she yanked the nose up just in time to dodge a missile. She had only pulled out of the turn when she realised Caesar's nose was pointing directly at the nearest Nameless ship. Slamming the engine into plus ten override, she charged directly at them.

"Skipper!" Dhoni called out in alarm, as the enemy ship loomed large on their display.

"Don't worry. Just hang on and find me a target."

The alarms gave a fresh whoop as a pair of missiles curved round onto their tail. Their two turret-mounted plasma guns spun round and blazed ineffectively back. The ship ahead launched another salvo directly at them. Alanna jinked the fighter left and right. With the range so short and changing so fast, the firing solution was impossibly complex, with the result that all the missiles flashed past. As before, their proximity fuses fired too late to effect Caesar. The two on their tail followed Alanna's manoeuvres with easy curves however. All the chaff and jammers around Caesar were still screwing up the gunnery radar, which was failing utterly to localise the two closing missiles. The impact was only seconds away and Caesar wasn't capable of dodging them.

As the fighter flashed across the nose of the ship that had fired, a solution suddenly presented itself to Alanna. She forced Caesar round into a viciously tight turn, curving in behind the starship. The fighter's frame groaned at the treatment and her peripheral vision darkened as the G-forces pressed down on her. Beside her, Dhoni gasped for breath. Then they were around, with the enemy ship between them and the missiles. The missiles self-destructed as their target disappeared and instead they found themselves facing a friendly contact.

"Good move Skipper!" Dhoni gasped. "I have a large contact at zero, three, seven, dash, three, four, three. It matches the profile of the tankers we saw before."

"On it!" Alanna called back as she swung towards the next enemy ship.

Steadily Caesar zigzagged across the combat zone, skimming from one enemy ship to another.

Chaff rockets burst and sparkled around *Dauntless* as the human ships fired them off as fast as their crews could reload the launchers. The three vessels had been amongst the Nameless for nearly one hundred and seventy seconds and so far had enjoyed an unreal immunity from destruction. Confusion reigned across the alien ships as the tight formation that had protected them from a conventional assault now worked against them. Enemy fire had been scattered and light with only small missiles directed at them. But now order was beginning to reassert itself as they changed formation, with minor ships clearing the firing lanes of the larger vessels.

"I have a tracking glitch on five."

"Switching to band two."

"God damn! Someone light a bloody fire underneath them. I need those launchers now!"

"Two on the left!"

Brian allowed the flow of orders and reports wash over her as she watched the tactical display, but subconsciously she heard the stress rise in her officers' voices. Abruptly one of the larger enemy ships turned and unleashed a full salvo at the fleeing humans. Four cap ship missiles and over twenty of their smaller companions charged down on the three human ships.

"Multiple inbounds!"

"Priority target the larger missiles!" O'Malley snapped out. "Concentrate point defence. I want a wall of steel into that arc!"

The firing pattern of the point defence guns shifted as they attempted to lay a protective screen of metal shrapnel into the path of the approaching missiles. The destroyer's plasma cannons speared out at the large missiles. One, then another, blew as plasma bolts punched into them. Around them, most of the small missiles shattered on impact with shrapnel, but six found their way through and bore down on the Battle Fleet ships.

Dauntless lurched as one went into the middle of the starboard side hangars and blew. The six hangars on that side were shredded and metal fragments from the hull were driven deep into the carrier. *Dauntless* was still shuddering from the force of the impact when a second missile went in, hitting the upper deck at a tight angle and gouging a twelve-metre furrow in the plating before disintegrating. Automatically Brian's eyes went to the main damage control display. Several sections were blinking red for fire while others showed blue as they haemorrhaged air. Damage so deep into the ship would have killed or maimed many of the crew but no truly critical systems had been hit. The reactor, engines and jump drive were still on line. Before Brian could feel any sense of relief however, the other four missiles plunged into *Piranha*.

The destroyer rocked as the missiles slammed in, but the worst was yet to come. The two remaining cap ship missiles followed hard on the heels of their smaller brethren. Desperately *Piranha* began to weave and throw out more chaff, but her foot was effectively nailed to the floor by the need to shield the *Dauntless*. The first missile missed by less than a hundred metres, but the second clipped the starboard engine, and detonated.

A groan went up on the Bridge of *Dauntless*, as *Piranha* staggered under the force of the impact. Debris tumbled away from the ship. Then with a fresh shudder, so violent that it was visible on *Dauntless's* optical display, the entire starboard engine ripped loose and fell away astern. Immediately the destroyer started to fall behind. O'Malley looked towards Brian and a request was clear in his eyes: to give the order to cut acceleration to allow *Piranha* to keep up. Brian met his eyes squarely with a small shake of her head. She had decided from the outset that should one or both of the destroyers be damaged, she would not wait for a cripple. The small squadron could offer little protection to a lame duck, while cutting acceleration would give the Nameless a better chance to nail them all.

Several officers on the Bridge started to object, but a glare from Brian silenced them all. Mercifully, for her at least, *Piranha* also remained silent, understanding they'd just been written off. Or perhaps her coms systems were smashed. Either way, and despite the strains of her remaining engine, the destroyer dropped steadily astern. The red numbered display in her armrest indicated that they were only one minute away from the mines going active. If *Piranha* could only last that long they might stand a chance.

It was a small faint hope that was quickly dashed. As the distance between them opened, the ability of *Dauntless* and *Hammerhead* to cover their battered companion declined. Despite her own point defence being gutted, *Piranha* tried desperately to defend itself. Her end was neither swift nor merciful as a hail of smaller alien missiles slowly took her apart. Brian forced herself to watch as each missile slammed in. Finally it all proved too much. There was no flash of a reactor letting go and instead *Piranha* simply came apart at the seams. Brian knew that in all likelihood some of her crew had probably still been alive when their ship disintegrated around them.

"Mines go active in five seconds!" The tactical officer called out.

Payback time, Brian thought to herself.

The mine's countdown reached zero and immediately its passive sensors came on line. Nanoseconds passed as it processed the information provided by the sensors. There were multiple contacts in the space all around it. The vast majority didn't match known profiles, so were tagged as unknown, while two contacts accelerating away registered as friendlies. The mine's targeting computer compared the readings to its database and found that the situation fell within the parameters of an authorised attack.

The small thrusters mounted along the outside of the spherical casing fired, swinging it to face the largest contact within two thousand kilometres. For the alien, there was no warning as a piece of apparently empty space suddenly belched out a missile. The Nameless capital ship hadn't even started to react when the missile struck and eviscerated it. All across the surrounding space, mines were going off like firecrackers. Most of the Nameless had being readying missiles to be launched at the fleeing humans. Instead they suddenly found they needed those same missiles for their own defence. Seconds were needed for fire control systems to calculate firing solutions on the approaching targets but many vessels didn't get that long. All across the combat zone Nameless ships died.

It was like a switch being thrown. One minute waves of missiles were coming at them and the next all was calm and serene. No one relaxed though. They were still in the middle of an enemy fleet. Alongside *Dauntless,* temporarily relieved of the need to defend, *Hammerhead* stabbed out with her own guns and missiles, adding in a small way to the havoc being wreaked. Much as she knew she should be displaying the calm aloof manner of a flag office who didn't for a moment doubt her plan, Brian couldn't help but let out a giant sigh of relief. O'Malley reached over to her and offered his hand. Brian shook it firmly.

"I honestly didn't think that was going to work," he admitted.

"Well I'm glad you were wrong," she replied. "I think we've played our part Captain and it's time we took our leave."

"I certainly don't think they're going to remember us with any fondness," O'Malley agreed.

"Sign of a job well done. Signal the courier to stay on station as long as they can and transmit their sensor data towards the Home Fleet."

A glimmer of concern appeared in the Captain's eyes.

"Do you think we've done enough?"

Brian's elation faded.

"I hope so," she said, "because I think we've pulled our last rabbit out of the hat."

"Thirty seconds to jump out," called the Navigator.

Before O'Malley could acknowledge, there was a sudden urgent buzz from the Engineering repeater board. The green icon for the jump drive suddenly went red.

"Christ Skipper! The jump drive has just gone off line!" shouted the Navigator.

Brian and O'Malley shared a look of pure horror.

"Engineering, report!" he bellowed down the intercom.

"We have an indicator light on the jump drive. It's showing a fault on the intermix chamber. The safeties have cut it out of load," the intercom crackled back.

O'Malley glanced toward his Navigator.

"How long until *Hammerhead's* drive?"

"At least another ten minutes Skipper!" the officer shouted back.

"We don't have that long," Brian snapped. The main Nameless fleet was in chaos but their outer picket, the one *Dauntless* had bypassed by jumping in, was unshaken. In less than five minutes they were going to clear the back of the fleet and then they would be out in the open.

"Bypass the safeties," O'Malley ordered.

"Sir that breaches regulati..."

"*God damn it*! I am not asking you mister! I am ordering you to bypass the bloody safeties or I'll go back there and shoot you!" he roared back.

There was a pause.

"Understood."

Seconds crawled by and agonisingly, the jump drive availability indicator continued to glow red.

"We have incoming!"

On the tactical display missiles were coming in from the front. The Nameless picket had locked on.

"Tactical, how much chaff do we have?" O'Malley asked quietly.

"Enough for two full spreads, sir."

"Hold for my order."

"Yes si..."

"Drive back on line!" butted in the Navigator.

The helmsman didn't wait for the order as his finger stabbed down and the *Dauntless* and *Hammerhead* disappeared into the safety of jump space.

"Skipper, the *Dauntless* has just jumped out," Dhoni reported.

"Good, that means we'll have somewhere to land," Alanna grunted. "Damn it D, I've lost track of the tanker, gimmie me a bearing."

"..."

"Dhoni?"

"Working on it skipper. There's a lot of interference out there."

Alanna looked around frantically. Several Nameless ships were close enough to be seen with the naked eye. She desperately wanted to turn to bear and put her missiles into them and get the hell out. A mine's missile whizzed past and instinctively Alanna jerked her control stick. C for Caesar was too small for the mines to target but there were now so many Nameless counter missiles flying about that they stood a good chance of getting pulverised by accident.

"Whoa! We have a contact coming up astern… it's the CO"

"*Caesar this is Anton are you receiving me? Over,"* crackled the radio.

"Anton this is Caesar, receiving loud and clear. Good to see you, sir. We spotted an enemy tanker but we've lost track of them. Over."

"*We have them locked in, Caesar. Form up on my wing. Over.*"

"Roger leader."

Alanna decelerated slightly to allow Anton to pass, before tucking in behind. Together the two fighters wove through the chaos of the enemy until suddenly a huge tanker appeared out of the darkness. On either side of it two small escort ships were firing frantically at mine missiles. They clearly hadn't yet twigged the presence of something more dangerous.

"All four of them are there skipper," Dhoni said. "Lead ship is carrying a wound."

"I can only see one, D."

"Skipper they're in line astern, one after the other."

"That saves us having to hunt around for the others," she grunted.

"*Caesar this Anton. The first one looks to be on fire. You take the second one and I'll take the third in line. Over.*"

"Anton don't you want to hit all four? Over."

"*Negative Caesar. I want two taken out completely, not four damaged. Over*"

"Understood Anton, am engaging. Over and out."

Alanna pushed the engine back into plus ten override and brought up the missile-firing computer, then swore softly as JAMMED lit up on the screen.

"Dhoni, they're jamming all targeting frequencies. Put the missiles into dumb fire mode."

"How close are you planning on getting, Skipper?"

"As close as I can."

Caesar came streaking in and only belatedly did the Nameless realise the danger. Missiles homed in from all sides only to self-destruct as Caesar's radar signal merged with that of her target.

"Let's see how much of a bang we get out of this," Alanna muttered as she fired. There was a whirr as the rotary launcher spun round and missiles shot out. Caesar sowed missiles down the length of the tanker, ripping open and igniting the fuel cells. Caesar was buffeted as she flew through walls of flames. Fire flowed and surged over their cockpit canopy as they pushed through. Then suddenly they were clear. Behind them the tanker was engulfed in flames. Ahead the third tanker was also in its death throes.

"Wow! I always wanted to do that," Alanna breathed.

"*I* didn't!" Dhoni complained

"Can you see Anton?

"Yes, he's at three, five, five, dash, zero, zero, three."

"Forming up on him."

Within a few seconds Caesar drew alongside Anton, close enough for Alanna to see Squadron Commander Devane give a thumbs up.

"*Caesar this is Anton. Prepare a full spread of countermeasures and cut to silent running. We're going to ghost out of here. Over.*"

"Dhoni?" Alanna asked.

"Countermeasures ready, Skipper."

"Anton this is Caesar. Countermeasures ready on your mark."

"*Mark.*"

Chaff and plasma flares fired left and right as both fighters cut their engines and disappeared into the night.

All four plasma bolts slammed into the Nameless ship, shattering hull plates and wreaking havoc in the interior beyond. Atmosphere and flames gushed out of the breaches as the alien's forward velocity checked violently.

"Fire Control, switch target to Alpha Three and engage," Willis barked out in a hoarse voice.

"Roger, Skipper. Switching to Alpha Three!" the gunner shouted back excitedly over the intercom. "We'll nail this one too!"

The gunner wasn't the only one getting excited. Everyone felt the same. After over an hour of being used as an overgrown live-fire target, they were at last getting a chance to hit back. As the aliens closed, they had finally got within the effective range of *Hood's* antiquated fire control system. With the Nameless tracking directly up *Hood's* wake their closing speed was low. As a result, *Hood's* previously wild and ineffective fire now becoming punishingly accurate. Added to this, the alien's missile magazines were clearly starting to run dry and the massed salvos they had been throwing had diminished to the occasional shot. Of what they were firing, only the small missiles were being directed at the Geriatrics, with the cap ship missiles being aimed past them at the rest of the fleet. Willis guessed that they were trying to get at the rest of the Home Fleet and didn't want to waste the few missiles they had on relics. For the moment however, the aliens were being checked by the ferocity of *Hood's* fire.

The nervous excitement was such that Willis kept wanting to jump out of her command chair. Only the seat restraints prevented her from bouncing off the deckhead. As *Hood's* turrets finished traversing round, there was a pause as the targeting computer made final adjustments, then the four guns punched out again. Ten thousand kilometres away the alien's hull plating buckled and shattered.

The distance between the two survivors of Cruiser Squadron Eighteen and the rest of the Home Fleet was narrowing slowly and had closed just enough for the rear elements of the Home Fleet to fire back in support. Willis regarded this as something of a mixed blessing, since several of the bolts had passed dangerously close, forcing her to send several sharp signals back to the fleet to watch their shooting. *Hood* herself wasn't in direct danger due to the proximity of *Hurricane*, but if the latter were hit, then at the very least her remaining engines would probably fail and that would be the end for Vince and his crew.

"Coms, any luck on establishing a laser link up?" Willis asked.

"Sorry Skipper. *Hurricane* keeps breaking the beam," replied the Coms Officer. "No luck with the radio either ma'am, there are still too many active jammers."

"Next time we get a link up, I think we might be better to tell them to stop trying to support us," Commander Horan suggested. "If I have to get killed, I'd rather it was the enemy that did it."

"I don't know about that. A bit of supporting fire might encourage them to keep their distance. Next time we get a link up, give them firing solutions that put their shots well clear of..."

"Sensors, Bridge. The main enemy fleet is turning. They're holding a course parallel to that of the Home Fleet."

"What range?"

"Only ten thousand kilometres ma'am."

"The railguns are going to have field day against them at that distance."

"Surely they can't be that stupid," Willis muttered to herself.

"Ma'am?"

Willis glanced at Horan with a slight frown on her face.

"They must have realised how powerful we are at short range."

"That's not our problem for the moment Skipper," he replied.

"Sensors, Bridge. Two of the ships astern of our track have just gone full burn."

"Sensors, what ships?" Willis asked quickly.

"Ships Alpha Three and Alpha Seven.

"How long since those ships fired?"

"What?" The voice at the other end of the connection sounded confused by the question.

"Damn it! Just answer the question," she snarled back.

"Err…. Neither of those ships have fired for ten minutes."

"Plotting, put up the projected course of A Three and A Seven on the main display."

"What are you thinking?" Horan asked.

"That they've used as many missiles on us as they're willing to."

On the main holo, brackets appeared round the blips for the two aliens in question. A pair of lines appeared on the display, starting at the aliens and terminating at the blip representing *Hood*.

"Profile matches ramming attack ma'am."

"No kidding," she muttered beneath her breath. "Sensors, bring up their trajectory on the main display. Helm, start running an evasion pattern."

"Ma'am that's really going screw up fire control's shooting."

"That's fire control's problem, helm," Willis replied evenly, "you worry about your own job."

"Yes ma'am."

Immediately the *Hood* started to jerk left and right, and up and down, as the helmsman threw the cruiser about. On the main display, the lines from the Nameless ships to the *Hood* writhed as they attempted to follow the cruiser's movements. One of the Nameless ships was masked behind the other. *Using it as cover*, Willis thought grimly to herself. Whatever the Nameless were, they weren't reluctant to lose ships. Those two ships emptied their mags and now they were going to take *Hood* out the only way they could. Yet in the face of such utter cold-bloodedness, Willis felt strangely calm.

"For God's sakes, how the hell can they be willing to sacrifice a ship to take out this relic?" asked Horan with honest bafflement in his voice.

Willis shot a grim smile at him.

"They're running out of missiles. They've already fired more at us than we're worth and they aren't going to waste anymore. They're going to try to smash us out of the way the only other way they can. Coms get on to *Hurricane* and order them to put some distance between us. I'm going to need some room to manoeuvre."

"Roger, Skipper."

She flicked on her intercom to the engineering channel.

"Bridge, Engineering. Chief how're we doing back there?"

"Busy, busy, busy, Skipper. How are things going up front?"

"It's getting fun. We have a pair of enemy ships lining up to try and ram us. I need a few minutes of absolute reliability from the engines."

There was a long moment of silence.

"Oh well, it's always a good thing to face an enemy willing to die for their cause. That way you both have the same aim in mind," Guinness commented. There was an extra tension in his voice that hadn't been there a moment before, but on the whole it was still remarkably even. Despite herself, Willis let out an amused snort.

"How long till they arrive, skipper?"

"Six minutes."

"Right I'm cutting three out of load, I need to replace a couple of firing coils, you'll have it back in four. Engineering out."

"Skipper," called out the helmsman, "Engine Three just cut."

"I know. The Chief needs a few minutes. Manage as best you can."

Two shots from *Hood* punched into the lead Nameless ship. This time there was no recoil. The alien ship continued to close, even as atmosphere streamed from its hull. The follow-up salvo missed completely.

"Ma'am, we might be better off steadying down our track. Give the guns a better chance of hitting," Horan suggested.

"No we wouldn't," Willis replied sharply. "This bucket is none too manoeuvrable. We need some momentum. We can't dodge from a standing start."

Hood continued to lurch clumsily back and forth. On the holo display, the range between it and the Nameless dropped to four figures. Once again *Hood's* guns punched holes in the nearest alien,

"Engine Three back on line captain," the helmsman called out. *Hood's* evasion became more vigorous, but still the Nameless closed.

"Helm, stand ready for instructions. I intend to favour the wounded enemy ship. The damage they have sustained should make their terminal manoeuvres slower. Countermeasures, prepare to fire a full spread of chaff right into their faces."

"Yes ma'am," the helmsman replied, his eyes locked on the display. As the range dropped below a thousand kilometres, the second Nameless ship slid back into view on *Hood's* starboard bow. Simultaneously, it fired a single cap ship missile, which arced out onto the opposite side of the wounded ship, offering *Hood* a choice of targets, on one side a missile and on the other a fully capable ship. Willis chose the missile.

"Helm side-slip to port! Side-slip to port!" Willis snapped, "countermeasures now!"

Thrusters along *Hood's* flank fired furiously to push the cruiser out of the way. Chaff rockets burst out of their launchers and detonated directly in front of the closing missile. Thousands of foil strips became a glittering wall in front of the approaching missile, scattering their radar signals. As it cleared the chaff, the missiles' guidance system saw *Hood* again clearly and attempted to steer in. But it had lost precious seconds in which to make corrective course adjustments. It skimmed past only fifty metres from the hull, and blew several kilometres behind them. Unable to match *Hood*'s manoeuvre, the damaged Nameless started to overshoot. The alien braked hard and swerved towards *Hood*, but as it did so its velocity relative to the cruiser crashed downwards. Both *Hood's* turrets swung round and put a broadside into it at point blank range. A pillar of flames burst from the alien's hull, then the entire ship disappeared in a flash as the reactor breached.

When the Nameless ship detonated, it was less than thirty kilometres away from *Hood*, far too close to an exploding fusion reactor for comfort. The starboard wing folded, and the upper and lower wings buckled under the force of the blow. Although the hull plating shielded the crew from the flash of radiation, they were violently buffeted. A piece of the alien's hull tumbled out of the explosion and slammed into the starboard side hangars. A clang echoed through the hull and on the Bridge, and even the very deck plating seemed to jump. Deep within the engineering compartments, circuit breakers for the electrical systems did as they were designed and tripped.

Radar, weapons, and engines all died instantly. Willis's bridge was plunged into near total darkness as the tactical holo flickered out. All around the Bridge ratings and officers found themselves facing blank screen.

"Damage Control, report!" Willis called out.

"All circuit breakers have tripped, we've lost everything!" Horan shouted back.

Willis flicked on her suit radio.

"Chief Engineer Guinness, are you receiving me?"

The radio connection hissed.

"Guinness here. We're resetting all of the breakers right now. I'm sorry Skipper. I didn't test them. They got over sensiti..."

"Never mind that now chief! How long to power?"

The main lights flickered on again. Around her came the hum of electronics powering up again.

"We've just reset the last of the breakers. All systems should be coming back up."

"Good work, Chief."

Willis looked towards her holo display. It was still blank. The screens around the Bridge were filled with scrolling letters and numbers.

"*Chief!*"

"*Oh Christ*! Skipper, the main computer lost power and the backup battery didn't kick in! The whole system has to reboot!"

"How long?"

"Two minutes."

"We can't wait that long!"

"It's a silicon system. It's hardwired in, Skipper! I can't give you a better offer."

Willis cut the connection.

"Sensors do we have anything?" she shouted cross her bridge.

"I have visual sensors ma'am," a rating called out.

"Put it up!"

The main holo lit up but in place of the usual orderly array of radar blips was a far busier display of the sphere of space surrounding the ship. While beautiful, the visual display was generally useless for tactical work because its range was so short. Which meant the second Nameless ship, that was visible, was right on top of them.

Like the one they had destroyed, the alien ship had overshot *Hood* but was now braking hard for another attempt. The visual display couldn't provide her with any information on range or velocity but it looked like the alien was going to make contact in a lot less than two minutes. This time they weren't going to be able to dodge the Nameless, assuming the alien didn't wise onto the fact that they were helpless and swing round and put a missile into them.

Willis looked around the Bridge… looked around *her* bridge. Her crew looked back at her. There was fear in most of their faces and Willis was shaken by the realisation that she knew the names of less that ten of her people. People who were now looking to her for answers and she had not a damn thing to offer them. Her first ship, her first crew and she was going to lose both.

She could save her crew. If she ordered them to abandon ship, there might be just enough time for them to reach the escape pods and get clear. But that would seal *Hood's* fate. If they remained at their posts there was a chance, a slender chance, that their CPU would complete the reboot in time for them to attempt evasive manoeuvres. But if it didn't the crew wouldn't stand a chance.

The rest of the Home Fleet wasn't visible on the visual display, but she could see explosions and the flashes of plasma cannon fire far astern. Off their bows another seven Nameless ships waited. *Hood* was the fleet's rearguard. If they abandoned ship, they would also abandon that responsibility.

"Steady everyone," she said quietly. "Steady. The reboot will be in time people."

The range was dropping steadily. The Nameless ship was moving along approximately the same vector but was decelerating hard. It was going to be far from the classic ram. Both ships would be moving in roughly the same direction, but *Hood* would be going a lot faster when they ploughed into one another tail to tail.

Then another engine flare appeared on the display. It was a single engine and, going by the stutter in the plume, one in its death throes. It was also very close to the Nameless ship.

"Tactical, what ship's that," Horan called out.

"It's the *Hurricane*," Willis replied quietly.

"They must have patched up a gun."

"No," said Willis, shaking her head. "I don't think they have."

On the visual display, the two engine plumes edged towards each other. *Hurricane* was closing as fast as her engine could drive her. The alien's initial charge had carried it beyond *Hurricane* as well as *Hood*. Then it had started to decelerate at maximum burn to close once again on *Hood*, but now *Hurricane* had interposed herself between the alien and its objective. Belatedly, the Nameless realised *Hurricane's* intentions and started to manoeuvre away from the mutilated cruiser, but there were upper limits to their engine thrust and the laws of physics were carrying them remorselessly towards the cripple.

"If they have even one missile, they're going to swat her like a fly," Horan murmured.

"If they had a missile, they would have already let fly," Willis replied
equally quietly.

The *Hood's* bridge had gone silent. In a sense they had been reduced from a warship, to a passive observer. Everyone present was now aware that their fate was now in the hands of a ship that was little more than wreckage held together by inertia. It was obvious that the stutter in her engine was getting worse, but still *Hurricane* bobbed and wove, striving to match the alien's manoeuvres.

"Coms, can we speak to *Hurricane*?" Willis asked without taking her eyes off the display.

"No, ma'am. Not until we get the computer back," came the equally quiet reply.

Hurricane was also slowing. Her rate of deceleration was much lower than that of the alien but it did mean that they were converging only very slowly.

"How much longer till reboot?"

"Perhaps one minute, ma'am."

"Right…"

Abruptly, the alien changed heading, pointing its bows directly away from *Hurricane*, its engines still firing at full power. Willis felt some of the tension leak out of her body. Several of her crew also realised what had happened.

"Looks like they've given up on trying to ram us," said Horan

"They're willing to exchange a ship for us, but not for a cripple," Willis agreed quietly.

"We'll have rebooted by the time they've gone around and lined up for another go."

Hurricane however was clearly not deflected by such concerns and continued to close. The alien's manoeuvring became more frantic as she closed.

"Oh God. What the hell is Vince doing?" Willis asked out loud. "Coms. Get on to *Hurricane* and tell them to break off their attack. Tell him to stop being a hero!"

"Still no…"

"GOD DAMN IT!"

The visual display blinked out. Willis opened her mouth to shout just as the holo came back on, this time with the welcome blips and icons of the radar display.

"We have the compu…"

"Coms order Hurricane to break off her attack!" she shouted across the Bridge.

"Too late!"

The two radar blips merged.

The Nameless ship was significantly out accelerating *Hurricane*, with her single labouring engine. But the alien had shed velocity after overshooting *Hood* and this had given *Hurricane* the chance to close on them. Even a second or two more and the alien would have started to pull away, but instead, with an overtake velocity of only seventy kilometres per hour, *Hurricane* grazed the alien ship.

Steel plates ripped and twisted like tin foil as the lower surface of *Hurricane's* hull opened up like a tin can as far back as the engines. The entire ventral turret was ripped clean out of its barbette and sent tumbling away. What little atmosphere remained in the cruiser gushed out of her ruined hull.

For the Nameless it was worse.

For all her terrible damage, *Hurricane* was still armour-plated, whereas the Nameless was unprotected. The entire upper surface of its hull was shorn away. The two ships tumbled away from one another trailing wreckage.

"Coms?" Willis whispered.

"Checking all frequencies ma'am." He shook his head. "I'm sorry ma'am I'm getting nothing."

As he spoke *Hurricane* snapped in two just forward of the conning tower.

"Skipper."

"Skipper!"

Willis looked round.

"Two more enemy ships have gone full burn. Profile consistent with a ramming attack."

The Nameless were going to keep coming until they succeeded.

"I'm not sure which ship, sir, but one of them definitely rammed an enemy vessel after the alien tried to ram its compatriot.

Err… several more have just started to make a run at the survivor," Sheehan said.

Lewis grunted a reply.

On the face of it, the Home Fleet was doing well. The Nameless fleet had lost well over half their number. The space behind them was littered with the drifting wrecks of gutted starships. The thinness of the enemy counter fire indicated that their magazines were near empty. Yet Lewis could take no satisfaction from the situation. The cruisers *Isis, Vali, Amazon, Tempest, Whirlwin*d and now either *Hood* or *Hurricane* were all gone, as were the destroyers *Shark, Black Widow, Cuckoo* and *Oak*. The cruiser *Nile* was staggering along astern of *Warspite*, her armament reduced to a single point defence gun, which blazed away defiantly at anything that came close. She wasn't the only ship so reduced. Only approximately one third of his ships were fully combat worthy. The rest were a mixture of the battered, the lame and the gutted. Reducing power to allow the cripples to hold formation had slowed the fleet's acceleration to a crawl and the Nameless were now overhauling them.

The ramming attack on the fleet's rearguard was probably just a foretaste of what the rest of the fleet would experience. The Nameless would soon turn to cross the Home Fleet's T and then come at them head on. They would likely be wiped out but they would take a hell of a lot of human ships with them. The Home Fleet would be finished as a fighting force.

"Admiral we're picking up an FTL transmission. It isn't one of ours," Captain Sheehan said. "Probably their main fleet reporting that they are jumping out for Earth."

"Yes," Lewis replied heavily

"I wonder whether they'll break off?"

"It makes little difference. They'll reach Earth hours ahead of us," Lewis said with despair clear in his voice.

Lewis continued to morosely watch the battle on the holo.

"That's strange." The bemusement in Sheehan's voice roused Lewis out of his hopelessness. He gave his staff captain a curious look.

"What is it."

"There seems to be quite a conversation going on, sir. There have been three clear transmissions from the direction of the second fleet and this lot has sent three separate replies."

Lewis pondered what Sheehan had told him. Strange but true. The middle of a battle wasn't best place for a discussion even if their FTL transmitters were better.

"Sir, look!" Sheehan was pointing at the holo. "They're turning away, all of them!"

"Sensors, Flag. Passive sensors are registering power build up in the majority of enemy ships," the senior sensor officer reported across the intercom.

"Sensors, are they powering up jump drives?" Lewis demanded.

"Unknown, sir. They could be, but the analysis system isn't sure."

"Sir, I think they're bugging out!" Sheehan exclaimed. "Should I order a pursuit?"

Lewis didn't answer immediately. The human ships were still firing. The aliens were still well inside the range of their guns and the Battle Fleet ships continued pound them. The alien fleet had been gutted, with more losses than survivors, but the ones that were still alive were in better condition than the surviving human ships. A glance at one of the tactical readouts told Lewis what he already suspected: their fleet speed, the maximum acceleration at which the Home Fleet could hold together, was a lot lower than the rate at which the Nameless were speeding away.

"No. We aren't pursuing, Tim," he said heavily.

"Sir..." Sheehan started to object.

"It could be a ruse, to get us to string out. Besides this is only a decoy force. They've done their job. They've succeeded in wasting hours of our time."

"What... what are your orders, sir." The brief elation in Sheehan's voice was gone.

"Order all ships to continue firing but start powering up their jump drives. Are they still jamming the radio bands?"

"Not any more, sir. They've lost too many ships to blanket all the bands."

"Send a transmission to the tug ships to jump to our position. We'll tow back any ships with combat capability, but cripples will have to be scuttled. We have to pray that somehow planetary defence manages to hold off their second fleet." The Admiral's voice was tired and without hope. The hours of worry, the moments of elation and knowledge of just how profoundly he had failed had taken their toll. He had reached his limit. He felt mentally and physically exhausted. He'd risked everything in a single throw, based on bad information and fallen into a colossal trap. He'd hurt the Nameless badly, no doubt about that, but he's also delivered Earth to its enemies. Possibly the greatest military error in the plant's history and he'd made it. It would take at least a day for even his lightly damaged ships to make it back to Earth. There was no possibility that they would return in time.

Lewis watched the holo morosely, his normally straight shoulders slumped. The fighting was still going on but there was nothing more he could do. The radar was detecting small contacts appearing from damaged Nameless ships and travelling to undamaged vessels. Presumably crews abandoning ships that no longer had jump capability.

"Sir," Sheehan said in a quiet voice. "Enemy ships are starting to jump out."

"I see them Tim."

"Flag, Communications. We're receiving a radio transmission from outside the Home Fleet."

"What ship?"

"ID is showing it as coming from one of the couriers sent to support *Dauntless*."

"Probably still trying to tell us there's a second fleet," Lewis replied wearily.

"Err… I don't think so, sir," replied the Coms Officer from the other end of connection. "It seems to be a data stream of current sensor readings. There's also a sensor recording file. The attached text file says it's eighteen minutes old, plus transmission time."

"Put up the current readings."

The display of the battleground around *Warspite* disappeared, to be replaced by a mass of new signals. The courier's sensor display lacked the definition of *Warspite's* analysis package, offering not much more than a collection of blips. But Lewis immediately saw a pattern in the dots.

There was a reasonably organised outer sphere that formed a screen, but in startling contrast, the inner formation was in complete chaos and lacked any coherence or order. Some ships were tagged as seriously damaged, while others were standing off to offer assistance. It looked like a fleet that had already fought a battle, and come off second best.

"What in hell's name has happened here?" Lewis whispered in wonder. "Coms, did you say there was a second data stream?"

"Yes, sir. Shall I put it up?"

"Yes."

"It's a compressed file being repeatedly transmitted, sir. Putting it up now."

Once again it was the second Nameless fleet on the holo. This time however both the inner and outer formations were in good order, all calm and orderly. Within the inner formation there was a cluster of ships tagged as a tankers. Then abruptly another blip appeared, between the inner and outer formation. A flashing label identified this new contact as the *Dauntless*.

"Christ, the woman's mad," Lewis muttered to himself.

In disbelief, he watched *Dauntless's* kamikaze charge, expecting to see the carrier destroyed at any moment. Then suddenly Nameless ships started exploding.

"What the hell?"

The courier's data wasn't telling him why, but suddenly Nameless were dying in droves. Two of the assumed tankers disappeared. Within minutes the fleet was reduced to a confused mob.

The Flag Bridge of *Warspite* had gone silent as every man and woman watched the recording. *Dauntless's* signal disappeared as she jumped out. Even after the carrier's departure, aliens kept dying.

"What in the name of God did they do?" Sheehan murmured.

"I don't know, but I look forward to asking Vice Admiral Brian," Lewis replied quietly. "I think she might have done it Tim. I think she's stalled their advance. At the very least she's given us the chance to get back to Earth in time. Get the fleet into cruising formation. We've done what we needed to do here. We're going home."

Chapter Fifteen

The Lost

Dauntless and *Hammerhead* drifted, their engines powered down, most of their radiators closed, all radar, communications and running lights off. On one side of the carrier the fighter bays had been reduced to a jumble of twisted metal. On the other, half the bay doors were gone, leaving dark gaping voids.

They'd decelerated to a halt shortly after re-entering real-space, to lick their wounds and wait for the fighters to reach them. Even from the other side of the system, they'd been able to 'hear' the sounds of the Home Fleet's battle: radio chatter, distant radar emissions and the faint but unmistakable emissions of fusion reactor explosions.

Soon they would be jumping away again, to the rendezvous with the *Samuel Clemens*. From there, they would start the journey back to Earth.

Brian sat in her command chair, staring moodily into the middle distance. O'Malley was watching his commander with open concern. They had waited nearly three hours for the fighters to reach them. The last radar reading taken before they jumped out had shown four fighters were still alive. But only two had made it back to *Dauntless*. Of twelve fighter crews that had arrived less than two days previously in Alpha Centauri for a training mission, only one crew of trainees and one of instructors survived. Added to this already sobering statistic were the losses suffered on the ships. Seventeen of *Dauntless's* crew were now in a hastily prepared morgue, while another thirteen were wounded in sickbay. Finally there were the fifty-three officers and crew of the *Piranha*, all gone.

Brian had seen action before. She'd fought in most of the major battles of the Contact War. She'd seen people die, friends included, sometimes horribly. Yet this had been different. Back then she'd been a junior officer, one cog in a great machine. This was the first time that she'd been the one formulating the battle plan and giving the orders. The one deciding how many lives would represent 'acceptable' losses.

"Ma'am, do you want to attend the pilot debriefing?" O'Malley asked, as much to break the silence as anything.

"Mmm?" Brian roused herself.

"The pilot debriefings, do you want to attend?"

"No. No thank you Captain. How long until *Hammerhead* is ready to jump again?" she replied after a pause.

"They need another hour to fully purge their heat sink," O'Malley replied. "The other two fighters might…" He left the words hanging.

"Mmm, I think I'll leave you to it for a while Norman. Once *Hammerhead* is ready… we leave," Brian told him before slowly rising from her seat and limping from the Bridge.

She wanted sleep, she needed sleep. After more than forty hours on her feet, her bad knee was aching fiercely. Despite this, she didn't go down to her cabin and the welcome oblivion of her bunk. Instead her feet carried her down and out of the centrifuge into the main hull.

The ship was quiet now. Only a skeleton crew were still on duty, while the majority were in their bunks, where she should be if she had any sense. Being in zero G at least took the load off her knee and the pain from it started to ease. She drifted gently down the passageway until she came to a sealed hatch. Above the hatch were two indicator lights, green and red. The red light was on. The chamber beyond, was one of those now open to space.

Eventually she found herself in one of the two hangars that still had an occupant. The Vampire fighter inside was pretty battered looking. There were several long score marks down the side of the starboard engine housing. One of the scratches had cut through the fighter's name, changing it from C for Caesar, to C for Ce. Almost all of the paint on the fighter's belly was scorched and blistered. Brian pushed herself off the hangar bulkhead and drifted over to it. Reaching out she pulled herself up and into the cockpit. She didn't buckle in, instead she allowed herself to float gently above the seat. Slowly she drifted into sleep.

Alanna stopped just inside the hatchway of the pilot's barracks. When first they had embarked aboard *Dauntless*, the mess had been filled to bursting. There had been constant noise of people coming, going and living, but now there was only the crew of Caesar and the silence was crushing. Dhoni plodded past her and sat down heavily on the first bunk. He looked around and shook his head.

They'd both hoped that someone else might have made it. After the debriefing was done, they'd both hung around the Operations Room waiting for news, putting off this very moment. They waited and waited, then a call came down from the Bridge and the operations officer drew thick black lines through the names of the missing fighters on the out board.

The barracks was far from the usual standards of military precision and clothing was scattered across unmade bunks. With the rush to mount the attack, tidying up hadn't been on anyone's priority list.

"Do you think we should... you know... clear up their stuff?" she asked hesitantly.

Dhoni looked around slowly.

"Really, I don't think I want to," he replied quietly.

"I think we have to, D," she replied.

She started to pick up items of clothing and pack them back into storage lockers. As she put away a shirt, her eyes fell upon a photograph on the bulkhead. *Dauntless* had served as the fleet's fighter training ship for most of twenty years. Mounted on the bulkheads were group pictures of graduating classes of fighter crews from the last ten years, all of them taken inside this very room. Proud smiling faces displaying their new flight stripes. The thought crossed her mind that this year's picture was going to be very small. Sickened, she turned away.

A red light blinked on and off for several seconds, before the siren in the hangar belatedly started up. Brian jerked awake as the banshee like howl echoed painfully off the hangar's metal walls. It took a few seconds of looking around in confusion before her memory kicked in.

"Bridge, report!" she shouted into her intercom.

There was no reply, not even static.

Glancing down she cursed as she realised that in her sleep, she'd managed to pull the wire for her intercom ear/throat piece out of its socket. She violently rammed the contact back into place and immediately a signal came across the command channel.

"... iral Brian, contact the Bridge! Admiral Brian, contact the Bridge!" It was O'Malley's voice on the other end and he was shouting.

"Brian here. What the hell is going on?"

"Ma'am, they've found us!"

She felt her spine turn to ice.

It's hard to rush in zero G, but once alarms start blaring, instinct cuts in and tells you to move fast and accept the bruises you are about to receive. As Brian dashed back to the Bridge, she felt the ship swing round and the engines go full burn. All the while she could feel irreplaceable seconds flowing away. Finally she slammed open the hatch into the Bridge.

"Report!"

O'Malley turned towards her. His face was expressionless but she could see fear in his eyes.

"Admiral, a force of eight enemy ships has just jumped in. They're currently two hundred and ten thousand kilometres directly astern of us," he said in an unnaturally calm voice.

"Strength?"

"Tactical is estimating two cruisers and six escorts."

"Hell."

"They're already out accelerating us."

Brian stared at the holo display. The two human ships had completed their turns and were now starting to accelerate. They'd been almost stationary and even if the aliens held their current speed, it would take *Dauntless* at least twenty minutes just to match it. Which was a moot point as far from holding speed, the Nameless were accelerating. While *Hammerhead* might have had the pace to match and then pull away from them, there was no prospect of *Dauntless* doing the same. The destroyer started to zigzag back and forth across the stern of her lumbering companion.

She turned away from the holo.

"What's our jump status?"

"We deployed nodes just before they jumped in. We need another twelve minutes before we can jump."

Twelve minutes. Just twelve more shitty little minutes and they'd have been clear. They'd already survived so much, taken so many risks, yet now, just when the danger had seemed past... Brian forced herself to stop thinking. She needed to be taking action, not feeling sorry for herself. If they could see the Nameless, then the aliens already had them in missile range.

"I don't understand how they even found us," O'Malley was muttering. "We had almost everything closed down. Unless they caught a glimpse of the radiators..."

"It doesn't much matter," Brian said cutting him off. "They didn't get a good enough fix to drop right in on top of us. That might give us some kind of a chance." She tried to believe her own words.

"Contact! Contact separation, we have missiles inbound! ETA three-and-a-half minutes," called out a sensor operator.

"Tactical, what's the state of point defence and counter measures?" O'Malley asked after visibly shaking himself.

"We have fifty-seven percent point defence ammunition left. We're putting the last of our chaff into the aft launchers, sir."

"We just need to buy eleven minutes," Brian said in a firm voice. "Captain, arm the fighters for space superiority. Targeting priority, those big missiles.

"If the fighters are out, they might… no probably, won't be able to get back," O'Malley objected. Behind him the operations officer hesitated.

"Get on with it, Lieutenant," she snapped at him, before looking back at O'Malley. "We've lost most of the squadron already Norman. This ships' more irreplaceable than what's left."

"Sensors, Bridge. *Hammerhead* is firing."

"Navigation, Bridge, we are ten minutes from jump capability."

A for Anton's hangar was a hive of activity as the deck crew raced through the launch preparations. The fighter's reactor was already running and with the radiators venting, the hangar was getting uncomfortably warm. A pair of armourers were trying to get a twisting belt of sustainer rods into the upper turret magazine, while below them other work crew manhandled Starstrike missiles onto their pylons with the fuses already in place. Dozens of safety protocols were being broken but Anton was going to ready in record time. In a corner of the hangar, the last four squadron members were briefing.

"Shermer!" Moscoe barked. She snapped her head back round towards the Commander. "Focus, damn it!"

"Yes, sir. Sorry, sir," she replied quickly.

"Right, we'll be launching as soon as our birds are ready. Once we're out, Anton will take the port, Caesar starboard. Stick tight to the carrier, no more than ten K, but for Christ's sake stay out of *Dauntless's* firing lane. If you get in the way, they aren't going to stop shooting. Save your Starstrikes on any big missiles and your guns for the small stuff. Try not to waste your fire on anything that's going to miss…"

"Sir, fighter ready!" A shout from one of the hangar crew interrupted the Commander.

"All right." Turning to his gunner, Brengtsson, "Get her started up, I'll be with you in a second." He turned back and looked Alanna straight in the eye. "Keep it tight out there. Once the jump drive is spun up, they aren't going to wait around for any of us. But remember, if the carrier dies, so do we. Now get moving and good luck."

The deck crew were just finishing with Caesar as Alanna and Dhoni pulled themselves through the hatch. Procedure said they should do a visual inspection, but without communication between them both Alanna and Dhoni headed straight for the cockpit. Just as they pulled themselves up, there was a boom from a shockwave hitting the bay doors. Three small holes appeared in the hangar's bay door and something whizzed past Alanna's nose. The pressure alarm buzzed as air started to rush noisily out into the void.

"That's it, we're out of here, all hands, clear the bay!" she shouted before snapping her suit visor shut. As the cockpit canopy closed she spoke again. "Launch control, we're ready."

Launch control didn't wait to depressurise the hangar, the bay door slammed open, venting atmosphere and a few discarded tools out into space. A few more seconds and Caesar was away and clear. Their radar did a quick sweep and immediately found *Hammerhead*. The destroyer was already heavily engaged. She'd given up on zigzagging and instead had gone full astern on engines to complete an about-face and present her armament.

"Skipper, look." Dhoni pointed at the visual display. It was a close-up of *Hammerhead*. The angle was awkward but Alanna immediately saw what he was referring to. The destroyer's bows, and the jump drive they had contained, were gone.

"God help them," Dhoni said quietly.

Alanna didn't have time to think about that. They were reaching their assigned position and Caesar's tactical systems were already tracking missiles entering their zone of control. There was no more time to think. Instead she allowed training and instinct to take over. A few moments later their first Starstrike missile cleared its pylon.

On *Dauntless's* Bridge, Brian sat silent in the command chair while around her the officers and ratings worked their systems. They were still five minutes from jump out. The two fighters were out on either flank bobbing and weaving, while *Hammerhead* continued to bring up the rear. So far, aside from some fragment strikes, *Dauntless* had taken no hits, but for *Hammerhead* it was a different story. The destroyer was too far away to get anything more than her engines on visual but she could see the explosions bursting. *Hammerhead* was dying on her feet. She'd been able to stop the incoming cap ship missiles but the small missiles were saturating point defence, taking her apart a piece at a time. This time there were no objections on the Bridge of *Dauntless* as the distance between the carrier and the beleaguered destroyer started to open.

But as Brian watched the main holo, the situation was altering. The Nameless ships were shooting as a group, firing slow, rippling salvos that sent a steady stream of missiles charging after the human ships. A mistake in her opinion, as a single massive salvo fired from every launcher at once would have left the humans with no way to stop, dodge or decoy them all. There would be a long gap between such salvos but by opting for a steady stream they might have made a tactical mistake, one that might allow *Dauntless* to get away. Her impassive expression twisted into a wince as another missile went into *Hammerhead* and one of her engines died. They were going to get the destroyer though, there was no way *Dauntless's* clapped out jump drive could hold the portal open long enough for *Hammerhead*. Perhaps if the destroyer's shuttle had survived the crew might be able to… Then abruptly, *Hammerhead* ceased to be part of the equation.

"Helm, ke… keep… keep the wreckage between us and the enemy," O'Malley stuttered out the order as twelve thousand kilometres astern *Hammerhead* died.

Even in death, the destroyer continued to shield them. Missiles already locked onto her continued the pile into the explosion. It bought them another two minutes, but then the explosion cleared, leaving nothing between *Dauntless* and the Nameless.

"Three minutes! Caesar pull in tight! Keep it tight!" Alanna heard the order and obeyed.

"Confirmed Anton, pulling in," she responded.

"Skipper, I'm getting an overheat alarm on the dorsal gun," Dhoni snapped.

"Roger, rolling," she replied tersely.

She briefly glanced up at *Dauntless* and her point defence pouring weapons fire back. The pulse guns were sending out visible streams of plasma bolts, while the projectiles from the charge throwers were invisible until they detonated. Between that, the chaff and exploding missiles, it looked like one hell of a fireworks display.

"We're nearly there skipper," Dhoni shouted, "we need to get closer to the carrier to get into the jump conduit."

Caesar had been running all astern, with her nose pointed towards the aliens. Now Alanna yanked Caesar round and side slipped towards *Dauntless's* scarred hull.

"Hang on D, this is going to be a bumpy jump!" she warned.

"Just don't get us smeared against the hull, that's all I ask," he replied tersely.

"Jumping out in thirty seconds," called the Navigator.

No one was celebrating yet. The guns were still firing furiously and every few seconds the hull was shaken by near misses. They'd taken two hits from small missiles: the first had demolished four of the port side hangars and knocked out an engine; the second merely stirred the exiting wreckage on the starboard side. The two fighters were on either side, only fifty metres from the hull.

"Guns, keep firing! All hands, brace for ju..." O'Malley was shouting when there was a sudden screech of metal from the front of the ship and a small explosive report echoed through the hull. "What the hell..." he started to ask.

"Skipper!" the Navigator shouted. Even through his helmet visor Brian could see the man's face was as white as a sheet. "Sir, the jump drive has just gone off line!"

Brian and O'Malley shared a look of horror.

"Oh my God! Engineering, report!" O'Malley bellowed into the intercom.

There was a burst of coughing at the other end of the line.

"Engineering what the hell's going on?" O'Malley almost screamed down the link.

The tone of the engineer's voice told Brian all she needed know.

"Captain, the charging chamber just blew, I told you it was..."

"For Christ's sake, never mind that! How long to repair?" O'Malley shouted him down.

"Skipper you don't understand. It's fried! The whole thing! The jump drive will never run again!"

The other bridge officers had heard the engineer's report. They looked to their Captain for instruction, but O'Malley had frozen up, his mouth opening and closing like a beached fish.

"Norman!" Brian shouted at him but he merely goggled at her. She swore savagely before flicking her intercom onto the command channel. "All officers, be aware we just lost the jump drive. Engineering, put all power into the engines. We're going to have to try to make a run for it in real-space. Operations, order the fighters back out onto our flanks. Coms, send out a distress signal, there might be a part of the Home Fleet that can get to us." No one believed that last bit, herself least of all. "Download our logs into a message drone and the black box. Prepare them for launch."

"Sensors, bridge, we have cap ship missiles inbound.

A groan went up across the command channel. Those missiles had proven mostly immune to point defence guns. Only plasma guns and their own missiles had been powerful enough and *Dauntless* had neither. As the old ship ran for her life, Brian could feel the deck plating start to tremble as the engines redlined.

Alanna had seen the explosion. It wasn't a big one, but it had lit up the bows for a moment and sent a small piece of hull plating tumbling down past Caesar. She guessed immediately what had happened. She'd read of *Dauntless's* exploits in the Contact War when she was a child, now they'd finally asked too much of the old ship. The message from the carrier was they were having a problem with the jump drive and needed a few more minutes. Neither of them believed it for a moment.

"We aren't getting out of this," Dhoni said so quietly she barely heard him.

"Yeah I know D," she replied as she pushed the button and their last missile blasted away. "We'll make them work for it though."

Four big missiles, flanked by over a dozen small one closed on *Dauntless*. The two fighters dropped back from the carrier and closed on them. Anton reached them first and started working through the small missiles, striving to reach the cap ship missiles at the centre of the wave. Then abruptly two small missiles turned on Anton, forcing her to defend herself as the cap ship missiles passed by. Both the closing missiles were destroyed short of their target but the second blew far too close. On her head up display, Alanna saw the icon for Anton change as the fighter's engines failed.

"Anton!" she shouted. "Anton, are you receiving me!"

"*Confir... Caesar... can hear you. I'm hit b... engines destro...*"

Alanna glanced at her radar. Another two blips were closing on Anton.

"Anton, you have missiles inbound! Punch out! Punch out!" she screamed into the radio.

"*Negative Caes... we're not getting ta...n alive. We're leaving now, goodbye Caesar and good lu....*"

On the Head Up Display the icon for Anton blinked out. *Dauntless's* last surviving pilot didn't have time to grieve. The missiles were entering range. Tears streaming down her face, Alanna picked one and fired, even as the missile exploded she was targeting another, the turret guns claimed another two. The surviving small missiles turned towards the fighter. Alanna threw Caesar into a desperate spiral, around them, missiles died as their guns picked them off. All but one.

"Skipper, from belo...!" Dhoni shouted just before the missile swung in and exploded twenty metres below the fighter.

His last warning was broken off in a choked scream. A red spray hit the front of the canopy and Dhoni slumped across his instruments. Half of Alanna's control board blanked out, the other half flashed red.

"Dhoni! D!" She twisted around and pulled him back. His eyes were open and staring, and blood leaked out of a gaping hole in his suit. There was a hiss of atmosphere leaking from the cockpit.

"Oh God! Oh God!"

Movement outside caught her eye. The HUD flickered for a moment and stabilised. As she watched four cap ship missiles passed less than ten kilometres away. Then all power died, Caesar's guns didn't respond, and neither did the engines. Helpless, Alanna could only watch the missiles plunge after the fleeing carrier.

Brian had watched the last of the fighters die and knew that the final slender hope was gone. In the remaining seconds before impact, the missiles were spreading out, like a clawed hand opening, leaving *Dauntless* with nowhere to go. There was only one more order to give.

"Launch message drone and black box," she ordered before closing her helmet visor. She limped back to her command chair, seated herself and looked up. The Captain hadn't moved since the jump drive failed. "We didn't do bad," she said to his uncomprehending face.

The missiles arrived, crashing through the defensive barrage. The first clipped one of the port engines, then exploded with a force that split *Dauntless* in two just forward of the engineering space. The second hammered into the starboard side, crushing the hull like an eggshell. On the Bridge, atmosphere howled out through tears in the hull and men and women died at their posts, some shouting, others in silence. Brian looked up just in time to see a support beam smash down on her.

Epilogue

The Price

6th August 2066, Earth Orbit

Dear Mr and Mrs Ermler

I regret that I must inform you that your daughter, Petty Officer Laura Ermler, was killed in action on thirty-first July, twenty sixty-six during an engagement with enemy forces in the Alpha Centauri system. Your daughter was under my command for only a short period and regrettably, I did not get a chance to personally know her. Her comrades have spoken well of her and I can assure you that she was killed instantly and did not suffer...

Willis hammered at the backspace key with increasing force, as she deleted the entire message. Getting to her feet she stretched, her hands striking the deckhead above her and glared at the computer screen. Two hours work and she had yet to find words that didn't sound trite or indifferent. Worse still, some of them were flat out lies.

She hadn't expected or really even hoped to survive the action, with good cause. She'd taken a ship that was basically a museum piece, into the biggest battle the fleet had ever fought and brought it home with minor damage and five fatalities. Space had been alive with missiles and plasma bolts, yet laughably, the damage had been caused not by weapons fire but a piece of wreckage striking the hull.

The lump of alien hull had smashed into and through the two starboard side hangars, impacting the main armoured belt. The strike didn't penetrate the belt itself and had instead dislodged a scab of armour plate massing, perhaps half a ton, and sent it crashing across the ship. The spray of metal splinters, sent out as the armour broke loose, cut down Ratings Dormy and Baudelaire. Lieutenant Hidaka was almost pulped as it smashed through the centreline bulkhead, while Rating Tuite was decapitated by a fragment of the metal. The final victim, Petty Officer Laura Ermler, was hit by a piece of a computer console before the mass of metal finally came to a halt, after putting a five centimetre deep dent in the armour on the opposite side of the ship.

Unlike the others, Laura Ermler not only could have, but should have survived. If *Hood* had carried a doctor she would have done. However in the dash to make the ship ready for action, one sickbay orderly, but no doctor, had been assigned to them. Medical supplies had been limited to out of date painkillers, and whatever else had been left in the ship when she'd been decommissioned. There hadn't been time or means to transfer Laura to another ship before they jumped out to Earth. The sickbay orderly had been helpless to stop her internal bleeding, and somewhere between Earth and Alpha Centauri she died in agony.

A tap at the door interrupted her line of thought.

"Who is it?" Willis snapped.

"Just me. Can I come in?" said a voice through the hatch.

"Certainly." A welcoming smile appeared on her face as Vincent Espey stepped in. He was dressed in a borrowed and ill-fitting lieutenant's uniform. He looked a hell of a lot better than he had a week earlier. Although for Willis, who knew him so well, he was still noticeably pale beneath his tan. While the haunted look in his eyes had faded, it wasn't gone yet.

Within twenty minutes of the end of the battle, the Home Fleet had jumped out for Earth. *Hood* plus the other cripples had been left behind, waiting for the tugs. They had busied themselves picking up escape pods and checking wreckage for survival suit distress beacons. The failure of their computer had fouled their plotting but finally *Hood* had come across what was left of *Hurricane*. Up close the cruiser had been a pitiful sight. Less than half her hull had remained and what was left, looked like a single touch might cause her final disintegration. Looking out at her Willis found herself doubting that even a single hull plate remained unbuckled. As gently as possible, they matched course and edged alongside the one remaining airlock. Technically she shouldn't have abandoned her bridge to go over to *Hurricane*. There had been no guarantee that Nameless stragglers weren't still in the system and it had been her duty to stay on her bridge. But she had to know for herself whether her friend had survived.

As she'd stepped through the airlock into *Hurricane*, a small red light on her helmet display had lit up, indicating air pressure outside had dropped below survivable limits. It was scarcely necessary, she'd felt her suit expand slightly as the airlock cycled. The inside of *Hurricane* was a dark and lifeless vacuum. Bodies had drifted, ghostlike, down twisted and torn access-ways. Worse were the crushed arms, legs and, on one occasion, a head protruding from the hatchway of a caved-in section.

There had been no response to their calls but she had refused to give up. The metal structure of the ship, she'd reasoned, could be blocking the weak transmissions from their suit radios. At her order, they'd split up to search the wreck. Out of the corner of her eye, she saw the ratings and officers accompanying her exchanging looks, clearly wondering whether to tell their commanding officer that it was hopeless. Then she'd heard a crackle on her radio that didn't seem to be one of her people. Tracking back towards the source of the transmission she'd wriggled into a compartment that at first glance appeared to have completely caved in.

Inside, were what was left of *Hurricane's* crew, all twelve of them. Almost all of them had been hurt. They'd seen the flash of the Home Fleet departing and known that they'd been left behind. There, in the centre of the survivors, trying to turn three shattered escape pods into one working one, was Commander Vincent Espey. The way she threw her arms around him would have left an observer wondering who was rescuing whom. As the two commanders embraced, a cheer went up across the radio as the news that there were survivors filtered over to the *Hood*.

Although clearly close to a state of near collapse, Espey had been the last to leave his ship and insisted that he be allowed onto *Hood's* bridge, to watch as they finally put *Hurricane* down. There hadn't been any explosion or even flash of atmosphere as *Hood* pumped a salvo into her. The little cruiser simply disintegrated, one moment a ship, the next an expanding cloud of fragments. Espey hadn't spoken and instead just watched.

When they'd returned to Earth, the wounded had been taken off. But there had been no orders for Espey, leaving him to drift around *Hood* like a purposeless but very solid ghost. Willis spent as much time as she could talking to her friend, trying to help him through the guilt. There were still deep shadows under in his eyes. For any captain to have their ship shot out from under them was a terrible blow. She could only hope that Espey would be given time to come to terms with it and time to silence the ghosts of the people he failed to bring home.

"A shuttle is finally turning up to take me dirtside," he said, sitting down on the bunk. "I should be out of your hair in half an hour."

"Any idea what next?" she asked.

"You mean after the court martial?" he replied, just for a moment looking as bad as he had when first brought aboard.

"Vincent, they won't blame you for not achieving the impossible."

"You brought *Hood* home, Faithie. I couldn't do the same for *Hurricane* or most of my crew," he replied bitterly. "Most of them died directly because of my decision to ram."

"I'm sorry Vince, you had to..."

"I don't blame you, Faithie. I just wish..." He shrugged before picking up Laura Ermler's file and looked at it distractedly. "We don't even know who was on *Hurricane*, all the personnel records went up with her."

"It wasn't your fault," Willis told him quietly.

Espey waved the personnel file in his hand at her.

"I've been hearing that a lot. It wasn't your fault they died," he replied, waving the personnel files of *Hood's* fallen. "Doesn't make it any easier though does it?"

They were both silent.

"*Commander Espey, please come to Shuttle Bay Four. Commander Espey, please come to Shuttle Bay Four.*" The intercom crackled with all the clarity of a railway PA system.

"I've *got* to get the Chief to fix that bloody thing," Willis muttered to herself.

"Well it sounds like you've got enough to keep you out of mischief. I guess I'd better go," Espey said as he got to his feet.

Willis quickly got up and placed her hand on his shoulder.

"Make sure it's not too long before we see you out here again Vince."

Espey suddenly grinned, like his old self almost, and threw his arms around her.

"Don't worry, Faithie, I'll be okay," he whispered before giving a peck on her cheek. On his way out he nearly walked into Guinness, who stepped aside to allow the Commander to pass before peering into the cabin.

"Skipper, we've finished patching the centre line bulkhead. I'm just going off duty," he said, his eyes not meeting hers.

"Please come in Chief. We need to have a word."

Guinness hesitated as a look of dread crossed his face.

Willis waited until the hatch was closed and Guinness was standing at parade rest looking deeply uncomfortable.

"I know we should have had this conversation days ago Chief, but..."

"I'll ask for a transfer Captain," Guinness cut in quietly, "or for discharge."

"Why do you say that Chief."

Guinness swallowed hard before answering.

"I didn't check the back up battery, Skipper. I topped up the fluid level, but I didn't stop the think why it needed topping up."

"There was a leak?"

"A crack right down the rear face. When I looked afterwards, the whole chamber was flooded in battery fluid. I don't make any excuses ma'am."

"And nor should you Chief. We lost the computer at a critical time and it could have cost us everything. That kind of mistake generally costs an engineer their job, even in peace time." Guinness's eyes remained fixed on the far bulkhead. "On the other hand, how long did we get to make this ship combat worthy?"

"A few days ma'am."

"Yes, only a few days to turn a relic into a warship again. We succeeded, or at least you succeeded." For the first time in the conversation Guinness met her gaze. "This ship is obsolete and so is most of the equipment onboard. I can't seriously hope to get another engineer who can match your familiarity with the technology. I don't want you to leave Chief, but if you feel you have lost the trust of the crew and myself... I will not block a transfer request."

"With respect ma'am, I don't know how you could trust me after this."

"Because I don't think you'll make a mistake again, not on my ship."

"You're right ma'am, I won't," Guinness replied his voice thick with emotion and an expression of open gratitude.

"Alright Chief, you're dismissed. I'll see you in the morning."

Guinness drew himself up and marched out.

The small smile on Willis face lasted until she sat back down at her desk. She stared at the late Laura Ermler's file for several minutes before starting the type again.

Mr and Mrs Ermler

By the time this message reaches you, you will already have received official notification of your daughter Laura's death on the thirty-first July twenty sixty-six. So I write to you to personally express my sympathy. Laura served under my command for only a short period and I regret I did not personally get a chance to know her. I know that there is nothing I can write that will make the coming days and months easier for you. I can only hope that the knowledge that she died defending you will offer some comfort and that as a person, as a professional, she will be missed.

The sky about Dublin was a brilliant blue, and the air was warm and dry. It was going to be a beautiful day. The first lump of soil hit the top of Rear Admiral Emily Brian's coffin with a flat thump. Slowly the mourners made their way past the open grave, each adding another handful of soil. With the funeral over, the mourners started to drift away, some of them heading for one of the three other funerals being held in the fleet's graveyard.

Lewis stood under one of the trees some distance from the funeral. It had been made clear by Brian's daughter that his presence was unwelcome and much as that hurt, Lewis respected her wishes.

He waited until the young woman dressed in black had left before approaching the grave. His wife was still there and as he stopped beside her, she looped her arm through his. The two of them stood in silence for a time.

That there was a body at all was due to the *Samuel Clemens*. The transport ship had picked up the beacon from *Dauntless's* black box and came in looking for survivors. There was one. It wasn't Emily.

Above them, beyond the blue sky, the Home Fleet and the Second Fleet orbited the planet. Most of those ships that had fought at Alpha Centauri were now in dockyards. Putting right their wounds would require months of repairs, but those ships would remerge better prepared to fight this new kind of war.

Immediately after the battle, *Warspite* and the other lightly damaged ships had raced back to Earth. The rest of the fleet trailed back at the best speed they could manage. For nearly twenty hours after their return the Home Fleet had remained at high alert.

The Nameless War

Uncertain as to whether the advance of the Nameless really had been checked, they paused only to rearm, before standing ready to fight again. Crews, tired almost beyond human endurance, snatched sleep where they could before returning to their posts. The Nameless did not come. Instead, there was the welcome arrival of the Second Fleet. Finally, battered ships and their exhausted crews could stand down and allow others to take up the load.

In the days that followed, the survivors of the Third Fleet began to arrive. Either individually or in small groups, often their ships barely holding together, they mostly told tales of horror. But one, *Deimos*, brought news of her clash at Junction and of the limitations of the Nameless's jump drive. Now, dozens of officers and technicians were poring over the ship's radar and passive sensor logs, trying to make sense of what it meant.

One of two hard learned lessons. As a consequence of the second lesson, a vast minefield was being laid in high Earth orbit, to give the fleet a safe harbour in which to rest and repair. The Nameless would be learning as well, and now that their opening move had failed, the race would be on to see who could learn fastest.

There was a polite cough from behind them. Lewis turned to see Sheehan waiting in front of a staff car. His arm was still in a sling.

"Sir, I'm very sorry to interrupt," He said apologetically.

"It's all right Tim. What is it?" Lewis replied.

"The Council is gathering sir. Admiral Wingate wants you there."

"Alright," Lewis nodded, before turning to his wife.

"I know Paul," she said, "I'll see you at home."

Before he left the graveside Lewis knelt, picked up a handful of loose soil and threw it into his friends' grave.

Inside the Gemini construction platform, the shuttle glided slowly down the length of *Deimos* as Crowe stared through the viewport at the buckled hull plating and shattered weapons mounts. His crew were all off the ship now. He'd been the last aboard and once the ship was handed over there was no reason for even him to remain. Space-suited dockyard workers were jetting back forth across the damaged areas, assessing, analysing, deciding how repairs could be effected and what improvements could be made. Crowe felt a stirring of pride in his ship. She wasn't the *Mississippi*, but she and her crew had achieved... greatness. Putting right her wounds would need months in docks, but if the past few days had taught him anything, it was that *Deimos* was a good ship, the right ship, a ship that would be in the thick of things and one he would continue to command. Now he had time to think and reflect on how much had changed in one year. He had taken out *Mississippi* full of optimism and innocence and now he had brought *Deimos* home maimed. End of an era. An overused phrase but in this case, the only appropriate one. No longer would people look up at the stars to see beauty and mystery, they would see only a source of danger.

"Pilot, you can take us down now," he ordered.

As the shuttle pulled away from Gemini, Crowe leaned back in his chair and pulled the blind down over the port. There was nothing out there he wanted to see, he'd be back soon enough.

Flying Officer Alanna Shermer sat in Terminal Three of Dublin Airport. Around her humanity in all its forms rushed for their flights, mooched around the shops, talked, read, ate and drank. Many cast curious looks at her, sitting there in her Battle Fleet uniform. A few had tried to talk her, to ask questions, wanting to know if what they saw and read in the news was true. Her responses had been monosyllabic and after a few minutes most people gave up. Only one person got a serious response. A man in his twenties, he started ranting at her, calling her an imperialist warmonger. He had been at least thirty centimetres taller than her and outweighed her by perhaps half as much again, but when she rose to her feet, he saw her hands close into fists. He looked her in the eye and saw the violence there. Wisely he's backed off.

After the destruction of *Dauntless* the Nameless immediately left the area. For nearly thirty hours she waited in what was left of Caesar, beside the body of Dhoni. Once the Nameless had left, she activated the distress signal but there was no way to know whether the transmitter was sending anything. The air pressure inside the cockpit slowly bled away and with every minute she grew a little colder, and with every breath the air grew a little staler.

The hours flowed into one another and after a while she stopped looking at her watch. Near the end the cold and the bad air started to affect her. She'd talked to Dhoni and even now, she could have sworn he'd replied.

She woke in the *Samuel Clemens's* sickbay, where they told her she'd been lucky. The transport ship had heard *Dauntless's* last desperate transmissions, the chatter between Anton and Caesar and finally, the carrier's black box beacon go active. They'd waited over twenty-seven hours for the solar system to go quiet again and only then did they dare approach.

They found what was left of *Dauntless* and searched the wreck for survivors. Strictly speaking, they lingered far longer than was wise, but recovered only bodies. They were about to leave when a radio operator heard a very faint signal. They could have ignored or disregarded it, but instead they investigated and found her.

Now, after several days in hospital, she was going home to see her parents. They'd given her fourteen days survivor's leave. She had vowed to herself that she would enjoy them because after Alpha Centauri, she could not make herself believe that on her return to the fleet that she would survive the war ahead.

A police escort from the cemetery had been laid on, so within a few minutes Lewis was being driven through a rear entrance and down into an underground car park. With equal speed he was escorted up to Wingate's office. It was the first time he'd landed since the battle and those officers and ratings he passed in the corridor stepped respectfully aside. Some saluted him, a few cheered. Lewis acknowledged them with a nod but didn't slow his pace.

As he entered the office Wingate stood up and when Lewis saluted he offered his hand.

"Paul, welcome home and congratulations," he said as they shook hands. "Sorry about having to sneak you in, the bloody press are crawling all over the front gate. We've already had a couple of dozen requests for interviews and two offers to help you ghost write your story about how you won the war."

"Thank you, sir," Lewis replied as he took a seat, "but we know that the congratulations belong to someone else."

Wingate gave a faint grimace,

"She was a good officer, Paul."

"One of the best, sir," Lewis replied quietly. "If Emily hadn't… improvised…" He broke off and shook his head. "Well, we certainly wouldn't be patting ourselves on the back."

"We haven't released many details to the press. With only one survivor from *Dauntless's* group, they haven't yet found out just how close it was." Wingate paused. "We always knew it was a flimsy plan Paul. It was based on intelligence that was poor at best. But it was enough." He slid a file across the desk to Lewis. "This arrived just in the last hour or so. We sent it up to *Warspite* but you'd left the ship by that stage."

Wingate waited patiently as Lewis read. Finally he looked up with relief on his face.

"So, now we know, sir."

"Yes."

There was a tap at the door before Wingate's Staff Captain stepped in.

"Sir, the Council is gathering."

"Thank you Anna, we're on our way down."

The last of the Council holograms was just flickering on line when the two admirals entered the room.

"Gentlemen, please be seated, I expect we have a lot to discuss," President Clifton said as they both saluted.

"Firstly, Admiral Lewis, congratulations on your victory in Alpha Centauri. Possibly the greatest threat this planet has ever known has been turned aside by the bravery and skill of your crews. Please express both the Council's and my own gratitude to your crews."

"Thank you Madam President," Lewis replied nodding slightly.

"The next point however is: has it been enough to end this conflict?"

"We have part of an answer for that." Wingate activated a display holo. "Before the engagement in Alpha Centauri, we deployed a number of couriers across the enemy's probable line of advance. This was both to maintain contact with the Nameless and additionally, to re-establish contact with the retreating elements of the Third Fleet. Approximately thirty hours after the end of the battle, one of those couriers, located in system Alpha one, eight, three, dash, one, nine, one observed an enemy fleet jump into the system, which after refuelling, jumped out in the direction of Landfall. Many of these ships were visibly damaged and, going on a rough number count, this fleet represented an amalgamation of both enemy fleets engaged in Alpha Centauri."

There were smiles and sighs of relief.

"So, they're in full retreat," someone said gratefully. "They've lost."

"That's an optimistic assumption," Lewis replied in a voice that was both flat and loud. It abruptly broke the mood.

"Admiral, your own report estimates that a least forty enemy ships were destroyed, while most of survivors were damaged to at least some extent," Clifton replied sharply. "This represents a very substantial portion of their invasion fleet. How can this be anything other than a major defeat?"

"Yes ma'am, they did take significant losses. Unfortunately for us, I believe they were willing to accept those losses in exchange for pulling the Home Fleet out of position. By using the lead fleet as a decoy, they fooled us into leaving Earth undefended. But for the efforts of *Dauntless*, their main fleet would have been left unmolested to strike at Earth."

"But their plan has failed, why would they continue?" asked the German Chancellor.

"In Nineteen Fourteen the German Schlieffen Plan failed to land a knockout blow against France, sir, yet the Great War continued for another four years," Lewis replied. "Setbacks in warfare, even big ones, are a practical reality. In the Contact War, the Aéllr were always hamstrung by their unwillingness to accept casualties. Regrettably, the Nameless do not appear to be so constrained."

"I don't believe we should rule out peace, Admiral!" the German replied sharply.

"Neither do I, Chancellor. If the Nameless contact us with peace proposals, I will be the very first to cheer, but unfortunately I do not believe this will happen. The information we have to hand indicates the Nameless have already wiped out one race. We have seen for ourselves a willingness to suffer losses, which I admit I find frightening. All of this speaks of the deepest possible commitment."

"Okay Admiral, answer me this," Clifton asked sharply. "If this is just a temporary blip for the Nameless, why are they retreating?"

"The logistical brake," Wingate cut in.

"I don't follow you."

"Before her own destruction, the *Dauntless* eliminated or crippled at least four enemy fuel tankers. Given that they were refuelling at the time they were hit, it is likely the Nameless were left without enough fuel to sustain their advance. It is our belief that they are now falling back along their own supply lines."

"How far are they going to retreat?"

Wingate glanced toward Lewis, who gave a half shrug.

"We guess, and we stress this is only a guess, that Landfall will be about as far as their retreat goes."

"What's the basis for that guess?"

"They have already eliminated our forces in that area. They likely had a muster point close to Landfall in preparation for their attack on Baden."

"We've hurt them badly though. Didn't that cruiser that fought them at Junction show that there are limits to their wonderful jump technology?" Clifton asked hopefully. "That is correct isn't it?"

"Possibly ma'am," Wingate replied.

"Possibly? How the hell can it be possibly?" she demanded angrily

Lewis sighed and sat back in his chair.

"Council members, the answer is 'possibly' because to give a clear answer we have to make three big assumptions and so far, we haven't had a good track record with our assumptions. The first assumption is that we have seen the bulk of their first line strength. The second, that we can return all surviving elements of the Third Fleet to service. The final assumption is that the Nameless aren't going to pull any new technological tricks out of their hat. If these assumptions are correct, then we have perhaps evened the score. If not, when the fighting resumes, we will remain at a disadvantage."

Several members of the Council looked annoyed at Lewis's almost lecturing tone and Wingate shot his subordinate a look of warning.

Clifton fiddled with her papers for a moment, before angrily throwing them down.

"Where do we go from here?"

"We prepare for the long haul ma'am. It's my belief this war will be both long and brutal." Wingate replied.

"Will it be winnable?"

Everyone looked round at the question. The speaker was Prime Minister Michael Layland.

"Can we win?" he repeated.

All eyes returned to the two officers.

"I will not lie to this Council." Wingate said. "We don't know the strength of their fleet, the strength of their economy, the will of their people. We don't even know whether they even are people in any sense we'd recognise. Worst of all, we don't even know why they have chosen to go to war against us. Finally, with the surviving elements of the Third Fleet still arriving, we don't yet know how badly we've been hurt. We need to answer all of these questions before we can judge what the future holds. In essence Council members, the past two weeks have only been a beginning, nothing more. The weeks, months and possibly years ahead will establish whether we have a future."

THE END

Glossary

Aèllr: Carbon based oxygen breathing mammalian life form. First intelligent alien life form encountered by humanity. Population: 32 billion (approx.), across eight major and six minor planets. Government type: democracy.

Battleship: Large gun armed ship, carrying heavier armour and guns than any other category of vessel. In human service this vessels frequently serve as fleet flagships.

Chaff: Standard passive counter measure, aluminium strips which give false returns or swamps radar systems. Chaff bursts are usually deployed by rocket.

Coms (Communication) Laser: Low powered lasers used for communications at short range (up to 70,000 kilometres). Standard feature of all human starships, coms lasers transmission can not be jammed.

Concussive Maintenance: The application of blunt force to a piece of equipment that is not working to an acceptable standard. Not recommended for use on live ordinance.

Contact War, The: Humanities first interstellar conflict, fought against the Aèllr Confederacy. Largely fought with Earth's solar system the conflict ended inconclusively with the Treaty of Mars. Battle Fleet was founded during the early stages of the conflict.

Cruiser: A category of vessel that can be loosely defined as the largest ships to be built in significant numbers. This classification is given to the workhorse of every fleet.

Dryad System: Human controlled solar system close to Mhar Union and several of the Tample Star Nations. Dryad Two is borderline habitable and has large Zillithium deposits.

EMD, Emergency Message Drone: Missile sized drone equipped with a one use jump drive and a small transmitter. EMD's are for the vast majority of ships the only means of communicating across interstellar distances.

Fire Control: A ship's weapon control systems.

Governing Council: Political leadership of Battlefleet. The council is composed of rotating eight members, two from each continental block.

IFF, Identify Friend or Foe: Identification system designed for command and control. It enables military and civilian- interrogation systems to identify aircraft, vehicles or forces as friendly and to determine their bearing and range from the interrogator.

Landfall System / Planet: Human controlled system. Initially called Fortune, the system is now largely known by the name of its principal planet. A Earth-like body, Landfall is being colonized by several nations. The Battle Fleet base Baden orbits at the edge of the system.

Light Speed: 299,792,458 metres per second.

Local Control: Targeting systems built directly onto each gun mount. These systems are a back up measure should a ship's main Fire Control be knocked out. They lack both the sensitivity and accuracy of main fire control.

Mass Shadow: The 3 dimensional area surrounding a planet or large spatial body that prevents a vessel from making transit into or out of Jump Space. The size or 'depth' of a mass shadow is proportional to the mass of the spatial body generating the shadow.

Mhar: Carbon based oxygen breathing mammalian life form. Third sentient race to be encountered by humanity. Technologically inferior to humans in most respects. Relations between Humanity and the Mhar are friendly. Government type: centrally planned democracy.

Plasma Cannon: Standard anti ship weapon used by Battlefleet and the Aèllr Defence Fleet. Light plasma cannons as carried by destroyers are effective out to 60,000 kilometres, cruiser scale weapons to 100,000 kilometres. Heavy plasma cannons as carried by battleships ships are effective out to 130,000 kilometres. Plasma Cannons will not function in atmosphere.

PO, Petty Officer: Non-Commission Officer.

Point Defence Guns: Active defensive system designed to protect a ship from fighters, missiles and small astronomical hazards. Standard feature in both military and civilian vessels, although military vessels will carry significantly more point defence guns.

Railguns: Projectile thrower which uses two charged super conductor rails to accelerate metal projectiles. Used principally as secondary armament on Battle Fleet battleships and cruisers.

Rating: Lowest rank of fleet personnel, equivalent to an army private.

Real Space: Conventional Newtonian space.

Red line, The: Standard terminology for the outer edge of a planet's Mass Shadow, thus the closest to a planet that a ship can make transition in or out of jump space.

Scram: To shut down a nuclear reactor rapidly in an emergency.

Silent Running: A state in which a vessel powers down and reduces all emissions to avoid detection.

Skipper: Unofficial term for officer in command of a vessel. As such can apply to officers of virtually any rank.

Tample: Carbon based oxygen breathing life form with both Lizard and Insect characteristics. Broken down into seven separate and competing. Star Nations the Tample were the second sentient race to be encountered by humanity.

Ships and crews

Dauntless: Glorious class fighter carrier.
Crew (in order of rank):
Rear Admiral Emily Brian,
Captain O'Malley
Commander Vardakas (engineer)
Squadron Commander Moscoe
Wing Commander Devane
Staff Lieutenant Gore (Staff Officer to Brian)
Flying Officer Alanna Shermer (pilot C for Caesar)
Wasim Dhoni (Navigator / gunner C for Caesar)

Deimos: Luna Class Flak cruiser
Captain Ronan Crowe
Commander James Hockley
Lieutenant Colwell
Bosun Wallace Benson

Hood: Admiral Class Cruiser.
Commander Faith Willis
Commander Alex Horan
Chief Engineer David Guinness

Mississippi: River Class Cruiser.
Captain Ronan Crowe
Commander Berg
Chief Engineer David Guinness

Warspite: Warspite Class Battleship.
Vice Admiral Paul Lewis
Staff Captain Tim Sheehan
Captain Holfe

Harbinger: Messenger Class Scout Cruiser.
Captain Marko Flores

Commander Faith Willis
Marine Commander Major Tigran
Professor Bhaile (head of civilian delegation)
Alice Peats (civilian language expert)

About the Author

Edmond Barrett is a techno-phobic science fiction writer who is quietly proud to be British, while happy to acknowledge his entire ancestry is Irish. He copes with the contradictions in his life by not thinking about them too much. *The Nameless War* is his first published work, he is currently work on the sequel *The Landfall Campaign* which is due for release in October 2012. A resident of Dublin, Ireland, he is life long fan of science fiction and fantasy as well as being a amateur student of military history.

You can find Edmond Barrett on line at:

http://edmondbarrett.wordpress.com/

Facebook:

http://www.facebook.com/#!/profile.php?id=100003044323873

Book Two of the Nameless War Trilogy:

The Landfall Campaign

Available from Autumn 2012

Also by this Author:

The Job Offer